THE GODS CHECK IN

Hawk gloomily surveyed the hotel lobby. While he was trying to register them—under whatever aliases he could think of—the Olympians were disporting themselves with alarming rowdiness. An arrow whizzed across the lobby and pinned an old gentleman's hat to the back of his chair.

"A fair hit!" boomed Bacchus. "Well done, Diana!"

Venus and Hebe were making advances to any presentable men they found; Neptune was haranguing a hotel guest who did not seem to appreciate fish as much as he should.

As Hawk watched, he saw Mercury unobtrusively transfer a fat wallet from an innocent bystander's pocket to his own.

"A nice little selection of the gods we made," he muttered.

By Thorne Smith

Published by Ballantine Books:

TOPPER

TOPPER TAKES A TRIP

THE NIGHT LIFE OF THE GODS

*THE STRAY LAMB

*TURNABOUT

*RAIN IN THE DOORWAY

*Coming soon from Del Rey/Ballantine Books

THORNE SMITH

The Night Life
of the Gods

A Del Rey Book

BALLANTINE BOOKS • NEW YORK

this book is in gratitude offered to a couple of
GOOD COMPANIONS
Neal and Dorothy Andrews
To borrow from Mr. J. B. Priestley

A Del Rey Book
Published by Ballantine Books

Copyright 1931 by Thorne Smith, © renewed 1958 by June Smith Delaney and Marion Smith Conner.

Library of Congress Catalog Card Number: 79-55331

ISBN 0-345-28726-6

Manufactured in the United States of America

First Ballantine Books Edition: July 1980

Cover art by Norman Walker

Contents

CHAPTER   PAGE

    I   CRITICISING AN EXPLOSION 1

   II   BLOTTO'S TAIL ASTOUNDS 7

  III   RELUCTANT STATUES 20

  IV   THE LITTLE MAN AND THE SCARECROW .. 32

   V   A FURIOUS RECEPTION 45

  VI   THE INVASION OF HAWK'S BED 55

 VII   PLAYFUL PETRIFICATION 63

VIII   MEG REMOVES HER PULL-OFFS 74

  IX   A NUDE DESCENDS THE STAIRS 88

   X   AN EPIDEMIC OF ESCAPES 98

  XI   THE PURSUING BEARD 120

 XII   LOOKING THE GODS OVER 128

XIII   THE GODS STEP DOWN 139

XIV   THE GODS GET DRESSED 153

 XV   THE GODS GET HOUSED 164

XVI   NEPTUNE GETS HIS FISH 176

XVII   MEG, MERCURY & BETTS, INC. 191

XVIII   A DEMORALIZING TANK PARTY 206

XIX   THE GODS LEAVE TOWN 221

 XX   BATTLE AND FLIGHT 240

XXI   THE GODS ON TRIAL 252

XXII   THE LAST SIGH 262

CHAPTER I

Criticizing an Explosion

THE SMALL FAMILY GROUP GATHERED IN THE LIBRARY was only conventionally alarmed by the sound of a violent explosion—a singularly self-centered sort of explosion.

"Well, thank God, that's over," said Mrs. Alice Pollard Lambert, swathing her sentence in a sigh intended to convey an impression of hard-pressed fortitude.

With bleak eyes she surveyed the fragments of a shattered vase. Its disastrous dive from the piano as a result of the shock had had in it something of the mad deliberation of a suicide's plunge. Its hideous days were over now, and Mrs. Lambert was dimly aware of another little familiar something having been withdrawn from her life.

"I hope to high heaven this last one satisfies him for this spring at least," was the petulant comment of Alfred, the male annex of Alice.

"I've been waiting and waiting and waiting," came a thin disembodied voice from a dark corner. "Night and day I've been waiting and expecting——"

"And hoping and praying, no doubt, Grandpa," interrupted Daphne, idly considering a run in her stocking and wondering what she was going to do about it if anything, and when would be the least boring time to do it if she did, which she doubted.

"Alice," complained Grandpa Lambert from the security of his shadows, "that baggage has no respect for her elders."

Stella, femininely desirable but domestically a washout, made one of her typical off-balance entrances. It started with a sort of scrambled hovering at the door, developed this into a mad dash into the room, and terminated in a tragic example of suspended animation somewhere in the immaculate neighborhood of Mrs. Alice Pollard Lambert.

"Been an explosion, ma'am," announced Stella in a deflated voice. "Mr. Betts says so."

"Now all you need to do is to fall dead at our feet to make the picture complete," remarked Daphne.

"Yes, Miss Daffy," said Stella brightly.

"And if Mr. Betts says there's been an explosion," Daffy continued, "then there must have been an explosion. Betts is never wrong. You go back, Stella dear, and thank him for letting us know so promptly."

"But, Miss Daffy, what shall we do about it?" asked Stella, vainly looking for some light to guide amid the encircling gloom.

"About what, Stella?" asked Daffy.

"This explosion, miss," and Stella extended her hands as if she were offering a young explosion for the inspection of Daphne.

"Stella," that young lady explained with sweet but jaded patience, "one doesn't do things about explosions. Explosions are quite competent to do things for themselves. All sorts of things. The most one can do for an explosion is to leave it entirely alone until it has decided to become a ruin. Also, you can blink at an explosion respectfully in the news reels and feel good about its ghastly results. You'll probably gasp at this one on your night off next Thursday." She paused, then added, "With that stout fellow Tim breathing heavily in your left ear."

This last realistic observation was enough to effect the untidy departure of Stella.

"Oh, Miss Daffy," was all that maiden said.

"I do wish she would refrain from calling you by that vulgar sobriquet," said Mrs. Lambert.

"Why, Mother?" the daughter asked. "I am. Very. That's why I like myself, and that's why I like him. He's daffy, too."

She pointed in the general direction of the explosion.

"In that you're right, for a change," agreed her father. "He belongs in some institution. What does he mean by getting us here in this house and then having explosions all over the place? I call it downright inconsiderate."

If Mr. Alfred Pollard Lambert had forgotten the small detail that after having lost his wife's fortune in various business misadventures he had sought sanctuary for himself and dependents in his brother-in-law's previously tranquil home, Daffy had not been so remiss. However, out of an innate sense of sportsmanship she rejected the opening her bumptious parent had offered her, merely contenting herself by observing:

"Well, if I had a home of my own I'd explode all over it as much as I jolly well liked. I'd explode from attic to cellar just as long as I felt the least bit explosive."

"I know, my dear," said her mother. "No one is saying your uncle hasn't a perfect right to explode whenever and wherever he pleases, but you must admit there's a certain limitation, certain restrictions of decency. One explosion, even two, we could understand and condone, but a series, a constant fusillade—it isn't normal. Good taste alone would suggest a little less boisterous avocation and a little less dangerous one."

"But, Mother," protested the girl, "he has never invited any of us to participate in one of his explosions. He's been very decent about it and kept them entirely to himself."

"Most of these scientific johnnies are content with a couple of explosions," said Alfred, "but your uncle is never satisfied. He seems to think that life is just one long Fourth of July."

"The day will come," intoned the devitalized voice from the corner. "Mark the words of an old man. The day will come when we'll find ourselves completely blown to bits."

This dire prediction struck Daphne as funny. She allowed herself several contemplative giggles.

"I can see it all," she said. "A lot of bits rushing busily about in a mad scramble to find one another. Hands collecting feet, legs, livers, and such, and putting them aside in a neat pile until all the bits have been assembled. Well, I hope I don't find some of this," she continued, spanking herself resoundingly. "I'm getting altogether too self-assertive in that quarter."

"Daphne!" Mrs. Lambert exclaimed. "You're positively obscene."

For a moment the young lady stood in rapt contemplation of some inner glory.

"I have it," she said at last. "Listen:

3

"Said a certain king to his queen:
'In spots you grow far from lean.'
'I don't give a damn,
You've always loved ham,'
She replied, and he said, 'How obscene!' "

From the dark corner inhabited by Grandpa Lambert issued a strange and unexpected sound, a sound which partook of the nature of both a cough and a cackle, such a sound as might clatter from the lipless mouth of a skull well pleased by some macabre memory.

"Why, Father!" exclaimed Alfred Lambert. "You're laughing, actually laughing."

"And at such a thing," added Mrs. Lambert with deep disapproval.

"Can't help it," wheezed the old gentleman. "Always had a weakness for limericks. Got a few of my own if I could only remember them."

He promptly fell to brooding not uncheerfully over those lost limericks of other years.

"You old darling," said Daffy, going over to the thin, crouched figure. "You've been holding out on me."

"Disgraceful," sniffed Alice Pollard Lambert, "Demoralizing."

Alfred made no further comment. He had a well defined suspicion that the old chap was holding out on him something far more desirable than limericks. If he could only lay his hands on his father's bank book. For some years now an inspection of that little book had been one of Alfred Lambert's chief aims in life. Just one little peek was all he asked. After that he could order his conduct according to the size of the figures in the book. As things stood now he was being in all likelihood dutifully and enduringly filial without any assurance of adequate compensation. Yet there was always that chance, that slim but not impossible chance. Hellishly tantalizing for an acquisitive nature. Alfred's was such a nature.

"There's one about the Persians," the old man was saying to his granddaughter. "Oh, a delightful thing, my dear child, an exquisite bit of vulgarity. Of course, I couldn't repeat it to you. Maybe after you're married.

4

I'll tell your husband, and he'll tell you—if he's the right sort of a husband."

"I'm sure Alfred never sullies my ears with such indecencies," said Mrs. Lambert with a rising inflection in her overcultured voice.

"He doesn't get out enough," grated the old man. "Do you both good."

"Your suggestion, Grandpa, is the greatest inducement to matrimony I've ever had," said Daphne, patting the old man's shoulder. "I'll look for a victim immediately."

"A full-legged girl like yourself shouldn't have far to look," the old man said with an unedifying chuckle. "In my day young men had to depend almost entirely on the sense of touch in such matters. Nowadays the sense of sight seems to play a more important part. It simplifies things, perhaps, but robs courtship of a lot of adventure."

"Disgusting!" pronounced Mrs. Lambert, then added with a view to changing the subject, "Don't you think, Alfred, that Stella was right? Shouldn't we do something about this explosion?"

"Perhaps," agreed Alfred. "He usually comes out after he's had one."

"Rather rapidly," remarked Daffy. "The last time he came out through the side of the house with a couple of bricks in his pants."

"But he hates to be disturbed," went on Mrs. Lambert. "You know how he is."

"I know how he was," replied Daffy. "How he is now, God only knows."

"Perhaps it got him this time," suggested Grandpa Lambert, not without a touch of complacency.

"Think we should go, Alfred?" asked his wife.

"Well, if that explosion failed to disturb him," Mr. Lambert observed, "I don't see how the intervention of mere mortals could make much of an impression. But why ask me? You're his sister. You should know best what to do about his explosive highness."

At this stage in the deliberations Alfred, Junior, age seventeen, lolled into the room. He tossed his hat at a chair with which it failed to connect. He thrust his hands deep into his pockets and looked ugly. He confronted his mother and began to speak in one of those voices which had it been a face one could have instinctively slapped.

"How long am I going to be made a laughing stock out of?" he demanded. "How long, I ask you?"

"If you asked me," put in his sister, "I'd say as long as a suffering world allows you to live."

"What is it now, darling?" Mrs. Lambert asked with cloying solicitude.

The youth laughed unpleasantly.

"You ask me that?" he exclaimed. "Does another explosion mean nothing to you? Am I to have my friends saying, 'That loony uncle of yours has blown up his house again'? Am I to be made the butt of all the humor and wisecracks of the community? Do you know what all my friends are saying? Would you like to know?"

"No," said Daffy. "Emphatically not."

"Shut up, you," snapped her brother. "They're saying that they wouldn't be caught dead in this house. That's what they're saying."

"If they're caught in this house they will be dead," remarked Daffy with a great decision. "I'll jolly well blow the whole kit and boodle of 'em to smithereens."

"Children, children," Mrs. Lambert protested.

"We've got to put a stop to it, Mother," announced Junior. "We've got to have a talk with him. I can't afford to be saddled with the stigma of a mad uncle."

"Yes, darling," his mother agreed. "I know how you must feel."

"Why don't you go yourself, dearie, and have a talk with him now?" asked his sister. "Lace it into him good and proper. Give him what for. Also, a microscopic portion of your infinitesimal mind."

"Think you're funny, don't you?" retorted the hope of the Lamberts.

"I do," replied Daffy. "I am."

"What I want to know is why does he have all these explosions?" Alfred Lambert inquired in an injured voice. "Are they essential to his happiness? What is he trying to prove, anyway?"

"Cellular petrification through atomic combustion," quoted Daphne weightily, "and vice versa. It's highly

6

electrical and can be, when it feels like it, no end smelly."

"And noisy," came from the corner.

"I'll tell you what let's do," suggested Mr. Lambert with the verve of one who has just conceived a bright and original idea. "Let's all go see him."

"Why not?" replied Daffy with a slight shrug.

"All but me," amended Grandpa Lambert. "I'll sit here and think up limericks. It's safer."

"And naughtier," said Daffy as she led the way from the room. "Horrid old man."

"Wanton," he retorted.

CHAPTER II

Blotto's Tail Astounds

FROM THE METHOD OF PROGRESS EMPLOYED BY THE Lambert family, one would have gained the impression that the correct way to approach an explosion was on tiptoe. There was something reverential yet subduedly daring about the small procession as it silently moved down the long hallway leading to the laboratory. It was as if its members were preparing themselves to gaze upon the face of an important but erratic corpse.

Daphne alone of the expedition's personnel was sincerely concerned about the safety of her uncle. She had no desire to find him scattered all over the place. Daphne was fond of her uncle. He constituted the larger part of her world—the more inhabitable part. Without him she would be thrust back into the narrow confines of her immediate family. Under such circumstances, she felt, life would hardly be worth the effort. Hunter Hawk was for her an escape and a revelation. He appealed to her imagination and added a small dash of color to her rather empty days. She entertained for him the healthily selfish devotion of her twenty-one years, the majority of which, she decided, had been shamefully wasted—the years before she had been brought to live in Hunter Hawk's home. Yet she was well aware of the fact that he was not much of an uncle. He was neither whimsical, dashing, nor debauched, one of which, at least, she had gained from her voracious reading, an uncle had to be, or else he was hardly any sort of an uncle at all. It was only on rare occasions that this uncle of hers realized she was alive. For the most part he went silently about his wondering way and did strange and mysterious things with impossible looking instruments in the privacy of his laboratory. Occasionally he indulged in an explosion. Daphne had come to believe that what a periodical binge meant to some men these explosions meant to her uncle. They served to relieve his feelings, and she was surprised at his moderation in confining them to only one section of the house. Quite frequently Daphne Lambert felt like blowing up the entire neighborhood, especially that part of it which at the time chanced to be inhabited by her mother, father, and brother.

Sometimes she would catch her uncle looking at her with an expression of mild astonishment in his dark, biting, and invariably delving eyes. Whenever this occurred, the girl for some inexplicable reason experienced a sensation of inner elation. There was always something maliciously challenging in his gaze, some derogatory reservation. She more than a little suspected that since the ruthless incursion of her family he had dimly felt that his home had been more or less taken away from him and that this side of bloodshed he was unable to figure out just what to do about it. Also she suspected that Hunter Hawk almost constantly carried about with him great quantities of violent yet unexpressed exasperation engendered by his sister, her husband, and their son. The three of them were enough to do terrible things to the most loosely constructed system of nerves.

Between her grandfather and her uncle there seemed to exist a sort of acrimonious bond of sympathy. True enough, the old man would have gladly seen him dead and welcomed the occasion as a pleasant interlude in the monotonous march of time. However, this meant nothing. The old man would have welcomed virtually anyone's death with the exception of his own. His son, his daughter-in-law, and the horrid results of their combined efforts to create an heir in the semblance of man he heartily detested. He had been forced to listen to their conversation for too many years. For Daphne he entertained the envious regard of the unregenerate and senile male.

This young lady now paused with her hand on the knob of the laboratory door.

"Perhaps we should have brought a basket," she suggested as she grimly surveyed the expectant faces.

"How can you!" exclaimed her mother in a tremulous voice.

The girl threw open the door, and the four of them stood gazing in upon the wreck of the laboratory. It was a long, high raftered apartment filled with more than enough instruments and paraphernalia to satiate the lust for descriptive detail of an avalanche of Sinclair Lewises.

There were several long tables supporting innumerable objects only remotely connected with life. Much of the equipment Hunter Hawk had been forced to devise himself. There were test tubes, Bunsen burners, pressure tanks, dynamos, mixing slabs, and all sorts of electrical appliances. In fact, almost everything seemed to be in that laboratory except a vacuum cleaner and Hunter Hawk himself. Most of the objects now lay smashed and twisted on the floor. It was like the disintegration of a bad dream. All of the windows were shattered, and innumerable jars and bottles carpeted the floor with their fragments. Heavy, evil-smelling clouds of gaseous vapor drifted casually about the room, while through these clouds from time to time appeared various bits of wreckage.

At the far end of the room a small but intense white light streaming from a huge wire-filled glass tube was splashing its rays against a silver ball about the size of an adult pea. From the other end of this tube a green light of equal intensity was treating another little silver ball in a like manner. These balls were poised about one foot from the floor at the ends of two thin rods. How they retained their positions during the violence of the explosion remains one of the many mysteries that Hunter Hawk never saw any occasion to elucidate.

"It must have blown the poor chap clean through one of the windows," remarked Mr. Lambert at last, in an awed but hopeful voice. "No man could have lived through such a shock as that must have been."

"Poor, poor Hunter," murmured the exploded one's sister. "We did everything we could to discourage him, but he would persist. I knew this would happen some day."

She hesitated and looked appraisingly about the long room. An acquisitive light was growing in her eyes.

"This place could easily be made into a perfectly charming lounge and breakfast room," she unconsciously mused aloud. "Long yellow drapes and the right sort of furniture. We might even try this modern stuff for a change."

"Make a bang-up billiard room," commented Alfred Lambert with a trace of wistfulness in his voice. "I could entertain my friends here."

"Say, Mom," demanded Junior, his tongue growing thick with anticipation, "does it all come to us—the house and the money and everything?"

"Everything," replied Mrs. Lambert with crisp finality. "All. I am his next of kin."

"You're his only of kin, aren't you?" her husband demanded in sudden alarm.

"I am," said Mrs. Lambert complacently. "The poor boy's only sister. Of course, there's Daphne and Junior."

"Then that settles that," said Mr. Lambert with obvious relief. "No legal complications. Lucky for us he never married, eh, my boy?"

Mr. Lambert slapped his son jovially on the back.

"Lucky for some poor girl," was Junior's bright reply.

A sound like a strangled sob, only more frustrated and inarticulate, drifted weirdly through the room.

"Did anyone hear that?" Alice Lambert demanded with a startled light in her eyes.

Apparently no one had.

"Must have been the wind," replied her husband impatiently. "Now what about the size of his estate, roughly speaking?"

Daphne had been peering through the various broken windows in the hope of finding her uncle or some part of her uncle.

10

"Of course," she remarked, sensing the drift of the conversation as she approached the self-congratulatory little group, "it will be necessary for you to produce the body before you can claim the estate. Anyone who knows his R. Austin Freeman even sketchily must realize that *corpus delicti* is one of the first essentials."

"My god!" Alfred exclaimed. "Daphne's right. We've forgotten all about the body."

"And perhaps there still flickers within it a small glimmer of life," said Daffy. "What then?"

At this uncongenial suggestion Alfred's cheerful face darkened perceptibly.

"He couldn't possibly have lived through this," he replied, as if striving to reassure himself. "It wouldn't be normal."

"He never was normal," Mrs. Lambert observed gloomily.

A furious chattering sound suddenly broke out somewhere above in the smoke-draped rafters. It was almost animal in its inability to express the full burden of its emotions.

Daphne's heart skidded round several sharp corners and came up with a thump against her ribs. A triumphant smile lighted up her face as she gazed aloft. Her mother, father, and brother stood looking at one another in guilty desolation. Each was trying to recall exactly what had been said and exactly who had said it. A heavy reluctance now weighted their tongues which only a moment ago had wagged so glibly. With an effort they brought themselves to follow the direction of Daffy's delighted gaze. A gas cloud drifted away revealing the long, lean, angular body of Hunter Hawk precariously draped on a rafter. It was like the unveiling of a statue of impotent rage. The man's mouth was opening and shutting without any apparent reason. Every time he endeavored to bring gesticulation to the aid of speech he lost his balance and nearly fell from his perch. The frantic clutching necessary to restore his equilibrium served only to increase the violence of his anger. Exhausted at last by the uselessness of his efforts he fell face forward on the rafter and lay there panting.

His straight black hair fell in a dank shingle over his

11

left eye. He made no effort to remove the obstruction but gazed balefully down at them with his free one. It was big, black, and smoldering. An expression of utter weariness lay across his tanned, deeply lined face. Sweat beaded his forehead. His hollow cheeks were unbecomingly dappled with dark smudges. There was a large rent in the right sleeve of his jacket. It hung down over his hand and interfered with his grip on the rafter. This had added to his irritation. He had now abandoned all effort to keep the sleeve up and was grasping the rafter through it. His large, ungainly nose showed evidence of having recently bled. In his present state of disrepair he looked many years over the thirty-seven that rightfully belonged to him.

"Oh, Hunter," his sister began with a desperate rush. "You've made us all so anxious. We were just——"

"Yellow drapes," he gritted.

"Yes, my boy," Alfred cut in throatily. "Thank God you're alive and safe. I was beginning to fear——"

"Billiards! Billiards!" Hawk spluttered. "Ha!"

He fixed Junior with his one clear eye and proceeded to bore into the very marrow of that uneasy youth.

"Go on!" he said in a dead voice. "Go on, you little nit. Make your speech. It's your turn. Tell me some more about that lucky girl I didn't marry."

Junior dropped his gaze and became absorbed in contemplating the extreme tips of his collegiate sport shoes.

"Don't know what you're driving at," he mumbled.

"I'll drive at you if I ever get down from this rafter," said his uncle.

Daffy grinned her appreciation. Her uncle darted a one-eyed glance at her, then disconcertingly closed that eye. It immediately snapped open again and came to rest on his sister.

"Now don't start in on Junior," she began defensively. "You've upset us enough as it is for one day— you and your silly explosions. The whole neighborhood is talking about it. Isn't it about time you gave up this sort of thing?"

"Yes, Hunter," spoke up Alfred, emboldened by his

wife's words. "You're subjecting us all to danger, you know. My boy here says his friends are laughing at him now—the nephew of a mad uncle."

"Oh-o-o-o-o," mouthed Mr. Hawk, unable to form words. "Oh-o-o-o—down—down—I wanna—at him."

His poorly expressed wish was almost granted. Mrs. Lambert uttered a little cry as he swayed perilously on his rafter. Junior placed a hand on his father's arm and tried to strike an attitude of outraged youth. The room became quiet save for the gasping of its presiding deity on the rafter. He rallied gamely, however, and made an effort to pull himself together.

"Oh, shut up," he said at last, somewhat inanely inasmuch as no one was saying a thing at the moment. "Shut up and go away somewhere. Go soak your heads. Get the hell out of here, or I'll blow the whole damn house up. Daffy, you stay with me."

"Well, I must say this is hardly the treatment one would expect after all our trouble and anxiety," Mrs. Lambert announced huffily.

"Yellow drapes," shouted her brother. "Modern furniture. Bah! Nothing goes to you. Not a plugged nickel."

His sister hastily swallowed a projected retort and, closely accompanied by her son and husband, sailed majestically from the room. They were altogether too wise in the ways of life to attempt to enroll the sympathies of Daphne or to coerce her to join the ranks of the insulted and injured. After all, Hunter Hawk was tremendously wealthy in his own name, and he did seem to be rather fond of his niece, the least lovable member of the family. It was just like him. Now, if only it had been Junior . . .

"Hello, aloft," called Daffy as soon as the door was closed, "do you want me to get you a ladder? I know where one lives. A long one. Betts could help."

"A ladder," repeated Mr. Hawk, blinking down at her. "I don't like ladders. I don't trust ladders. And if Betts gets a look at this room he'll make remarks. I can stand no more remarks. No. No ladder. Don't need one."

"Would you care to have some dinner flung up at you and a couple of sheets for to-night?"

13

"I'm coming down directly."

"How, down?"

"Listen," said the scientist ingratiatingly. "It's all very simple. There's no occasion for any excitement or rushing about. I hate excitement and rushing about."

"I suppose being blown about is an entirely different matter?"

"It is. I don't choose to be blown about, you know. In spite of what the rest of your family says, I really have no fondness for explosions. They are merely the less agreeable results of scientific research."

"Don't be an old hypocrite. You know perfectly well you couldn't get along without your explosions."

"I'm afraid I won't be able to get along very much longer with them. But, listen. I've figured it all out. It's simplicity itself. All you have to do is to come over here and stand directly beneath this rafter. Then I'll drop my feet down to your shoulders . . ."

"And then?" inquired Daffy.

"And then?" here a rather vague, covering note crept into his voice. "And then we'll manage to get down the rest of the way without the aid of the ladder."

"What do you mean by 'we'? You're the one on a rafter, not I."

"I realize that," said her uncle amicably. "And I'm depending on you to do something constructive about it. Come on over here, Daffy. You're a great, strong, strapping young girl. You can get me down somehow. Come on over."

Daffy, with the resignation of one accustomed to temporize with inebriates, children, and maniacs, placed herself beneath the rafter occupied by her uncle.

"I hope to God your divine confidence isn't misplaced," she remarked.

"Everything will be all right," Mr. Hawk assured her as, with the reckless abandon of a man who has little left to live for, he heavily dropped his large feet upon Daphne's shrinking shoulders and released his hold on the rafter. The celerity with which this maneuver was performed took the girl entirely by surprise.

"What goes on? What goes on?" she managed to get

out as she strove to keep her knees from buckling beneath her.

"Stop prancing about like that," the man of science complained. "This is no time for larking."

"Larking," came painfully from between the girl's clenched teeth. "Lolling about, why don't you say?"

After this there was no more conversation for some moments, packed with intense anxiety for the fluctuating Mr. Hawk. The silence of the room was broken only by the sound of unsteadily shuffling feet, a flight of staccato grunts, and several long, tremulous sighs.

"Well," gasped Daffy bitterly. "What are you going to do, live there?"

"Damn it all, what can I do? You've got a strangle hold on both my ankles." Hawk's voice was equally bitter. "Can't you crouch down gradually?"

"Oh, God, what a man," groaned his niece and collapsed unconditionally to the wreck-strewn floor of the laboratory beneath yard after yard of unupholstered uncle.

"Didn't hurt me at all," he announced triumphantly as he uncoiled great lengths of himself from the small of Daffy's back. "How did you make out?"

"Not at all well," replied Daffy. "Rather poorly, if you must know. But I'm glad it didn't hurt you. Would you like to try it again?"

"It saved all the bother of getting the ladder, anyway."

"You certainly must loathe ladders to subject another human being to such brutal punishment," replied the girl. "Did you ever get into any trouble with a ladder?"

With another unladylike grunt she rolled over and struggled to a sitting position beside her uncle.

"Well," she observed, surveying him critically, "you must be a tough son of a gun to have come through that alive."

"Do I look all mussed?" asked Mr. Hawk.

"You're not quite at your best," she replied.

"I'd like to see you after an explosion," said Hawk.

"You see enough of me as it is," answered Daffy. "After a thing like that you'd see too much."

Hunter Hawk gazed about the laboratory with professional interest.

"This is about the best yet," he remarked philosophically.

"It is, Hunter. It is. You should feel greatly encouraged. This is about the biggest thing you've done so far in the way of explosions."

"Thanks, Daffy. Wonder what became of Blotto? The poor beast was here when the thing happened."

"If it blew you up to the rafters, Blotto must be well on his way to Mars."

"Hate to have anything happn to Blotto," said Hunter. "Here, boy, where are you? Blotto, you dumb clown!"

From a corner of the room came the sound of diligent scraping. Presently the head of an animal not totally unlike a dog, yet far from being the living image of one, cautiously appeared above the rim of a table. With deep suspicion two black beady eyes studied the pair on the floor. A moist nose quivered delicately as it sniffed the malodorous air. One tan ear pointed starchily aloft. The other, a solid white, was not doing nearly so well. The farthest north it was able to achieve was a rakishly tilted flop. As the dog shifted his gaze and looked about the laboratory something like an expression of dismay came into its eyes.

"He doesn't like it at all," commented Hunter. "Come here, Blotto, for a minute."

Blotto placed two putty-like paws on the edge of the table, let go of them, and allowed their weight to drag his rump into view. It was a most disreputable-looking rump, shaggy, unenterprising, and hurriedly patched here and there with odd scraps of black and tan. There was a large tail on the extreme end of it, a willowy object composed chiefly of hair and burrs. Originally it had been white.

When Blotto had finally surmounted the obstruction he undulated across the room and stood looking inquiringly into his master's face. Hunter took the dog in his arms and felt him carefully, while Blotto, with his tongue sprawling out, gazed from his inverted position at Daffy, the whites of his eyes unpleasantly displayed.

16

Releasing the low-geared, supine creature, Hawk arose and stretched his long legs.

"No bones broken," he announced.

"All bones broken," said Daffy, "and flesh bruised."

She followed his example.

Blotto, as if trying to satisfy himself as to exactly what had happened, ranged busily about the room. His tour of inspection completed, he stood at the far end of the laboratory and wagged his tail in appreciation of the fact that he was still alive. Suddenly and most disconcertingly for everybody concerned, but much more so for Blotto, of course, the mop-like appendage refused to wag. For one brief moment it had dipped its extreme tip into the rays of the white light on its blinding passage to the little silver ball.

"Look!" exclaimed Daffy, pointing at the dog. "Something has happened to Blotto."

Something had happened to Blotto. To be exact, something had happened to Blotto's tail, but just what it was the astounded dog was unable to figure out. Concentrating what little power he had on this recalcitrant member, he strove desperately to make it perform its proper functions. Not a wag. Not even a quiver. An expression of sharp anxiety sprang into Blotto's eyes. He cocked his head over his shoulder and thoughtfully scrutinized his tail. Yes. He could tell at a glance that there was something radically wrong with it. It neither looked the same nor felt the same. Instead of the white, fluffy brush in which he was wont to take so much pride, the tail was now a formidable, implacable looking club. Not one hair that contributed its quota of glory to the *tout ensemble* even so much as stirred. It might as well have been a thing of stone, bereft of life and purpose. And the affair was heavy, decidedly heavier than could be conveniently managed. Obviously it was no sort of tail to go carrying about with one. Apart from the ill conceived merriment it would evoke, there was the question of fatigue. Would he be forced to remain in one place because of an abnormal tail? Were his amorous excursions at an end? Competition, God knows, was close enough, but with such a tail—impossible!

Unwilling to entertain this tragic thought, the over-

17

wrought Blotto made a final effort. This time he completely reversed the familiar order of the operation. Instead of wagging his tail he violently wagged himself. Behind him the tail swung ponderously, so ponderously in fact, that Blotto was thrown off his balance and was forced to do some pretty clever footwork to keep from falling over. This was just a little too much for the dog. He sat down heavily and washed his hands of the tail. But Blotto was to discover that no dog can completely wash its hands of its tail. His, for example, clattered noisily on the floor behind him. The dog looked seriously disturbed. He stealthily curved his head back over his shoulder and approached his shrinking nose to the tail. Then with a great effort he touched it with the extreme tip of his tongue. To his horror he discovered that it was as cold and unresponsive as a stone. He suspected it was a stone.

It speaks well for the dog's strength of character that in spite of his obvious disinclination to have anything further to do with that tail he pursued his investigations to the end. With a tentative paw he reached back and gently pushed the unnatural manifestation. The noise it made as it scraped across the floor caused him hurriedly to avert his eyes. Blotto was sweating. His gaze sought his master. If he wanted a dog with a stone tail it was up to him to do something about it—put it on wheels or something. Blotto could do no more.

"By all the gods," said Hawk in a hushed voice, "I believe I've done it at last, Daffy."

"What have you done now?"

"Turned that dog's tail into a statue, or, at least, a part of a statue."

"I never knew that turning the tails of dogs into statues was one of your aims in life."

"You don't quite understand. I have succeeded in achieving complete cellular petrification through atomic disintegration."

"You mean Blotto has."

"Observe," continued Hawk, seizing the outraged dog and holding him upside down. "Isn't it a beauty? Regard that tail. As if carved by a sculptor's hand. The white ray turns it to stone. The green one changes it back to its normal state. I can now make both rays invisible and retain the same action."

"I think Blotto would appreicate a slight dash of green," said Daffy. "I know I would, under the circumstances."

"I'll fix him up in a minute," said Hawk enthusiastically.

He turned and dipped the dog's tail into the green ray. Instantly, and to Blotto's intense relief, the tail returned to its former unlovely state. Hawk then set the dog on its legs. For a moment Blotto regarded his restored member reproachfully. What had the damn thing been doing with itself anyway—trying to make its owner look foolish? Then Blotto did a very silly thing. He viciously bit his tail. The sudden yelp of pain and indignation arising from this shortsighted attempt at retaliation eloquently testified to the complete success of the restoration. Then, with a sudden revulsion of spirit for which he was noted, Blotto bounded to his feet and performed hitherto unachieved altitudes in the line of wagging. It would be just as well, he decided, to register his satisfaction with his tail as it was, or else the same misfortune might overtake it again.

Thus did Blotto, a dog of low and irregular birth, contribute to one of the most spectacular discoveries of modern science.

"I hate to seem to fly so unceremoniously into your ointment," remarked Daffy, "but now that you've got it what are you going to do with it?"

For a moment Hunter Hawk's face went perfectly blank. "What am I going to do with it?" he repeated slowly. "Why, I hadn't thought about that."

"Well, you'd better begin to think about it."

"Right off, for one thing," he said, his face clearing and a malicious light gleaming in his dark eyes, "we can have a bit of fun with it."

"Nice man," remarked Daffy, for the first time permitting herself to smile. "Lovely character. And just for a bit of fun you've been cheerfully blowing yourself to pieces for God knows how many years."

Mr. Hawk looked at her broodingly.

"You know what happened to Blotto's tail?" he asked her.

"I'll never quite forget," replied Daffy. "Neither will Blotto."

"Well," continued Hawk, looking warningly at what he was thinking about, "if you don't want to chip when you sit down you'd better keep a respectful tongue in your head, or I'll splash yours with a dash of white."

"Sweet scientist," said Daffy. "Lofty mind."

CHAPTER III

Reluctant Statues

"Finished?" asked Daffy.

"Finished," replied Hawk. "Finished in spite of the fact that for the past three quarters of an hour you have been breathing with monotonous regularity on the back of my neck."

"I was so interested," the girl explained.

"And well you should be, my girl," said her uncle. "You have been privileged to witness the most unusual scientific discovery of all times, compared to which the Egyptians with their jolly old mummies were slapdash morticians. I do not claim that it is a useful discovery, but even you will have to admit it's a most diverting one."

"Yes," agreed Daffy. "It offers no end of pleasing possibilities."

"Practically inexhaustible," said Hawk. "I am contemplating one right now."

He turned to his work bench and picked up the two rings on which he had been working. In each ring was deeply imbedded one of the small silver balls most potently charged with its remarkable properties.

"I have merely to direct the rays emanating from this ring," he continued, "at any living object and that object, whether man or beast, will immediately be turned to stone. A slight pressure of the finger on the back of the ring is all that is required to release the ray. With this ring I can achieve either partial or complete petrification. For example, I could turn your left leg to stone if I felt so inclined."

"Think of something else," said Daffy.

"Now with this one," resumed her uncle, "I can

restore the subject or subjects to their former state of cellular elasticity, which in this world is none too happy. I dare say there are many persons who would consider it a favor just to be allowed to remain things of stone forever."

He paused and considered the rings with a dreamy expression in his eyes, then shifted his gaze to the girl.

"You," he said, "would make a lovely statue. I could keep you in the garden. Might even make a fountain out of you."

"You mean, let me stay out there winter and summer in the rain and snow and all?"

"Certainly. Why not? Are you particularly pleased with your present state?"

"No," admitted Daffy. "My present dull mode of existence is not an enviable one, but your alternative is even less attractive."

"For the present, then, said Hunter Hawk, "we shall keep the idea under consideration. There are other things to do."

"Yes," replied Daffy. "Let's do them all before we take up the matter of the fountain."

"Good," said her uncle. "On second thought you might make a better sundial or rustic bench."

"Sure," put in Daffy hastily. "There are ever so many things. If I wasn't so large you could make an ash tray or a book end out of me."

"Out of part of you," corrected Mr. Hawk. "Such utilitarian articles can be easily devised with a little chiseling and hacking here and there. Take Blotto's tail, for instance. I could easily have cracked it off and made a paper weight out of it, a most attractive paper weight. The same could be done——"

"I do wish you'd lay off this constant association of that hound's tail with my own personal anatomy," Daphne protested.

"As I remember it," replied her uncle, "you were the first to suggest the comparison."

"Well, I'm sick of the subject now," said Daffy. "Let's leave out tails altogether."

"It might be just as well," observed Mr. Hawk. "Would you like me to explain to you the fundamental principle on which this momumental discovery is based? There is a complicated part and a simple part, but they are so inextricably mixed that the whole thing becomes amazingly confusing. Some of it I've forgotten myself. To be quite frank I'm not altogether clear in my mind yet as to just what has happened. The explosion has left me a trifle dazed."

"I think we might profitably omit any attempt to understand the fundamental principles of this, as you say, diverting discovery of yours," said Daffy, "and put them to a practical demonstration instead."

"As you like," replied Mr. Hawk. "Go now and tell your mother, father, brother, and grandfather that I would like to have a word with them in the library. I have stood quite enough."

As the girl departed on her mission the scientist slipped one of the rings on the index finger of his right hand and the other one on his left. Had he realized at the moment the ultimate outcome of what he was doing it is barely possible that he might have hesitated, or at least thought twice about it, but in the end it would have made no difference. Destiny had made arrangements for a radical change in the even tenor of Hunter Hawk's days at this time. If it had not come to him in one way, it would have come to him in another. Nothing that he could do now could retain for him the cloistered, unworldly order of things. Mr. Hawk, had he but known it, was already well launched on his last and greatest discovery—woman and all of the complications she trails in her wake.

At thirty-seven Hunter Hawk was still rather a decent, unspoiled character. Although there was not one handsome feature in the composition of his face—save perhaps his eyes—the general effect was not displeasing. He was tall, lean, untidily crumpled, and permanently stained about the fingers. His disposition was evenly somber, and he had an infinite capacity for quietly but thoroughly disliking a great many persons and things. His laboratory was his life. It also served as a means of shutting out life. In it he moped, puttered, dreamed, and experimented most of his days away. He belonged to several scientific societies, and occasionally contributed to scientific quarterlies and reviews. By his fellow scientists he was considered a brilliant but erratic worker. This was perhaps due to the fact that he approached his researches with a certain element of humor.

"Wouldn't it be amusing if I could do this?" he would say to himself, and then devote much time and money endeavoring to find out how funny it would be. Quite frequently he would discover that it was not funny at all, whereupon he would abandon his experiments and be greatly upset for several days. He was fully satisfied that his latest discovery was the funniest thing he had done so far and, also, the most important. It was much funnier than the dissolving safety razor blade he had invented as a result of a wager with a certain derisive column conductor.

Until the arrival of his sister, Mrs. Alice Pollard Lambert, and her family, he had lived contentedly alone under the proprietorial management of Mr. and Mrs. Betts, two nice old creatures who knew a great deal more about Mr. Hawk's infantile explosions than the scientist did himself. Daphne had compensated him in part for the punishment involved in being forced to associate with his sister, his brother-in-law and nephew. Old man Lambert he could understand and appreciate.

Hunter Hawk's chief relaxation was tramping about the countryside and not acknowledging the salutations of his neighbors. He felt much more at home with strangers, and made many chance acquaintances by the roadside. Although he had little to do with women, he had an alert and observant eye and was able to distinguish with unerring accuracy between a possible and a probable. He would have made an eminently successful rake. Occasionally he would mix himself strange potions in the privacy of his laboratory and become slightly inebriated. At these times he could be heard to sing, yet no one, not even Betts, had ever been able to tell the name of the song. He was a strange, wrongheaded, acidulous man with a sardonic sense of humor which he kept for the most part to himself. He was fond of Blotto and Daffy in almost the same way. Both amused him. Because of his wealth and scientific prestige he was much sought after in the community in which he lived, but seldom gotten. His money alone lent warmth to his anti-social nature. He was not essentially a selfish man, but so far he had lived an entirely self-centered existence.

He now rose, and going to a wash basin, effaced the marks of the explosion. After sketchily combing his hair he donned a more presentable jacket and left the laboratory. As he made his way to the library he was more elated over his discovery than he cared to admit even to himself. It was stupendous, and he knew it.

"There is no need to apologize," his sister began when he had slouched into the room. "That explosion must have upset you."

"I know there's no need," he answered, his white teeth glittering wolfishly against the dark background of his face. "Nor any occasion."

"Of course, if you feel that way," she began.

"I do," he interrupted. "Very much that way. Let's drop the subject. I have no desire to add to the almost general disappointment arising from my inconsiderate escape from death."

"You told Daphne you had something to say to us," Alfred Lambert suggested.

"I have. Better still, I have something to do to you—the successful results of more than seven years of research and experimentation. Inasmuch as you all have suffered somewhat from these experiments, I have decided that you are at least entitled to be the first to witness the conclusive demonstration of my discovery. I may even allow you to take an important part in it."

"Very nice of you, I'm sure," Mrs. Lambert murmured.

"Mother, may I borrow Uncle Hunter's roadster?" demanded Junior in his high whine of a voice.

"No," replied Uncle Hunter, "you may not. I want you here—you especially."

He looked grimly at his nephew, whose gaze speedily sought the carpet in an effort to avoid the pent-up hostility blazing in his uncle's eyes.

"Now, listen," continued Hawk. "I have at last achieved complete cellular petrification through atomic combustion or disintegration. How I have achieved this incredible thing would overtax my capacity to explain and yours to understand. The important part is that I have done it. From now on there will be no more explosions. As a matter of fact, this house is going to be a quieter and happier place."

He paused to consider his small audience with a disconcertingly enigmatic smile.

"Much quieter than it ever was before," he went on. "Much, much quieter. It will be like a museum at midnight, if that means anything to you."

"I knew you'd be reasonable once we had spoken to you," said Mrs. Lambert uneasily. "But, Hunter dear, you don't have to go to extremes. We can stand a certain amount of noise, and after all, Junior is still a boy. We can't expect him——"

"He's going to be the quietest one of all," Hunter interrupted grimly.

Junior's scared eyes instinctively sought his mother's. Mrs. Lambert smiled reassuringly.

"It's one of your uncle's jokes, darling," she said. "You know how he is."

Junior was afraid that he knew only too well how his uncle was.

"Well, I'm delighted to hear that you've got hold of something at last," said Alfred Lambert heartily. "Has your discovery any commercial value? If so, my experience in promoting products and organizing companies is freely at your disposal."

"Thanks," replied Mr. Hawk dryly. "Wait and see."

The voice of old man Lambert came querulously from the corner.

"No nonsense, now, young man," it said. "I don't like all this. I don't like that look in your eye. It's a mean look. I've seen it there before."

"You have nothing to fear," replied the scientist. "You're practically petrified now as it is."

"Too much so," complained the old man. "I don't want to be any more than I am."

Hunter Hawk advanced into the center of the room.

"I am now going to turn myself into a human statue," he announced. "This is the first time it has ever been done. To all intents and purposes I shall be a thing of stone although retaining my mental faculties. Only my left hand will escape petrification. I shall need

25

that to restore myself to the bosom of my devoted family."

"Half a moment," interrupted Daffy. "Suppose that left hand doesn't work? What do you want me to do then?"

"Chip me up into small pieces and fling my remains at the neighbors," Hawk replied. "Be sure you hit them."

"Not a bad idea, that," said the girl.

"Horrible," breathed Mrs. Lambert.

A tremulous chuckle came from the corner. Grandfather Lambert was amused.

Hunter Hawk, arranging his features in a malevolent grin, folded his arms and, pressing the ring on his right hand, allowed the invisible rays to pass through his body. It was a delicate piece of work. He had to be extremely careful not to overdo it. Later, when he became more familiar with the action of the rays, he would know exactly how much his body could stand. At present he had no data from which to judge.

The effect of the ray was almost instantaneous. The terrible grin became fixed and solidified on Mr. Hawk's face. His body stiffened and turned to the color of marble. Even his clothing became white and ridged under the influence of the powerful ray.

Mrs. Lambert gave a gasp of horror as she looked at her brother's face.

"Now he will kill us all," she said. "His face is the face of a murderer. Look at it."

"I can't keep from looking at it," replied Alfred Lambert, "but God knows I don't want to. The only comforting thought is that if he's right in what he was saying he's more helpless now than ever before."

"Then why don't you knock his head off and say it was an accident?" suggested the old man.

A small but ominous rumble seemed to drop from the distorted lips of the statue.

"Oh, my God!" The words came from Alice Lambert, and they were nothing if not sincere. "Did anyone hear that?"

"I heard a very disagreeable something," replied her husband.

"You heard him," she declared, dramatically pointing at the hard-shelled Mr. Hawk. "It's just the sound he would make if he turned into a statue—a disturbing, sinister sound."

"Perhaps the beggar can hear you," suggested the ancient Lambert.

Alice Lambert shivered slightly.

"If he can," she replied, "I think it's downright indecent of him."

"Why does he have to look that way?" whined Junior. "Do you think he's gone mad?"

"I suspect he has always been mad," said Alice Lambert.

Once more the diminutive rumble rolled from the statue's lips. In it there was a note of warning.

At this moment Blotto, with the air of a strolling player, ambled into the room. He gave one look at his inanimate master, then showed the whites of his eyes and sat down heavily. A loud lament ascended to the ceiling from his elevated muzzle. The dog seemed to realize that the same misfortune had overtaken his best friend that had temporarily deprived him of the use of his own tail. Only in the case of his master it was much more so.

The howling of the dog did not add to the general merriment of the situation. Once more Mrs. Lambert shivered. Even Daffy became a little worried.

"For the love of Pete, dog," she exclaimed, "take that to a graveyard somewhere, won't you?"

Evidently Blotto wouldn't. His place was beside his master. He strained his throat desperately in another display of grief. This dismal cadence was interrupted by the tense arrival of Stella with the tea things. The sight of so much food made the dog thoughtful. When had he last eaten? When would he ever eat again? Perhaps Daffy might be prevailed upon to do something about it. He glanced significantly in her direction.

As for Stella, that comely maid was in great trouble. One look at Mr. Hawk had been sufficient to convince her that something was radically unorthodox in his appearance. After receiving the full force of the hellish smile on his twisted lips she froze in her tracks and outwardly became as much of a statue as he was. It seems unfortunate that at this moment Mr. Alfred

27

Lambert nerved himself to investigate this miraculous phenomenon. Leaving the comfortable security of the lounge, he approached the statue with the alert trepidation of an explorer drawing near an unknown shore. With a reluctant forefinger he pushed Mr. Hawk in the neighborhood of his diaphragm. A ghostly grunt emerged from the depth of the statue. Mr. Lambert hastily withdrew his finger. Stella, retaining her rigidity, began to breathe heavily.

"As hard as a rock," announced Mr. Lambert. "He couldn't have felt it."

"No, but he knew it," his wife replied.

"If he ever hits you a clip with one of those stone fists of his there'll be one less Lambert left to trouble my days," Alfred's father remarked. "Here, why don't you use my stick?"

The unpleasant possibility embodied in the old man's words effected a watchful retreat on the part of his son. When he returned to his investigation of his petrified brother-in-law he was in possession of a stout stick heavily mounted with a silver knob. With this he briskly tapped the statue. The statue responded with a hollow sound. What Mr. Hawk had accomplished only after seven years of dangerous and laborious experimenting Stella now accomplished through the simple medium of fear. She became perfectly white, her eyes became fixed in her head, and an expression of suffering congealed on her face. A stranger entering the room would have been tempted to applaud her warmly for her realistic impersonation of a statue. Once more Alfred Lambert tapped the man of stone, this time on his nose. The result of this was a cold click followed by a faint sneeze. Then the statue spoke and said in a far-off, eerie voice:

"Not on the nose, you fool," it said. "Tap hard enough for experimental purposes, but for God's sake don't chip me."

"Saints preserve us!" came from the numbed lips of Stella. "The thing will be moving next."

She abandoned all further responsibility for the safety of the tray and its burden and allowed it to drop on Blotto. For the dog it was like manna descending from heaven or the gentle dropping of dew. He escaped the hot water and found himself virtually surrounded by sandwiches. Amid the confusion resulting from Stella's unconsidered action Blotto sat and did what he decided was the wisest thing under the circumstances. He expeditiously consumed sandwiches. When order had been restored the company was amazed to see Hunter Hawk comfortably seated on the floor beside his dog and greedily wolfing down a large piece of cake while deftly snatching a sandwich from under Blotto's disgruntled nose.

"That sort of thing makes one hungry," he announced. "You see, I gave myself only a surface treatment. My material processes continued to function. Well, what do you think of it?"

"All very well for a side show," remarked his sister, "but hardly the sort of thing one would expect at tea time."

"A bit of devil work, it was," murmured Stella.

"It was very good," commended old man Lambert. "Very good indeed. I only regret I wasn't able to take a whack at you myself."

Hawk looked up with a grin.

"I heard your thoughtful suggestion," he said.

The old fellow chuckled wickedly.

"I meant it, too," he replied.

"It's all very interesting," said Alfred, "but I can't see any commercial possibilities for the thing—no practical application."

"Oh, you can't," exclaimed the scientist. "How about putting an end to the activities of objectionable individuals? Think of what it could do for humanity. If I had made this discovery previous to the World War I could have turned a flock of statesmen to stone, and then there wouldn't have been any war. And the economic as well as artistic waste entailed by eventually making statues of those self-same wholesale butchers would have been eliminated. The majority of statesmen should be born statues, anyway."

Alfred's face began to glow avariciously.

"Got it!" he cried. "Got it! The United States government would give you millions in cold cash for the use of your discovery. We could play up the bloodless side of the thing. That sort of drip is popular right now. Victory without death, you know. Do you want me to get in touch with the right parties and arrange for a demonstration?"

"We haven't quite finished with our own little demonstration here," Mr. Hawk replied darkly. "But why don't you try to sell it to Mussolini first? He'd put his country in hock to see himself as a statue and to experience while still alive something approaching the adulation of posterity."

"I'm serious," protested Mr. Lambert. "Provide me with the formula, and I'll make a fortune for all of us."

"Yes, Hunter," spoke up Alice. "You can trust Alfred. I can see his point now. Why, this discovery is a gold mine, but of course you could never do anything with it yourself. Executive ability is required to make it mean anything, and the man who has that and who can put your discovery over is entitled to share equally in the glory and financial reward. It's lucky Alfred is not doing anything at present."

"You have no idea how lucky it is," replied Hunter, rising.

"Are you going to do it, Uncle?" asked Junior, unable to restrain his eagerness.

"I'm going to do something," Mr. Hawk replied. "I'm going to put an end to long years of insufferable boredom. You go first."

He raised his right hand and crooked its index finger at the youth. Alfred Lambert sprang to his feet as he saw his son turn to stone.

"I say," he began, but his voice failed as he followed his Junior's example. His mouth remained open as if still framing a protest. Mrs. Lambert was next to go, and after her the old man solidified comfortably in his chair. Mr. Hawk turned and considered his niece.

"Don't pick on me," she told him. "I'm going to make a heavy date for myself to-night if you keep them frozen long enough."

"With whom?" asked her uncle.

"Cy Sparks," she replied.

Mr. Hawk considered.

"All right," he said at last. "Cy's not altogether impossible. Try to get back in the general direction of

30

midnight." He turned to Stella. "You may go now, Stella," he told her.

"If I can," replied the maid. "My knees are all wrong. They wobble."

Cautiously she crept from the room. At the door she halted and cast one swift, awed glance at the petrified family.

"Saints preserve us," she muttered and diligently crossed herself.

Hunter Hawk stood regarding the statues he had created. There was a gleam of triumph in his eyes.

"That," he said at last to his niece, "greatly simplifies matters. Your father is a particularly arresting study. I'm rather proud of him. Grandpa isn't half bad either. His venerable appearance gives him the dignity he ordinarily so lamentably lacks."

"Can they hear us?" asked Daffy.

"I hope so," Hawk replied. "I gave them just a dash. My dear sister would love to make a few choice remarks, I'm sure of that. When I turn my laboratory into a breakfast room and lounge, as she suggested, I'm going to put her in an alcove just as she is. She can have the room all to herself."

A blotchy pink color crept for a moment into the cold pale cheeks of Mrs. Lambert, then faded away. A dry croak came from the corner in which her father-in-law was sitting. Alfred Lambert looked on in stony silence.

Of all the statues Junior pleased Blotto the most. Blotto particularly disliked Junior. Junior had kicked him once, and Blotto still remembered that kick. Junior was a detestable young man. Something should be done about him. The dog hoped that the transformation was permanent. He could do without a lot of Junior. As he busily sniffed the feet and legs of the statue Blotto forgot his manners for the first time in years. Daffy uttered a scream of delight.

"Why, Blotto!" she exclaimed. "What a thing to do."

Blotto with head and tail erect marched proudly from the room. The kick had been avenged.

"Dogs do enjoy certain advantages over human beings," observed his master as he followed Blotto.

31

"On occasions their lack of formality is greatly to be envied."

"If not emulated," added Daffy.

CHAPTER IV

The Little Man and the Scarecrow

DINNER THAT EVENING WAS ONE OF THE MOST EN-joyable meals Mr. Hawks had taken into his attenuated body for many a long day. It was attended only by himself and his niece. That was the reason. Blotto lurked in the background.

The scientist was in excellent fettle, and his mood seemed to have communicated itself to the equally ex-cellent Betts, who moved about the table with unaccus-tomed briskness. A quarter of a century had dropped from the old servant's shoulders.

"It's like old times, Betts," remarked Mr. Hawk, "with the exception of Miss Daffy here."

"It is, Mr. Hunter," replied Betts beamingly. "And a very pleasant exception it is, to be sure, if you'll par-don my saying it."

"Go on and say it, Betts," said Daffy. "Say it loud and often. I'll pardon you as much as you like just as long as you keep on making such encouraging little speeches."

"Thank you, Miss Daffy," said Betts.

"And, Betts," commanded Mr. Hawk, "descend into the bowels of this structure and return with a couple of bottles of something sort of especially that way. You know what I mean, Betts."

"La vie mondaine," gloated the girl. *"La vie joyeuse.* Oh, my! Wine is good, and my uncle the salt of the earth."

Betts's beam was almost audible as he hurried to carry out the most congenial instructions he had re-ceived in a long time. Stella, who assisted at dinner, en-tered with a bowl of soup. It was plain to see that she looked upon Hawk as a none too minor demon. Her reluctance to linger in his vicinity caused her to spill a plate of soup as she nervously snatched it from under the tureen. Hawk fixed her with a stern eye.

32

"What do you think of what happened in the library?" he asked her.

"I'm trying not to think of it," she replied, dabbing at the carpet with a serving cloth. "It's all right for Mr. Betts. He didn't see what I saw."

She rose from her crouching position and almost sprang across the room.

"Would you like to make a fifth?" Hawk demanded.

"Mary, Peter, and Joseph!" gasped Stella, putting in a three-alarm call for heavenly succor. "I would not, Mr. Hawk."

"Then stop flinging soup about the place, or I'll damn well turn you to stone," he assured her.

"She'd make a lovely Venus," suggested Daffy. "I've seen her that way."

"Miss Daffy!" admonished Stella, her outraged modesty momentarily overcoming her fear. "You shouldn't say such things."

"Rubbish, Stella," replied Daffy. "You're as proud of your shape as a peacock. Wouldn't she make a bang-up Venus, Uncle Hunter?"

"Not having enjoyed the same opportunities as you," Mr. Hawk answered judicially, "I am not in a position to say without considerable research and investigation. However, purely superficial observations would lead me to believe that perhaps you are right. She'd bang as a Venus."

Under the penetrating scrutiny of Mr. Hawk's glittering eyes Stella sought refuge in the kitchen.

"They're a couple of black-hearted devils, the pair of them," she informed Mrs. Betts.

"What are they up to now?" inquired that good woman.

"Miss Daffy said I'd make a lovely Venus," Stella replied with a rush. "A bang-up one."

Apparently this meant little to Mrs. Betts.

"And who might that party be?" she asked.

"Some naked heathen she-goddess," explained Stella. "I saw a statue of her once."

"Oh, that one," said Mrs. Betts, peering into the oven. "I remember her now. Well, a worse thing might have been said. She used to have a clock in her stomach."

"But the way he looked at me," continued Stella. "You don't know. There was ruin in his eyes."

Mrs. Betts rested her hands on her hips and looked steadfastly at the large-eyed girl.

"Listen, my fine young wench," she said. "If Mr. Hunter wants to ruin you, which I doubt, supposing such a thing was possible, which I also doubt, you can consider yourself ruined and a very lucky girl at that. It's not every woman he ruins. He's not ruined a maid since I've kept house for him, and that's been all of his life. He's been a great disappointment to me in that direction."

"What do you know about it?" Stella demanded a little defiantly.

"All," said Mrs. Betts with admirable compactness. "Everything."

"I'd rather sleep with the devil," declared Stella.

"There'd be little sleep with that busybody," replied Mrs. Betts, "if we're to believe the half of what we hear about him."

Deriving scant comfort from the unedifying observations of the elder woman, Stella returned to the dining room, where she made herself generally unhelpful and kept getting in the way of the exasperated Mr. Betts. Occasionally she would dart speculative glances at the prospective source of her approaching ruin. If only he were not in league with the powers of darkness the future would not have been altogether unendurable.

Unconscious of the delicate office allotted to him Mr. Hawk proceeded cheerfully through his dinner. This finished, he rose and, wishing his niece good hunting, sought the seclusion of the back veranda. As a result of the wine and the complete success of his discovery the scientist found himself in a slightly elevated mental condition. There was a tingling sensation in his veins. He felt as if something unusual were going to happen, that some remarkable adventure was already on its way to him. Ordinarily Mr. Hawk, when thus assailed by this inexplicable exaltation of spirit, would have retired to his bed and endeavored there to return to reason through the medium of some abstruse scientific treatise, but to-night he was in no mood to share his bed with a book.

34

Across the dark tops of the trees a brute of a moon was casting bolts of golden gauze. An August night filled with haze and the scent of moistly breathing vegetation lay around him. Clouds scuttled across the sky and cavorted weirdly in a far-away wind only the lingering breath of which moved among the trees.

In front of him stretched the country and the night. His eyes followed the familiar path that twisted up a grassy slope and dipped into a grove of trees only to appear again on the margin of a cornfield. That path had a fascination for Mr. Hawk. He never grew tired of treading it—of thinking about it. To him it was like some huge serpent that never got anywhere but which in the fullness of time would move along to some dangerously enchanted place. Mr. Hawk was one of those persons who retain a keen awareness of the impressions and sensations of early youth. He still remembered a patch of sun-baked mud that had exerted over him a spell of attraction far stronger than the gardens and orchards surrounding his home. He could still recall the cracks in its tawny surface and the smooth, hot feel of it against the soles of his bare feet. The acrid, febrile smell of the weeds that flourished round its margin frequently drifted back to him from the past. This path had something of the same influence on his imagination. A whisper seemed to be running down it now, summoning him out to the woods and fields where unknown but pleasant things were waiting.

In obedience to some inner prompting he went back into the house. Unhesitatingly he descended to the cellar and returned presently with two bottles of Burgundy. For more than half a century these tubes of magic had lain under old dusty dimness dreaming of vineyards gratefully ripening beneath the far, fair skies of France.

On the way out he looked in at the library to see how his petrified encumbrances were getting along. Silently he displayed the bottles to them, raised one bottle to his lips in a dumb show of drinking, then appreciatively patted his stomach. Mr. Hawk was enjoying every moment of his revenge. As he left the room something like a groan followed him from the cold lips of old Grandpa Lambert.

Crossing the back lawn he passed through the fragrance of an old-fashioned garden and, opening a small white gate set in a hedge of box bushes, set out along the path. He had no definite destination in mind. He had hardly anything at all in mind save a floating, hazy sensation of well-being, an intimate relationship with the night and the world around him. All he knew was that he was going to some place and drink a lot of wine and, perhaps, sing a little to himself and the trees, if he felt so inclined.

On the summit of the hill he paused and looked back at his long rambling house sprawled peacefully out in sleep beneath the yellow flood of the moon. For a moment he stood silhouetted against the sky, a tall, lean figure of a man with two large bottles dangling at the ends of his arms—a rather enigmatic outline in the night. Then he dipped down into a grove of trees and became lost in the darkness piled up against their trunks. As he passed through the grove an expectant hush lay about him, a sort of breathless hesitation trembling on the verge of some strange revelation. But Mr. Hawk did not linger in the grove. For some blind reason he continued along the path. It was as if a muted voice at the end of it were endeavoring to get his ear. Presently the trees were left behind and, coming out into the full flood of the moon, he followed the course of the path as it circled a vast cornfield, and then, as if suddenly changing its mind, took a short cut through it.

Dark, keen-leafed stalks rose and rustled on either side of Mr. Hawk. He caught the pungent scent of corn silk and absently decided that he was inordinately fond of corn—preferably on the cob. He came upon a scarecrow, and on a mound beside the scarecrow a little tattered man was sitting. And the little tattered man was crying bitterly, his tear-stained face raised to the distinguished figure flapping against the stars.

Under ordinary circumstances the scientist would have been slightly mystified by this encounter. In his present all-embracing frame of mind it struck him as being the most natural thing in the world. Why shouldn't a little tattered man be sitting in a cornfield in the moonlight crying bitterly at a scarecrow? And why shouldn't he, Hunter Hawk, stop and ask this little tattered man what the devil he was crying about? Hunter Hawk did.

"Why all the lachrymose moisture?" he demanded. "Speak, little tattered man."

The little man gasped and looked startled. He promptly ceased crying and seemed on the point of flight. Some wayward strain in Mr. Hawk's nature must have reached out to the other, however, for he remained alertly poised on the mound.

"Why all the what?" he faltered.

"The tears," Mr. Hawk explained.

"Oh, those," said the little man. "I shouldn't have taken on so, but sometimes I get so furious I can't help it."

"What were you furious about just now, if it isn't too long a story?"

"I'm furious about that scarecrow. I want his clothes. I especially want his hat."

Mr. Hawk glanced up at the scarecrow. It was wearing a beaver hat in rather a fair state of preservation. As a matter of fact, the scarecrow was about the best dressed specimen of his deceitful tribe Mr. Hawk had ever seen. It was decked out in a morning coat, gray-striped trousers, and patent-leather shoes. There were spats. A withered gardenia decorated its lapel, and a gray Ascot tie adorned its neck. It was stoutly stuffed with straw.

"That's about the most up-stage scarecrow I ever met," Mr. Hawk observed.

"Isn't it?" exclaimed the tattered individual eagerly. "And look at me—a living creature. Rags and patches. More of a scarecrow than it is."

"Then why don't you assault this scarecrow?" asked Mr. Hawk. "Lay the beggar low and strip him to his straw? I know the person who owns him. Man named Brightly. It would give me no little satisfaction to see his scarecrow outraged. He's a rich, profiteering, shot-and-shell sort of a chap, and he belongs to the League for the Promotion of Class Distinction. Also, he has warts and an exceedingly dizzy wife. In short, he makes me sick. Why don't you despoil this scarecrow? It looks too damn smug."

The little tattered man shook his head sadly.

"Can't do it," he answered. "I'm afraid. You see, I'm one of the last of the Little People, and it's against our magic to rob scarecrows. It would bring us some great misfortune. And God knows we've had enough already. Only a few of us are left now. We're the last family in the neighborhood, although we're older than the oldest settler. We're even older than your family. I knew your father well by sight. He was much like you, only by this time of night he usually staggered more."

"Thanks," said Mr. Hawk rather dryly. "I can tell you must have known him. Exactly what did you say you were—one of the Little People? I've heard of them or read of them or something."

"Yes," replied the little man. "We emigrated from Ireland long before the great-great-grandfather of Christopher Columbus ever climbed through a bedroom window."

"I never knew he did," said Hunter Hawk.

"Neither do I," replied the little man, "but I imagine he must have done. Most every man does at one time or another, if it isn't too far to the ground. Haven't you?"

"You're getting a bit personal," Hawk replied with a grin, "but now you've asked me, I'll say that I never left that way."

"Then you've missed one of life's most illegitimate thrills," said the little man, sighing reminiscently. "Also spills, perhaps. I'm disappointed in you, my dear sir. Once at least to every man, you know. But perhaps she wasn't married?"

"I make a practice of never asking," Mr. Hawk hastened to assure him. "You get lied to less that way. But were you saying you came over from Ireland?"

"I was saying exactly that," replied the little man, with a note of sadness in his voice. "The country virtually belonged to us then. We didn't have to listen to 'Mother Machree,' or 'Come Back to Erin,' or 'The Rose of Sharon,' or to any bum jokes about It Seems There Were Two Irishmen, Pat and Mike. Taking the good with the bad, we were quite happy and contented.

In later years the uninterrupted wailing of those songs over on the other side was one of the reasons for our migrating. Of course, we had the Indians here to deal with, but they were an essentially simple-minded lot, and we were soon able to get around them. Everything went along well until the police force came over from Ireland. After that we began to wane. Our magic gradually weakened, until we have only a little left with which to eke out a bare existence. Most of our people have moved away to China or to South America for the revolutions. Many of them just crawled into caves and crevasses in rocks and went to sleep forever. Is there wine in those bottles?"

"There is," replied Mr. Hawk, thinking the little man deserved at least a drink of wine after his long speech. "Do you want some?"

"Yes," answered the little man. "I want some, and then some more."

"So you're that kind of a little man," observed Mr. Hawk, eyeing him with approval. "A regular winebibber."

"In my time I have bibbed a little," he modestly admitted.

The quiet of the cornfield was broken by the pop of a cork. A small patch of moonlight was splashed by the spray of the wine.

"It's a heartening sound," said the little man.

"One of the sweetest sounds I know," said Mr. Hawk.

"How does the sound taste?" asked the little man.

"After you," replied Mr. Hawk with admirable self-control.

The little man accepted the bottle and, tilting back his head, drank long and deeply. Mr. Hawk watched the proceeding with a mixture of admiration and concern. At last the bibber returned the bottle and drew a deep breath. Then he faced about and aggressively eyed the scarecrow.

"I feel like knocking your block off," he muttered. "You big toff."

"Let's give him the bum's rush," suggested Mr. Hawk, wiping the tears from his eyes as he set the bottle down in the path. "I can't bear the sight of that scarecrow."

The little man shook his head.

"You're big enough to do it alone," he said. "Why don't you reach me down that hat?"

"I will," replied Mr. Hawk, taking another swig at the bottle. "I'll strip the devil mother-naked, and you can have all his clothes. How do you go in spats?"

"Oh, thank you so much," breathed the little man, his hand reaching out for the bottle. "I don't know. I never went in spats. How do you think I'd go?"

"Dandy," exclaimed Mr. Hawk ecstatically, and coiling his long body he released some hidden spring suddenly and dived through the air at the scarecrow. For a moment the figure flapped frantically in the moonlight, then toppled among the cornstalks beneath the weight of its assailant's body.

"Got him!" cried Mr. Hawk, thrashing about among the corn. "Now we'll undress his nibs. Wonder if he wears drawers?"

"Don't wear them myself," said the little man. "I'm much more interested in that hat. Hope you didn't smash it."

"Here it is," announced the man of science, rising triumphantly from the corn with the scarecrow's coat and trousers. The hat was tilted rakishly over his left eye.

He flung the garments at the little man, passed him the hat, then dived back in the direction of the scarecrow.

"No. No drawers," he called out. "I'm afraid you'll have to do without drawers, but here's his shoes and spats and necktie."

"You will insist on my wearing drawers," the little man replied, "when all the time I keep telling you that the Little People wear no drawers."

"Not even the little ladies?" asked the cornfield.

"They least of all. Couldn't get a pair on 'em."

"Then they're not such little ladies."

"And they don't pretend to be. That's why they're superior to your brand of women."

"I should say so," Mr. Hawk replied, emerging from

40

the cornfield with the last shreds of the scarecrow's wearing apparel. "He's as clean as a whistle now."

"Half a minute," replied the little man. "Thanks a lot. I'll be ready before you know it."

Rapidly he divested himself of his tattered clothing, and Mr. Hawk discovered to his amusement that his companion of the cornfield had spoken no less than the truth. The little man wore no drawers. In almost less than half a minute he was fully attired in what had once been perhaps the most fashionable scarecrow that had ever given a crow a raucous, ribald laugh.

"How do I look?" asked the little man. "Are the spats on right?"

"Splendid!" cried Mr. Hawk. "Perfectly right, only they're on backwards."

"Necktie, too?"

"A neat knot."

"I'm so pleased," murmured the little man. "My daughter will be quite surprised."

"Have you a daughter?" asked Mr. Hawk.

"A howling hell of a daughter," replied the other. "She was born in this country, so of course she's much larger than the native-born Little People. And she's taken up American ways. Dresses and talks like the modern young girl, but in spite of all that she can still turn a pretty trick of magic when she has a mind to."

"How old is this daughter of yours, this howling hell of a daughter?" Mr. Hawk inquired in a casual voice.

"Not more than nine hundred years, I should say. The exact date I don't rightly remember, but she's still just a girl."

"Oh," said Mr. Hawk a little blankly. "I see. A mere flapper. Shall we open the other bottle?"

"You practically took the words out of my mouth," said the little man admiringly.

"I hope I won't have to do the same with the bottle," Mr. Hawk said without any attempt to disguise his meaning. "You almost inhaled the bottom out of the last one."

"I was afraid you might think I didn't like it."

"You may dismiss all such qualms now," said the scientist, most unscientifically fumbling with the cork

41

of the second bottle. "I'm convinced that the stuff doesn't revolt you."

"Far from it," said the little man. "I am very fond of your wine. I shall probably steal your wine now that I know you have it. You must understand, sir, we live by stealing. It's our only recourse. Although I wouldn't touch that scarecrow, I'd steal the eyeteeth out of your head."

"Thanks for your frankness," said Hunter Hawk. "Would you like my eyeteeth now?"

"I do not need eyeteeth," replied the little man.

"Well, any time you'd like to have a couple of eye-teeth—or are there four of them?—I'll have them packed up and sent around to you. 'An eye for an eye and a tooth for a tooth.' I'll do even better than that. I'll give you all my teeth—the whole damn set—and not ask for even an eye."

"Any gold in them?" the other asked.

"Filled with gold," replied Mr. Hawk, and collapsed in such a surge of laughter that the night became alive with the cacophony of his mirth.

"That wasn't so funny," said the little man when Mr. Hawk had pulled himself together.

"No? Wasn't it?" he replied weakly. "Well, I'll get much funnier later on. Wait and see."

"And not laugh," said the little man.

"Oh, all right," replied Mr. Hawk. "Have it your way. Entirely your own way."

Once more the pop of a vigorous cork ricocheted against the astonished cornstalks and once more the venerable bubbles renewed their youth as for a brief moment they lent grace to the moonlight before falling in foam to the soil.

"The call to arms," said Mr. Hawk. "By the way, just what is your name?"

"Name?" replied the little man. "I used to have lots of names—Lim, Shawn, Angus, and Mehal. There's safety in having a change of names. Since the World War I've rather fancied Ludwig Turner."

"Sounds extremely un-Irish to me."

"It is. It does. Where were we? Oh, yes, the wine. Let's drink it. My name saves a lot of nationalistic, or should I say racial, singing. No one knows where I come from, what I am, or who I am. I once knew an English barmaid——"

"Not interested in low memoirs of a personal nature," proclaimed Mr. Hawk. "Don't want to hear about your English barmaids. Have you ever gone through an explosion?"

"On and off for two dozen centuries as time is inaccurately reckoned by mortals, I've been a married man," said Ludwig Turner. "Most of them were explosive. All were explosive. One after the other exploded herself into premature ugliness. I have no wife now. Only one spawn. She is on the explosive side also, but it seems to do her good. It damn well agrees with her. More beautiful every day."

"Well, I've just been through a most thorough explosion," said Mr. Hawk, not without pride. "A real one. The seventh. I'm still a little bit dazed. Not sure of anything. Not sure of you or the night or this cornfield full of corn stalks——"

"What would a cornfield be full of?"

"Wouldn't surprise me if it was full of azaleas," said Hunter Hawk. "It might not be real at all. Nothing seems real. Nothing quite is."

"If you don't pass me that bottle there'll be another explosion," the other one remarked. "That will be real enough."

Mr. Hawk absently passed the bottle to his small companion.

The scientist had spoken truly. Nothing seemed real to him. And perhaps on that strange night nothing was quite real. Otherwise there seems to be no rational explanation for all the things that took place. Certainly this little man could not be real. Obviously. Wrapped opulently in the drapery of much wine Hunter Hawk no longer cared to question the reality of things. He had a strong impression that he was sitting in a cornfield drinking wine with a little man in a top hat who declared that he was twenty-four centuries old. It was a great age to Mr. Hawk, but not an impossible one. He chose to believe the little old man. Had not he himself just achieved the impossible? Had not he accomplished a miracle of science? Perhaps the impossible came to those who did the impossible. Perhaps not. Or maybe it was the other way round. Anyway, the little man's spats were on backward. That fact, assuming the reality of the wearer, was as plain as the nose on his face. Mr. Hawk would establish reality on the backwardness of his friend's spats. That was something if not much. He reached out and seized the bottle from the avid Mr. Turner. The wine tasted real enough, though perhaps that also was just a little too marvelous to be real. Anyhow, what did it matter? What did matter was that he wanted to sing. In fact, he would sing. But what song? Try as he would, Mr. Hawk, what with the wine and the moonlight and the natural perverseness of a man's mind, could think of no song save "Mother Machree." It would have to be that song. He began to sing it not well but willingly.

"Oh, for God's sake, don't sing that!" exclaimed the little man, rising.

Mr. Hawk stopped and looked impatiently at his friend.

"Then what shall I sing?" he demanded.

"Almost anything but that."

"I've tried to, but I can't think of anything but that at the moment," Mr. Hawk explained. "Won't you sit down?"

The little man sat and thought, and the scientist sat and thought, and presently the little man looked up brightly.

"I have it," he announced. "The very song. Heard it the other night when I was stealing vegetables from your garden. I remembered it because it's the most non-partisan song I ever heard. The most impartial. It means nothing and it goes: Boop-Boop-a-Doop. I love it."

"Sounds like a motor boat lulling its young to sleep," said Mr. Hawk, "but I'll try it if only because you heard it on my radio while stealing my vegetables from my garden."

"We'll both sing it," said the other, and they did just that.

A late stroller suffering from insomnia heard the strange noise issuing from the heart of the cornfield. It had a salutary effect on him. He no longer was a late stroller, but became a man of actions, a man of single

44

purpose. So briskly did he return to his home and jump into bed that the exhaustion caused by his exertion speedily brought the sleep that had eluded him.

Unaware of the favor they had done the man, Messrs. Hawk and Turner back in the cornfield blissfully continued Boop-Boop-a-Dooping until the bottle of Burgundy was no longer able to lubricate their hard-working throats. It was drained to the last drop. The scientist lifted the empty bottle and held it between his eyes and the moonlight.

"All gone," said the little man.

CHAPTER V

A Furious Reception

Doesn't sound so good without wine, does it?" observed Mr. Hawk at length, stopping to replenish his exhausted lungs.

"No," admitted the little man gloomily, "nor feel so good, either. Let's go to your house and get some more."

"Don't you live anywhere?" Hawk demanded. "No home?"

"Oh, yes," replied the little man. "I have a home of sorts."

"Then why don't you go there and take me with you?"

"We might do that," was the skeptical reply. "Only applejack there, and not so much of that."

"Let Providence take a turn," said Mr. Hawk. "After what you've got is all gone we'll think of something else."

"And I know just what we'll think of," returned the other. "We'll think of me struggling through the dark in search of more drink."

"Your daughter, perhaps?"

"She might—if she's in a good humor, which she seldom is. Still, she might. Anyway, we'll try that. Sure you won't go to your house?"

"Not now. Later, perhaps."

"Then I guess we'll have to go to mine. Rightly

45

speaking, it isn't a house at all, but you'll see for yourself. I hope you'll not be sorry."

"Sorry? Why should I be sorry?"

"Oh, I don't know," said the little man evasively. "There might be many reasons."

There were, but no one will ever know if Hunter Hawk at any time seriously regretted his visit to the abode of his casual little friend of the cornfield. Certain it is that many a more intrepid soul, foreseeing the remarkable results of that visit, would have bade the little man good-night on the spot and returned to the safe, sane, and familiar surroundings of his own home. And, of course, it will never be ascertained now whether or not Mr. Hawk would have turned back or even hesitated, had he been able to read the meaning of the little man's prophetic words. Perhaps that appointment had already been made for him by some unseen, unknown secretary who, without consulting our preferences, makes all our important appointments, including the final one. Perhaps Hunter Hawk, even had he tried, would have been unable to avoid this one. The answer to these minor questions will never be known. Their answers do not matter. What is known and what does matter is the simple fact that on a certain night in August, Hunter Hawk, three sheets in the wind, accompanied an exceedingly small and queerly garbed creature to his home, and that there he met one Meg or Megaera, and that forever after he was never quite a free man. At times he even kissed the chains that shackled him. And rumor has it, he went a great deal farther than that.

The way was mostly moonlight and lurches. There were trees and a world of bushes, dense, aggressive bushes. There were patches of moon glow and tunnels of utter darkness. There was the sound of much sincere cursing and always the thrashing of leaves being crunched under foot. Both sounds were made by Mr. Hawk. The little man did his lurching with surprising silence and deftness. And he knew every twist in the mystifying way. Hawk was never able to return to the spot alone. Finally and most amazingly he found himself in a murmurous grotto—a secret pocket in the earth, remote from the world of men.

From the roof of this grotto a tiny stream splashed to the floor, and running through the center of the chamber, disappeared with a whisper through a small, bush-concealed opening. Straddling this strand of water was a rough table, and only those who were adepts could sit at the table without getting their feet wet. But few ever sat at that table now, although many had in the past. On either side of the table were two long benches, and somewhere in the remote shadows there was the suggestion of bunks made from the boughs of trees. And in this chamber there were the smell of moist earth and drenched bushes and the everlasting splash and murmur of falling water. And in this chamber, there was a small girl—or woman—one of the smallest and most furious-looking creatures Hunter Hawk remembered ever having seen.

Great eyes were hers, great black, fuming eyes, astir with sullen lights, eyes ready to blaze and flame, but seldom to caress. A dark skin. Short, straight, blue-black hair. A beautiful mouth and the appealing features of a delicate child. It was a face of confusing contradictions. And when this girl arose from the table at their entrance, Mr. Hawk needed only one glance at her slim but delightfully developed figure to appreciate the fact that here was a woman to deal with, not a child, not even a slip of a girl. This small thing with the hostile eyes, the child's face, and the provocative breasts of a well formed woman, could, he more than half suspected, be a highly diverting companion on certain auspicious occasions. It was only too immediately apparent that this was not going to be one of those occasions, for at the mere sight of the two strangely matched gentlemen she sprang from the table and words entirely unpleasant fairly sizzled off her tongue.

"So," she said, and again, "so. We're back, are we?" A pause to permit the gentlemen to receive the full benefit of her furious eyes. "And what do you think I am—dirt? Dirt to sit here in this filthy hole and wait?" Although neither gentleman attempted to answer these questions, Mr. Hawk felt strongly inclined to make the observation that that was usually what dirt seemed to enjoy most—sitting in holes and waiting. "Where the hell have you been?" she continued. "You look like the devil. Worse. And what's wrong with that person? Tell him to go away. Get out of here, both of you," the deadly voice continued. "Disappear!"

"A true explosive," Mr. Hawk remarked to his companion, at whom he was looking with increased respect and admiration. "Tell me, have you had that with you for nine hundred years?"

"That and more," said Mr. Turner. "Much. That's nothing. She's only playful now.

"Am I"?

Bang! A heavy mug whizzed past the left ear of the small man and shattered itself against a rock in the wall of the grotto.

This act of swift and efficient violence sobered Hunter Hawk considerably. He realized that at any moment his turn might come. It was a matter of dodge or die. Nevertheless, he regarded the enraged, but in every other respect most desirable young lady, with critical admiration. Instinctively he felt that he figured her out just a little, no more than that.

"You deliberately missed him," he informed her, his eyes no less dark and glittering than hers.

Startled and annoyed, she looked back at him. In that swift moment contact was established. It was never to be quite broken thereafter. She looked into his eyes and liked them. Not for a hundred years had she liked the eyes of a mortal. Those eyes, those black, quiet, sardonic eyes of Hunter Hawk both troubled and fascinated her. All of which made her more angry.

"A lot you know about it," she said, sullenly and sat down. Hawk made no attempt to answer. He stood there quietly looking at her. She knew it. She hated it. "I could have hit him," she said defiantly. "I have hit him and if you get fresh with me, I'll damn well hit you—you long-legged booby."

Hawk had a peculiar temper of his own. Certain words—not necessarily desperately insulting ones at that—had the power to throw him off poise, to stir up the usually placid springs of his nature. Booby was one of those words. The word always evoked for him the mental image of a fat, bubble-lipped boy.

"Booby, am I?" he retorted. "Well, what are you but an ill-natured little snip, a mere thing, a pea?"

48

"What!" cried the girl incredulously. "Me, a snip? A thing? A pea?"

Bang!

The crash of the second mug completely sobered Mr. Hawk. This conduct was unreasonable. It would have to stop. One of those mugs might find its mark. With the unfailing good fortune of a man who attracts women and never knows quite why, he played his trump card in spite of the muttered urgings of Mr. Turner to have nothing to say to her "just yet."

"Listen," he said. "I'm nervous as a cat. Got an awful hangover. Been drinking for a week. Have you got a little pick-me-up anywhere round?"

A light of morbid interest came into the mad black eyes. The girl considered him darkly but not venomously.

"Nervous, eh?" she said. "Headache? How are your eyes?"

"Bad. Awful." Mr. Hawk blinked rapidly several times.

"What you need is a good physic."

"I know, I'll take one, but I'll crack unless I get a pick-up right now."

"Got anybody at home to look after you when you get there?"

"Yes. Lots of 'em—too many."

"Well, I hope to God you don't go blabbing to them that you met some woman in the woods who got you drunk. Not that I give a damn," she added inconsistently.

She rose from the table and moved swiftly to the end of the chamber. There was the sound of secretive rummaging—things being swiftly moved. Soon she returned with a quart bottle two thirds filled with applejack.

"Here," she said, handing him a glass. "Pour your own. I don't know how much you take, but watch yourself."

"I'd prefer to watch you."

Ludwig Turner stood dumbly by, his eyes fixed wistfully on the bottle.

"How about——?" Hawk nodded significantly in the direction of his host.

49

"What—that one?" replied the girl scornfully. "What he needs is a good thrashing. Wouldn't you think that after twenty-four centuries he'd have sense enough, self-respect enough to give up this knocking about the country, staying out late at night and bringing home with him the first tramp he picks up? Present company not excepted."

"I refuse to answer that," said Mr. Hawk.

For a full minute packed with suspense for Mr. Turner she looked appraisingly at him while she drummed irritatingly on the table with the tips of her fingers. To relieve the strain of this protracted scrutiny, her father made an attempt at an ingratiating smile.

"Don't smile at me, you old dog," she said. "Come over here and get your drink. No pride, no shame, just a plain sot. I'm through with you. Here, swallow it down, bottle and all."

This invitation, in spite of the rough verbiage in which it was couched, led to one of the most pleasant nights Hunter Hawk had so far spent in the course of his rather confined if casual existence. One drink led to another, and by the time the story of the assaulted scarecrow had been thrice repeated at the special request of Miss Turner, who was able to extract from it at each telling fresh sources of enjoyment, the applejack had long dissociated itself from the bottle.

"Miss Turner," asked Hawk with elaborate politeness, "could you manage to rummage up another one?"

"If you'll call me Meg I might. Otherwise, no," she replied.

"I am fond of the name of Meg," said Hawk. "It sounds so old and hard. You are well named, Meg, my wench."

"I don't like that. Wench isn't nice," replied Meg. "And I'll have you to know that my name is a damn sight older than yours."

"It is," put in Mr. Turner mollifyingly. "It is, Meg. Yours is the oldest name of all. It dates way back to the days of pagan Greece, when life was worth living. You are a direct descendent of Megaera, one of the Three Furies."

"I was always under the impression," observed Mr.

Hawk, "that those ladies were so ill favored and disagreeable that propagation and that sort of thing was way out of their line."

"In that you are correct," replied the little man academically. "And that is what made them so furious. But Megaera seems to have been a little more fortunate than her sisters."

"Might have happened at a masked ball," Mr. Hawk observed speculatively.

"Possibly," replied Mr. Turner. "It's an interesting point. There are several possibilities."

"Never have I listened to such dull drivel in all my life," Meg broke in wrathfully, having established what was for her a record in temper holding. "Without saying a word I've sat here and listened to you insult my first and most famous ancestress. I've stood for that, I say. But when it comes to having to sit here and listen to such stupid, drunken drip, then I'm through. Get your own damn applejack. I'm going to bed."

"Be reasonable, Meg," pleaded her father, holding out a detaining hand as the girl rose to leave the table. You're altogether different. You're not like the original Megaera, the one we were talking about. Nothing in common. You've different tastes and different inclinations. And much better luck."

"What do you mean, much better luck?" demanded Megaera menacingly.

Mr. Hawk unfortunately was unable to restrain his mirth at this rather delicate point. She turned on him furiously, and for some reason the flames in her eyes had spread to her cheeks and neck.

"Shut up!" she said in a low voice. "You low-minded sot."

Mr. Hawk's laugh died to an appreciative chuckle as the girl turned back to her father.

"I said you'd be sorry you came," was the lament of that unhappy individual.

"I'm not, and you didn't," replied Mr. Hawk. "You said, you hoped I wouldn't be."

"What do you mean by much better luck?" Meg's voice cut in like a chilled knife.

"What I meant to say, my dear," propitiated Mr.

51

Turner, "was that you had better luck many centuries ago."

"It never was a matter of luck," said Meg. "It was looks and ability."

"Hear! Hear!" cried Mr. Hawk. "I agree entirely. How about that applejack, Meg? Good old Meg. A dear girl."

"Be quiet, you blotter," she replied, but there was the suggestion of a smile lurking round the corner of her mouth as she tossed a black cloak over her shoulders and slipped through the small opening. For several minutes thereafter Hunter Hawk had the uncomfortable impression that two large black and strangely compelling eyes were intently fixed on him from the night that curtained the entrance.

A sigh of weary relief escaped Mr. Turner's lips. He spread out his hands in a gesture of resignation.

"You see how it is," he said. "Such is my life."

"Not every man has a daughter who will go out at this hour of the night and steal applejack for him," was Mr. Hawk's answer.

"No," admitted Mr. Turner. "Nor is it every father who will allow his daughter to go out and steal applejack for him at this or any other hour of the night."

"When you put it like that," said Mr. Hawk, "there's something in what you say. You pride yourself on your liberal attitude, I take it?"

"Live and let live, say I."

"That's all very well for you who have had twenty-four centuries of it, but with us, our span is so short it's almost die and let die. What you meant to say is, drink and let drink, isn't it?"

"Well, it comes to the same thing. There're altogether too many crimes attributed to drink which rightly belong to natures that would be a lot more vicious without it. Drink doesn't create crime. It modifies it."

"Makes it more democratic," suggested Hunter Hawk. "Spreads it over a wider area and reduces its velocity."

"Absolutely," agreed Ludwig with enthusiasm. "If the world kept itself staggering drunk for a couple of centuries there wouldn't be any wars. Armies would

52

fall down and go to sleep before they could reach each other."

"And when they woke up," Mr. Hawk amplified, "the soldiers' hands would be so unsteady they wouldn't be able to do much damage."

"You've got it," said the little man. "You've gotten my point exactly. Instead of going over the top the soldiers would barely be able to crawl along on their bottoms."

"An inspiring picture."

"War has no inspiring pictures that cannot find their counterparts in peace." Mr. Turner looked exceedingly solemn when he brought forth this one.

"Then, as I understand it," summed up Hawk, "you hate war and love drink."

"Exactly, sir. Exactly."

"Well, I'm agreeable," the other continued. "Let's form a League for the Promotion of Peace through the Medium of Strong Drink."

"Light wines and beer, also," added Ludwig Turner.

Just as they were about to shake hands on this, a disturbing noise held their outstretched arms suspended. The deep-throated baying of a dog strained itself devilishly through the branches of wildly thrashing bushes. Both men sprang to their feet. The little man's face was pale.

"I think that's your friend Brightly's pet watchdog," he said, his lips grim and drawn. "God, if he gets at Meg."

This was too much for Hawk. He knew Brightly's watchdog. A big brute, a blood-letting brute, a creature of jaws and teeth and evil appetites.

"What a dog to be chased by," thought Hunter Hawk as he outlurched Ludwig to the opening.

"Here I am," Meg cried out in the darkness. "And here he is, too. He's following me."

Hawk, his long legs flashing with energy, waded through the bushes in the direction of Meg's voice. He ended by falling both over and upon her. A dog was baying in one ear, and Meg was screaming in the other.

"Look out!" she cried. "You'll break the bottle."

"Bottle hell," he replied. "This animal's trying to swallow my head."

53

"Wouldn't be much loss," came the muffled reply. "Why don't you file your knees?"

Brightly's dog was in a state of demoralization. He was not accustomed to so much thrashing and casual conversation. He wondered if these people realized this was an actual attack, that he was going to bite them, mangle them, perhaps.

"This is the second time to-day I've fallen on a woman," Mr. Hawk complained as he deftly placed a foot in the dog's ribs.

Then suddenly he remembered.

"My God, what a fool I've been," he said, and raising his right arm he put an end to the dog's offensive by speedily petrifying the beast.

"He can get at you but not at me," Megaera gloated from beneath Mr. Hawk.

"He can't get at either of us now," said Hunter Hawk complacently.

"What have you done, killed him? You almost have me."

"No, I haven't killed him. I've turned the beast to stone."

"What?"

"Turned the dog to stone, I said."

"How did you manage that?"

"Easily. Want to see?"

"No—to breathe."

Now that the danger was past Mr. Hawk removed himself from the crumpled object and permitted it to uncrumple. Meg was gamely clinging to the bottle.

"Very good," she said when she had carefully felt the stony body of the dog in the darkness. "Some of your own magic?"

"My latest," replied Hawk proudly. "I can turn people and animals to statues and back again."

"Very good," repeated the girl with professional appreciation. "Unusual for a mortal."

"I'm a very unusual mortal."

"So I've decided," said Megaera. "I've got a trick that goes yours one better. I can turn statues to people and back again. Come inside, and I'll show you. And," she added impressively, "because you saved me from

54

that dog I'll show you how to do it. Then you'll have two tricks, both knockouts."

On their way back to the grotto a small voice arrested their progress.

"Would you mind tugging me out of this unfortunately placed hole?" asked Mr. Turner. "What with wine and applejack and dogs and darkness and daughters I'm completely undone. The night has been too much for me."

Mr. Hawk collected the little man, and together they proceeded to the grotto, leaving the forest richer by the addiiton of one rather absurd stone dog caught in an attitude of pained surprise.

The events of the night had not dealt kindly with Mr. Wetmore Brightly. He had sustained a double loss. His scarecrow had been outraged and his watchdog turned to stone. On the other hand, the squirrels in the forest had a new mystery to solve and Mr. Ludwig Turner a new suit of clothes to wear—after radical alteration. Meg made them with both plain and fancy stitching.

All of which goes to support the almost universal impression that a wind has to be ill indeed not to turn over a new leaf.

CHAPTER VI

The Invasion of Hawk's Bed

BY THE TIME MEGAERA HAD INITIATED MR. HAWK so well into her magic for turning statues into people and back again that he would remember the simple ritual even when not quite sober, no one was quite sober, not even Megaera herself. As she had previously told him, it was really a bang-up trick and not so difficult to master if taken without applejack. With his own discovery and Meg's magic literally at the tips of his fingers, Hunter Hawk, with an emotion of exaltation not entirely unbeholden to applejack, felt himself well equipped to face a new and eventful life.

"An eminently satisfactory night," said Mr. Hawk, an hour or two later, extending his hand to his friend Ludwig, who with Meg had falteringly escorted him home. "I would ask you in, but the hour forbids and the flesh fails, the spirit flags and the body swoons. Good-night, my dear Ludwig, good-night. And you, my charming Meg. Bring your father to see me soon. If he insists on hiding his face in that top hat, cut eyeholes in it for him."

"You talk too much," replied Megaera softly. "Look at me, Mr. Magician."

She came close to him and placed a small, firm hand on either shoulder. Her dark, smoky eyes, half concealed by drooping lids, caught and held his.

"I won't," exclaimed Mr. Hawk. "Not if you look at me that way. It isn't a good look. Bad things lurk behind it."

"Look at me," she repeated. "Good things lurk behind it, O mortal pig."

Mr. Turner had wavered down the path and had now lost himself in shadows. Megaera came still closer. Her small, delightful body clung to the lanky scientist.

"Look at me," she commanded.

"Listen," replied Hawk. He was extremely uneasy. "Do you have to come so close? I can hear you without effort at the customary conversational distance. First thing I know you'll be perching on my shoulder."

He heard her low laugh and felt her arms slip round his neck. He backed away and dragged her with him. The toes of her small sandals scraped across the gravel. The sound caused him to stop.

"This is no way to act on a warm night," he objected.

"You are a pig," she murmured.

With a light, unexpected jump she bounded up into his arms. He was forced to hold her in spite of himself. Both of his arms were thus engaged. Thus, having him at her mercy, she calmly proceeded to give him anything but a calm kiss.

"Now say you didn't like it," she said when at length he had placed her on her feet.

"If you don't get off my property," he told her, "I'll begin shouting and throwing rocks."

"It's a brutal pig, at that," she jeered. "Listen," she continued, her voice sounding suddenly serious, "I've placed my seal on you, Hunter Hawk, you're my man, such as you are, and I don't pride myself any on my selection. But for some reason I can't explain even to myself we belong to each other. You'll fight against it and go through no end of unnecessary moralizing, but in the end you'll give in and know I was right. Good-night now, dim mind. I'll see you soon—sooner perhaps than you expect. You can't lose me."

"Good God!" groaned Mr. Hawk.

Then, with amazing swiftness, she was gone into the shadows where the estimable Ludwig Turner still lurked beneath a top hat which rightfully belonged to the demolished scarecrow of Mr. Brightly. Hawk was a little bit stunned and no end perturbed. Still he was thrilled. The blood in his veins raced waywardly. This almost goes without saying. After nine hundred years of varied experience a pretty woman should know a little something about kissing and the allied arts.

"Cripes," he muttered, mopping his brow with his coat sleeve, to which some leaves were still clinging. "Dear me. Wonder if she meant that stuff. That would be just too bad."

Perhaps, after all, he had better go to sea forever.

For a moment he stood looking after her in the darkness; than he turned and entered his house.

"No more of this sort of thing," he assured himself as he switched on the light. "Old enough to be my grandmother ten times over. Wonder if she is? Wonder if anything is? To-night, for instance. Did it really happen? Seems like a drunkard's dream. One of the pleasanter sort. Opium."

The light from the hall partially illuminated the library, and as Mr. Hawk passed the door he was brought to a sudden standstill by a glimpse of his congealed brother-in-law standing in an attitude of frozen indignation.

"My God!" breathed the long man of science. "I'd forgotten about them."

His distaste for the heavy reproaches of those four still figures when restored to their natural state tempted him to leave them permanently petrified. He stood and considered this possibility. No, it wouldn't be quite right. There was old man Lambert. He wasn't such a bad sort. And from the strange sounds that were issuing from his lips he must be the toughest of the lot. The old fellow was still battling against the effects of the powerful ray.

"No," Mr. Hawk decided. "I'll give them a suspended sentence first."

He approached Grandpa Lambert. Pressing the ring on his left hand, Hawk allowed the restorative or contra-active ray to play for a moment over the figure seated in the chair. In an instant the old gentleman was back again, his mouth filled to spluttering with insults and invectives.

"Now, listen," said Hawk quietly. "If you don't want to go back where you came from you'll cut all that out. Understand me, Grandpa?"

Apparently the old man did. A startled look came into his eyes, and the spluttering died away.

"Damn you," he muttered. "You and your devil's tricks."

Hawk then turned to Alice, his superior sort of a sister. Although it pained him to do it he would give her another chance. As he was about to raise the left hand he was arrested by the voice of the old man.

"Wait!" he cried. "Wait! Why don't you love her as she is, she and the other two? Think of the life we could lead without them, Hunter—the peace and quiet and freedom—just you, Daffy and me."

Hunter looked at the unregenerate old fellow sympathetically.

"I'd like too," he told him, "but they're in the way here."

"Then take them down to the cellar and turn them back to stone," the venerable gentleman pleaded, "or lure them down to the lake, then petrify them and tip the lot of them in. We'd be rid of them for good."

"I'll think it over," said Mr. Hawk and, raising his hand, released his sister.

Mrs. Alice Pollard Lambert returned to herself in full cry. Her jaws were wagging before the rest of her body was completely restored.

"Of all the outrageous conduct," she began. "I'll sue you for this."

Without a word Mr. Hawk raised his right hand and

Alice Lambert's voice died away as she once more turned to stone.

Alfred Lambert restored was a more tractable subject altogether. He stretched himself wearily and looked respectfully upon his brother-in-law. He even grinned a little weakly.

"The joke's on us, all right," he said, "but, for God's sake, don't do it again."

"Then watch your step," replied Hawk as he passed on to Junior.

"If you have any heart at all, you won't change that pest back," exclaimed the boy's grandfather. "Carry him up to bed and drop him on the way. Let him shatter to bits."

Hunter Hawk hesitated. He realized that life would be a great deal pleasanter without Junior, and that the world would never miss him. After all, it wouldn't be such a crime to drop Junior on some hard surface. It would be an act of divine justice and a public benefaction. Yet Hunter Hawk, in spite of all that he had suffered at the hands of these people, could not bring himself to do away with anyone of them—with all of them later, perhaps, but not at present. He shook his head at the old man and gave Junior back to the world. The boy, whimpering like a kicked dog, ran to his unresponsive mother. This was too much for Hawk. He promptly restored Alice Lambert to her son. This time she had nothing to say as she clung to her offspring and looked fearfully about her.

"You may all get to bed now," Hawk told them. "I'm sorry I forgot you, but no harm's done. Remember this, however, from now on I hold the whip hand. If you don't want to take up a permanent existence as statues, walk lightly and pay strict attention to your own affairs. Now clear the decks, or I might change my mind."

The company moved hastily toward the door. Alice paused and looked back.

"May I have a word with you in the morning?" she asked. "Something happened last evening. Callers. Most humiliating it was."

"Drop in to see me in the morning," said Hawk. "This morning, in fact. Lots happened last evening."

Alone in his own room, Hunter Hawk undressed triumphantly and prepared himself for a much needed rest. Never had his bed looked so inviting. In one corner of the room Blotto, undisturbed by the arrival of his master, was snoring volubly, a thing he did quite well.

"Wish he'd try to break himself of that habit," Hawk idly mused, "but he doesn't even try. Perhaps he doesn't know. Stupid dog. A great bother."

Still pondering over the bad habits and abysmal stupidity of Blotto, Hunter Hawk threw open all the windows and, turning his back to the night, sought the safety and sanctity of his bed.

"He sleeps at night just like a gross human being," his thoughts ran on as he maneuvered his ungainly body alongside the bed preparatory to that most grotesque of all actions—the lifting of the leg that swings one on to the mattress. "Doesn't care whether I live or die. Look at him." At last he was completely ensconced. "What the hell!" he said aloud, his face going blank. "How in the name of all that's——"

He was unable to finish his sentence. Megaera, her great eyes astir with the night from which she had emerged, was sitting on the ledge of one of the windows.

"At its best getting into bed isn't pretty," she observed, "but you make it unnecessarily unpicturesque. People should have sunken beds like sunken tubs."

"I'm not here to discuss the æsthetic side of bed-going with you," replied Mr. Hawk in a low voice.

"Oh, no?" she replied. "You're not, eh?"

She stripped off her dress and stood before him in a ragged shift. Mr. Hawk promptly closed his eyes and switched off the light.

"Leave this room by the way you entered," his voice commanded through the darkness. "I don't know what sort of magic you used, but if you flew up, you'd better damn well fly down again."

In answer to this he received a violent jab in the ribs.

"Ug!" grunted Mr. Hawk. "What the devil are you trying to do, stab me?"

"Don't get me mad," a small voice gritted in his ear.

60

"Move over now and be quick about it. I'm getting into this bed."

"Then I'm getting right out. This bed would be too small for the both of us if it were as wide as the Sahara Desert."

"No bed could be too small for us," she whispered. "You and I could sleep on a straw."

"There'll be no sleep for me to-night, my dear young lady."

"You've said it!"

"What do you mean?" Hawk's voice was weak with alarm. "Out I go."

"I mean just that. Budge from this bed, and I'll scream so loud every damn neighbor within a radius of five miles will come pelting in here to see what we're doing."

"We?" replied Mr. Hawk. "I'm not going to be do-ing a thing."

"We'll see about that," Megaera said grimly.

"Just like your ancestress," Mr. Hawk groaned.

Meg giggled, and one small hand stole playfully along his ribs. For such a large man Mr. Hawk gave vent to a surprisingly small shriek.

"Don't do that," he told her. "No familiarities. If you insist on staying in this bed, stay just where you are."

"I can't. You're so attractive. Don't turn your back on me. I'll kick it."

She did.

"Oh, for the love of Pete," exclaimed Hunter Hawk indignantly. "You'll be having me black and blue. As if I hadn't been through enough bangs and explosions al-ready."

"Then turn over."

"I will not—not on your life. Why, you're just a de-praved woman crashing your way into my bed like this without even so much as an invitation."

"You deliberately set out to make me. You know you did."

"Horrid little liar. Just like a woman."

"Exactly like a woman," agreed Megaera gloatingly. "Only a whole lot nicer than most. You should thank your lucky stars."

"For what?"

"For me, of course."

"I don't want you."

"You do, but you don't know it."

"Perhaps I do."

"Oh, you dear."

"Easy there with that hand. A kind word doesn't constitute an invitation to an orgy."

"Nothing like a good old orge occasionally."

"Don't be common. And here's something else. You've been doing this sort of thing on and off for nine hundred years. For me, it's almost an entirely new experience."

"It hasn't been even that yet," replied the girl. "And you said, almost. Who was she?"

"None of your damn business. Anyway, I've forgotten."

"Well, this will be one you won't forget."

"That's the truest words you've ever spoken. I'm going to lock my windows hereafter. Wish that dog would stop snoring. It keeps me awake."

"Good for the dog," said Megaera.

Mr. Hawk had an inspiration. He flashed on the light just long enough to petrify Blotto's nose. The snores diminished to the mere whispers of their former selves. The dog opened one eye and squinted down his nose. Yes, it had happened again. From one extreme to another. Blotto closed his eye, allowing the lid to drop heavily and did the best he could.

"Now, let's try to get a little sleep," said Hunter Hawk. "I'm all in."

Megaera was concentrating all of her magic on Blotto's nose. She wanted that dog to snore, and she meant to see to it that he did. Her magic proved successful in counteracting the potency of the petrifying ray. Before Mr. Hawk had settled himself comfortably Blotto was snoring with increased volume, so much so, in fact, that he woke up even himself.

"What? Is it working again?" he asked himself. "Well, I wish it would stay one way or the other."

Hunter Hawk was thoroughly aroused. He flashed on the light and redirected the ray at the dog's nose.

"I'll petrify that damned dog's nose so hard he'll

wish to God he'd never even sniffed," declared the scientist.

Megaera was sitting hunched up in bed, looking for all the world like a wicked child. She said nothing. She was calling on centuries of magic to bring back those snores. She was proudly pitting her pagan powers against those of modern science. For some minutes the contest continued, Blotto alternately sparking and stopping like a willing but broken-down motor. Finally the bedeviled animal, abandoning all attempts at sleep, raised his head and looked with moist, reproachful eyes at his master. The poor dog's nose was in a state of the utmost confusion. One minute it was a thing of life and vigor, the next a cold, unresponsive stone. Blotto felt that his nerves would prove hardly equal to the strain. The wail of protest he attempted to register was cut off in its prime only to burst out unexpectedly and frighten him out of his wits. As proud as he was of his scientific achievement, Mr. Hawk was unable to resist the mute entreaty of his dog. After all, why should their differences be taken out on Blotto's nose?

"I give up," he said at last as he switched out the light. "Snore your damn head off. Go on. Shake the walls and rattle the windows. I give up."

"Do you?" cried Megaera. "Then so will I."

Between Blotto and his uninvited bedfellow there was scarcely any sleep at all for Hunter Hawk that night.

CHAPTER VII

Playful Petrification

WHEN AFTER SEVERAL FLUTTERING ATTEMPTS MEG-aera succeeded in lifting the long lashes from her heavy eyes some hours later she found herself gazing up at no less a personage than the outraged Alice Pollard Lambert. This excellent lady, remembering her brother's invitation, and hoping to propitiate him before attempting to carry out her fell purpose, had quietly arrived at his bedside armed with a cup of coffee. This she now set down on a small table and devoted all her attention to the amazing joint occupant of Hunter

Hawk's bed. It had been her dark design either to wheedle the formula for his disagreeable discovery from him or else to destroy it. She was not going to permit anyone to hold the whip hand over herself and her family. Even though a dependent, she intended to be the dominating factor in the household. Now, however, here was another situation to face.

"What are you doing in bed with that man?" she demanded in a voice of chilled reproof.

"What do you usually do under the circumstances?" Megaera asked lazily.

"I don't go to bed with men," said Mrs. Lambert, her chin elevated virtuously.

"For goodness' sake," said Meg with innocent interest. "What do you go to bed with?"

"Don't be low and ridiculous," replied Mrs. Lambert.

"Well, if you think it's ridiculous," remarked the girl, "you've got something on me. I think it's the most natural thing in the world."

"Perhaps you do," said Mrs. Lambert. "I repeat my question. What are you doing here?"

"I wouldn't like to say," replied Megaera with one of her wickedest smiles.

"How did you manage to get yourself in?" Mrs. Lambert continued inflexibly.

"If you must know," said Megaera, indulging in a small but frank yawn, "your son deliberately dragged me in here last night and threatened to strangle me if I screamed."

Mr. Hawk's disorderly head popped up from the pillow as if suddenly jerked by a wire.

"Oh, what a lie!" he exclaimed.

"Furthermore, he's not my son," said Mrs. Lambert whose indignation at this reflection cast on her age had for the moment made her forget the moral issue involved.

"Sorry," said Megaera, "but how was I to know? Perhaps he's your lover. If he is, I'm sorry for him."

"He's neither my son nor my lover," Mrs. Lambert announced with great dignity.

"Then who is your lover?" asked Meg. "All this puzzles me."

"I want you to know I have no lover," Alice Lambert hurled at the girl in bed.

"I'm very sorry about that," replied Megaera. "But why do you want me to know it? I can't help you out."

"That besmirched creature on the bed beside you is my brother," said Mrs. Lambert.

"Well, madam, all I can say is, you've got some brother."

"Oh!" breathed Mrs. Lambert as Meg reached out a bare arm and took several appreciative sips from the cup of coffee her companion's sister had so considerately placed within her reach.

"So thoughtful of you," she remarked with a sweet smile. "How did you know I liked it?"

"Are you going to wallow there and allow this creature to insult your own sister?" Alice Lambert demanded of her supine yet interested brother.

"Yes," he replied, "I am. And when she's finished I'm going to try my hand."

"Do you realize that the Ashleys called on us last night?" continued his sister. "Stella forgot the terrible condition you left us in and brought them right into the library. There they sat for fully fifteen minutes, asking about this and that and trying to be pleasant. And do you realize we were unable to say a word back, not one word?"

"That must have been hell for you, dear sister."

"It was," agreed Mrs. Lambert. "It was. Suddenly Mrs. Ashley—you know how nervous she is—uttered a piercing scream and cried out, 'They're all dead! Stone dead!' With that she rushed from the room, the rest of the Ashleys right behind her. I could have fallen through the floor from mortification. By this time the news must be all over the countryside. Alfred and Junior and myself are ashamed to go to church, to be seen on the streets. And you are responsible for that, you and your silly discoveries. Now we have a fresh scandal on our hands, this creature you are openly flaunting in our faces."

"Cheer up, Sis," Mr. Hawk grinned as he thought of the Ashleys' call. "I'll go to church with you. Forgot it was Sunday."

"We'll all go to church with you," put in Meg. "That

is, if I can get some decent clothes to cover my nakedness."

"Good!" cried Hunter Hawk. "You, Daffy, and I will form ourselves into a hollow square and protect the respectable members of the family from the gaze of the curious public. And now, my dear sister, if you will be good enough to withdraw, I might try to get a little something done."

"Open and shameless iniquity," his sister replied, looking directly at Megaera, who met her gaze with a pleasant smile. "I don't know what to make of it. I'm sure you must have taken leave of your senses. What will Alfred and Junior say?"

"I haven't the slightest idea," replied Mr. Hawk. "Something dull and hypocritical, no doubt, but you can tell them both for me that they'd better be damn careful what they say or I'll petrify 'em beyond recall. And that goes for you. Now clear out." He turned abruptly to the girl beside him. "Say there, you wench," he continued, "quit hogging that Java. Give Daddy Long-legs a sip."

"Oh," breathed Mrs. Lambert once more as she hurried from the room. "Oh—Daddy Long-legs—this is too much."

The moment the door was closed Megaera attempted to become violently demonstrative. Mr. Hawk foiled her, however, through the simple expedient of kicking her out of bed.

"See that window," he said, pointing dramatically.

"What about it, you big bully?" asked Meg from the floor.

"Well, out you go, my girl," he replied. "Fling yourself through it, and make it snappy."

"Ah, Hunter darling, you said you were going to take me to church—you, Daffy, and myself."

The girl's eyes were large, round, and reproachfully pleading. Mr. Hawk considered her with something more than a parental interest. She was a bad one, no doubt, nine centuries sunk in depravity, but what a refreshing creature, what a relief from the undercover impulses of everyday life. Hastily he ran over the experiences of the past twenty-four hours. Events marched. First there had been the explosion and

66

Blotto's bewitched tail. Then he had petrified the family and gone walking with two bottles of Burgundy. There had been a little man crying in a cornfield for the clothing of an overdressed scarecrow. The assult had followed, the visit to the grotto, Brightly's dog, new magic, more applejack, and the trip home. The latter was still a trifle vague to Mr. Hawk. Then there had been the release of the family and the entrance of Meg through his window. Then the battle over Blotto's nose and—no sleep. Yes, he remembered it all, but somehow it still did not seem quite real. The whole thing was too incredible. Events were certainly marching. He grinned inwardly as he quickly made up his mind. Church it would be. Surely there could be no harm in taking a nine-hundred-year-old girl to church, even a small, pagan, and utterly unmoral one.

"We go," he said at last. "Slip on one of my dressing gowns. In there—that's a closet."

"And that?" she pointed to another door.

"Bathroom. Tub, shower, and everything."

"Oh, good! What a grand life!"

Meg rose from the floor and became very active in exploring the room, its contents and possibilities. Presently she disappeared, and the voice of the shower was heard in the land. Hunter Hawk pushed a bell.

"Betts," he said when that old gentleman appeared, "bring me three things: lots of breakfast, two of Burgundy, and all of Miss Daffy. Bring also innumerable plates and cups and eating tackle. There will be three of us breakfasting here."

Betts received this command with a decided elevation of spirit. He felt even more elated when, just as he was leaving, Meg, lost in a trailing dressing gown with dangling arms, emerged flappingly from the bathroom.

"Good-morning," said Meg with a smile. "I like you. You look nice like me. I'm Meg."

"Thank you, Miss Meg," said Betts and hastily withdrew.

"A beauty," he told the interested Mrs. Betts when he reached the kitchen. "Small, but a rare beauty. Makes one feel that life is still worth living."

"Doesn't it just," mused Mrs. Betts. "A girl and Burgundy before breakfast. I know he was a chip off

67

the old block, even if he did take a long time chipping. Stella, my child, you've lost your chance. The master's gone and done it."

"Done what?" demanded Stella, who had just come into the kitchen.

"Started in ruining," replied Mrs. Betts complacently.

For a moment Stella's face fell, then she rallied.

"I should think you two old people would feel ashamed," she said, "talking like that to an honest, high-minded girl like me. What does the ruin look like?"

"She's small," offered Betts with a reminiscent eye. "Small she is, but, oh, how succulent."

"Small," repeated Stella with manifest satisfaction. "Venus, I'm told, was a large, full-bodied woman."

She threw out her breasts and walked majestically from the room.

"She's got those, too," Mr. Betts flung after her.

"Apples," was Stella's cryptic retort. "Grapes."

Daphne, in a scarlet kimono, sped down the hall like a living flame. Betts's report had thrilled her. It seemed too good to be true. All her life she had been fed up with so many smug hypocrisies and so many arbitrary taboos that a little open shame appealed to her sense of proportion. She rejoiced in this heaven-sent opportunity to share in her uncle's depravity.

"Come in," called Mr. Hawk when she had tapped lightly on his door.

"Good-morning everybody," said Daffy in the most offhand manner in the world as she entered the room. "I hear that a little moral leprosy has broken out in here. Is this the lepress? She's sweet."

"Hardly that," her uncle replied. "She's nine centuries deep in iniquity. She's a scheming, unscrupulous, and sometimes violent woman. At present she's hungry and without any decent clothes. The three of us are going to eat here in this room, then we're going to church with the family. Without any further explanations, however, let me introduce you to Meg or Megaera. Her last name doesn't seem to matter. Sometimes it's Turner. Related remotely to the Furies. Bar sinister, I suspect."

68

Meg, who had been studying Daffy hopefully, now spoke.

"The man's a liar, to begin with," she said quite calmly. "In the second place, he suffers from delusions, and, finally, he's no fit person for decent girls like you and myself to associate with. Nevertheless, we'll associate. He has ordered Burgundy. That's why."

"Can you fix her up?" asked Mr. Hawk.

Daphne considered Meg with an appraising gaze in which she made no attempt to conceal her admiration.

"You're about one of the cutest little tricks I've ever seen turned out," she said at last. "No wonder you're not quite respectable."

"Listen to her," Meg complained. "You've got her calling me names now."

"Complimenting you, my dear," said Daffy briefly. "Let's see. I'm just about twice of you. That makes it easy because it means doing things by halves. I've always done that. You'll need everything."

"Except drawers," put in the scientist dispassionately. "Her father says she wears no drawers—none of them does."

"If they're pretty I might," said Meg. "I'll go that far."

"A great concession," Hawk replied.

By the time the girls had returned Hunter Hawk was dressed and shaved. The breakfast was growing cold, but the Burgundy was just right. Betts had been allowed to hover in anxious attendance. His master felt that he owed him that much, at least. As the girls entered, the old domestic was replenishing Mr. Hawk's glass. Hawk was sitting by the open window breathing deep of the morning air. Sunday was resting gracefully on the countryside spread out before him. Down in the orchard a number of birds were making agreeable noises. The air was faintly tinged with the scent of blossoms. Life was not at all bad. Sunlight and sparkling Burgundy made a cool little hell in the depth of his glass. He was committed to a life of sin. And he was content. Few men, he felt, were better equipped.

"He could not wait," remarked Daffy.

"I told you he was a pig," said Meg.

"I'm a pig who couldn't wait," Mr. Hawk replied

with a pleasant smile. "Catch up. You've done a good job, Daffy. The girl looks fine."

"Mrs. Betts helped," Daffy replied. "She can sew and fix slick."

"The loveliest pull-offs," Megaera began.

"Step-ins," Daffy corrected.

Betts was heard to make strange noises.

"Oh, yes. How silly of me," the girl continued. "Step-ins, of course. Must have been thinking of something else. Want to see them?"

"Come, come," frowned Mr. Hawk. "We're going to church now. Snaffle down some food and try a glass of this wine. You know, the more I think of church, the more the idea appeals to me."

"Yes," responded Daffy. "We should do well at church. Never drank wine before in the morning. It's a good idea."

"An old, old custom," observed Megaera. "Much older than church."

The small creature looked really presentable in a black and white georgette thing. A small hat, also of the black and white color motif, had been slashed to fit her head. There was something a little amiss about her feet. They were loosely confined in a pair of pumps Daffy had retrieved from the attic. Small as they were, they were still too large for their present incumbent. The general effect, however, was not displeasing. In fact, quite the contrary.

Betts's report of the breakfast is all that is necessary.

"They sat there drinking wine and crunching toast and enjoying themselves for dear life," he recounted to his wife and Stella. "Never saw the master in such fine feather. He's a changed man since he met that little girl, Meg. Claims she's nine centuries old. Well, the way she went for her breakfast you'd think she'd never had a bite to eat in all that time. She's a queer one, she is, but you can't help liking her."

"Then what did they do?" Stella interrupted.

"Nothing," replied Betts anticlimactically. "Miss Alice spoiled everything. She tapped on the door, and off they all trotted to church. Mrs. and Mr. and the boy walked on ahead. The other three followed jeering quietly and whispering and giggling. Mr. Hunter tried to look dignified, but he couldn't keep it up. Looks like trouble to me."

And trouble there was, but it did not start until it was time for the collection. Even then it began gently. It so happened that Mr. Hawk and party sat in the two front pews near the center aisle of the church and that Mr. Brightly and his beautiful wife sat directly back of Mr. Hawk, Megaera, and Daffy. Nothing could have been more unfortunate—for Mr. Brightly, who was deep in the bad books of Hunter Hawk. It was one of those fashionable churches one occasionally finds in a semisuburban community largely inhabited by snobs. It was smart to be seen there occasionally. Members were forever returning to it from Palm Beach, Deauville, St. Moritz, or Park Avenue. It was their way of officially registering the fact that after having spent oodles of money in fashionable travel they were once more honoring the neighborhood with their presence from the upholstered seclusion of their country estates.

"Look well while you have the chance," the set of their backs seemed to say. "We will soon be expensively on our way again."

Mr. Hawk did not like this church, and he did not like its preacher, and he felt strongly inclined to do something about it. The impulse was especially strong because he realized his sister and brother-in-law and even their son looked upon being seen in church as one of the high lights of the week. Yet no one looking at his dark, thin, and serious face would have suspected him of contemplating retaliation for all the weary hours he had passed in that pew.

The first note of discord was struck when the plate was being passed. Meg, dutifully remembering the training of her father in matters of money, made a rather clever snatch. Mr. Hawk, very much upset by this display of cupidity, promptly seized the small offending hand and squeezed it. A shower of coins fell back into the plate. At that moment Meg would have bitten Hunter Hawk's hand had not Daffy restrained her. However, the ancient young lady's attempt was not without some reward. She successfully retained in the palm of her hand a neatly folded five-dollar bill.

"Try and get that," she muttered, giving Mr. Hawk

a glimpse of the bill, "and I'll knock you into the aisle."

"If you need money why don't you ask for it?" Hawk demanded in a furious whisper. "I'll give you as much as you want."

"All right, give me some," she retorted.

"After," said Mr. Hawk.

"Ha!" she laughed nastily and noisily. "I knew it would be that way."

By this time the usher was presenting the plate to Mr. Wetmore Brightly. Hunter Hawk turned and petrified them both from the neck down. They formed an interesting group, Brightly and the usher. The suppliant stood with extended plate while the rich man slouched in his seat, one hand stubbornly thrust in his pocket as if to protect its contents. Both regarded each other with expressions of suspicion and growing animosity. Necks began to crane and eyes began to peer. What was the meaning of all this? Why was the rich Mr. Brightly refusing to contribute to the collection? Something like a murmur began to stir through the church. Brightly grew red in the face. What the devil had happened to him? Hunter Hawk turned and looked severely at the man.

"Go on, be a sport," said Mr. Hawk in a voice intended to carry. "Give the usher some money and let him go."

"I can't get my hand out of my pocket," gasped Mr. Brightly.

"What's wrong with it—too full of money?"

Mr. Brightly looked pleadingly at the usher.

"Please take that plate away somewhere," he said. "I'll see you later."

"I can't" replied the usher.

"Why can't you?" demanded Brightly. "Trying to make a fool out of me? I'd like to break your damn neck."

At this moment Mr. Hawk released the usher so swiftly that the poor man lost his balance and toppled over into Brightly's lap. This was the right moment for the release of Brightly. Hawk restored his power to him. There was the sound of falling coins. Brightly and the usher became entangled in an effort to retrieve the money.

"By Jove," said an old gentleman aloud. "Looks as if the beggars are actually fighting over the money.

"Disgraceful!" exclaimed a lady.

"Oh, good," muttered Megaera, rapidly concealing coins about her person.

"Stop! Stop!" whispered Mr. Hawk. "I told you I'd give you some money."

"One dollar in my stocking is worth two in your purse," breathed Meg. "I hope I don't jingle when I walk."

Order was at last restored, and the usher, with a sadly diminished collection in his plate, proceeded on his way. Mr. Hawk sat watching the minister closely. The moment he started to rise the scientist promptly froze him in a half-sitting position which of all positions is perhaps the most grotesque. It was in this unprepossessing pose that the man of God was so ill-advised as to announce:

"We will all rise now and sing——"

Exactly what it was expected to sing the congregation never found out. Mute with astonishment, the Reverend Dr. Archer turned and took a quick, frightened look at his ecclesiastical rear, which for the first time in its life refused to do his bidding. Then he turned a white face to his congregation, a strained, white, bewildered face. Although not quite as strained and white as his, the collective face of the Reverend Archer's congregation was equally bewildered.

"Looks as if he was going to spring at us," observed the old gentleman to his wife. "What's going on in this church, anyway?"

The minister licked his dry lips and cleared his throat several times. Finally he gained command of his voice.

"Something extremely odd has happened to me," he said. "Don't know what it can be. Perhaps it is some divine manifestation. Whatever it is, I certainly won't be able to preach to you in this position. It would be too trying for all of us."

At this point the nervous Mrs. Ashley, remembering her previous experience with the Lamberts, uttered a little scream and fainted. She was carried from the church.

"In view of this mystifying occurrence," continued the Reverend Archer, "I think it would be best for you all to leave me now. In the meantime, I trust you will pray for my speedy recovery."

When the church was empty, six members of the choir carried the Reverend Doctor to the vestry and deposited him tenderly on a sofa.

"I implore you not to drop me," said the Reverend Archer as he was being lowered. "I am sure it would smash to bits."

CHAPTER VIII

Meg Removes Her Pull-Offs

THAT SUNDAY ESTABLISHED HUNTER HAWK'S UN-disputed sway over his home and household. A counsel of war had come to nothing. That is, it had ended in unconditional capitulation. Mr. Hawk was given to understand that he was at liberty to have as many mistresses and explosions as his heart desired and physique could stand. It was the secret hope of the three opposing Lamberts that the general wear and tear involved in the overindulgence of these two luxuries would soon make a wreck of the man. So long as he refrained from practising his black arts on them the Lamberts would tolerate if not welcome the establishment of a harem.

Hunter Hawk, after listening to the magnanimous sentiments of his sister, expressed his gratification and gave her to understand that in view of the circumstances her concessions were rather pointless. The Lamberts could hardly do otherwise. He himself offered nothing in return. To quote him verbatim he said, "You'll do as I damn well please, and so will I."

Alice Lambert did not like this attitude at all. She felt that her brother should have shown more gratitude for being allowed to do as he pleased in his own home. However, she very wisely refrained from giving expression to her feelings. She withdrew with a gracious smile while he watched her departure with a cynical one.

Megaera become more or less a member of the household, although her vagrant ways made it impossible to count on her presence. Twice she had taken Mr. Hawk to the grotto in the woods, and on the latter occasion Daffy had been brought along to admire the stone dog. Mr. Turner profited by the cementing of the unconventional relation between the two houses. He was provided with wine, food, and raiment and a supply of ready money with which he made various little purchases through the agency of a mysterious friend who later turned out to be the proprietor of a still. He throve and prospered and quarrelled a little less frequently with his daughter. So, considering everything impartially, it would seem that when Megaera swung a slim leg over Mr. Hawk's window ledge she was acting in the best interests of everyone concerned. The conventional demands of the community were more or less satisfied by the shallow deception of foisting Megaera upon it as a visiting school friend of Daphne's. Often with murder in her heart, Mrs. Lambert found herself conversing with neighbors about her daughter's sweet young friend and how delighted she was they could be together for the remainder of the season, if not longer, a possibility she very much feared.

Events marched.

This evening Megaera and Mr. Hawk were returning from the village after the consumption by the young lady of several ice-cream sodas. Where the pavements yield to grass they encountered the charming and voluble Mrs. Wetmore Brightly, looking more possible and cosmetic than ever. After she had finished congratulating herself on her good fortune she announced the fact that she had been simply dying to meet Megaera ever since she had seen her in church.

"You're such a beautiful creature, my dear," she said. "I'm sure you must be such company for Mr. Hawk's delightful niece—or shall I call you Hunter?"

The eyes came in very effectively here. Meg hated the woman from that moment, and knowing herself as she did, she naturally suspected the purity of the other's motives. Her intuition was amply justified in

75

this, for Mrs. Brightly's motives were notoriously low. On her part, Mrs. Brightly regarded the official report concerning the visit of Meg to Daffy as being nothing more than an entirely justifiable lie concocted on the spur of the moment to conceal a much more interesting situation.

"And now," announced the lovely woman, "I'm going to ask you a special favor, one that I ask only extra special people." Here her voice dropped to a note of confidence. "We are opening up Greenwood next week," she continued. "I do wish you would come. You and my husband were once awfully thick."

"Your husband is still awfully thick," Mr. Hawk replied, "or is that why you're opening up Greenwood? I didn't know he was even sick."

"Hunter, you're such a cynical person," Mrs. Brightly pouted, "and such a wicked one. Of course my husband isn't sick. Our camp was named long before the cemetery. It's been in the family for years."

"Well, you've got nothing on the other Greenwood," said Hawk. "Many a family's been in it for years."

"What a ghastly sense of humor you have," exclaimed Mrs. Brightly. "But I'll forgive even that if you'll only say you'll come—you and Miss Turner and your niece and an extra pair of pants."

"Trousers," corrected Mr. Hawk. "Women wear pants."

"Panties," replied Mrs. Brightly. "What do you know about it, anyway, you old bachelor? And you didn't say I could call you Hunter. I have been—"

"I know you have," said Mr. Hawk. "Now that it's become a habit, why not keep it up?"

"You're so gracious," observed Mrs. Brightly. "You may call me Tom."

"Why that?" asked Mr. Hawk.

"A hangover from the days of my youth. I was once a great tomboy. The name stuck. I think it's rather cute."

"So do I," agreed Meg, with a much too sweet smile.

"I don't know a thing about it," said Mr. Hawk, "but I do know this: if anyone called me Flo or Gracie or Glad I'd knock his damn block off. Don't see why the same reasoning doesn't apply both ways."

"You've an exceptionally agreeable companion," Mrs. Tom Brightly said, addressing her remark to Meg.

"Isn't it?" replied the girl.

"Will you come?" asked the elder woman. "Say, yes."

"No," said Mr. Hawk promptly. "I'm afraid it can't be done. I don't go to riots. A good old-fashioned stag party is bad enough for me. The performers there get paid for their folly."

Something sharp and painful was making its way into Hunter Hawk's ribs.

"Accept," gritted a low voice in his ear, or rather a low, gritty voice drifted up to his ear. "Accept, damn you, or I'll drive this knife clear through your bladder."

Mrs. Brightly, who had unexpectedly moved a pace to one side, suddenly turned pale.

"For God's sake!" she cried out. "What are you doing, child? Don't murder the man."

Mr. Hawk smiled falsely. "She's merely scratching my back," he explained. "Can't reach it myself. And by the way, I accept your jolly old invitation. My second thoughts are always best."

"I'm glad," said Mrs. Tom Brightly. "Does she always scratch your back with that desperate-looking blade?"

"She carries it for that express purpose," said Mr. Hawk.

"My family has always carried knives," said Meg, slipping the knife in a sheath attached to a startlingly well turned leg. "Good in cases of assaults and such. Lots of times a girl doesn't feel like being assaulted."

"I didn't know," murmured Mrs. Brightly. "The women of your family must have led such interesting lives."

"I'm afraid they were a pretty hard lot," Meg answered with a small smile. "I'm quite different. I'm really a very nice girl. You'd be surprised."

"I'm sure I would," Mrs. Tom replied with a world of meaning in her voice. "Then it's all settled?"

"We'll be there," replied Mr. Hawk, "even though it kills me. So long, Tom."

Mrs. Tom flashed them both a smile and turned

down the street, her shapely body swaying to advantage. Mr. Hawk's gaze followed her.

"Take your eyes off that," amended Meg.

"Off what?" asked Mr. Hawk.

"You know very well what I mean. Take your eyes off it and keep your eyes off it, or there'll be a whole lot of trouble. Just remember that."

"I'll do my best," Hawk replied, his thoughts centered on the knife. "The only thing wrong with that leg of yours is that murderous weapon you carry on it. I never knew you toted a dagger."

"You'll find out lots of things about me before I'm through with you," Meg commented darkly.

Mr. Hawk found scant comfort in this remark.

Greenwood was situated on a wooded hill. There was a tracery of pine boughs around the house, and a constant whispering could be heard from a breeze that moved among them. From a long wide veranda one looked down on a silver lake lying like a coin tossed among the trees. And from the veranda one could trace the graceful course of a smooth gravel road twisting leisurely down to the pavilion and boat house rising like a fairy palace from the waters of the lake. The wind seemed cooler on this hill than elsewhere, and the sun warmer and more friendly—the air sweeter and more stimulating to the lungs. The house was an ancient and immense structure. It dominated the landscape, thrust itself up through the trees, and scrutinized the countryside with a baronial eye. It was a mansion of many chambers—large, fragrant rooms, intimately associated with boughs and birds. Their windows framed the sky and were forever capturing for awhile little wind-blown clouds. Wild woods and terraced gardens lay below these windows. Huge wide-treaded stairs walked up through this house, their turnings watched by empty niches that had once held statues of unrivaled ugliness. The first step of this ample staircase, or the last, as the case may be, rested on the smooth, solid surface of an immense assembly room used for dancing, mass drinking, and associated revelry. It was a vast room with intimate corners, a place of windows, convenient tables, and divans that defied fatigue. In this huge hall one could enjoy life. The floor made a splendid place for crap games. Almost always, from midnight until dawn, dancing couples were forced to circle round groups of vociferating gamblers.

To-day Mrs. Tom Brightly, surrounded by a number of guests, was leveling a cocktail glass and gazing through its amber-colored contents at the Emperor as it made its way majestically up the drive. The Emperor was Mr. Hawk's carry-all. He could never discover why he had bought this barge on wheels save for the fact that barring a van it was the largest motor-propelled vehicle he had ever seen. It was utterly out of proportion to his needs. There is something satisfying in being able to afford a thing for which one has no earthly use. It lends that meretricious touch to a purchase without which few pleasures can be fully savored.

The Emperor was now transporting its owner, slumped behind the wheel, Meg curled up quite a little too close beside him, and Daffy trying to recline in the back in the arms of a young gentleman who looked upon her advances with disapproval and mistrust.

"He's always protecting me from myself," the young lady had complained of Cyril Sparks throughout the course of the trip. "Has a quaint idea that my neck was made only to swallow with."

"You deserve to be hung by yours," Mr. Sparks had growled. "Can't you leave a fellow alone?"

"No," had been the emphatic rejoinder, "I can't. What is a fellow for if you've got to leave him alone? Might just as well have a mummy for a boy friend."

Cyril Sparks was a large lad, horselike and rangy. A seemingly endless supply of arms and legs was attached to his body. He had a long, honest face, prominent cheek bones, and startlingly blue eyes, always a little troubled. Situations got the better of him. He seemed to jerk along through life on the minimum amount of words. Few persons suspected that behind those blue, perplexed eyes lay a world of acute and devastating observations. Little if anything escaped those eyes or failed to register a definite impression on the brain that directed them. He was interested in two things—Daffy and bugs. He knew no tricks and could play no games.

Many miles a week he tramped and wandered. When Mack Sennett stopped producing his slapstick comedies a source of genuine enjoyment was removed from his life. He was one of Blotto's warmest admirers, contending that a dog, to be so completely dumb, must necessarily possess some human attributes. His hair was red, and his father was rich. He himself seldom had more than a couple of dollars in his pocket at one time, but he had the happy faculty of being able to dig up money from the various women who dwelt in his house. His three brothers, all of whom were competent but essentially decent sorts, gave him large checks which he usually kept in his pockets until they became so soiled and dog eared the teller at the bank handled them with shrinking fingers. When he had money he spent it on presents, candy, nuts, books, and an especially vile brand of rum of which he was inordinately fond. He was always so distrait and inarticulate his family could tell he had been drinking and was pleased about it only when he was heard to croon wistfully to himself about some laddie who kept going away somewhere and never coming back. On such occasions his mother and his various aunts would smile sympathetically and hold their peace. His father never grew tired of quietly observing Cyril and trying to follow the workings of his mind. He realized that the boy, though very much a part of the household and more dependent on it than any other member of the family, nevertheless lived in a world entirely apart from the others. Recently Mr. Sparks had come to regard this son of his as a rather gifted animal that eluded classification. Hunter Hawk was fond of young Sparks, and, strange to say, Sparks lost much of his restraint in the presence of Mr. Hawk. The boy would converse with him long and laboriously, preferably over a bottle of something. Next to his rum, Cyril Sparks loved the ethyl alcohol he found in Mr. Hawk's laboratory. Whenever he entered the place he would rove about with deceptive inconsequence until he had located a bottle labeled with the familiar C_2H_5OH. This satisfactorily accomplished, he was able to answer questions and exchange ideas with a surprising degree of intelligence. It was his hope that in time Daffy would take up the subject of marriage and perhaps make arrangements. Also he hoped that these arrangements would not include Mr. and Mrs. Lambert and the boy Junior. It was a puzzle to him how three people could be so thoroughly undesirable on all counts. Mrs. Lambert both despised and venerated him on account of the Sparks fortune.

"Don't forget," he now said anxiously to Mr. Hawk. "You said you'd get this Brightly woman to give us some bottles for our own use. Don't like this punch-bowl business. Always step on some woman. It's better to go up to one's room and take off one's coat and talk and drink——"

"And spit and swear and tell bad stories," supplied Daffy. "Wouldn't you enjoy yourself even more if we hit you over the head with an ax at the start and put you to bed? The results would be about the same, only quicker."

"An ax is hard, and it would hurt," he answered reflectively. "It might do for once, but you couldn't keep it up. No head could stand much of that sort of thing. No, I'm serious about those bottles. A lot of people fatigue me. Bottles in the room will be much the best."

"In other words," said Daphne, "you prefer to drink furiously with a few rather than foolishly with the flock."

"Frantically," amended Cyril. "Your alliteration remains intact."

"Don't worry about your private supply, my boy," said Mr. Hawk in a large manner that Cyril greatly admired. "I'll attend to that."

"Do," put in Meg sweetly. "And only that. Observe that leg."

She gave her skirt a flip and displayed the businesslike dagger snugly sheathed against a sheer silk stocking.

"Ah, there!" cried Mrs. Tom from the veranda. "Crawl out of that hearse and join a live party."

Hawk led his three charges up the gracious steps and accepted a cocktail, which he courteously passed to Megaera.

"Yum," she mouthed avidly. "This is so much nicer than school, isn't it, Daffy?"

Daffy, over the rim of her glass, agreed that it was.

81

"Well," said Sparks, eyeing her drink critically and wishing it was composed entirely of alcohol, "here's gobble, gobble."

Down went the cocktails with admirable precision and dispatch.

"You four appear to be snappy drinkers," Mrs. Tom observed. "I can tell by the way they went down that you'll make fast friends here."

"The faster the better," said Mr. Hawk.

Meg was completely hidden from view by a circle of knickers and white flannels.

"I'm already meeting a few," she said. "Call off your pack, Tommy. Haven't these gentlemen ever seen a small woman before?"

She broke through the circle and joined her hostess just in time to hear her say, "You're my neighbor, Hunter Hawk. Your room is next to mine. If you get frightened in the night by all these bad people just knock three times on the wall and I'll send my husband in to keep you company."

"That's the most appalling anticlimax I've ever heard," he replied. "Why not come yourself?"

"Why not be yourself?" Mrs. Tom replied. "But if you really do need me, just scrape on the wall very, very gently."

Wetmore Brightly approached none too pleasantly.

"It had better be damn gently," he rumbled. "I sleep with one ear open, Hunter."

"Hello, there," said Mr. Hawk. "Has your hand fully recovered the use of its pocket?"

Brightly's face darkened.

"That's far from funny," he answered, "unless one has a sophomoric sense of humor."

"Did you get much in the scramble?" asked Meg. "I made out fine, but dear Mr. Hawk, noble Mr. Hawk, made me return it later. It's not often one gets such a chance."

"Oh," said Mr. Brightly, "I remember now. You're the cute little thing with the busy hands. You snatched a coin right out from under mine."

"It was fifty cents," replied Meg quite seriously. "A nice bright new one. That's a worth-while piece of change, fifty cents. Two of them make a dollar."

Hunter Hawk took the avaricious young lady by the arm and forcibly led her down the veranda.

"Don't," he pleaded, "don't go on in that horrid way about money. It sounds terrible coming from your sweet young lips, even if centuries of lies have slipped through them."

"I'm sorry," replied Meg, this time with sincere humility. "You can't understand what money has meant to us. You see, it's the hardest thing to get. We can't work for it, and still at times we must have it. Once we had no need of money, but now, with our magic running low, it seems to stand for everything. The Little People have gotten a tough break in your so-called Christian Era. We are neither fish, flesh, nor fowl. You see how it is? You belong to me, but I don't belong to you. I just keep on going, and sometime you'll stop . . . come to an end . . . and I'll go on raising hell, no doubt loving but yet not wanting to love . . . living yet fed up with life."

She flung herself down in a large leather chair and looked with unseeing eyes at the panorama stretched out before her. Through a French window leading into the great hall drifted a haunting and rather pathetic little air. Mimi was dying gracefully somewhere in a Vocalion, her tiny hands being quite frozen. The small, broken voice, poignantly sad because reminiscent of happier times, carried in its note of suffering a yearning still to live and to share the warmth of life. The sad voice was appealing directly to Megaera and the tall man looking down at her. Mimi, dying, her love story ended, was saying farewell to them. Meg's large eyes, touched with a new depth and just a little frightened, were gazing into Hawk's.

"I want to belong to you," she said in a low voice that crept close to the man's heart. "I want to end with you or before you. I don't want to go on and on . . . hell raising and all that."

"There's a few breaths left in me yet," Hawk forced himself to reply.

"I know, but what is that to me, my tall? . . . a moment snatched from time. What is the name of that damn tune, anyway? It's made me feel awfully low. You never saw me cry, did you?"

83

"Don't," said Hawk hastily. "Think of your lovely new pull-offs and cheer up."

"Oh, be quiet and bring me another cocktail or I'll have an emotional breakdown all over the place."

Her modifying grin was rather forced and fragile. Hunter Hawk who suspected her every move and mood studied her intently. She seemed so thoroughly downcast at the moment, yet could he trust her? If he made the slightest display of his own emotions she might toss them brazenly in his face and do some terrible thing—kiss him, or climb a tree, or start in picking pockets. Feeling a bit upset himself, he silently departed in search of cocktails. And all the time he had the uncomfortable sensation of being intently watched by a pair of dark brooding eyes.

When he returned with the cocktails—four of them on a silver tray—Meg's mood had altered but not improved.

"Put them down," she said impatiently as he held the tray before her. "Put them down on that table and listen well to me—if you so much as touch a finger nail to your wall tonight the blade of this knife will be red with blood. Understand that now. I won't put up with any monkey business."

"Don't be silly. As if I'd do such a thing."

"Silly nothing," she snapped. "And you would do such a thing. Look at me. Before you bought me body and soul I was a decent girl. My father sold me into shameful bondage, and you persuaded him to do it . . . you and your tainted money."

"For goodness' sake, don't go on like that. Here, have a drink. If I gave you clothes and money it was only to keep you from stealing them. I had——"

"So that's how you feel about it. I suppose if I hadn't asserted myself with the last shred of my pride you'd have let me go naked and hungry."

"Naked, perhaps, my dear, but never hungry."

She cast him a quick look, then her face darkened again.

"Don't try to get around me," she answered, "and don't be lewd. Talk to the Brightly woman that way if you want, but if you do I'll cut your tongue out. You've gotten me into an awful fix. I'm going to be a

84

mother . . . and my child will have no name. I'll make you pay for this through the nose, just see if I don't."

"If you succeed," Mr. Hawk replied, "you'll have discovered a new source of revenue. Anyway, about that having a baby business, it's all a lie."

"What if it is?" she answered hotly. "I might have a baby—I might have a flock of babies, great seething litters of them for all you care. You don't have babies. I have babies."

"I understand, dear," Mr. Hawk's voice was placatory. "I didn't claim I had babies. You have babies."

"I don't have babies," Meg replied furiously. "Never had a baby in my life, but I wish to God you'd have some—wish you'd have a cartload."

"I'd do anything to be agreeable, but having a cartload of babies, or even a small carriage full, is out of my line altogether."

"That's it!" she exclaimed. "That's it! Just like a big hulking brute of a man. You go round giving people lots of babies and then wash your hands of them. What are we going to do with all these babies? I ask you that—what are we going to do?"

The small creature looked tragically about her, as if literally surrounded by babies. Wherever Mr. Hawk's eyes rested he could see a small bald head. He was lost on a sea of babies, the immensity of which dazed him.

"How," he asked rather wearily, "how did so many babies get into the conversation?"

"What conversation?"

"I don't know even that."

"Well, you brought it up, and now you're trying to lie out of it. It's all because you insist on scratching on that wall."

"No such thing. I told you I wouldn't even breathe on that wall."

Meg laughed nastily.

"That's not because you wouldn't like to. It's because you don't want to have your throat slit." She paused and fixed him with her suspicious eyes, then continued: "And see that your bed's pulled out into the center of the room. Those long tentacles on the end of your feet might start in scratching the wall in your sleep, then in she'd pop. And that's another thing—

your toes are too damn long. They make three of my fingers."

"It's too late to do anything about that now, isn't it?" Mr. Hawk asked mildly.

"Well, keep them tucked under to-night or off they come, too."

"Don't get started on toes," Hunter Hawk pleaded. "Let's keep to the point."

"I will talk about toes," Meg replied passionately. "Don't try to stop me talking about toes. I suppose splendid Mr. Hawk's toes are too fine to be talked about—long, knobby, stalks like the twisted limbs of trees."

This revolting picture of his toes got under Mr. Hawk's skin. Nevertheless, he still endeavored to keep his temper.

"I never claimed my toes were works of art," he said with some show of dignity. "I know very well they're not lilies, but still they're not so awful as toes go."

"They are! They are!" she cried frantically. "They're the most terrible toes in the world. Don't tell me. I know."

"I'd like to place five of them where they'd do you the most good," was Hawk's heartfelt reply to this.

"So that's how you feel, is it?" she answered and snapped down the second cocktail. "Like to kick me, would you? I knew all the time you were a bully and a brute. Well, place those five horrible toes where you want to and see what happens."

She had risen and now stood confronting the man, her eyes mad with rage. Hunter Hawk was outfaced. He ignominiously wilted. Taking her soothingly by the arms, he smiled down upon her as if she were a child.

"Now, now," he said. "This is no time to get yourself all worked up and angry. Think of all the lovely things you have to wear and all the fun we're going to have. Think of those snappy pull-offs you got from Daffy. I'm just——"

"If you're going to keep throwing those pull-offs in my face," she cried, "I'll damn well throw them in yours."

She wrenched herself free, and before he could stop

86

her she had ripped off the flimsy garment and flung it in his face.

"Take that," she said, rushing down the veranda, "and if you make another wisecrack I'll rip off all my clothes and tear 'em to shreds."

"What goes on here?" came the unperturbed voice of Mrs. Tom.

"You mean, what comes off here," said Hawk, emerging with a grin from the step-ins. "Are all girls like that?"

"All that count," his hostess replied.

"Then do me a favor," he told her very earnestly. "Send up to my room about three quarts of the strongest grog you have in the house. I'm going to take off my coat and talk and drink with men."

"Certainly," said Mrs. Tommy. "I understand. I might even join you later. Being on parade becomes such an awful bore. I'll see about it right away. Any one of the servants will direct you to your room. Your things are already there."

She moved gracefully away. Hawk looked about for Cy and Daffy. They were just entering the hall. He started to follow them.

"And I'm not coming back," said a small, positive voice. It came from the shrubbery at the edge of the veranda. "You've seen the last of me."

"Well, if you change your mind," replied Hawk, addressing the shrubbery at random, "you'll find me in my room with three quarts of grog."

Silence a moment, then from the shrubs, "Where's that?"

"One of the servants will tell you."

"I'll find it, never fear, but you don't get me back." A pause. "I said, you don't get me back." Another pause. "Just for that I will come back, damn you," the voice continued. "Be careful what you do with those pull-offs."

Hawk smiled, thrust the step-ins into his pocket, and walked down the veranda.

"I think I'll give them to Tommy," he tossed over his shoulder.

Behind him the shrubbery seemed suddenly to have gone mad.

CHAPTER IX

A Nude Descends the Stairs

MR. HAWK WAS SINGING TERRIFICALLY IN HIS TUB. He was quite a little drunker than that well known lord one hears so much about. The three bottles of grog had been removed empty. Mr. Cyril Sparks had been removed full. Across the hall in their spacious chamber, Daffy and Megaera were dressing, were probably dressed and dancing, for all Mr. Hawk knew. He was far above time and circumstance. In his present mood he believed in doing one thing at a time and that thoroughly. From the great hall below came the sounds of music, dancing, and what not. Vaguely he wondered if people no longer ate, then he remembered he'd already eaten. Dinner had been served in the room. The remains of it were still outside. Tommy Brightly ran her place like a hotel.

Hawk's bath was concluded on a crashing climax of vocal ferocity. He emerged from the tub, rubbed himself down until he lost his balance, decided to abandon the effort, and knotting a bath towel around his waist made for the nearest door, his eyes still smarting from an overgenerous application of soap.

Now unfortunately for Mr. Hawk's evening it just so happened that the nearest door opened into the bedroom of the Brightlys. Even more unfortunately, it continued so to happen that Mrs. Tom Brightly had chosen this moment to shift to another and lighter gown, the night being what it was. She had progressed very satisfactorily to this end and was looking her best in hardly anything at all when the bathroom door, which she had forgotten to lock, was suddenly opened, and a man even a little more naked than she staggered briskly into the room. He was singing.

Mrs. Brightly glanced quickly in the mirror to see if her wind-blown was okay—she was not a woman to overlook essential details—and turned smilingly to deal with the situation.

"I hope your knot is on tight," she said easily. "That

towel doesn't make much difference, but it does make some difference."

Mr. Hawk brought his song to a close and eyed the fair revelation reproachfully.

"I didn't scratch on the wall," he observed. "This towel makes all the difference."

"What do you mean, scratch on the wall? This isn't your room."

"It's mine as long as I stay under your roof. An Englishman's home is his castle. Don't try to kid me just because I've been drinking a little—a very little."

"My dear man, you must have been drinking a lot if you can't tell this room from your own."

A heavy footstep sounded outside, and the knob of the door shook. Mr. Hawk with great presence of mind leaped grotesquely to a corner, where he froze himself in the attitude of Greek pugilist, his features distorted almost beyond recognition in a scowl.

Mr. Brightly also had been drinking a lot. Always nearsighted, he was now more fog eyed than ever. He lurched into the room and asked his wife why the hell she wasn't downstairs entertaining their guests. Then, unfortunately, his eyes fell upon the frozen but bellicose figure standing threateningly in the corner.

"Oh," said Mr. Brightly in a nasty drawn-out manner. "So-o-o-o. Well, I've got the low-down on you at last."

He lurched over to the statue and stood confronting it.

"Want to fight, eh?" said Mr. Brightly also striking an attitude of hostile intent. "Got anything to say for yourself before I give you the licking of your life?"

Mr. Hawk's silence increased Mr. Brightly's rage.

"Don't be an ass, Wetty," said his wife. "That thing's a statue. No human being could have a face like that."

"He won't have any face at all when I've finished with him," Wetty flung over his shoulder. "Nothing to say, eh? Well, take that."

Brightly's fist smashed against the stony chin of the statue.

"Godamighty!" cried Mr. Brightly, holding his damaged fist in his left hand. "Why didn't you tell me the damn thing was made of stone?"

He turned and glared at his wife.

"I did," she replied sweetly. "And if your head wasn't made of the same substance you'd have known it right off. No man could be made like that. Look at those funny legs and those long skinny arms. I had it made especially for tonight. We're going to have some fun with it."

Mr. Hawk's temper was rushing busily about in the hard shell of his body. Megaera had said unpleasant things about his toes. He had stood for that, but damned if he was going to have comparative strangers hold up his arms and legs to ridicule.

Brightly turned back to the statue and examined it closely. To Hawk's indignation, the man felt his face and slapped various parts of his body. Then he began to laugh drunkenly.

"You're right," said Brightly at last. "Should have known it right off, but my eyes are not so good. That's the silliest looking statue I ever saw. A physical wreck. He looks like Mutt in the funny strips."

He turned beamingly upon his wife.

"You're a great kid, Tommy," he told her. "That thing will be the hit of the evening."

This was just a little more than Hunter Hawk was willing to stand from Brightly. Taking advantage of the man's unprotected rear, he released his right leg and, still retaining his rock-like sledge hammer of a foot, delivered upon Mr. Brightly's person one of the most devastating kicks ever received by man. The recipient lunged forward and descended on his face. Mrs. Tom Brightly was as astounded as her husband. Up to this moment she had been too preoccupied with the situation itself to be impressed by the strange and sudden metamorphosis of Mr. Hawk. Now, however, when she came to think of it, there was something decidedly odd about the man, something inexplicable.

On all fours Brightly regarded the statue; then, after scratching his head in perplexity, he transferred his hand to his injured quarter.

"What the devil happened?" he asked.

"You tripped and fell," lied Mrs. Tom.

"I distinctly felt a kick," replied Brightly. "I'll bear its mark to the grave. If you don't believe me, look."

"I believe you," said Mrs. Tom, hastily averting her eyes. "Fix yourself up and go downstairs. I'll be with you in a jiffy."

The situation was becoming too complicated—too Rabelaisian. One naked man was enough at a time. If her husband didn't stop his solicitious inspection, she'd have one naked man and at least a half on her hands. A derisive chuckle floated from the statue. Mr. Hawk was feeling ever so much better.

"It's nothing to laugh at," Brightly complained.

"I'm not laughing at it," Mrs. Brightly replied rather coldly. "I agree it is nothing to laugh at. It shouldn't even be seen."

While Brightly was rearranging his toilet, Mr. Hawk took advantage of the intimate little interlude to make a spasmodic dash to the door. Brightly turned at the sound and looked over his shoulder. Hawk cleverly froze himself on the spot. But this time the man's suspicions were not to be lulled. He looked long and thoughtfully at the statue. There was something vaguely familiar about it. Mr. Hawk in his haste had made a slight mistake. He was grinning now instead of scowling, and this reversal of expression made a decided difference in his appearance.

"The damn thing's moved," said Brightly in an awed voice. "Statues don't move by themselves."

"Nonsense," replied Mrs. Tom. "It hasn't moved an inch."

"Don't tell me, my dear. I'm not as drunk as all that. Furthermore, the damn thing's laughing at me right this minute."

Brightly stopped and felt the place of the kick. His face cleared, then darkened suddenly.

"I see it all now," he said grimly. "That statue isn't a statue at all. It's a plot. It's your lover, and by the living God he kicked me in the pants. I'll kill him for that."

He rushed to a chest of drawers and snatched out an automatic, blue-black and mean looking. At the same time Mr. Hawk made an earnest endeavor to reach the door and thus to put an end to a situation which, painful as it was, had in it the possibilities of becoming even more painful. He flung open the door and, in his overwhelming desire to keep on moving as rapidly as possible, forgot to close it behind him. This gave Megaera, who was just emerging from her room, a splendid opportunity to see what was what. Mrs. Brightly in step-ins, Mr. Hawk in less, and the husband mostly gun—that is what she saw. And being a young lady of no little experience she placed upon the situation the only interpretation that seemed reasonable. Fire leaped to her eyes, and her dark face was flooded with the crimson of her rage. Flashing out her dagger, she blocked Mr. Hawk's passage to his room.

"So you couldn't even wait," she taunted. "I'd like to cut your liver out, and hers, too, for this."

Hunter Hawk was keenly appreciative of the importance of speed. He realized perhaps better than anyone present that this was no place to dally. One look at that gun had convinced him of this.

"Can explain everything," he gasped as he sprinted for the broad staircase leading down to the hall. As he sprang into one of the niches he prayed to God that the knot in the towel would remain steadfast to its purpose.

Bang! Zing! The scientist became morally as well as physically petrified as Wetmore Brightly, gun in hand, came bounding down the stairs. A sea of upturned faces seemed to be washing at Mr. Hawk's feet. Dancing had ceased to interest its votaries. All eyes were fixed on Messrs. Hawk and Brightly.

"I never remembered a statue being in that niche," a primitive-looking blonde remarked.

"What is it supposed to be?" another girl demanded.

"Starving Apollo," replied her companion.

"Oh," said the young lady in a disappointed voice. "I thought he wore a leaf."

"You shouldn't think of such things," she was told. "That towel might be the Greek for a dinner jacket."

"But what's the matter with Brightly?" another male inquired. "What on earth does he want to go shooting at a statue for?"

"I'd shoot at that statue myself if I had a gun," another voice stoutly declared.

"My God! Look!" a woman cried hysterically. "Brightly has turned to a statue now."

It was true. Mr. Hawk in desperation had been forced to petrify his host. Brightly stood motionless before him, the gun leveled at his head.

"I can't be as drunk as I seem to be seeing," one of the guests confided to anyone who cared to hear. "Brightly actually turned white and became as rigid as a block of marble."

"He damn well is a block of marble or something," replied another observer.

At this moment Megaera appeared at the head of the stairs. Her large dark eyes were fixed on Mr. Hawk. She was concentrating desperately, putting all her will power into her eyes, calling upon her reserve supply of magic to overcome the potency of Hunter Hawk's ray. She was determined to play an exceptionally dirty trick on this man who had betrayed her trust. Her heart glowed with triumph as she felt herself succeeding.

Hunter Hawk reluctantly came back to himself, sweating. A moment later Meg effected the restoration of Mr. Brightly. And a moment later than that there was the report of another shot. Bang! Zing! Going at great speed something small but hard buried itself in the wall less than an inch from Mr. Hawk's ear. Accustomed as he was to explosions, he was nevertheless unable to regard his present predicament with equanimity. He found himself in the position of a man who is forced to do several difficult things at once. One of these things was to maintain his towel in the important capacity it now filled. The knot, he feared, was working loose. Another thing was to continue rapidly down those stairs regardless of the throng awaiting him at their base. Finally, it would be helpful if he could repetrify Mr. Brightly. That should be done without further delay.

At the sound of the shot Meg underwent a sudden change of heart.

"What the devil do you mean by shooting up my man?" she demanded.

"Watch," said Brightly with an unpleasant laugh as he took careful aim at the diligently descending Hawk.

Before he could make the gun work, however, Meg had seized a huge vase which never should have been made and dashed it at Mr. Brightly. From the floor of the hall Hawk turned and directed the ray on the stricken man. The result was a rather interesting statue remotely resembling the Dying Gladiator. At the sound of the crash Daffy appeared, supporting her friend Cyril Sparks. That gentleman selected the top of the stairs for a base and sat there cheering. Mr. Hawk felt himself being closely examined by many pairs of bright and penetrating eyes. A less modest man would have passed through the crowd as quickly as possible and lost himself in the night. Hawk felt that he could go no farther. He had consumed a little more than his share of three quarts of strong liquor, and in spite of his activities he was far from being himself. Assuming the pose of wing-footed Mercury, one arm aloft and one foot delicately raised from the floor, he balanced himself skilfully on the ball of the other foot and, sending the ray through his body, remained in that position. Interested spectators crowded around him. Incredulous hands caressed him intimately. Fingers poked. One enterprising wag went even so far as to attempt to dislodge the towel. It clung with commendable loyalty to the middle section of the scientist. Meg was standing at his elbow, and in her hand she held a gun—the gun that Wetmore Brightly had relinquished upon the descent of the vase. There was a cynical smile on the young lady's face and a look of determination in her eyes. She would teach this man the lesson of his life.

Once more Mr. Hawk found the strength of the ray failing. And once more he appeared before the amazed guests as a creature of flesh and blood. At this point Meg discharged the revolver at his feet. Hawk leaped high in the air and cleared a space for himself on the great floor of the hall. From his place on the stairs Cyril Sparks redoubled his cheering. The sound fell ironically on Hunter Hawk's ears. For the security of the towel that wild leap had proved disastrous. The knot became merely two disconnected ends. With one hand Hawk seized these ends, with the other he wiped the sweat from his forehead. He looked about him for some means of escape, but wherever his anxious eyes searched they encountered the amused gaze of a group of guests. Cut off from escape in every direction Hawk lost hope and with it he lost all presence of mind. He became blindly and unreasonably enraged. Deliberately he removed the towel and flung it to the floor.

"So you won't stay on, won't you?" he shouted. "Well, damn you, you will!"

Then to the surprise of everyone he executed a dance of wild abandon. Suddenly he changed his mind and snatched up the towel. A man with nothing but a towel, even though it is strategically arranged, is a figure to give pause to any party. It did.

His rage expended in his dance, a great calm settled down on Mr. Hawk. He seemed to realize that everything was lost now and that he could lose no more. He felt much like a man who having been thoroughly drenched in a rainstorm can afford to loiter by the wayside. With unhurried dignity he walked to a table and, picking up a tray full of cocktails, made his way into the night through one of the French windows. Mrs. Brightly, now fully clothed—for Mrs. Brightly—arrived on the scene in time to witness Hawk's classical exit.

Ten minutes later a servant in striped drawers and the remains of a tattered undershirt rushed heedlessly into the hall, where an interested crowd immediately collected. The servant was white and trembling as he recounted his story to Mrs. Brightly.

"I was walking up the drive," he said, "keeping an eye on the cars. It happened just at the turn. That's where I lost my pants."

"And almost everything else," added Mrs. Tom. "But go on. What happened at the turn?"

"It was a madman—a maniac," continued the despoiled domestic, "and if you'll believe me, madam, he was mother naked."

"Not even a towel?" asked Mrs. Tom.

"Not even a towel, madam."

"Better and better," the primitive blonde remarked.

"He flung himself upon me, this madman did," went on the servant, "and began to undress me. I was so shocked and surprised I wasn't able to defend my-

95

self. Presently, after he had stripped off my coat, I thought I would try to reason with him like they say you can do sometimes with lunatics. 'What do you want to undress me for?' I asked him, and I remember his exact words. 'Your curiosity is justified,' he said, 'but have no fear. I don't want to undress you. It's most repugnant to me, but I must do it. It's your nakedness against mine, and I prefer yours. Turn about is fair play. Look out or I'll bite.' Well, of course, nobody wants to be bitten by a madman, that being a very dangerous thing, so I kept still. When he had gotten me down to my drawers he looked at them considering like for a long time. 'I leave you those,' he said at last, 'I can't imagine where you ever got such drawers. Consider yourself lucky,' and believe me, madam, I did."

The man paused and gulped.

"Go on," said Mrs. Brightly, her eyes dancing.

"Well, there's not much left," replied the man. "He took everything else except my undershirt, which had gotten torn in the first scrimmage. Then he insisted on having me help him to dress, which I did very nicely, tie and all. After that he gave me a cocktail, which I took just to please him."

"I dare say you needed one by then," observed Mrs. Tom. "You may withdraw now if you have nothing further to add. You're excused from duty for the rest of the evening. Try to keep those drawers. They're priceless."

As the servant departed Mr. Hawk nattily appeared. He had selected his victim with a discriminating eye. If anything the dress suit he was now wearing fitted him better and was more presentable than his own. Considering all it had been through, the stiff shirt front made a brave showing. His white tie was much more dexterously arranged than ever he had been able to achieve himself. He was slightly drunk but perfectly collected. About him seemed to glow the aura of a conqueror. In his right hand he held a long glass vase whose rightful occupation was flowers. At present it contained about two dozen cocktails.

"I poured them all in," he explained easily. "It made things less difficult."

"What a mind!" said the voice of Daffy. "That man's my uncle."

Mr. Hawk turned to Megaera.

"I have danced once already this evening," he said, "but unfortunately that was alone. Would you care to join me and my cocktails now?"

Megaera handed him the revolver and smiled almost shyly.

"Yes," she said. "Especially the cocktails."

"Before you go," Mrs. Tom asked, "won't you please try to do something about my husband? He's in a terrible state up there, and he's blocking up the stairs. One gets so tired stepping over him."

"Doesn't one just," replied Mr. Hawk. "I'll try to do something about him if you guarantee he'll do nothing about me."

"I fancy he's about through for the night," Mrs. Tom assured him.

Mr. Brightly was indeed in a terrible state, and he was very much in the way. He was lying in a stiff, distorted attitude amid the ruins of the shattered vase. Mr. Hawk restored him to the use of his body, but he could do nothing with the man's mind, which seemed to have been seriously affected by the events of the night.

When he had risen painfully to his natural position he looked wildly about him. His eyes finally rested on Mr. Hawk. A look of fear and loathing came into them. Without attempting to utter a word he turned and staggered up the stairs to his room. There he tried to puzzle out some of the various things that had happened. Eventually he gave it up. However, he was sure of one thing. Hunter Hawk was at the bottom of it all.

In the meantime the mysterious subject of his thoughts had once more descended the stairs—this time in a less original manner—and after circling the hall with the diminutive Meg disappeared with her through one of the French windows.

"We have a lot to thank them for," Mrs. Tom observed as she followed the disappearing couple not without a trace of envy in her eyes. "Already they have made the party a success."

"Yes," replied the primitive blonde in a tone of an-

97

ticipation. "After what we have seen to-night one can't blame any girl for standing for anything, can one?"

"Well, hardly, my dear," said Mrs. Tom, casting about for something fresh in the line of masculinity.

CHAPTER X

An Epidemic of Escapes

FROM A DISTANT ROOF GARDEN IN THE HEART OF a glowing city a waltz was throbbing over the air—Victor Herbert's "A Kiss in the Dark," many of which were being exchanged at that moment between Mrs. Brightly's guests, Mrs. Brightly herself being by all odds the most indefatigable exchanger.

Neither Meg nor Hunter Hawk was in the mood for such mild pleasantness. On the low hanging limb of a tree the small creature was perched. Hawk was standing beside her. This arrangement made it possible for them to converse almost as equals so far as height was concerned.

Below them in the dying light of an old moon the little lake lay fitfully glimmering. The white pavilion rising gracefully from the silver-flecked water looked like an enchanted barge that had gently drifted to shore from another world. Silently it floated on the surface of the lake, like a little prayer or dream passing in the night. Then, as the man and girl watched, the white pavilion became very much a thing of this world. Suddenly there burst from its doors a rout of white bodies. Flashing for a moment in the wan light, they sped like naiads across the platform and plunged into the quiet water, the ivory of their supple forms momentarily silhouetted against the night. Faint sounds of shouts and laughter drifted up the slope.

"Pretty," commented Meg, her eyes fixed on the lake.

Hawk considered. He was a trifle shocked.

"If I had the nerve I'd like to try it myself," said Hawk.

"You've contributed about enough nudity for one night," replied Megaera. "That dance of yours was almost more than mortal eye could bear. I didn't mind it in the least."

"You were responsible for it."

"Perhaps," she admitted, "but you were really at fault—you and that shameless woman."

"I keep on telling you it was all a mistake, Meg. I barged blindly through the wrong door. Soap in my eyes and all that. Wouldn't believe her when she told me it was her room."

Meg laughed mirthlessly.

"And naturally you stayed to argue the point in a friendly way," she observed sarcastically. "And no doubt you'd have arrived at an agreement perfectly satisfactory to both sides if himself had not arrived first with his gun."

"How many times do I have to tell you——"

"No more times," she interrupted brusquely. "You could keep on telling me until that horselike face of yours turned blue, and still I wouldn't believe you. When I see a man and a woman strutting about in nothing at all or nearly, with a bed in the background, it doesn't take much imagination to put one and one together."

"Evidently not," remarked Hawk bitterly. "You just naturally fling them together."

"I don't have to," she replied, "but I know what's what, never fear. However, my lanky lecher, you're forgiven this time. I can't help admiring your singleness of purpose. Just a real good time is all you're after— the playboy of the Christian Era of which you speak so highly."

Hopelessly Hawk regarded his companion. A nature such as hers would never credit the truth of the unfortunate affair. Even if he did succeed in making her believe him, he would in all likelihood lose caste in her eyes. She would not be able to understand. He shook his head and gave it up.

"All right," he said, "you win. Have it your way. What I would like to arrange right now if we could would be some sort of working agreement between you and myself. You can see for yourself how silly it is for your magic and my discovery to be forever clashing, working against each other. See what I mean? If I don't interfere when you want to turn a trick of magic I wish you'd give me a free hand with my science. When we work against each other the results are most unexpected—even dangerous. That chap Brightly nearly blew my head clean off of my shoulders when you brought him back to himself."

"You'd gotten me properly aroused," Meg explained. "What girl wouldn't be, in the same circumstances? I wanted that madman to blow your head off. The ugly thing deserved to be blown off, but what did I do instead? I almost knocked his ugly head off with an overgrown vase."

"And very neatly done it was, too," commented Hawk, inwardly smiling at the memory. "It must have been a scene of astonishing activity. I was rather busy myself."

"As busy as a drunken jumping jack," she said, laughing softly in the darkness. "Yes, you certainly had your hands full. The old man would have enjoyed seeing you. His sense of humor runs to violence. He enjoys the uncouth, and you were about the most uncouth object I ever saw. And I was so ladylike and well poised myself—bashing my drunken host over the head with a couple of tons of clay. Hope he has no hard feelings."

"Doubt if he knows who did it. Things were happening far too fast. I very much fear, though, he'll never be the same man, although God knows he can't be worse than he was."

A man and a woman, closely linked, passed by. They were unaware of the presence of Megaera and Hawk.

"If the maid answers," said the woman, "tell her it's the dentist calling up to let me know that Thursday will be all right for an appointment."

"But suppose himself should answer?"

"Then ask him to play golf."

"Where is he now, by the way?"

"On the business end of a cocktail," the woman replied. "I encouraged his libations to-night. The dear man thinks I'm a good sport."

"Think it will be safe to go swimming?"

"Have to take a chance on that," she replied with a

light little reckless laugh. "If he finds out and tries to get stuffy I'll pull an attack of hysterics and scare him out of a year's growth."

"That's the way I like to hear you talk," her companion said triumphantly. "If all wives were like you——"

"You'd have a much easier time."

Both of them were laughing as they passed out of earshot. Meg looked after the couple. There was a scornful expression in her eyes.

"You know," she said at last, "there are lots of things about this party I don't like, and most of them are people. They don't strike me as being wicked because they can't help it, but because they feel that they should be. Seem to have an idea that they're missing something unless they follow the mob. You're not like them."

"Thanks."

"No. You're just naturally a wicked man."

"The hell you say."

"Yes. You can't help being wicked. You don't try to be—probably you don't want to be. It just comes to you spontaneously, and there you are—wicked. And that's why you're so much better than these so-called good men—the moral sort. People who are not naturally wicked don't find it so hard to be good. I can stand good people and bad ones but these trollops up here with their dancing darlings, they bore me overmuch."

"You mean the kind that park their suitcases on Friday, have an interview with their bootleggers, and then start out to have one hell of a wild week-end. They're always throwing parties or being thrown at parties and having a nice vicious time generally."

"I guess so," said Meg, "but I haven't had much experience with them, after all. I've a feeling that they never just find themselves in bed with each other casually and clubbily. They make all sorts of elaborate arrangements, scheme, whisper, and telephone like those two that just passed. It must be an awful anticlimax. No zest. No element of surprise. They don't drift into depravity. They deliberately wade out to find it. Are the cocktails all gone?"

"Not quite."

"Give me a gulp."

Mr. Hawk passed the vase but kept one hand on it, while the girl drank, after which he refreshed himself.

"That's much better," she sighed, wiping her lips with her bare arm. "Whee!" She blew out her breath and gave her thigh a smart slap. "You know," she continued, waxing philosophic, "almost any man if he stays in bed long enough and enjoys sufficient privacy will find some woman alongside of him sooner or later."

"Trouble is," said Mr. Hawk, "the majority of men are not so optimistic as that—or so patient."

"Then they don't know women," Meg replied in a decided voice.

"Some of my best friends have been good people," said Mr. Hawk reflectively. "You know what I mean—really good people."

"Most good people have wicked friends," put in Meg. "They seem to attract them and to understand them. It sometimes takes a really good person to appreciate a wicked one. That's why I appreciate you."

Mr. Hawk laughed scornfully.

"You're the worst woman I ever met," he declared with unchivalrous sincerity. "I put nothing past you."

"Nonsense!" exclaimed Meg. "You don't know anything yet. Compared with this mob up here I'm a back number. Really good people like myself are all right, and really bad people like you are all right. It's the exploiters of either class that are all wrong. They're what you might call white-collar sinners. They lack distinction in their vice. They're just party people, if you know what I mean."

"I get what you mean," said Mr. Hawk. "They have to throw a party to get their courage up. A sort of I-will-if-you-will idea. Mass production of an inferior grade of sin."

"It's mostly vanity and competition that get the best of the women," went on Meg. "That and bad booze. These girls to-day will give up almost everything if not all to keep from losing a man even when they're sick of him. They're so constituted that they just can't bear to let the world see some other woman trotting the poor deluded ass across the floor. It galls them."

She reached for the vase, shook it, and turned it upside down.

"Empty," she said. "Damn. Just as I was getting moral, too. In the old days, before it was considered quite the proper thing for nice women to advertise their wares, men had to damn well fight for their folly. A lover of any consequence had to qualify first as a successful poisoner, knifer or clubber. Women were really apreciated then."

She sighed and sniffed the empty vase.

"Oh, well," she went on, "I dare say I'm getting old. I wouldn't have talked like this perhaps a couple of centuries ago. Something seems to have gotten the best of me tonight. I have a suspicion that you depress me. You're lots too long and much too sober. Let me down, and we'll refill that vase."

She flung her arms around Mr. Hawk's neck and, slipping from the limb, clung to him.

"See here," he began, but she interrupted him.

"Aw, shut up," she said. "Do you know what's wrong with me? No. Well, I don't belong. These women are so much prettier and bigger than I am, and they seem to know just what to do and how to do it. I feel sort of out of things and a little bit envious. Even if they are a bunch of petty, sneaking adulteresses they don't have to live in a hole in the ground like I do."

"Drop off, won't you?" complained Mr. Hawk. "Your knees are jabbing me right in the stomach. They hurt like anything."

"What do I care about your old stomach?" she cried, and silenced his further protests with her lips.

As they passed back through the trees towards the house they encountered numerous couples posed in attitudes of varying degrees of amorousness. The prediction of the primitive blonde had been a conservative one. With admirable fortitude every girl seemed to be standing for everything. The man who could calmly stand for any amount of explosions became more

103

alarmed as he progressed. He did not know what he might run into next. His fears were not without some justification.

"The other day," he told his unperturbed companion, "they ran in seventeen girls for spooning along Riverside Drive."

"Then, if the law ran true to form," said Meg, "these couples here would get the chair, or at least a life sentence."

"No," replied Mr. Hawk. "The difference between the conventional thing and dissolute conduct is the difference between Saturday night on a country estate and a park bench in the city. I beg your pardon, sir. I didn't know you were there."

Mr. Hawk hastily removed his foot from the dark figures beneath him and hurried on with averted eyes. A slow giggle followed after him on the wings of a muttered oath.

They passed through the great hall, now a place of wild disorder, and ascended the stairs. Cyril Sparks was seated on the top step. He was crooning dolefully about the laddie who kept on going away and never coming back. Daffy, who had been hearing about this nonreturning Scotchman for some time, was looking a trifle fed-up. Already she had rejected the oily suggestions of numerous gentlemen who had approached her with a view to getting her to indulge in activities that offered a little wider latitude to her talents. To all of these disinterested individuals her answer had been the same.

"I am sorry, sir," she had replied, "but I'm about to become a mother."

This answer had proved most effective. The gentlemen, shocked by this revelation, had hastily withdrawn.

"Hasn't it moved from this step?" inquired Meg of Daffy.

"It goes occasionally to get drinks when I won't bring them to it," she replied. "It is sitting here because it hopes it will all happen again."

"Wouldn't miss such a spectacle for the world," said Cyril with a bland smile. "First you appear with a towel, then you turn to a statue. I saw it with my own eyes. Don't tell me. Then Brightly arrives with a great big gun, takes a pot shot at the statue, and then plays statue, too. I've got it all down by heart. Can't think of anything else. Then, by gad, both of you come to life again and he starts in shooting. You sprint down the stairs, Meg wangs him over the head with a vase, and down he goes, once more a statue. You follow his example for a moment, then probably you feel like dancing, because you come back to life again. After that you pull off a real snappy dance and snaffle a tray full of cocktails. The surprising part is that you disappear into the night, naked, and presently return better dressed than I ever before saw you. Tell me, did everybody see all this? If not I'm going to stick to good old $C_2 H_5$ OH, a comparatively mild stimulant."

"It happened that way," said Mr. Hawk. "You didn't miss a trick, but let's retire now to my room and discuss several bottles."

When the jaded servant had brought the bottles and everyone was arranged according to his or her idea of comfort, that of the ladies being a flop on the bed, Mr. Hawk advanced a proposal.

"Let us," he said, "shake the dust of this place from our feet. Let us go out into the night and seek adventure. Roadhouses are still roading, and the night is not too far advanced. I know where the Emperor is parked."

"And I know where there is a secluded side entrance," contributed Daffy.

"It shall serve as an exit in this case," said Hawk. "Shall we escape without further procrastination?"

"Shalt," agreed Cyril readily, "avec bottles."

"Escape!" cried Meg, her dark eyes dancing. "That's my idea exactly. I'm ready now. When friend Brightly wakes up in the morning he will be in a none too agreeable mood."

There followed several minutes of rather scrambled packing, several more of earnest drinking, and a few devoted to stealthy retreating before the four departing guests found themselves rolling smoothly down the drive in the capacious interior of the Emperor. As the huge car circled round the lake the party watched with interest the sportive antics of the bathers. One stout youth was busily engaged in the pursuit of a slim girl. Mr. Hawk leaned out of the car and petrified the two figures in their tracks.

"They willl never be missed," he remarked, "and they will add materially to the artistic value of Mrs. Brightly's garden."

"Adequate recognition of indifferent hospitality," said Cyril as the car gained headway and moved towards the wide flung gates of the estate.

The main highway practically flung them into the arms of a roadhouse, and from that time on the stages of their journey were measured by the last roadhouse and the next.

At about three o'clock in the morning they were enjoying the advantages of a ringside table at an especially swanky resort. Money was running low, but spirits were still mounting. They were hungry and consumed by thirst. Mr. Hawk regarded the waiter not like the bird whose name he bore, but more like that predatory nocturnal one. He demanded the speedy satisfaction of both hunger and thirst, and without any undue delay his demands were abundantly satisfied.

It was then that the petty misfortunes which were to dog them for the rest of the trip began to arrive. Mr. Hawk was performing something hitherto unattempted in the line of dancing when a large lady planted her high heel heavily upon his instep. In addition to this the lady remarked to her partner that there seemed to be a number of drunken couples on the floor. Her partner gallantly assured her that there would be one less drunken couple if it bumped into them again. To put an end to what promised to be an unpleasant situation Mr. Hawk firmly froze the lady to the dance floor. Her partner, in endeavoring to proceed with the dance, found his gyrations suddenly arrested. The lady refused to budge. Redoubling his efforts, he tugged at her manfully, but still she remained glued to her tracks.

"Come on," he grunted. "Get started. What's the big idea?"

Receiving no answer to what he justly considered a reasonable question, he summoned his strength and, putting his weight behind his shoulder, grappled with

106

the lady. The general effect was more that of an assault than a dance. Several couples, observing the man's energetic actions, preferred to watch instead of dancing. Thus an interested little group gathered round to witness the unequal contest.

"Refuse to budge, do you?" panted the man who had not spent the evening unrefreshed. "Well, I'll damn well see that you budge."

He lunged at the petrified woman. His shoulder coming into violent contact with her received damaging punishment.

"God!" breathed the man, standing off and observing the immovable figure. "What's happened here?"

One of the watching ladies, who at that time of night would have found it difficult to stand under the most advantageous conditions, now yielded to the law of gravity and sank to the floor.

"Look! she screamed hysterically. "He's trying to dance with a statue. That isn't a real woman."

"God," repeated the man, thoughtlessly touching the petrified woman with a long finger. This action elicited general merriment on the part of the low-minded spectators.

"If she's a real live lady she'd never let you do that," someone remarked.

"No," agreed another voice. "Not even if you were married to her."

The man flushed.

"Wasn't thinking," he said apologetically.

"I should say not," said a lady indignantly.

The man's eyes sought and found Mr. Hawk, whom he regarded as the author of his misfortune. The scientist's gaunt features were registering his amusement. This did not improve the temper of the man.

"What did you do to her?" he demanded, advancing on Mr. Hawk.

"Who, me?" asked Mr. Hawk in a surprised voice. "My dear man, what do you think I am, a magician? If anyone is responsible for the unresponsive condition of your partner it obviously must be you, who were dancing with her at the time it happened."

"Is that so?" replied the man, making a wide pass at

107

Mr. Hawk, who, ducking adroitly, allowed the fist to continue on over his shoulder and into the face of an interested spectator standing directly behind him. With a howl of indignation and surprise the assaulted man seized Mr. Hawk and pushed him violently into his assailant. This gentleman, on plunging back, succeeded in inflicting painful injury upon another eyewitness. Thus several unpleasant contacts were established. The result was a brawl in which all present eventually became involved. It was one of these brother against brother conflicts in which every participant was for himself or herself for no good reason that they could discover. Mr. Hawk, taking advantage of the confusion, released the innocent cause of hostilities from her petrified condition. Meg and Daffy seized her by either arm and, whispering something in her ear, hurried her unnoticed to the Ladies' Room. Above the din of the battle rose the amazed voice of the woman's partner.

"My God!" he shouted. "She's gone entirely. She's not here."

Blows were arrested and oaths swallowed. Hostilities came to an abrupt end as the embattled participants, forgetting their meaningless fury, made a common cause of looking for the disappearing statue.

"Damn if I'm going to fight any more," announced the partner at last in a thoroughly discouraged voice. "There's something funny about this business."

With that he returned to his table where, sitting down heavily, he tried to think the thing out. As no one could discover any reasonable pretext for the resumption of the fight the various couples repaired to their seats, where they remained for some time earnestly discussing the strange occurrence. While this was at its height the large lady, flanked by Daffy and Meg, came unconcernedly across the floor. The three women seemed to be the best of friends and were laughing inanely together as women seem to find it helpful to do when getting acquainted. The partner of the large lady watched her approach with dazed eyes.

"'Later," he said as he hurried her to the door of the roadhouse. "Not here. Explain outside."

The poor man was mortally afraid that the lady

108

might take it into her head to turn into a statue again. This would be most inconvenient. He would never be able to explain the affair satisfactorily to her husband.

As the couple departed the waiter appeared before Mr. Hawk and presented him with the check. There was hardly enough room on it to edge in another figure. Mr. Hawk glanced at the total and gulped. Then he smiled weakly at the waiter and became an inanimate thing of stone.

"Look," whispered the waiter. "It's happened again."

Cyril removed the check from the nerveless fingers and looked at it to see what had so affected his friend. One look was enough.

"I want to join you, brother," said Cyril, and Mr. Hawk accommodated him.

There remained the two girls and the waiter. Within the hard shell of his head Mr. Hawk was doing some quick thinking, but think as he would he was unable to think himself and his party out of that room without paying the check, and this he could not do. The girls looked into the two stony faces of their escorts, then looked at each other. The waiter was visibly upset. His knees were trembling under him. In petrifying himself Mr. Hawk had still retained partial control of his lips. A sound now issued hollowly from them.

"Go away," he said to the waiter. "Be gone, you dog, or I'll petrify you for life."

The waiter made an honest effort to be gone, but his limbs refused to function.

"It seems he's already petrified," observed Daffy.

"Go away," repeated the hollow voice. "Make those legs work. Snap 'em into action."

This time the waiter succeeded in getting himself started. He did not stop until he had collapsed in the manager's office. There, in garbled form, he gasped out what had happened.

"You say he turned to stone and then began to talk?" asked the manager.

"He did, sir," replied the waiter.

"What's gotten into this place?" the manager went on. "Are all you waiters drunk to-night? Just a few minutes ago one of the men was telling me a cock-and-bull story about some woman who turned to stone.

109

The stuff we serve here is rotten, God knows, but I didn't know it was as bad as that."

"It's God's own truth," declared the waiter. "I saw her do it myself."

"Well, God's own truth is hard as hell to believe," remarked the manager, rising from his chair. "I'd better go out and see these petrified birds for myself. Take me to their table."

"I wish you would, sir," said the waiter. "I'm worried about their check. It's a knockout."

After the manager had devoted several minutes to making minor improvements on his already immaculate self he turned from the mirror and, beckoning the waiter to precede him, quitted the room.

In the meantime events had not stood still at the table of the petrified birds. Meg had taken decisive steps. She had accepted the invitation of a fat gentleman sitting at a table on the opposite side of the dance floor. This invitation had been extended and rejected several times during the course of the night or rather the morning. Now, however, Meg reversed her decision. She smiled sweetly at the fat gentleman and nodded. Unsuspectingly that individual approached, Meg rose to meet him, and in a moment she was circling the floor in his putty-like embrace. A low growl of suppressed rage broke from the lips of Mr. Hawk. He was tempted to return furiously to himself, but thought better of it. The unpaid check lay on the table before him. So far he had been able to think of only one way out of the difficulty—flight. The odds were greatly against the success of such an enterprising move, Cyril Sparks being one of the odds—at this stage of the game his legs were unreliable.

"Damn bad jam," said Hunter Hawk to himself. "Wonder what she's up to?"

The music stopped, and the manager arrived at about the same time. Meg returned to the table. Her face was flushed, and her eyes sparkled, and strange to relate her left breast seemed to have outgrown its fellow. Daffy was the first to notice this rather disconcerting change.

"My dear," she whispered. "You're getting over-breasted on the left."

110

"Yes," agreed Megaera with a gin-induced giggle. "I'm what you might call busting out."

In her enjoyment of her little joke she slapped Mr. Hawk on the back.

"Ouch!" she cried, blowing on her fingers. "This man of mine is certainly hard boiled." Then in a lower voice she added, "It's these damn low-cut, tight-fitting dresses. A girl nowadays can't hide a thing."

The manager, who had been an interested observer, now made his presence known. He picked up the check and rapidly ran his eyes down the column to the only place that mattered. At the sight of the total his face darkened. Still he retained his poise.

"I hope everything has been satisfactory," he said, with one of his Ittest smiles, virily showing his white teeth.

"No, it hasn't," snapped Daffy. "This place is altogether too rough for a woman of any refinement. I've been greatly perturbed by the conduct of some of these lousy bums." She waved her hand at the room and attempted to look indignant.

The manager opened his eyes wide, then blinked rapidly. The lady's miscellaneous selection of words made it difficult to place her exact position in the social scale. He tried again.

"Sorry," he said, running a hand through his boyish bob, a gesture he had always found effective when dealing with women. "Are the gentlemen quite well? If you'll excuse me for saying it, there seems to be something wrong with them."

"Nonsense," replied Daffy. "They're as hard as a rock—as hard as a couple of rocks. We want some drinks here. What's happened to the waiter?"

"Stop scratching your head in public," put in Meg, "and get down to brass tacks."

The manager nervously handled the check. Evidently these two women were not of the impressionable type. So many women nowadays considered themselves lucky to be singled out by managers of roadhouses, leaders of orchestras and other, for the most part, God-fearing and hard-working members of a restaurant's staff. He gave up all attempts to It the ladies and came to the point.

111

"It's about the check," he said quite frankly. "It's a whale of a check, and I wouldn't feel at all disappointed if a little something were done about it."

A deep sigh came from the direction of Mr. Hawk. The manager stepped back a pace and regarded the scientist suspiciously.

"Oh, the check," said Meg indifferently. "Let's have it."

She reached out and took the check from the manager. Then she dived into the bosom of her low-cut dress and produced a fat wallet—pin seal trimmed with gold and bearing the irrelevant letters T.H.G.

"I have to keep it from him when he gets this way," she explained. "It's an awful bore. Makes one left breasted. See, I'm all right now, Daffy. Not a penny's worth of difference between 'em."

As she rapidly examined the contents of the purse a delighted smile lit up her features.

"Why," she continued in a pleased voice, "he has ever so much money. We can drink gallons more. Here's one hundred and twenty dollars, and don't let me see any change. Take that check away and frame it. You're in luck. And, waiter, bring us a flock of drinks."

At the sight of the strange wallet, Mr. Hawk had returned to himself with a click. He had then resuscitated Cyril Sparks. Both of them now sat staring at the fat roll of bills in Meg's brown hand.

"For the love of all things sacred," said Hawk when the manager and the waiter had withdrawn, "get that wallet and money out of sight. Where did they come from?"

"Oh, so you're back, are you, you coward?" replied Meg. "Well, don't worry about this money. It's an old game to me. If you want any more I'll get you lots."

She crammed the bills into the wallet and carelessly returned it to her breast.

"I say," put in Cyril Sparks to Daffy, "your uncle just did the most surprising thing to me. He actually turned me to stone."

"And you weren't any more useless than you ever are," Daffy hastened to assure him. "We didn't miss you at all."

The waiter, also a changed man, returned with the drinks. These were dashed down with avidity and more ordered.

"Now you lugs are going to turn into a couple of gigolos," announced Meg. "I'm paying for this party, and I insist on being entertained."

"About that money," began Mr. Hawk as she led him from the table.

Disaster had been delayed but not averted. It descended swiftly as Meg was whirling past the fat gentleman with whom she had just danced. It was not the final disaster, but rather the prelude to disaster. It began with a plop as the well stuffed wallet slipped down through Meg's dress and landed on the floor. Quick as a flash the girl ducked and seized the lost article. Mr. Hawk, taken by surprise, hurdled on over her and sat heavily on the floor. The fat man, recognizing his wallet, uttered a strangled cry and strove to retain Megaera's hand. She eluded his grasp and darted across the floor. In her own mind she was satisfied that she had a moral right to the wallet and all it contained. On the other hand, the fat gentleman had certain definite ideas of his own concerning the rightful ownership of the wallet.

"Run!" cried Meg to the recumbent scientist. "I've got it."

"Then give it back," called Hawk, rising hastily from the floor and sprinting after the girl.

"Thieves!" shouted the fat gentleman, as was only just and proper. "Robbers! Stop those two!"

"They seem to be running," observed Daffy to Cyril Sparks. "Perhaps we'd better run after them."

"I've already started," said Cyril who at that moment was in entire agreement with the law of self-preservation.

"Wait for me!" cried Daffy, dashing after him to the door.

As she sped along in the rear of the retreat she encountered several waiters standing in attitudes of petrification. Apparently they had been so ill advised as to attempt to place themselves between Mr. Hawk and liberty. Behind her she could hear the shouts and excited voices of the multitude. From in front came the

113

sound of ground being scraped energetically by several pairs of flying feet. Her companions were toeing in. Redoubling her efforts, Daffy succeeded in overtaking the main body of the retreating party just as Mr. Hawk was getting the Emperor under way. A long arm reached out and hauled her aboard as the car gathered speed and shot down the drive. Nothing was said until they were well clear of the roadhouse. Mr. Hawk then became vocal.

"Well," he announced nastily. "You've succeeded in making thieves of three honest people. You never were honest yourself."

"I know it," said Meg, still panting a little. "We're all in it now. If they catch us I'm going to swear you made me do it."

At this information, Mr. Hawk increased the speed of the already flying car.

"Damn these new-fangled dresses, anyway," Meg continued. "They might have certain advantages, but they're no good for plunder."

"Hadn't you better get rid of that wallet, dearie?" casually inquired Daffy. "And wouldn't it be a good thing to distribute some of that money among the rest of us?"

Although Meg was far from enthusiastic about the latter suggestion, she complied with both. The wallet was hurled through the window into the bordering woods, and the money was unequally divided among the four. Meg tucked the lion's share alongside the dagger and took the precaution to warn Mr. Hawk about his hand.

"Not that I object," she assured the indignant man, "but it's a sin to fool with money."

And all this time a motorcycle policeman was burning up the road behind them while several brother officers were approaching from in front. Telephone communications had been established between the roadhouse and the various headquarters of law and order along the road. The hue and cry was out. As fear of apprehension grew farther from the minds of the Emperor's passengers the actuality of such an occurrence was taking more definite shape.

Cyril Sparks was the first to voice his relief.

114

"I feel that we all deserve a drink," he announced as he drew a bottle from some mysterious place of concealment. "I'll bet no one knew I had hidden this."

"You win," said Daffy. "Occasionally you have a brain wave. Pass it around."

She elevated the bottle, then handed it forward to Meg. That young lady drank without reluctance and asked her companion what he was going to do about it. He stopped the car and proceeded to show her. This was an unwise move. It could not have been better timed for the convenience of the elements of restraint. Three of its members jumped into the glare of the headlights and a fourth sprang to the running board of the car.

"Oh, Goddy," breathed Mr. Hawk as he dropped the bottle to the roadside.

Then he did about the most effective thing he could have thought of to annoy and baffle the officers. He petrified the entire personnel of the Emperor. When the investigation officer shouted out the customary no-monkey-business warning, he found himself looking into a face of stone. And when he glanced at the others in quest of some explanation of this incredible occurrence he was prodigiously shocked to find their faces equally stony. For a moment he thought he had gone mad or lost the sense of touch, then, being an officer of no little resource, he summoned his colleagues to a conference.

"This isn't the mob we're after," he told them. "This damn car is full of abandoned statues."

"The hell you say," exclaimed another officer. "There's some funny business about this. These things can't be statues. They're all sitting."

"Why can't statues sit?" asked a third officer, remembering his Bulfinch days. "There's crouching Venuses and flying Mercuries and leaping fawns and a hell of a lot of other funny statues."

"Then I suppose you'd call these Sitting Automobilists?" the second speaker put in sarcastically.

"Not necessarily, but they might have been removed from someone's garden," was the nearly impossible reply.

"Well," replied the other, "from the looks of them

they might have been removed from a graveyard suffering from an attack of acute cramps."

This was too much for the fourth officer, who up to that moment had been content to remain in wondering silence.

"Who ever heard of a corpse having cramps?" he demanded.

"Who ever heard anything to the contrary?"

The fourth officer was not prepared for this essentially unfair question.

"Oh, of course," he hedged, "a corpse might have cramps, for all I know. I've heard that their teeth keep on growing."

"Not teeth, you dunce, hair." Mr. Hawk had been unable to restrain himself. His voice fell like a ghostly whisper among the officers.

"Who said that?" one of them asked nervously.

Receiving no reply, he backed hastily out of the car, his interest in the problem completely evaporated. Let those who would carry on the investigation so far as he was concerned. He would be satisfied to remain at a modest distance and watch the car, the number of which he took as a pretext for his absence.

"There's something fishy about this," said the senior officer of the group. "Statues or no statues, I'm going to put the lot of 'em under arrest. We got to show something to the chief."

"He'll be tickled pink to put that outfit behind the bars," remarked the mythological expert.

"Yeah," put in another. "What are you going to charge 'em with, resisting arrest?"

"No," replied the senior officer quite seriously. "I'll charge 'em with obstructing traffic. Get in there, Delaney, and drive this bus to the lockup."

"One of you guys lend a hand and help me push this statue or corpse or whatever the devil it is over," complained Delaney. "Damned if I'll sit on its lap."

With much puffing and panting the two officers succeeded in prying the unhelpful Mr. Hawk clear of the steering wheel. He clattered dangerously against Megaera. Then Officer Delaney, feeling none too happy at the prospect of the drive that lay ahead of

116

him, slid down in the seat by the petrified scientist and set the car in motion.

Everything went well for the first mile or so, then Officer Delaney began to have an uneasy feeling that eyes were fixed watchfully upon him. It was an unpleasant feeling to have, and it became even more so when it grew from a feeling to a conviction. He turned his head quickly and could have sworn he detected an ironical flicker in the sightless eyes of the figure beside him.

"Nerves," muttered the officer, beginning to sweat profusely. "Shouldn't have gone on that party last night."

Then, to his profound discomfort, he distinctly felt himself being tapped on the shoulder. The first three taps he allowed to pass unchallenged, but at the fourth and most impatient of the series he spun round in the seat and looked behind him.

"Eyes on the road, Delaney!" a ghoulish voice commanded. Officer Delaney whirled back to the wheel and looked numbly at the road ahead.

"That's better," said a feminine voice. "Have you enough room, Delaney?"

"No," said Delaney in a hoarse but positive voice. "I haven't near enough room, but I'm going to get a lot more."

He brought the car to an abrupt stop and signaled to his escort.

"Listen," he told its leader, "these damned statues are talking and asking me foolish questions, and one of them had the nerve to go tapping me on the back. Get somebody else to drive this car. I'm a sick man."

"Nonsense," said the senior officer. "This won't look at all well on your record, Delaney."

"I'll turn in my resignation before I'll touch that wheel again." Delaney was firm about it.

"All right, Brownell," snapped the officer. "Get in there and relieve Delaney."

Brownell reluctantly obeyed. With a shrinking feeling he climbed into the seat and squeezed over to the door as far as possible. With the starting of the car his ordeal was begun.

He didn't think, he actually knew someone was

117

breathing heavily on his neck. Also he was certain that the gaunt figure beside him was scrutinizing him disapprovingly out of the tail of its eyes. Then the officer had a bright idea. He raised his eyes quickly to the driving mirror and uttered a wild cry. Over his shoulder was peering a white grinning face.

"Great Godamighty—whew!" rushed from the lips of the officer as he endeavored to bring the car to a stop.

"What, again?" demanded a disgusted voice. "Drive on, Brownie. Have we far to go?"

"None of your damn business," Brownell shouted. "But if you want to know *we* don't go one inch farther. I don't know what you are or who you are, but whether you're human or devils you should feel damn well ashamed of yourselves, carrying on like this."

"Come, come, Brownie," said an admonitory voice from the back of the car. "Don't you carry on like this. You're making yourself ridiculous. Hurry up and drive this car, or something decidedly unpleasant might happen."

"Something unpleasant is happening," vouchsafed Officer Brownell. "If you were any sort of statues at all you'd shut up and act like statues. You're more talkative than a bunch of drunks."

"What an unpleasant officer," came a woman's voice from the back of the car.

"My God, is there another one of you?" demanded the officer.

"There is," said another voice, this time a man's. "Do you want any more?"

"No!" shouted the officer.

"Your voice, Brownie, your voice," said a soft, reproving voice from the front seat. "Do something about it. We don't want any trouble, you know. And you'd better lay off making these wisecracks about what sort of statues we are. We're about the finest body of statues yet uncaught. If you don't believe it, just take a look at that leg."

Officer Brownell was so heavily married he even depressed his wife. This ribald invitation on the part of a female statue shocked him more than anything else so far. The color mounted to his face; he elevated his chin haughtily and drove on in silence. The statues were singing a drinking song when he pulled up before the police station.

By the time the last statues had been lugged into the charge room and seated in a chair Chief of Police Mc-Gowan was almost crying with rage.

"I'll break the whole damn lot of you," he shouted. "What are you trying to do, anyway, turn my jail into a goddam museum?"

The motorcycle policemen had filed into the room and now stood facing their chief. There was an expression of dismay on their faces. Suddenly from among them came a wild, insulting noise, sounding like the neighing of a demented stallion or a sail being ripped in a mighty wind. The chief's face went white.

"Who did that?" he thundered. "Speak up, or I'll strip you clean of every damn button you own."

A shriek of feminine laughter greeted this dire threat.

"That settles it," said the chief. "I break you all. Tear each other's buttons off. Start in."

The officers were about to obey this drastic order when the sound of an engine starting outside the door of the station house attracted their attention.

"They're gone!" an officer suddenly shouted. "Look! Their chairs are empty."

"Go out and round up those statues," commanded the head of the motorcycle squad.

"Come back here, boys," called the chief in a weak voice. "Let's forget the whole damn thing ever happened. I'll stand for a certain amount of skylarking, but, for God's sake, don't bring m eany more statues. We don't want to get this town laughed at in the newspapers."

"Do we keep our buttons, chief?" sang out an officer.

"Sure you do," grinned the chief. "And be sure to keep 'em buttoned."

"Say, you guys," announced a bright young officer coming snappily into the room, "every damn one of your motorcycles is punctured both fore and aft."

Far down the road four limp and drunken occasional statues were speeding through the dawn and singing at

119

the top of their lungs a song derogatory to the morals, antecedents, and personal appearance of Chief of Police McGowan.

CHAPTER XI

The Pursuing Beard

HUNTER HAWK SENT THE EMPEROR BOUNDING across one of his most inaccessible fields. In the slanting light of dawn four stiff and disheveled figures emerged from four separate doors. They stretched, yawned, and held their respective heads. Then they assembled in a compact little knot like battered football players after a tough scrimmage.

"This will never do," declared Cyril Sparks. "Have you any ethyl alcohol at home?"

"As a last resort, yes," said Mr. Hawk.

They decided without being invited temporarily to collapse upon the hospitality of Meg and her father. It would be unsafe to appear en masse at Hawk House until their status in the criminal class had been more definitely established. In the grotto they would entrench themselves and await developments. Cyril Sparks was all for setting fire to the Emperor and thus destroying one of the most damaging pieces of evidence against them. But Mr. Hawk was sincerely attached to the Emperor. In its lumbering way the car had served him well. As ungainly as it was, it concealed a heart of gold, and, even more important still, a reliable and responsive engine.

Meg greatly preferred a comfortable bed to the grotto, but when Hunter Hawk tactfully pointed out to her that his body might be seized and placed in a dungeon, the comfortable bed lost much of its attraction.

"Come along, then," she said at last. "We'll all crowd in somehow."

They trailed away to the forest through a rising flood of sunlight. A fresh breeze soothingly stroked their foreheads and brought momentary relief. Meg, with an arm around Hawk's waist, was allowing him to drag her along.

"Did you have a good time?" she asked.

120

"One of those times that is good only after it is over," he replied. "Good in the retrospect."

"I thought you were awfully clever, the way you manipulated that ray," she went on, her eyes fixed admiringly on his unshaven face.

"It kept me pretty busy," replied Hawk, "but I'm getting better at it all the time."

"Do you like knocking about with me?"

Hawk's face grew serious.

"Listen," he said. "Since you climbed into my room and took a mean advantage of my yielding nature and aversion to publicity, I have been living what I call dangerously—on the fringe of some startling dénouement. Already I'm beginning to feel just a wee bit déclassé. It's been amusing at times, I'll quite readily admit, but where, oh, where, is it going to lead?"

"If we knew the answer to that," she said, "none of us would carry on, perhaps. I hope it leads to bed."

"Are you unable to entertain an abstract thought?" asked Hawk.

Meg laughed a little unchaste scrap of a laugh.

"And to sleep," she added.

Ludwig was squatting disconsolately at the entrance of his grotto as they approached. When he saw them he brightened up a little, but when pressed for food and drink, especially drink, he shook his head sadly.

"There is nothing, my friends, nothing," he announced, spreading out his small, clever-looking hands. "I have neither drunk nor eaten in twenty-four hours."

"Which is less than a second, as you reckon time," said Mr. Hawk.

"But not as my system reckons it," he answered. "My appetites are the same as yours."

"On even a grander scale," said Hawk admiringly.

"That would be difficult," he retorted with a faint smile, "if past performances count for anything—but what is my daughter doing? It looks unusually interesting."

He hurried over to Megaera, who, seated on a fallen log, was leisurely counting a fat roll of bills, wetting her thumb from time to time on the red tip of her pointed little tongue.

"Ahem," coughed Ludwig Turner. "Your old father has missed you, my child."

"Two hundred and fifty-five," said Meg.

"He has more than missed you," hastily continued Ludwig, his realization of how much he had missed her growing keener with the size of the figure.

"Two hundred and seventy," said Meg. "What?"

How his fingers itched. He thrust them into his pockets to keep them from making a diplomatic blunder.

"I was just saying it could be arranged," he replied. "All things can be arranged. Everything. And most agreeably. I have a friend. An invaluable fellow. Through him there is little that can't be done—for, of course, a purely nominal consideration—what would be a mere trifle to those who are—er—warm with money."

After a certain amount of noisy and unpleasant haggling and the exchange of a few mutually demolishing recriminations, the financial side of the bargain was struck. Mr. Turner disappeared into the bushes, and presently various baskets began to arrive. Eggs, bacon, bread, butter, coffee, and milk took up some but not too much room. The remainder of the space was given over to applejack, an arrangement to which no one made objection. While breakfast was in the course of preparation Cyril Sparks and Hawk took turns at holding their heads under the miniature waterfall in the grotto, Mr. Hawk observing that he wished it were Niagara. Breakfast served and dispatched in a rough-and-ready manner, the party unceremoniously slept. Meg's head, pillowed in the pit of the scientist's stomach, kept rising and falling like a wax figure animated by clockwork, as the long man sought for air. Mr. Ludwig Turner and his bottle sat companionably at the entrance of the grotto. In vain did the little man endeavor to perfect some plan whereby he would be able safely to transfer the roll of bills from his daughter's stocking to his own sock. At last he shook his head and gave it up. He had never been able to steal successfully from Meg. A most unsatisfying offspring.

After three days of this woodland existence Mr. Hawk came to a decision. He had been home and

122

learned to his horror from his sister that an officer of the law in plain, unbecoming clothes had called and made certain inquiries regarding the present whereabouts of Mr. Hawk. Mention had been made of a small dark woman who was wanted on a charge of theft. He had left with every assurance that Hawk House had not seen the last of him.

"Of course, when he asked me to describe your car I had to tell him the truth," said Mrs. Lambert. "Fortunately I was able to give him the number of your plates. Junior found it for me. Betts had told the man all wrong. He said your car was a small two-seater, sky blue, with pink trimmings. Of course, I couldn't let the man go away believing such a thing as that."

"Of course not," Mr. Hawk had replied. "Pity you didn't give him a photograph and a set of my finger prints."

"But we did," she replied triumphantly. "That is, we gave him a photograph. He said the finger prints would come later."

"Much later," was Hawk's reply. "Did Junior also find the photograph?"

It seemed that Junior had, but only after a great deal of diligent searching for which his mother gave him due credit. She had then mentioned in passing the talk that was going round about a man who had performed a nude dance at Mrs. Brightly's house party. She understood it was generally known that the dancer, the nude dancer, was her own brother. Of course, he had lost standing in the community—the whole family suffered from it—and now, with this arrest hanging over his head, oh, well, wouldn't it be better if he took a trip somewhere and stayed for a long time, until people had had a chance to forget? And while she was on the subject he really should do something about the poor Reverend Dr. Archer. In spite of the fact that he had had a chair built to conform to his odd position, the dear man was still very uncomfortable. Then, of course, there was his appearance. It wasn't very reassuring, especially for a man of God. Some respect should be shown for the cloth, even if a man had fallen so low as willingly to drag his family through the mire. Of course, she would make no reference to the effect of all this on her husband and her son Junior. After all, the boy was only his nephew, his own sister's child. Her remarks, she hoped would be understood, were made merely in passing. Naturally she had nothing to say. It was none of her business.

It was only with this last observation that Mr. Hawk was in entire agreement. He had then asked his sister if she in turn would like to take a long trip. But Mr. Hawk had been much more specific. He had been even good enough to name the place. She had not liked this. Few persons do like to be told to go to such a place, even when they are intellectually convinced that the place does not exist. It must be the spirit of the thing. However that may be, the invitation resulted in Mrs. Lambert's leaving the room, much to the satisfaction of her brother. Mr. Hawk rang for Betts and made known to that worthy and subtle domestic the decision to which reference already has been made. And it was this decision, made on the spur of the moment, that launched Mr. Hawk on the last and least credible stage of his not altogether commonplace experiences.

The quartet was disbanded. Cyril Sparks and Daffy returned to their respective homes. Mr. Turner was given nearly, but not quite all, of Meg's ill-gotten bank roll. All of it, that young lady could not be induced to give. Some she must have for herself. The woods were filled with her protestations of the necessity for a girl to have a little something in her stocking. Would they drive her out into the streets—force her into a life of shame? Although her father almost tearfully assured the company that to achieve this end neither driving nor force would be required, Megaera was allowed to retain a light little anchor to windward. Still protesting against a life of sordid commercialism into which circumstances would undoubtably precipitate her, she was virtually hurled into the Emperor and a thick veil pulled down over her indignant face.

"A gag will follow if you don't shut up," Mr. Hawk calmly assured her.

"Damn you, anyway," she mumbled. "If you'd had enough money in your pocket I wouldn't have had to become a thief."

Mr. Hawk was too deeply involved with a large, flowing beard to which he was attached, to reply.

"I'm afraid we'll have to sacrifice several inches of this damn thing," he told Betts. "It's getting all tangled up in the steering gear."

"Tie it behind your ears," Meg suggested rudely.

"You might button it under your vest, sir," Betts offered with admirable gravity.

"There are a number of things I might do with it," Mr. Hawk replied slowly and bitterly. "I might take it off and hang it on the radiator. I might stuff it under the seat or build a bonfire with it. I might decide simply not to wear the beard. The possibilities of this beard are endless, and your suggestions are not helpful." Over the rim of this startling disguise he peered passionately at them. His face seemed to be all eyes and beard, which, as a matter of fact, it was. It cannot be said that the beard had improved him, but it had made him a different man, so different as hardly to look human at all. "All that I want to do with this beard," he continued, "is to sit quietly and unobtrusively behind it and to drive speedily out of this state into New York City. After that I don't very much give a damn what becomes of the beard. You can raffle off the beard. You can take the beard to an art dealer or have it framed. The beard can be used to stuff a pillow with a picture of Niagara Falls on it. Or if you can think of nothing better to do with the beard, you can thriftily roll it up in moth balls and tuck it away in a trunk in the attic." He paused and looked searchingly at Betts and Meg. "Now," he added, "I hope you no longer feel that I need any further damn fool suggestions regarding the use and ultimate disposition of this beard." Another heavy pause. "I trust it is clear to you that I don't want to wear this beard. It's not a thing I naturally run to. This beard is most offensive to me. I wish to God you were both wearing one exactly like it." Mr. Hawk appeared to have said all he was going to say about the beard.

The thoughtful silence that followed was broken by the hopeful voice of Mr. Betts.

"Would you like me to carry one beard, sir," he asked, "so as you could snap it on when you needed it?

That would give your chin a chance to air out a bit."

Hawk shrank hatefully in his seat but still endeavored to control his anger.

"Think, Betts," he said in a cold, level voice, "think of what you're asking. Try to picture the thing to yourself. You are carrying the beard, let us say. I am driving at fifty miles an hour. A motorcycle policeman approaches—rapidly. I cry out, 'The beard, Betts, the beard!' You pass it forward to me. I stop the car and hastily attempt to don the beard. People stop and look. A small boy jeers. Laughter is heard. I grow confused. In the meantime the policeman arrives. He looks at me in a strange way. 'What is that?' he asks, pointing a soiled finger at the beard jumping in my hand as if impatient to be attached. 'It's a beard,' I answer, not because I want to, but because it's the only thing it could be. He looks at me more closely. A smile of satisfaction touches his cruel lips. I shrink back and wonder to myself, 'What on earth am I going to do with this beard?' Then the policeman speaks. He says, 'Well, you and your beard come along with me,' and he adds, 'and no monkey business.' Now, Betts, do you understand how unintelligent your suggestion was? I hope we shall hear no more about this beard."

"Yes, sir," said Betts. He glanced respectfully at his master, then quickly hid his face in his handkerchief. As the scientist listened to the sounds issuing from the handkerchief, his eyes took on an injured expression. The man was actually laughing. Hawk had never before realized that Betts had a perverted sense of humor. Bearing his beard proudly, Hawk gazed directly ahead.

"A man with a mind like yours must die a million deaths," Megaera observed.

"Since meeting you," he replied, "it's been one long, lingering death," was Mr. Hawk's reply. "If there are no more questions or suggestions regarding this beard, I shall now endeavor to drive with the damn thing."

Bracing himself grimly behind his streaming facial adornment, he viciously kicked the starter and drove the Emperor from the field. Once more he was on the road with a newly risen sun dead ahead. An hour and a half later, a long matted object was picked up in the

126

dead center of Holland Tunnel. Mr. Hawk had taken no chances, and so far as the scientist and his destiny were concerned, that was absolutely the last appearance save one of the beard, for which everyone devoutly thanked God, considering it the least that they could do. As the Emperor came to rest before the house on lower Fifth Avenue in which its owner maintained an apartment, a car which had been patiently following drove slowly past. A man at the wheel leaned out and, tossing the beard into Mr. Hawk's lap, sang out cheerily, "Here's your beard, mister. You look much funnier with it on." At the unexpected reappearance of the beard Mr. Hawk shrieked as if bitten by a snake. Between them Betts and Megaera succeeded in dragging the temporarily demented man to his apartment. On entering the place Meg, who had been carrying the beard carelessly, tossed it to a chair. Most unfortunately, Mr. Hawk selected this chair in which to collapse.

"Eh!" he exclaimed. "What's this?" and reaching down he withdrew the beard from under him.

For a moment he stared at the thing with dilated eyes. Meg and Betts stood speechless, rooted to the spot.

"Oh!" cried Hawk suddenly. "It's alive. It's pursuing me. Don't leave me alone. Yet don't come near. I'm crazy. I'm mad. Something has snapped in my brain. Bring me a drink, Betts, or I'll slit your gullet from ear to ear. Ha! ha, ha! I'm going to my room."

As he staggered from the library he was singing about Mother Machree and the dear silver he intended to kiss in her hair. Betts picked up the beard from the floor and thoughtfully examined it.

"I don't see anything so wrong with this beard," he said, turning to Meg. "It's almost as good as new. A little combing, perhaps."

"It's the color," she replied briefly. "Should have been red."

Undecided about this, Betts bore the beard from the room.

CHAPTER XII

Looking the Gods Over

MEG TOOK NEW YORK IN ONE DIMINUTIVE BUT buoyant stride. Nor was that all she took. There were things. All manner of things. Such things, for example, as handbags, stockings, brassières, lipsticks, perfume, underwear, even, and many other small articles her quick hands encountered as she demurely followed the tall figure of the impeccable Mr. Hawk along the aisles of the various department stores they visited.

Had the scientist but known of the petty pilfering in progress behind him he would have lost all poise and made a dash for the nearest exit.

There were articles Meg appropriated to herself for which she had no earthly need. Penknives, soup spoons, mousetraps, fish hooks, banjo strings, baby rattles—anything, in short, that appealed to her roving eye. Doubtless she was working on the theory that one never can tell what the future held in store.

With her, stealing was a point of honor, a racial instinct and family tradition. It seemed almost as if she were disinterestedly striving to get an even break for her benefactor by reducing the excess profits the stores made on his uninquiring purchases.

On one memorable occasion she nearly caused the poor man to swoon by staggering out of a shop with the great-grandfather of all portable phonographs tenderly strained to her breast. For one panic-stricken moment he debated whether to petrify himself or the entire neighborhood. Rather than risk a scene, he compromised by pushing both Meg and her plunder into the nearest taxi and offering the driver a five-dollar bonus to take them away from the scene of the crime with the least possible delay. Not until they were five miles removed from the spot did he breathe with any degree of freedom.

"This sort of thing," he said at last, "will come to no good end. You'll be taking up murdering next."

"That," she replied, looking at him darkly, "would be nothing new to me."

Mr. Hawk felt a little like screaming.

After this unsavory episode Mr. Betts became Megaera's shopping companion. Soon he developed a sincere admiration for her sleight-of-hand ability. "Well, what will we get today?" became his attitude. And they got plenty.

Always, after these cheerful little raiding parties, both would return with their arms laden with untidy packages, the legitimate ones having been opened to make room for certain articles which from the nature of things could not be wrapped in the store. Betts became redolent with new cravats and socks. From these Mr. Hawk turned a sorrowing eye.

The man of science lived in constant dread of being summoned to his telephone by a police officer and told that a couple of shoplifters had given Mr. Hawk's apartment as their address, and that he, the policeman, did not believe one damn word of it. For the sake of the records would Mr. Hawk kindly verify the fact that these two crooks were a couple of low liars? What! Mr. Hawk could not oblige? Then something must be all wrong with everything. Perhaps they weren't shoplifters after all, but just a team of kleptomaniacs. Would Mr. Hawk hurry round and talk things over? Thanks. The young lady was corrupting the force and swearing something terrible.

After one of these imaginary conversations Mr. Hawk would mentally put down the receiver and turn a blanched face to an empty room. Not until his two responsibilities were safely home did he have a happy moment. Meg had spoken rightly. A man who could imagine ghastly details as vividly as Hunter Hawk must die a million deaths before he called life a day and took the final plunge.

The very sight of a package made him shudder. Vaguely remembering something unpleasant about accessory after the fact, he refused to have articles legitimately come by or otherwise displayed in his presence. He was taking no chances.

"You've succeeded in making a thief out of your accomplice, Betts," he grimly informed Meg, "but I'm damned if you'll make a jailbird out of me. You seem to forget, young lady, that both of us are probably being looked for in another state for practically every crime except arson and rape."

"I could get you run in for the latter," she replied; and Mr. Hawk choked.

To vary the routine of shopping, night clubs, roof gardens, and talkies, Mr. Hawk began taking his charge to those eminently respectable places optimistically referred to in guide books as Points of Interest. He solemnly pointed out to her various fishes of the better class with the air of one who had brought them into the world. He made her gaze down upon his city from many unnecessarily lofty points of vantage. He tried to tell her intimate things about the past of the Statue of Liberty, only to discover that he was a liar by the clock. He showed her a large building in which a great quantity of books were knocking about and vaguely speculated in so doing upon the parentage of the silly-looking lions that graced its portals. Once he went so far as to take her for a long dull ride on a ferry boat and expatiated with profound inaccuracy upon the Narrows and Butter Milk Channel.

With surprising docility Meg accepted these little excursions. She intuitively knew that her guide did not know himself just what they were all about and that he cared even less.

The finishing touch was a visit to several museums specializing in this and that. Thus it came about that close to closing time one afternoon they found themselves wandering bleakly through a forest of marble limbs, busts, and recklessly applied leaves in the sacred precincts of the Metropolitan. By this time Mr. Hawk was almost morally certain that to walk six yards in such a place was equivalent to walking six miles in less edifying surroundings. Meg knew that it was. Her companion's face was lined and drawn, his eyes hollow and aching.

"Damned if I can understand it," he said at last, painfully easing himself to a bench, a hard, inhospitable bench. "I don't doubt for a moment that all these legs and torsos and busts and backsides are works of sheer inspiration, exquisite things, and all that, but some low element in my nature keeps me from responding. I find myself insufferably bored and, oh, so weary."

Meg looked with a considering eye at the offending thighs and torso.

"You know," she said, "I think the trouble between you and these statues lies in the fact that you can't use them. You can't put the women to bed, and you can't put the men to work. They've reached a sort of inanimate perfection, can't go any farther in either direction—neither forward nor back. They've no potentialities. They're just beautiful uselesses."

"Don't care much for the motives you ascribe to me regarding these lady statues," replied Mr. Hawk. "And as for their potentialities, I'm not so sure. Not at all so sure."

There was a brooding light in his eyes. "It could be done," he was thinking. He'd like to know more about these chilly-looking people of the past.

"An exquisite thing," continued Meg, "deserves the dignity of isolation. It should have at least a room and bath of its own. A lifetime would not be too long to devote to its contemplation. These gods and goddesses here, as well housed as they are, suggest to me a lot of men and women who have lost most of their clothes in a subway rush."

"More like a large but loosely conducted Turkish bath," observed Mr. Hawk. "I get a jumbled-up impression of a lot of perfect anatomical parts and wholes that must have been no end of fun to do, but to look at them all at once, to appreciate them as they deserve to be—that's beyond my capacity. I can see all of these things any night on Broadway, and there would be life in them—life, grace, and all sorts of agreeable suggestion."

"Dearie," said Meg, "you don't have to go as far from home as that."

She demurely fringed her eyes with their long lashes, then raised them with startling suddenness and flooded the dismayed Hawk with an unnecessarily passionate glow.

"My own," she breathed.

"Come, come," Mr. Hawk rebuked. "None of that now. Not here at any rate. Refrain from being an utter trollop."

"All right, my boy," she replied briskly. "Let's be
131

arty and instructive. I'll go on about these statues, get to the bottom of the trouble. And this is it: They bore us because they're complete and detailed reproductions of men and women. Our imaginations don't have to supply a thing. Even the fig leaves fail to suggest. We know. That's why it's easy. All one has to do is to gape, admire, and look seriously cultured. If someone should slip in among these statues a grotesquely comical figure people wouldn't have the spontaneous appreciation to laugh at it. They'd stand and stare and murmur, 'Exquisite! How gripping! Only the Greeks could do it. And some others.' The last they'd add just to be on the safe side."

She paused and looked as if she were about to spit on the floor. Mr. Hawk, watching her, grew a trifle nervous.

"Don't," he muttered. "Please."

"Don't what?" she asked.

"Don't spit," he faltered. "On the floor. There are people."

She looked at him uncomprehendingly for some moments, then burst out into a loud unladylike laugh.

"I wasn't going to," she explained. "That's the way I look when I'm being arty and instructive. As a matter of fact, I was thinking about that old boy you called Rodin. A clever devil. He never bores one. Why? Because he didn't give everything. Always held a little back—suggested something beyond the mere medium in which he worked. He leads us along and points out the rest of the way, but he doesn't take us there and plop us down as if to say, 'Here you are, damn you. This is good. Like it or be forever lost.' No. Rodin holds out and gives our brains a chance to shift gears for themselves. There should be a bar in a place like this. The streets are lined with speakeasies. Let's go and find the speakiest of the easies or the easiest of the speakies."

"Let's," sighed Mr. Hawk. "I'm greatly cast down about myself and art. We don't seem to click."

"Don't worry, old dear. It's your business to make statues, not to admire them."

Through the vast wing of the museum they made their defeated way. The place was now nearly deserted.

132

Even the usually alert guards seemed to have overlooked the two weary loiterers. Paying scant heed to their progress, Meg and Hunter Hawk followed their feet down a flight of stone stairs. Once more fate was guiding the footstep of Mr. Hawk, guiding him towards his last and most astonishing undertaking.

"What the hell!" he suddenly exclaimed. "No speakeasies here. This isn't the street."

They were in a long corridor, a section apparently not intended to be used by the public. There were many doors. One stood open. It was at the moment that Hunter Hawk set eyes on that open door that the idea which had been sprouting in his mind sprang to full flower. The step of a guard sounded from somewhere at the far end of the corridor. Hawk was moved to action.

"In there," he said, "and strip."

"What's the grand idea?" asked Meg, for once a trifle startled.

He pushed her through the door and quickly looked about him. An overhead light flooded the room. There were several benches and a low stand. A few feet from the door and at the right of it stood a long table.

"Strip," repeated Hawk. "And make it snappy."

"What, here?" protested Meg. "Well, of all things. Why now? And in such a place."

"Strip," he said in a fierce whisper. "Hide your clothes in that box. Crouch, use your hands, do anything a ladylike statue might do, but for God's sake don't be indecent or funny."

Meg's wits were quick, and her clothes were few. She made no further protest save to observe that of all unsuitable places a public museum struck her about the most unsuited. However, anything to please the king. Her stripping was a small matter. She sprang to the stand, crouched like a frightened virgin and did helpless things with her hands. A perfect pose.

"Hold it," whispered Mr. Hawk, and froze the figure in that position.

He ran to the box and snatched out one of Meg's garters. It was yellow. Good. When the guard entered he found Mr. Hawk industriously measuring the left calf of what even that blasé protector of priceless

133

property had to admit was an exceptionally charming figure. As the guard entered the scientist turned and holding up a hand for silence strode to the table and jotted down a few figures on the back of an envelope. For a moment he stood frowning down at the figures, his head cocked on one side. Suddenly he looked up and squinted at the man standing in the doorway.

"Yes?" said Mr. Hawk, slipping Meg's garter into his pocket. "Yes, my good man, you were saying?"

"I wasn't saying a thing," replied the guard.

"Then why begin now?"

"Begin what, sir?"

Hawk eloquently elevated his shoulders. "You're perplexing me," he said. "Is it deliberate?"

"I'm kinda slipping myself," said the guard.

"Then slip on," beamed Mr. Hawk.

"But it's closing time, sir. I got to lock up."

"What! Closing time already? Dear me, I fear I'll have to be staying on. Not half through here. So far my examination has been merely superficial."

"But I don't rightly recognize your face, sir," said the guard with some show of deference. "Nor that statue—she's a new 'un to me."

Apparently Mr. Hawk had not been listening. He was reverentially regarding the statue.

"What a bust!" he murmured. "What a thigh! But the face—an evil image." He paused and considered the puzzled man. "Pardon me," Hawk continued. "What is it you're having such difficulty in getting out of your obviously overripe system?"

"Your face is new to me, sir," the guard faltered, feeling sure now he was in the presence of some important maniac.

"And yours is to me," replied Mr. Hawk, "although," and here he scanned the man's face as if seeing it for the first time, "it is not a new face. The face itself is far, far from new. Not even second-hand. But you did not come here, I hope, to chat about faces, did you? If you did I'm afraid you're doomed to disappointment. Busts and thighs and torsoes are more in my line."

"Would you mind telling me, sir, if you are officially

134

connected with the museum?" asked the dispirited guard.

"Let these speak for themselves," replied Mr. Hawk.

He opened his wallet and selected five or six cards. It was an overwhelming array. Several were from members of the Board of Trustees, two gave Hawk's own important scientific connections, and one, hand signed by one of the Metropolitan's most important officials, gave Hunter Hawk the freedom of the museum. These tributes, long unheeded, had come to the scientist as a result of many a boring banquet and lecture. They belonged to the natural order of things.

The guard was visibly impressed.

"Want any more?" asked Mr. Hawk pleasantly.

"Beg your pardon, Mr. Hawk," the man replied. "Line of duty, you know, sir."

"Perfectly right. Perfectly right. You should have told me at once what you were after. How was I to know? I must go into the texture of this new statue now and find out whether the young lady is genuine or spurious. To-day, in such investigations, art recognizes the feeble existence of science, you know."

"She looks genuine to me, sir," the guard observed with a lewd smile. "Small, perhaps, but all there, I should say, if you'll pardon me."

"You shock me," said Mr. Hawk. "I can hardly pardon you. The face is bad. It's the face of a wanton of ancient times. A dangerous, destructive face."

"Never pay much attention to their faces," said the guard as if to himself.

"You continue to shock me," replied Hawk. "But I must get on with this texture business."

"Yes, sir," murmured the guard. "Think I'll go out and examine a little texture myself. Something not quite so tough. You know, sir, associating so much with these here nude statues keeps giving a man young ideas."

"Don't let them get the best of you," said Hawk. "You seem to be a bit of a bad egg. The air is tainted."

The guard grinned and departed. Hawk promptly released his prisoner, and his prisoner as promptly started in to abuse him for the aspersions he had cast on her face. As Hawk was about to take her in his

135

arms the guard reappeared at the door. Hunter Hawk never used his ray with greater swiftness. He froze the girl as she was and seized her in his arms. At the same time he turned a strained face over his shoulder and looked with bulging eyes at his tormentor.

"Lifting her down," he grunted. "Ah, that's better. The little lady is quite a weight."

"You fairly shocked me that time, sir," said the guard. "Looked as if she'd come back to life. Just wanted to say, Mr. Hawk, that you seem to be known at the office. Everything's okay."

As the guard left a second time he subjected the statue to a long and speculative look.

"That's about the most lifelike bit of marble I ever saw, Mr. Hawk," he observed, "and I've seen plenty. The guy who turned her out didn't miss a trick. He knew his women."

"And so do you it seems. Once more, good-night."

"Thank you kindly, sir," said the guard, accepting the proffered five-dollar bill with the air of a man who did not need to be told too much. "There's a private entrance—a small one—at the extreme end of the corridor. Hope you make out with the texture."

"Oh, that," said Mr. Hawk a little startled. "Thanks. Same to you."

This time he watched the man's retreating figure until it had mounted the stairs; then, feeling dimly disturbed by his somewhat significant parting remark, he returned to the statue. The guard seemed an unscrupulous sort of a chap. Might be wise to cultivate him. Unscrupulous people were always the most useful. With this thought in mind he turned the beautiful statue into an even more beautiful woman.

"You had your arms around me, I think," she said. "I liked that."

"On with that dress," snapped Hawk, "and be ready to yank it off at a moment's notice. The Board of Trustees might drop in to view the most dangerous statue the Metropolitan has ever acquired."

"A lovely invitation and an even lovelier compliment," Meg murmured as she wriggled her supple body into a scrap of silk and sat hunched up on the

136

edge of the stand idly observing the tips of her toes. Hawk switched off the light.

"Well, mister," she said at last, "what do we do next?"

"We wait," replied Mr. Hawk, "and after that we wait some more."

"For what?"

"For the most desperate of all adventures—the return of the gods." His voice sounded unnaturally solemn in the room now gradually filling with dusk. "And," he added on a less solemn note, "perhaps a couple of goddesses."

Meg's eyes gleamed.

"I thought as much," she said. "You'd have to work in a couple of those ample-breasted hussies. Nevertheless, it's an adventure worth waiting for. They never should have left us, those gods."

"And goddesses," added Mr. Hawk.

"One grows weary of your Christian Era day after day, year after year," observed Meg. "Too much of a strain for an effect."

"It doesn't seem to place any restraint on you," commented Mr. Hawk.

"But it does on my associates—you, for example. All inhibited."

Hawk grinned in the shadows.

"Yes," he admitted, "I can't bring myself to murder, and I'm still delicate about theft. Aside from those two undeniable forms of pleasure I'm fairly well broken in, thanks to you."

He crossed the room and seated himself beside her on the stand. Presently the small creature edged closer to him, until at last she maneuvered herself into his arms.

"By the way," she whispered, "what did you find out about my texture?"

"My examination so far has been merely superficial," said Mr. Hawk academically.

"I'm glad," she replied, nestling closer.

For a long time they sat thus in silence, then, with her dark eyes taunting his, " 'Lo there, long legs, whose lover are you?"

137

" 'Lo yourself, you runt. Let us merely say instead of lover that we have many things in common."

"Very common," she murmured.

Once more silence.

Above them the vast storehouse of the ages gathered the deepening dusk into its sprawling corridors. The dead eyes of Egypt, Greece, and Rome peered sightlessly into their respective pasts. Jewels, fabrics, and pottery fashioned by hands long turned to formless dust gave their beauty to the night that lay upon them. Death and oblivion were defied by the living works of the dead. The unbroken stream of life fed by the currents of genius showed the toughness of the spirit of man in his eternal quest of something to make, something to leave behind. In this dim place century followed century and era merged with era on a rising tide of beauty. Surging onward, surging onward, checked, yet always flowing, it advanced to add itself to the unborn beauty of centuries yet to come. There was a sort of hopeless sublimity about it all. The mighty works that man could fashion, and yet he was so small. Through the smoke at the mouth of his cave the hand of the original potter reached across the ages to salute his fellow craftsman of to-day. Time in the great museum became merely a family affair—not a matter of age or distance. Here beauty was neither old nor new, but a part of the creative whole, as ageless as genius itself.

Something of this feeling must have communicated itself to the two very much alive figures in the lower reaches of the building. For them there was neither time nor distance. Forever and always a man and a woman would be the same. From the rise of the first sun they had sought blindly for beauty and ecstasy, striven to burst through the confines of their bodies, at last to find what they sought only in themselves. Meg in the darkness gloated. No matter where his mind might lead him, she knew that his feet would return to her.

Presently they rose. Meg sighed and sought for garments.

"Snap to it," said Mr. Hawk. "The gods await our coming."

138

"Is my hat on straight?" asked Meg.

"It is," said Hawk without looking.

She thrust a firm little hand in his, and together they left the room.

CHAPTER XIII

The Gods Step Down

SOON THEY WERE AMONG THE STATUES, THE SYM-metrical relics of an age that had lived with the creative buoyancy of a conscience-free child, a precocious child, perhaps, but not pernicious. From Fifth Avenue the street lamps sent pale shafts of light against even paler bodies. Here a back was favored, there a breast. It was a still place, this spacious hall, made even stiller by the motionless figures standing or sitting or crouching there in the eternal grip of bronze or stone.

Megaera and Hunter Hawk walked on lightly. Their steps felt like whispers.

Presently they found themselves standing before the statue of Mercury, faintly discernible in the dim light.

"Competent-looking chap," observed Mr. Hawk in a low voice. "Looks as if he'd know his way about."

"I like his funny hat," said Meg. "Wonder if he'd lend it to me?"

"You should hit it off well with Mercury," Hawk continued. "Next to you and the once unblemished Betts he was one of the greatest thieves that ever went unhung. Also, he was the messenger of the gods, an office which demanded no end of finessing, not to say unobservance. I suspect he lived by blackmail. Altogether your sort. Shall we try him?"

"I think he might prove helpful," Meg conceded.

Then Hawk performed the incredibly simple yet effective rites into which Meg had introduced him back in the grotto on the night when he had first met her—the night following his own great discovery. It was fortunate that Mercury was not aware of himself, else he would have been surprised, if not a trifle shocked.

For a brief moment the statue remained motionless, then, with disconcerting agility, it came to life. Jumping

139

down from its pedestal it stood before its grateful liberators.

"My thanks," said Mercury, looking at Meg with suave admiration. "Standing poised on the ball of one's foot for Zeus knows how long is no Roman holiday. One is supposed to do that merely in passing, you know. If sculptors must continue to sculp they should favor the recumbent school. Of course, when they're doing mixed doubles they'd have to exercise a certain amount of decent self-restraint, but not much, if you get what I mean."

"Without a struggle," replied Mr. Hawk smiling pleasantly. "How have you been all this time?"

"Inactive, sir," said Mercury. "Hibernating, I think is the word. I long for some errand to run or some pockets to pick."

"I didn't know they used pockets in your day," interposed Meg.

Mercury smiled deprecatingly. "Figuratively speaking, my dear young lady," he replied. "In my day pockets were merely bare flanks, but I run on. What I wanted to ask," and here he turned hopefully to Mr. Hawk, "can I be of any service to you, perhaps? Some slight message to convey, a purse to snatch, a lock to pick or, if you'll pardon me, sir, an assignation to arrange. I am not unskillful in such delicate matters. The gods found me good."

"Mercury," said Meg quite frankly, "I've taken a fancy to your funny hat."

"It will be a pleasure to let you wear it sometime," answered Mercury, "but not now. By the look in your friend's eye it would seem there is work to be done. Your name, sir?"

"Hawk," said the scientist. "Hunter Hawk. This small thing is Meg. Your services will be exceedingly helpful."

"What, may I ask, is the exact idea?" Mercury inquired, tentatively scratching the head of one of the snakes on his caduceus.

"The return of the gods," said Mr. Hawk. "That is, the return of some of them. We would like a small, congenial group. Not too large to handle. Whom do you suggest, for instance?"

140

Mercury smiled smoothly.

"Few little groups are congenial without the presence of that debauched half brother of mine, Bacchus," he observed. "You may have heard of Bacchus. He is one of the few gods who is wise in his cups though gross in his habits."

"Certainly," replied Mr. Hawk. "Bacchus was in my mind."

The three of them found their way to the statue of the god of wine and social amenities. Mr. Hawk performed his rites, simple almost to crudeness, but powerfully effective. Mercury was alertly interested.

"So that's the way it's done," he observed. "I see. I see." He laughed softly. "Well, Bacchus wouldn't mind. He's the sort that stands for anything. But take Jupiter, there." Once more Mercury laughed, leaving his sentence unfinished.

"We'll take Jupiter next," said Mr. Hawk.

"Don't," replied Mercury shortly. "Too stuffy."

"Look!" breathed Meg. "Look! A noble paunch he swings."

As Bacchus stepped carefully but lightly down from his elevated seat he had the effect of making the vast hall seem less spacious and austere. A little feeling of intimacy had crept into the place. Vineyards seemed to be mounting sunward behind him. Low, provocative laughter floated in the air.

The huge god huskily cleared his throat and favored his half brother with an affectionately ironical grin.

"Up to some of your old tricks," said Bacchus in a deep, wine-warmed voice. "You always were a great hand at doing the inexplicable."

"You have Mr. Hawk to thank for your presence here," replied Mercury.

"And my name's Meg," put in the girl. "Megaera."

"How wonderfully you have improved, my dear," said Bacchus with a gigantic smile. "Couldn't bear the sight of you once."

"Oh, I'm just a poor relation," Meg hastily corrected the god. "A sort of long-distance hangover."

"I've had them," said Bacchus. "I've had them." He turreted his bulk on Mr. Hawk. "My dear sir," he continued, "my dear Mr. Hawk, we are happily met, and I

141

am deeply grateful. It hurts me, sir, it hurts me much to ask it, but have you anything to drink about you—a small flask or, even better, a large one? You can see how low I've fallen, I who have dispensed in the past veritable oceans of grog."

"You are at a considerable disadvantage," replied Mr. Hawk, placing a friendly hand on the great man's arm. "You are not, so to speak, in your own home town, and consequently you should not be expected to dispense hospitality. The pleasure is all mine."

Here Mr. Hawk produced a long, flat silver flask from his hip pocket and extended it to the already reaching Bacchus.

"Knew it was there all the time," said Mercury. "I felt it."

Strange things were happening to Bacchus. He had suddenly staggered back and was now clinging to his pedestal for support. In the pale light sweat could be seen beading his forehead like jewels.

"Zeus Almighty!" he exclaimed, looking with awe at the flask. "What was that?"

Mercury, unable to restrain his curiosity, removed the flask from his half brother's palsied hand and swallowed a generous drink. For a moment he stiffened, then quietly wilted to the pedestal beside Bacchus. From that position the two gods gazed inquiringly at Mr. Hawk.

"Are we poisoned?" asked Mercury in a strangled voice, "or merely disappointed?"

"Or both, perhaps?" added Bacchus.

"Neither," Meg assured them. "Just hold on for a minute or so and you'll feel yourself greatly improved. You'll be begging for that flask, Bacchus. We won't be able to pry you away from the end of it."

"Interesting if true," groaned Bacchus.

"Will the same thing happen to me?" asked Mercury rather wistfully. "It doesn't seem possible I'll ever feel well again."

"You will," said the scientist, retrieving his flask. "That whisky is gentle and kind in comparison with some of the stuff we habitually drink to-day."

"Well," replied Bacchus, his voice a trifle hoarse, "I'm generally credited with being the great-great-grandfather of all good bartenders, but I'll have to admit that was an entirely unknown beverage to me. However, you are correct. I'm beginning to feel slightly improved already."

The wings on Mercury's hat, which after the drink had suddenly flopped without even folding, began to show signs of life. Gradually they lifted until they had assumed their former position of poised alertness.

"I, too, have escaped the clutch of Pluto," he announced, "but only by the breadth of an exceedingly fine hair. Whether the game is worth the candle remains to be seen. That remark about the conformity of one's conduct when visiting Rome holds about as true to-day as it did when it was first made. We must learn to drink the stuff."

The party of four that had started as two wandered quietly about the hall and off jutting corridors. Mercury was looking preoccupied. The business of selecting the most congenial group of gods and goddesses was not as easy as it seemed. Suddenly an exclamation from Megaera arrested them.

"Aren't they lovely?" she said, seizing Hawk by the arm. "We must have those two."

"Why?" asked Mr. Hawk. "They look thoroughly unreliable to me."

They were looking at the figure of Cupid amorously bending over the recumbent figure of Psyche, no less amorous.

"That's why I like them," replied Meg. "They seem so wrapped up in what they're doing."

"Yes, agreed Mr. Hawk. "It's what they're doing that worries me." He turned to Mercury. "Doesn't that couple look a little—er—dangerous to you?"

Mercury shrugged his shoulders eloquently.

"It all depends on what you call dangerous," he said. "Some consider it rather a diverting pastime."

"Oh, quite," hastily agreed Mr. Hawk. "I understand perfectly. What I mean is, I can't rightly tell whether he's saying good-bye or hello. That makes a lot of difference, you know. Can we depend on Cupid's sense of the fitness of things? He's a determined-looking chap in spite of his pretty ways."

"We can but try," smiled Mercury.

143

"Go on, give the kids a break," urged Bacchus.

"Here goes, then," said Mr. Hawk.

Deftly he performed the double rite and stepped back to regard his handiwork.

Meg uttered a sharp exclamation of dismay.

"Why, Cupid!" Psyche cried.

Bacchus and Mercury were laughing silently. The scientist was stung to action. He turned the couple back to stone.

"Whew!" he muttered, wiping his forehead. "Just in the nick of time. What a bad actor that Cupid turned out to be."

"Well, obviously he wasn't saying good-bye," remarked Meg. "That's dead sure."

"He has a single-track mind," Mercury explained. "He can think of only one thing at a time. Always was that way."

"I wouldn't give a penny for his thoughts at this moment," Mr. Hawk observed with a sympathetic grin. "Poor fellow. Don't blame him a bit, but I hardly think that in his present frame of mind he'd work in very well with our plans."

"Depends on your plans," said Bacchus. "Mine are usually extremely inclusive. How about Neptune, now? He's by way of being an uncle of ours and not at all a bad sort. Minds his own business, enjoys a good time in a quiet way, and is a handy man in a brawl."

"Like him myself," commented Mercury. "He's no damn booster. Throw him a couple of fish and he's as happy as a lark."

"He's tiresome about fish," agreed Bacchus, "but he knows how to carry his wine, though God only knows how this stuff will affect him. By the way, Mr. Hawk——"

"Here it is," said Hawk once more producing the flask. "Help yourselves."

The two gods drank, smacked their lips, shivered slightly, and threw back their shoulders.

"If mere mortals can handle that brand of fire," said Bacchus, "it should prove child's play for an old-timer like me. I must try a whole lot of it, just to find out what it does."

144

"I've a suspicion it will do plenty," said Mercury. "Much more than enough, in fact."

Neptune, they discovered when he had been released from the imprisoning stone, was not at all interested in women. What he wanted was fish, lots of fish, lobsters and virtually anything that swam.

"Would you mind very much taking me to a good fish and chop house?" he asked Mr. Hawk after Mercury had managed the introductions. "Both of my nephews here are just crazy about fish, aren't you, boys?"

"Guess we are," said Bacchus, "now that I come to think of it."

"Good!" exclaimed Neptune, playfully prodding Mr. Hawk with his trident in a spot where it would prove the least painful if the most demeaning. "Then it's all arranged. Let's hurry up with the selection. I nominate young Hebe, the cup bearer of the gods, and that handsome devil Apollo."

Megaera looked upon Apollo with approval and Hebe with dark suspicion. She was altogether too pretty and too agreeable. So agreeable, in fact, that Meg feared she might agree to almost anything. At present, however, the amiable young goddess was a trifle distrait.

"Anybody got a cup?" she kept asking. "I want to bear a cup."

"If you limit your bearing to cups," remarked Apollo in his musically insinuating voice, "you'll be an exceptionally fortunate young girl."

"You would make some such remark as that," said Neptune. "Don't pay any attention to this advertisement for the latest thing in fig leaves, my child. We'll get you a cup pretty soon—about the same time as I get my fish. How will that do?"

"That will be fine, Uncle," replied Hebe with a grateful smile. "Just give me a cup and watch me bear it. It's been ages since I bore a cup or watched a god get drunk."

"You're due for a deluge to-night," Mercury observed rather grimly. "The stuff you used to bear in that cup of yours was flat and tepid water in comparison with the robust brew that goes into cups to-day."

145

"Oh, I don't mind so much what goes into the cup," Hebe replied quite cheerfully, "just as long as there's something in the cup and everybody gets sort of that way."

"We'll do our best to oblige," said Mr. Hawk. "Now let's drop the cup for a moment and get down to business. Any further nominations?"

"I nominate Perseus and Diana," announced Mercury. "Perseus is not only good at killing women, but also on occasion he can save them with equal charm and dexterity. As for Diana, she can run like hell, and she's got a level head on her shoulders. Also, since Hebe insists on getting us all slopped when Zeus only knows what might or might not happen, Diana will lend a touch of respectability to an otherwise demoralized party."

"I'm told she's chaste," said Neptune in a puzzled voice. "Now, I wonder why is that?"

"Don't worry too heavily about it, Uncle," Apollo observed casually. "There has to be a virgin goddess just the same as there has to be a virgin queen or a virgin martyr or a virgin priestess. In other words, there always has to be a virgin in the woodpile just to keep on reminding women of something they don't want. She and Venus tossed for the job and Venus cheated. Neither took the matter seriously, and I hardly see how they could, because by the time Diana assumed office I understand it was quite, quite too late."

"Scandal monger as well as home wrecker," muttered Bacchus. "I'll drink him under the table, damned if I don't."

Neptune's face cleared.

"That's better," he said.

It took considerable searching to locate Perseus, but eventually that godlike but gory young man was found. As usual he was clutching the unpleasant head of Medusa by its serpent's hair in one hand and displaying a mean-looking sword in the other. His pedestal was high, but he achieved the jump with surprising agility. Carefully placing the horrid relic of past heroism on the floor and laying the sword beside it, he straightened himself and rubbed his hands together. At his feet the serpents hissed and snapped spitefully. The gods stood back at a respectful distance and eyed the unattract-ively bobbed head with mild distaste. Perseus, noting their obvious disapproval, leaned over and slapped the snakes with the flat of his hand.

"That's the trouble with you snakes," he told them. "Always butting in and making a lot of noise. Don't give a man a chance to think. Coil up there and keep quiet."

At this moment Mercury unfortunately approached his caduceus a little too close to the sinister object on the floor. A terrible battle ensued. The serpents on the severed head rose to a snake and viciously attacked the two representatives of their race straining angrily at the end of the rod in Mercury's hand.

"Better take those feeble worms of yours away from my serpents," said Perseus, "or they'll get their foolish heads eaten off."

Mercury laughed unpleasantly.

"These two feeble worms," he replied, "will make a meal of the whole damn lot of your fangless fish bait. They're a disgrace to the reptile kingdom."

"Reptiles haven't any kingdom," said Perseus. "That shows how much you know."

"Then what have they got?" shot back Mercury.

"What?" repeated Perseus a trifle confused. "Ah, just places to crawl back and forth in—holes in the ground, trees to climb, and such like."

"Then I'd call that a kingdom," said Mercury.

"Go on and call it a kingdom," retorted Perseus. "Show the world how dumb you are."

In the meantime the battle of the snakes was pro-gressing with unabated fury. Mercury's two contestants were putting up a game fight in spite of the superiority of numbers they were facing. The gods had become in-terested in the little unpleasantness. They seemed to re-gard it in the light of a sporting event and were heatedly backing their favorites. The supporters of the Perseus group were forced to give heavy odds. Meg had become so enthusiastic she was betting on both sides.

"What shall we use for money?" Neptune asked her.

"Don't worry," she replied. "Daddy Long-legs has lots of money. He'll settle up for all."

"You mean our liberator Mr. Hawk?" asked Neptune.

"The same."

Mr. Hawk had the unpleasant sensation of feeling his legs being critically surveyed. He turned round just in time to catch the tail end of an appreciative grin vanishing from Neptune's face. The sea god bowed politely and looked away. So did Mr. Hawk.

The battle between the snakes was not adding to the peace and calm of the museum. Mr. Hawk viewed the situation with growing alarm. He feared that the gods themselves might become personally involved. Such a contingency must be avoided at all costs. Mr. Hawk had no desire for any undue publicity. It was his responsibility to get these freshly awakened immortals quietly and successfully out of the museum. How was he going to do it if they kept betting recklessly on a snake fight and losing their poise at the first opportunity? He could no longer depend on Meg's coöperation. The whole affair had proved too much for her unstable nature. She was as childlike as the gods themselves.

"That's the girl, Minnie," Mercury was saying with urgent encouragement. "Snap off a couple of heads. Come on, Jove. Get into it! Don't let your little sister do all the fighting."

"They're flirting," observed Apollo. "Dating each other up, those snakes."

Mr. Hawk decided it was high time to intervene. Hebe was growing nervous. Apparently she did not share her brother's passion for snake fights.

"I hate to spoil a good time for you gods," said Hawk, "but all bets are off. Watch those snakes."

He raised his right hand and petrified the warring factions. Perseus leaned back against his pedestal and grinned at Mercury.

"That saves you," he said. "In another moment you wouldn't have had an inch of snake left."

"You always were a braggart," retorted Mercury without rancor. "You and your rescuings and your slayings and silly expeditions. Publicity stunts, all of them. Without the aid of an unscrupulous press agent you wouldn't be the half god you are to-day."

"You forget, my dear brother," said Perseus, "I had no prenatal control over our common father's amorous delinquencies. But that reminds me. Are there any women about in need of rescuing or slaying? It doesn't matter to me which. I do both with equal enjoyment and precision. I'd like to tackle a couple of sea monsters if it could be arranged."

"What do you mean, arranged?" inquired Mercury. "Do you want us to bribe a couple of sea monsters to lie down at your feet and throw the fight?"

"I never bribed——" began Perseus hotly, but Hebe cut him short.

"Listen, everybody," she said, "I want a cup to bear."

"And I want a fish to eat," added Neptune.

"And I crave some bathtub hooch," put in Meg.

"I agree with the little lady," said Bacchus. "If we drink enough of this current grog we'll be able to see all the snake fights we want without even troubling to open our eyes."

When Diana was released from her gracefully poised position she sprang noiselessly to the floor and looked coolly about her.

"I'd like to take a pot shot at a deer," she announced, inspecting her bow, "if any of you happen to know where one is knocking about. If I had my hounds along I'd rustle up a deer for myself."

"There are enough hounds along as it is," observed Apollo. "We have fish hounds and meat hounds and cup hounds and grog hounds and all sorts of hounds in the party. We don't need any more hounds."

"Speak for yourself," said Magaera.

"I have," replied Apollo. "I'm the meat hound."

"That's the truest word you've ever spoken," said Mercury, then added as if it were an afterthought, "And that isn't saying much."

Meg inspected the beautiful Diana and felt herself growing small. She looked covertly at her lanky scientist to ascertain what his reactions were to this new and altogether delightful arrival. How could she hope to compete, she thought rather ruefully, when these well formed women went striding cheerfully about with nearly nothing at all on? Of course, she could flirt with

149

Perseus or Apollo, but after all, she was not really interested in them. They were the sort that appealed to the ordinary run of women. They were great big beautiful boys with hearts of gold and all that. Her long-legged scientist was different. He was homely and nervous and refreshingly bitter about things in general. She knew more than he did. She was able to get around him. No, she decided, the gods were all right in their places. Mercury was perhaps the most interesting of them all. But she loved Hunter Hawk. She was sure of that now. And she was a little bit afraid for him. She realized he had kicked over the traces for good, and she knew that a mere mortal would never be able to get away with it.

"I nominate Venus," came the deep voice of Bacchus. "She was always a good sort at an orgy."

"But she hasn't any arms," said Hebe.

"Venus doesn't need any arms," replied Bacchus with a low chuckle. "She has everything else that's necessary."

"Oodles of it," agreed Apollo. "Almost too much."

The gods and goddesses with Meg and Mr. Hawk gathered round the statue of the high priestess of love. A little self-consciously the scientist performed the rites. Low murmurs of amusement from the gods. Diana endeavored to look shocked but was unable to restrain a cynical grin. The beautiful goddess stirred on her pedestal. Life sprang to her eyes, and she looked languorously down at Hunter Hawk. The sea from which she had sprung was caught in her gaze, the blue, warm, dreaming Mediterranean, plunged with unknown depths. With voluptuous grace she moved her hips, then uttered a little cry. The drapery was falling. Being without arms, the fair lady did the next best thing and promptly turned her back on the audience. Then she glanced over her shoulder and giggled.

"For once it's not my fault," she declared.

"An unavoidable exposure," replied Mercury. "Forgivable and at the same time diverting. I don't know how it is exactly, but you can manage to look nakeder than any naked woman I ever saw."

"And you've seen enough," supplied Perseus. "What are we going to do about her?"

Venus looked sadly at the head of Medusa.

"She was a good old girl once," she said, "before she vied in beauty with Minerva. That one always did have a jealous disposition. And there were others not far behind." Venus allowed her gaze to linger for a moment on Diana. That slim creature merely sniffed scornfully and looked away.

"You've got me on weight, my dear," she said, "but I've got you on speed."

"I don't have to chase my men," drawled Venus.

"You don't even have to know them," said Diana.

"Oh, la, la," laughed her sister. "If I only had fingers I'd snap them. Now what are we going to do about the condition I'm in? Can't stand like this all night."

"Someone will have to hold the thing up for you," replied Mercury. "How about Hebe?"

"No," replied Venus promptly. "I'd much prefer a man."

"You would," said Diana.

"It's not that at all," Venus explained. "Men are more reliable. I know what to expect from them."

"And you generally get it," the moon goddess retorted.

"I'll hold it up for you," said Perseus, gallantly stepping forward. "Allow me."

"You always were a dear," replied Venus cooingly. "Especially with ladies in distress."

Perseus gathered the garment round the hips of the goddess of beauty and assisted her down from her pedestal. She was delighted with Meg and Mr. Hawk. She said nice things to them and complimented Mr. Hawk on his good taste.

"Size really doesn't count," she assured him. "It's a matter of being interested. That's all there is to it."

"What do you mean?" demanded Mr. Hawk, feeling somewhat uncomfortable.

"Ask the lady," replied Venus. "I'll bet she understood me."

"Miles ahead of you," said Megaera. "He's not quite so dumb as he acts. Nearly, but not quite."

"If everyone is agreeable," said Mr. Hawk, "I suggest we adjourn to surroundings that would give our various talents greater scope."

"He's not so dumb at all," commented Mercury.

"Oh, good," said Neptune. "Fish!"

"Cups!" put in Hebe.

"Women!" cried Apollo.

"Wine!" mouthed Bacchus, then added thoughtfully, "or any potent substitute."

"Don't peek," murmured Venus in the ear of Perseus. "That's not fair."

"Stop putting ideas into the young man's head," Diana told her, "and for the love of Pluto don't be girlish. You can't get away with it."

"Bet you wish you didn't have any arms," jeered Venus.

"Enjoy yourself," was the sarcastic reply. "I suppose you'll have to scratch next."

"Thanks," said Venus. "The idea had not occurred to me. It's a good one."

"Thought it would appeal to you," smiled her sister.

"If you ladies will stop your little unpleasantries," cut in Neptune, "we'll all go somewhere."

When Mr. Hawk had shepherded the gods and goddesses into the lower corridor he addressed them.

"Now you gods and you goddesses," he told them, "listen to me. You've got to get some clothes on. You can't go round as you are. I'm going to take you to a store, and I won't stand any skylarking. Grab anything you like and put it on, but put it on fast. If you don't we'll all get arrested. I'll help the men, and Meg here will help the women. You she-gods must understand that you can't linger over your toilettes at the start. You must cover your nakedness first. Later on, we'll see that you're rigged up swell." He paused and looked at Megaera. "Meg," he continued, "the Emperor is outside. The ten of us will have to squeeze in somehow."

"Oh, I don't mind," put in Venus.

Hawk regarded her with a sardonic grin.

"I didn't think you would," he said. "Meg, you lead the way, and I'll bring up the rear. Pile into that automobile and pull down the shades. What follows is going to be ticklish business. Nip and tuck with law and order. Now, snap to it, the lot of you."

He opened the door, looked out, then stood aside. Behind the back of the diminutive Meg the large Olympians strode innocently into the night in quest of clothes.

CHAPTER XIV

The Gods Get Dressed

"WHY THE HELL COULDN'T YOU HAVE LEFT THAT damn head behind?" demanded Apollo as the great Perseus, still clinging to Venus's precarious girdle, tried to snuggle down beside him in the back seat of the automobile.

Perseus carefully placed his ghastly souvenir in his lap and patted it affectionately.

"You know," he admitted quite seriously, "I'd feel lost without this head. And, anyway, why can't I have my head if I want it? Neptune has his trident, and Diana's brought along her bow, and Mercury still clings to his craven worms. I wouldn't swap this head for all of them put together."

"There's no accounting for tastes," remarked Diana from somewhere in the depths of the swiftly moving car.

"What's wrong with this head?" asked Perseus defensively. "Why does everyone keep on picking on my head?"

"Your head is a horrid head," retorted Diana. "Both of them."

"And to pick on either properly," put in Mercury, "one would be forced to use an ax."

"You're quite funny, aren't you?" replied Perseus after a moment's thought. "But for all that, I keep my head. If Mr. Hawk hadn't stricken my snakes flat, you'd be singing a different song about my head. You'd be smiling into its face, making much of it."

"There's too much of it as it is," said Apollo.

"Dear boy," put in Venus soothingly, "don't believe a word they're saying. All it needs is a haircut."

"What! Lose all my snakes?" cried Perseus in horror.

"Well, wouldn't they grow out again?" asked Venus innocently. "They might grow even longer, you know, and thicker."

"Yes, and I'd like to know what barber would take the job?" Mercury sarcastically inquired.

"We'd have to find some snake-loving barber," said Venus easily. "That's all."

"But if he loved snakes," observed Apollo, "he wouldn't like to snip 'em off."

"Then we'll have to find a barber who doesn't like snakes," replied Venus. "That's not so hard to figure out."

"But ninety-nine barbers out of a hundred don't care for snakes," said Mercury.

"All the better," replied Venus. "They'd welcome the opportunity to do 'em a bad turn."

"Not necessarily," retorted Mercury, who seemed to be thoroughly enjoying the argument. "They might hate snakes so much they wouldn't want to have a thing to do with them. Prefer to leave them entirely alone."

"I'm not listening to a word anybody is saying," put in Perseus. "This head goes to no barber. Only over my dead body."

"That would make it all the pleasanter," said Diana.

"How long, may I ask," inquired Neptune with dangerous mildness, "are you all going to keep on about those snakes and that head? While history is being made you all forget everything for the sake of a handful of low-caste reptiles. If you were talking about fish it would be an altogether different matter."

"But barbers couldn't do anything with a fish," objected Perseus, who apparently was not nearly so bright as he was heroic.

Neptune grew crimson with exasperation. "I know, I know," he said. "I didn't claim that barbers could do anything with fish."

"Might not be able to do anything professionally," Mercury observed judicially, "but socially they might eat them."

"Of course, of course," replied Neptune.

154

"Not necessarily," interposed Bacchus, drawn into the argument in spite of himself. "Did it ever occur to you that a great many barbers might not care for fish? I haven't the slightest doubt that there are as many anti-fish barbers as there are pro."

"Exactly," put in Mercury. "And you never can tell what might turn the scales in their favor."

Nobody laughed.

"I said," repeated Mercury, "you never can tell what might turn the scales in their favor."

"We didn't hear you," said Venus. "We don't now."

"And anyway," continued the sea god, "what does it matter whether barbers do or do not like snakes or fish? A hundred years from now who will even know whether any barber alive to-day ever expressed an opinion one way or another?"

"Of course, if you put it that way," said Diana. "But, just the same, the principle of the thing holds true."

"And that is?" inquired Neptune.

"This head goes to no barber," Perseus supplied with finality.

"Then don't take your head to a barber," snapped Diana.

At Fifty-ninth Street Mr. Hawk skirted the park and headed the car west. He knew of a store on Broadway that catered both to men and women in all things wearable. If he could only succeed in getting these scantily clad gods and goddesses safely inside all might be well. Once dressed they were safe from detection. On the front seat beside him Meg and Hebe were wedged. Meg had made friends with Hebe and was now explaining to her about stockings and step-ins and garters and allied feminine adornment. Hebe's eyes grew brighter as she listened, but suddenly a disturbing thought occurred to her.

"But they're easy to get off, aren't they?" she asked.

"Simplicity itself," Meg assured her.

Hebe sighed contentedly and once more became all attention.

"Meg," said Hunter Hawk, "once we get some clothes on their bodies, I will call the adventure a complete success. Help those women to dress. Stick 'em in booths and hurl things at 'em. You'll have to take care of Venus yourself."

"Wouldn't you like that job?" she asked a little spitefully.

"Don't be lewd," Mr. Hawk admonished.

"I will," said Meg, "at the earliest convenient moment."

At Broadway the Emperor turned south and joined the stream of traffic. The great car continued on for a certain number of blocks, then drew up before a highly lighted shop. Its windows attractively displayed raiment and accessories of all description for both men and women. Behind him in the body of the car the gods and goddesses were in a great state of excitement.

"As I understand it." Neptune was saying, "as soon as the doors are opened we're to pop out and run like hell."

"Correct," said Mr. Hawk. "And when I fling you a pair of trousers you're to yank 'em on your legs with a snap."

"Have these trousers you're talking about any possible means of escape?" asked Apollo anxiously.

"He means, have they any exits?" explained Bacchus.

"Adequate exits," Mr. Hawk assured the two Olympians. "But be careful how you use them."

"Oh, we know a thing or two," Bacchus replied confidently.

"Good," said Mr. Hawk. "Everybody all set? The women are to stick to Meg, the men follow me."

"What about this lady's girdle?" asked Perseus. "It seems too bad to let it slide at this late date."

"Diana will pinch hit for you," said Mr. Hawk.

"And I'll bet you an old sandal she'll do me dirt," quoth Venus.

"None of that sort of stuff," the scientist warned sternly. "As I said before—no skylarking. When I open these two doors, out you pop. Here goes, and may luck be with us."

A moment later the traffic policeman standing in the center of one of the world's most famous thoroughfares, and about half a hundred pedestrians received the shock of their lives. To this day a majority of the

156

witnesses of the unique scene are not sure that they actually saw the sights their eyes registered. Many of them believe they heard a nearly naked armless woman exhorting another woman wearing little more than a bow to do something about a girdle.

"Hold the thing up," Venus was panting. "I'm not ashamed of my feet, you know."

This interruption in the ordinary routine of Broadway's night life had a disturbing effect on the policeman. At the sight of the nude figures piling with nervous alacrity out of the automobile and hot-footing it across the pavement as if the devil himself were behind them, the officer stopped traffic in all directions. He had no belief that this was going to prove in any way helpful, but he urgently felt the need for some sort of drastic action. The sight of Bacchus lumbering delicately along behind his vast paunch at the heels of a beautiful but brazen woman caused the policeman to reverse his decision. He started traffic in all directions. As a result of this, Broadway in his vicinity became an extremely confused area. In the midst of this confusion, and totally disregarding it, the policeman stood diligently scratching his head.

"This Earl Carroll guy is getting too damn fresh," he mused to himself. "He'll be having his girls bathing under the fire hydrants next."

For a few moments he considered this possibility, while motor cars clashed and clattered about him.

"What are we to do?" asked one driver, leaning far out of his car and peering anxiously into the officer's blank face.

"Do?" said the policeman vaguely. "I don't know. What are you going to do?"

"That's what I'm asking you," replied the motorist.

"Well, don't ask me," said the policeman. "I'm thinking about something else. Go away and bother another cop."

The motorist obediently wedged himself inextricably between a couple of ill-temperedly bleating automobiles, and the officer returned to his thoughts. He had a feeling he was not doing exactly the right thing. Some effective action had been omitted. He had failed to take steps. Leaving the traffic to worry along for itself he walked slowly in the direction of the store into which he had seen the naked bodies disappear. A large crowd had gathered, and through it he toilfully made his way, wondering if all these people had seen the same thing as had he.

And in the meantime the gods were getting dressed.

Mr. Hawk at the head of a solid phalanx of nudity burst into the store and cornered an immediately interested individual who proved to be the manager. Behind Mr. Hawk's back crowded the bare Olympians, their eyes darting about the shop with acquisitive alertness.

"I'll buy everything," gasped Mr. Hawk.

"You'll need to," replied the manager, looking with amused admiration at his prospective customers.

"Close the doors," continued Mr. Hawk, "and lock them. I'll make it worth while."

"You have already," the manager assured him, stroking his smooth black hair as his eyes dwelt on Diana. "How did you manage to keep your clothes?"

"We won," said Mr. Hawk. "This lady and myself."

"You must have played your cards pretty close," remarked the man as he quietly directed a subordinate to close and lock the doors and also to pull down the shades in the store windows. The few customers remaining in the establishment were fortunate. They were the sole witnesses of a scene well out of the ordinary.

"I think your friends will take everything fairly large," continued the manager. "Shall we begin at the beginning?"

"Yes," replied Mr. Hawk. "And make it snappy. I expect a cop at any minute."

The manager appeared utterly unperturbed.

"I'm surprised the reserves are not here already," he observed with a bland smile.

"If the law steps in," Mr. Hawk told him, "don't be surprised at anything that happens. Just take your cue from me."

The manager nodded and signaled to the various members of his staff. By this time the Olympians had grown restive and had distributed themselves over the store. In one corner Apollo was busily engaged in trying on a high hat while close beside him Perseus was

158

strutting gallantly back and forth with a gold-headed cane. Neptune and Bacchus were sticking strictly to their instructions. Both were struggling into a pair of trousers. Hebe, in spite of the pleadings of Megaera, had managed to get her head through a pair of salmon pink step-ins, while Diana, with gales of laughter, was doing things to Venus with a flimsy brassiére. Meg saved the situation by dropping a black satin dress on the goddess's shoulders and helping her to adjust it. The dress fitted Venus perfectly and completely changed her appearance.

"If I only had arms," the poor creature murmured, surveying herself in a long mirror.

"How about me?" demanded Diana. "Get me something in white or green. I'd do well in both."

Mercury alone appeared to entertain no desire for clothes. He was standing near a cash register and regarding it with a glittering eye.

It was at this unauspicious moment that the traffic policeman rapped heavily on the door. Mr. Hawk was stung to action. He even forgot his customary urbanity.

"Will you two gods please stop messing about with hats and canes," he called out, "and snap on a pair of trousers?"

"What do you mean," asked Perseus, "one pair of the things between us?"

"No, a pair on each," explained Hawk.

"On each what?" called back the god.

"Leg, you blockhead! Leg!" shouted Hawk.

"Oh," said Perseus in an injured voice to Apollo. "How were we to know? Wonder if this wouldn't do as well?"

He snatched up a sports sweater from a near-by counter and endeavored to draw it over his massive limbs. The effect was engaging.

"Don't do that, you great ass," Apollo told him. "You're supposed to tie the damn thing round your waist."

"Give me a chance," heaved Perseus. "It will get to the same place in due time."

On the doors of the shop the knocking was growing louder and more imperative. Hawk's glance traveled swiftly about the store.

159

"Strike attitudes," he called out, "and don't try to be funny."

"How the devil can a god strike an attitude other than an amusing one with his trousers half on?" demanded Bacchus, red in the face from exertion.

"Are fish never to be?" complained Neptune, who was in an equally undignified condition.

The scientist darted swiftly from god to goddess and back again and turned them to their original composition regardless of the state into which they had gotten themselves. A busier and more lifelike group of statues had never before been seen by the eyes of man. He seized the head of Medusa and hid it behind a counter.

"That damn head," he muttered to himself. "It's always in the way."

Then he hurried back to the manager.

"If anyone gets stuffy," said Mr. Hawk, "just tell them they're a consignment of window models that has just been delivered. Get me?"

"I get you," replied the manager, "but damned if I see how you did it." .

He walked briskly to the door and allowed Traffic Officer Muldoon to enter.

"What's going on in here?" that worthy demanded, stepping into the store and looking quickly about him.

"Lots," replied the manager easily, closing and locking the door behind the officer's broad back.

"I saw a mob of naked men and women dash into this store," continued Muldoon. "Where did they get themselves to? That's what I want to know."

"Is it possible he's referring to these window models I just delivered?" Mr. Hawk inquired, stepping up to the manager.

"Window models me eye," said the officer. "The people I saw were running like hell, and as far as I could see they were mother naked."

"I fancy the officer has good eyesight for such things," Meg observed sweetly.

"Well, lady," said Muldoon, "a traffic cop ain't supposed to be blind. It wouldn't be a healthy job if he was."

"Then if your eyesight is so good," continued Meg,

"you must have seen my husband carrying these models into the store."

"He must have been busy as hell, lady," said the officer, "and even at that he couldn't have carried them all at once."

"Perhaps you were overtired," suggested Mr. Hawk. "Protracted standing in the midst of traffic will do that, for no matter what you think you saw, carry them I did. Otherwise they couldn't have gotten in here at all. Take a good look at 'em and see for yourself if I'm not right."

Traffic Officer Muldoon walked up to Hebe and inspected her with something more than mere professional interest. Suspiciously but respectfully he reached out and applied one finger to the cold tip of her nose.

"I seem to recognize this one," he said, turning back to Mr. Hawk.

"By what?" asked Meg innocently.

"By her face, lady, of course," replied Muldoon with a triumphant smile.

"Oh," said Meg. "I didn't know."

"But what the devil has she got round her neck?" he continued.

"Step-ins," supplied the manager. "The lady here was dressing her."

"Well, I wouldn't interrupt her for the world," said the officer. "A model as true to life as that deserves to be dressed just as soon as possible."

"You speak as one who knows, officer," remarked Meg in an offhand tone of voice.

"I've had five children," Muldoon retorted proudly.

"How you must have suffered," murmured Meg.

Muldoon eyed Meg with a half grin.

"Pretty smart girl you got there," he said, turning to Mr. Hawk.

"They don't come any smarter, officer," Mr. Hawk replied.

As Muldoon wandered from statue to statue the perplexity in his brain increased. He became so skeptical of his own sanity at last that he decided it would be far, far better if he did not think at all. Obviously these inanimate figures could not be alive. And it was equally obvious that if they were not alive he could not have seen them dashing across the street to the store. But see them dash he had. Therefore the only logical conclusion to be drawn was that out there in the middle of traffic he had momentarily gone mad and become the victim of hallucinations. The less said about this the better. When he came to Perseus, poised awkwardly with the sports sweater drawn halfway up his legs, the officer abandoned all attempt to read any reason into the situation.

"Whoever tried to dress this guy mustn't have known how to dress himself," he remarked.

"Oh, one of the boys was merely fooling," explained the manager.

"A peculiar sense of humor," replied Officer Muldoon.

He continued on until he came to Bacchus. The heavy god was seated on a bench in an attitude of complete discouragement. Even his munificent paunch appeared weary and disillusioned. A pair of golf knickers, several sizes too small, stubbornly refused to continue any farther up his legs. It looked as if it would be equally difficult to pull them off. Altogether Bacchus had succeeded in making quite a mess of himself. Neptune was little better.

"What are these two models supposed to represent?" asked Officer Muldoon. "Ready-made clothes for stout parties?"

"Exactly," replied the manager. "If you've any fat friends, just bring them round and we'll give them a discount. This store caters to all shapes and sizes."

"And sexes," added Meg.

"You have to on Broadway," said Officer Muldoon wisely. "I've got a fat wife myself." His eyes dwelt wistfully on the slim form of Diana, then passed with approval to Venus of the stony breasts slouching with voluptuous grace in her gleaming black gown.

"Just bring your wife in," said the manager, noting the direction of the officer's gaze, "and we'll make her look like that one."

Muldoon grinned good-humoredly. "Can't be done," he said. "The old girl needs a tent, God bless her soul."

"Then if you're perfectly satisfied that everything is

as it should be," continued the manager, "we'll continue with our dressing."

Muldoon took the manager's hint and Mr. Hawk's five dollars. At the door he paused and looked back.

"There's something wrong somewhere," he said, "but damn me if I know just where. If you see me suddenly tear off my own clothes out there and start to run about naked just put me down as crazy and let it go at that."

So departed Officer Muldoon, a tremendously puzzled man. The snarling traffic received him and spitefully tried to cut him down in his prime. And Officer Muldoon, sticking valiantly to his post, little realized that for a brief moment he had stood in the presence of the gods.

Back in the store Megaera and Mr. Hawk were busily engaged in returning these selfsame gods to life. This accomplished, the male Olympians were placed in the hands of several competent salesmen, while Venus, Diana, and Hebe followed Meg and a couple of intelligent young girls to a private dressing room where all things were done and well done.

When finally the gods and goddesses reassembled for inspection Mr. Hawk was as proud of them as if he had been their father.

"You're the finest looking outfit of men and women I've ever laid eyes on," he told them. "You look just as well this way as you did the other. Even the ladies do, and that's saying a lot."

"If I only had my arms," Venus lamented prettily.

Diana resplendent in white laughed scornfully.

"Now that you're fully clad," she said, "you suddenly discover you need your arms."

While Perseus was collecting his head Mr. Hawk went into conference with the manager.

"I suppose you'll accept my check for the damages?" asked the scientist.

"I suppose I'll have to," said the manager smiling. "It would never do to let your friends depart in the condition in which they arrived. That would be a poor advertisement for the shop. I don't mind if customers come in naked, but I'd hate like the deuce to see them go out the same way."

Before Mr. Hawk filled in his check he had a number of suitcases packed with clothes and placed in the Emperor. Then he settled the bill and called to his party.

"Come on," he told them, "we are drawing nearer fish and everything."

Neptune dashed to the door, and the others followed close behind. Perseus, with his head tucked under his arm, brought up the rear. He was nonchalantly swinging a walking stick in emulation of the immaculate Apollo.

CHAPTER XV

The Gods Get Housed

"WHEN YOU PROPOSE TO DO THE WORST," SAID MR. Hawk to Meg, "always use the best."

He dropped a nickel into the telephone slot and gave the operator the number of one of the toshiest hotels in town.

"Reservations, my dear," he told the girl at the switchboard. "Put me on to Mr. Stevens, if you will." A short wait, then, "Hello, Stevens, this is Hawk speaking—Hunter Hawk."

"Hello, Mr. Hawk. What can I do for you?" came the voice of Stevens.

"Stevens," said Hawk, "fix me up right away with a flock of rooms. I'm entertaining some friends for a week or so, and I want everything to run off smoothly."

"About how many rooms, Mr. Hawk?"

The scientist thought rapidly, taking into consideration the loose habits of the immortals. They should be allowed ample space, he decided, if only as a matter of self-protection.

"Oh, about fifteen rooms, Stevens," he replied. "We'll need a couple of large reception rooms, baths, and all that."

"Certainly, Mr. Hawk. I understand. I'll give you half a floor. Your own elevator goes with it, and a private entrance on a side street."

"Excellent, Stevens," said Mr. Hawk as he hung up

the receiver, then added to himself, "God help the other half of that floor."

He next got Betts on the wire.

"Betts," he said, "events march. It doesn't look as if they're going to stop for some time. Listen. Pack a couple of bags with Miss Meg's stuff and mine. You know what to do. Then you fill a steamer trunk with all the grog that's in the house and put in as much decent wine as you can lay your dishonest hands on. After that join me," and Mr. Hawk gave his man the address of the headquarters of the gods.

"Too bad his wife must miss all this," he said to Meg as he returned the receiver to the hook. "We might think about getting her in. She'd go nicely with the gods. Like them, she was born without morals."

"Everyone is born without morals," asserted Meg.

"I know," replied Mr. Hawk, "but they very soon develop a faculty for picking up a devil of a lot of superfluous morality on the way."

"You should worry," retorted Meg. "What's found can be lost again. I'm sure you don't miss yours."

"What do you mean?" said Hunter Hawk. "I'm one of the most moral men that ever breathed."

"In short, staccato gasps," added Meg. "Come on, let's get back to our gods, or they'll be swarming all over the city."

As they left the cigar store they ran into no less a person than Mercury himself. He had been mingling with the Broadway crowd and was now leaning against the store window, his hands carelessly thrust in his pockets.

"What did I tell you?" said Meg as they accosted the casual god.

Mercury looked at them innocently and grinned. There was something about this suave god's grin to which Mr. Hawk never grew quite inured. There always seemed to be a little something on Mercury's mind, some project of dubious honesty held lightly in reserve.

"Just taking a look round," he told them. "Thought I'd wait here while you were telephoning. Everything all right?"

"Fine," Hawk replied, studying the smile distrustfully. "Come along. Any other gods out, or goddesses?"

Mercury hesitated for a moment, then evidently made up his mind to speak.

"Well, I saw Venus walking down the street a piece with a tall, dark man," he admitted. "No harm in it, you know, but anyway, that one always was a bit of an old hooker."

At this moment Venus under full sail undulated up to the group.

"I just met the sweetest man," she exclaimed. "You should have seen him, dear girl. He was plush. Wanted to see me later, but I couldn't give him our address. Haven't the vaguest idea where we're going next. Wish I had a couple of arms. Do you think some drunken sculptor made me this way deliberately, or did I get damaged in shipment?"

"You got damaged in more than shipment," her brother replied. "What do you mean by letting yourself get picked up by a perfect stranger?"

"Who does one generally get picked up by?" asked the goddess in innocent surprise. "Certainly not old friends. And besides, I haven't any old friends in this town. A girl must put her best foot forward. Don't you agree with me, Mr. Hawk?"

The smile she favored the scientist with was a delicious thing indeed.

"Oh, certainly," he hastily answered. "So long as you confine yourself to your feet."

"Oh, Mr. Hawk," she murmured, gazing at him with archly lowered lids.

"And speaking of feet," said Megaera, "I think I can do something about your arms. It will be rough work, of course, but at that it will be better than no arms at all."

"You're a darling, Meg," cried Venus delightedly. "Without arms a girl's style is terribly cramped."

"You keep referring to yourself as a girl," put in Mercury. "Don't do it, you ancient dragoon."

"I'm still a girl at heart," Venus replied lightly.

"Hurry up," boomed a deep voice across the street.

"Uncle grows restive," observed Mercury as they moved in the direction of the parked Emperor.

166

The arrival of the gods at the hotel created a little stir among the guests. Instead of making use of the private entrance Mr. Hawk led them to the main lobby, where he with the help of his old friend Stevens succeeded in covering the register with a neat array of lies. Mr. and Mrs. Smith, Jones and Brown came in for a strong play. And for some strange reason, unknown even to himself, Mr. Hawk made the gods hail from Canton, Ohio. While this heavy work was in progress the Olympians disported themselves about the lobby, in their artless way endeavoring to make friends with anyone they chanced to encounter, regardless of sex or station.

"This man won't talk to me," Hebe complained loudly to Meg and pointed to a dignified-looking gentleman at the moment grimly engaged in hiding as much of himself as possible behind a newspaper. "I asked him if he had a cup, and he wouldn't even answer me."

"Don't mind him, my dear," said Venus soothingly. "He looks like a washout, anyway."

"And this fellow apparently has lost his tongue," Neptune thundered across the lobby. "Doesn't seem to know a thing about fish."

The unfortunate individual whose lamentable ignorance of fish had occasioned the sea god's criticism looked about him uncomfortably and edged away. As he did so a scream was heard, and a woman fell fainting to a sofa. Perseus in a moment of playfulness had thrust the head of Medusa in her face. An arrow whizzed across the lobby and pinned an old gentleman's panama to the back of the chair in which he was sitting.

"A fair hit!" boomed Bacchus. "Well done, Diana."

The moon goddess hurried across the lobby and retrieved her arrow.

"Did I frighten you?" she asked the old man sweetly as she handed him his hat.

"Did you frighten me?" said the old gentleman, looking up at her with an uncertain smile. "My dear young lady, if you must know the truth, you nearly scared the shirt off my back. Don't do it again, please."

"You're an old duck," replied the goddess, and

bestowed on the old gentleman a smile so gracious that he felt fully repaid for the damage she had done to his nerves and his hat.

The confusion created by the unconventional conduct of the gods caused Mr. Hawk to turn sharply from the desk. He was just in time to see Mercury unobtrusively transferring a fat wallet from an innocent bystander's pocket to his own.

"A nice little selection of gods we made," he muttered to himself as he hurried over to Meg.

"Collect the women," he told her, "and herd them into the nearest elevator. I'll get the men."

As the Olympians ascended in the magnificent cage gasps of dismay issued from them.

"It gets me right in the pit of my stomach," groaned Venus.

"Me too," said Hebe. "Whoop! There it goes again."

The moment they were ushered into their sumptuous quarters Diana pulled up her skirt and diligently began to undress.

"For God's sake!" cried Mr. Hawk. "What are you doing that for?"

"Want to save it," explained Diana thriftily. "It's too nice to wear about the house."

"Keep it on and I'll buy you a new one." said Hawk.

Meg was convulsed in a chair.

"Look!" she gasped. "Look!"

Hebe had opened a little cupboard in a stand by one of the beds and withdrawn a large vessel.

"I've found a cup!" she cried merrily.

Meg doubled up. Mr. Hawk clapped a distracted hand to his forehead. The attending bus boys were momentarily shocked, then quietly exchanged grins.

"Put it back!" cried Mr. Hawk. "Put it back where it belongs. That thing isn't a cup. I'll get you one. I'll get you a dozen if you'll only put it back."

"What! Not a cup?" said Hebe, inspecting the vessel with disappointed eyes. "Looks like a cup to me. It must be a cup."

"Hebe," explained Mr. Hawk as soberly as possible, "you can't bear that cup I tell you. Put——"

A fresh explosion of mirth from Meg interrupted Mr. Hawk's sentence.

168

"Neither can I," she managed to get out. "I can't bear that cup."

In spite of all objections Hebe clung to her prize. Finally Mr. Hawk turned to one of the bus boys.

"Will you please go downstairs," he told the boy, "and bring back as many cups as it is physically possible for you to carry."

Hebe's face brightened.

"Then I'll put this one back," she said, "though I'm sure I don't know what's wrong with it."

"Do," replied Mr. Hawk. "That's a dear, sweet girl."

With a pleased expression Hebe returned the vessel to its cupboard.

Weakly Meg made her way from the room. In a moment she returned, her eyes still moist from tears.

"Laughing makes me that way," she explained. "These people don't need any grog. They act drunk already."

"What are these things for?" asked Mercury, dangling two gold watches before Mr. Hawk's horrified eyes.

Once more Meg collapsed. Mr. Hawk was too full for either sound or speech.

"Where did you find those watches?" he managed to ask at last.

"Found them in my pockets," the messenger of the gods replied.

"Yes?" said Hunter Hawk. "And in whose pockets did you find them before that?"

"Can't remember the fellows' faces," answered Mercury with a winning smile. "They passed me by in the street. Watches, you say they are?"

"Yes, watches," gritted Mr. Hawk. "Stolen watches. They're supposed to keep time, and people who steal them are supposed to do time. Understand that? They do time behind bars in dark cells. Between you and Meg and Betts you'll have us all in jail."

"Who's Betts?" asked Mercury.

"This is Betts," said Mr. Hawk. "As big a thief as you."

Betts entered the room respectfully. Behind him came two boys bearing bags and suitcases, and behind the boys came another one balancing a trayful of cups. Mercury inspected Betts with lively interest.

"Can he steal as well as I can?" the god asked Mr. Hawk.

"Not quite," replied Mr. Hawk. "But he hopes to be able to soon. Meg is trying to teach him. She's in your class."

"I'll make a master thief of you, Betts," said Mercury. "Here, have a watch."

"Thank you, sir," replied the old servant, examining the watch appreciatively before thrusting it into his pocket. "I'll do the same for you, sir, at the first opportunity."

Once more Betts looked at the watch, this time with a peculiar expression—a mixture of amusement and embarrassment.

"Isn't this yours, sir?" he asked at last, extending the watch to Mr. Hawk.

The scientist took the watch, glanced quickly at it, then looked for a long, long time at Mercury, who skillfully avoided his gaze. The look finished, Mr. Hawk carefully put the watch away and turned to Betts.

"Thank you, Betts," he said quietly but distinctly. "It is my watch. Someone must have deliberately stolen it."

"Some low-lived god, perhaps," put in Megaera with an admiring glance at Mercury.

At this moment Venus came quietly into the room. A large and drunken man had an arm round her neck.

"Look what I found," the goddess announced proudly. "He lives across the hall. I'll take him to one of the rooms and try to sober him up."

Diana laughed cynically.

"You'll sober him up all right," she said.

"The little sweetheart of all the world," jeered Apollo.

"I'm sure I don't understand you," retorted Venus in an injured voice.

"Throw that drunk out on his ear," said Mr. Hawk in a voice of command. "Take him away from her and pitch him across the hall."

Snatching the head of Medusa from Perseus he

170

placed it at the inebriate's feet and made use of Meg's magic. The snakes came to life with a hiss and a snap.

"Look!" cried Hawk to the swaying man. "Look! Snakes! You've got 'em, and you've got 'em bad."

The man took one look at the fearful object at his feet, then, clapping a hand over his eyes, turned and staggered from the room. Venus looked after him regretfully.

"He was such a nice man," she said. "If you'd only given me a chance to sober him up. I'm sure he was a perfect gentleman."

"Oh, quite," Mr. Hawk assured her. "Sorry to have been forced to deprive you of him, but there will be quite enough drunks around here before the night is over."

A steamer trunk was brought into the room by one of the hotel porters.

"Take it to that large lounging room of ours," said Mr. Hawk, "and put it down there. Betts, you tip the men and then lock all the doors. My brain is threatening to crack. Hebe, if you want some cups to bear just bring that tray along and help Mr. Betts. The rest of you follow me if you want something to drink. Don't push me," he added hastily as the Olympians surged behind him. "There'll be grog enough for all."

"Dear Mr. Hawk," cried Venus, her recent frustration forgotten. "The sweet man thinks of everything."

The lounge was exactly that—a large room filled with lounges and easy chairs. It was a room for either revelry or reflection as the spirit inclined. Mr. Hawk surveyed it with approval.

"Ladies and gentlemen," he said, "please stop making such an infernal noise and sit down somewhere. Hebe will bear the cups, and Mr. Betts will mix. Break open that trunk, Betts, and start us off with some cocktails—strong and dry. I'm sadly in need of a drink. Running this outfit is worse than handling a circus with an infinite number of rings."

Megaera was at the telephone.

"Yes," she was saying. "I want plaster of Paris, and if you haven't that, putty will do. Oh, you can get plaster of Paris? Good! Send it right up. Yes. This is Mrs. Hawk speaking."

"Ask for a basket of fish," said Neptune, but Meg had hung up the receiver.

"You shouldn't have said you were Mrs. Hawk," the rightful owner of the name told her. "You're down on the book as Miss Turner of Canton, Ohio."

"Want to have them think I'm living in sin?" she demanded indignantly.

"Aren't you?" asked Mr. Hawk.

"What is sin?" Venus inquired.

"Almost everything that is worth while doing," Mr. Hawk answered, sinking back in a deep chair. "The word has no meaning for you. Neither has it for Meg, but she likes to pretend."

"Sin," came surprisingly from Mr. Betts, "is forgetting to pull down the shades."

"Oh," said Mercury, "I understand. It's not unlike leaving the door unlocked."

"Or grabbing the wrong sandals when you jump through the back window," Apollo added reminiscently.

"So it's that," said Venus, her face clearing. "Well, if you ask me, I think sin is nice. I'd like to live in it."

"You've never lived out of it," Diana tossed at her.

"Why bring up the past?" Venus again asked rather wearily. "Can't a girl make a remark round here without someone getting personal?"

"What girl?" demanded Apollo.

"Any," replied Venus. "It doesn't really matter. Let's drop the subject."

"A wise suggestion," quoth Neptune. "Sin is merely a matter of thinking out loud. It's always been the same. Some people thrive on it while others take it too seriously—make a sort of cult of it. Sin is nothing to revel in—it's essential to a comfortable and cultured existence. It should go without saying. But enough of sin. Here's fair Hebe, bearing at last her cups. How does it feel, my rosy hired huzzy?"

"Like old times, Uncle," said Hebe. "Take a couple while you're at it. There's lots more cups, and I'm going to bear them all."

When everyone had been served Bacchus rose from his chair and held his cup on high. His magnificent paunch was now swathed in a buff-colored vest. An

172

impressive figure, he stood there, an infectious smile
well set off by the ruddy background of his jovial face.

"To Mr. Hawk and Meg," he called out in his
husky, wine seasoned voice, "the liberators of the gods.
Bottoms up!"

"Oh, Bacchus!" said Venus coyly.

Neptune's polite but not overenthusiastic, "Hear!
Hear!" was lost amid a series of sharp explosive
coughs and exclamations. Perseus sat heavily down on
his head, then rose with a cry of pain. He had been
seized on in various places by several snakes, who had
blindly resented this uncalled for interruption in their
night's repose. Mr. Betts regarded the god with respectful concern edged with a touch of triumph.

"Did you find it strong, sir?" he asked.

"Zeus, yes!" gasped the professional hero. "Jupiter's
thunderbolts were as gentle sunbeams in comparison."

"And you, sir?" asked the servant of Apollo. That
gentleman raised a tear-stained face from his hands and
looked moistly at Mr. Betts.

"It's a far cry to nectar," he said, "but I suppose we
should be thankful the things weren't served in vessels
the size of that mysterious cup fair Hebe originally attempted to bear."

"You have another one right beside you," Betts reminded him.

"Yes, I know," said Apollo evasively. "I can almost
taste it from here."

"And to think," came the strained voice of Diana,
"that mortals subject themselves to that painful experience time after time throughout the course of an
evening and believe they're enjoying themselves."

"It's one hell of a commentary on the monotony of
modern existence," replied Apollo.

"I can't understand it," said Mr. Betts, pouring himself a large drink and sampling it with a convincing
show of relish. "If you'll pardon me," he continued,
"that's one of the best cocktails I ever made."

"Then may Zeus protect us when you're off your
game," came piously from Perseus.

"I thought it was swell," said Meg.

"Me, too, my dear," agreed Venus who apparently

173

had not turned a hair. "I don't see what they're all kicking about."

"You, you old hooker," exclaimed Apollo indignantly. "Anything alcoholic seems good to you."

"Well," she replied sweetly, "I don't believe in looking a gift horse in the teeth."

"Wisely spoken," said Neptune, struggling out of his chair. "That cocktail, whatever it was, might be hard to know at first, but it certainly seems to wear well. I feel quite bucked up already. I, too, drink to our host. There is only one thing wrong with him. He's slow on his fish."

Once more the party drank, this time with better grace. There was a knock at the door, and Betts hastened to open it. A bus boy stood there with a large paper bag on a tray.

"The plaster of Paris," he announced, as if the order were one of the most frequent the hotel received.

Megaera took Venus and the plaster of Paris to one of the many bathrooms.

"Set a couple of drinks outside the door at frequent intervals," she told Mr. Betts.

"Strong ones," added Venus as she followed Meg from the room. "Our stomachs are strong enough to stand them."

"Yours should be," Diana enigmatically flung after her seductively undulating form.

Half an hour later she swept back into the room the proud possessor of a complete pair of arms. How she had acquired them was never quite revealed, although Hunter Hawk had his suspicions. Of course, the plaster of Paris was a clue.

"It's rough work," said Meg with pardonable pride as Venus displayed her new acquisitions to the party. "The texture doesn't quite match, but we can pass it off as sunburn."

"There'll be no holding her now," said Diana. "She'll drag them in by the hair."

Venus was too pleased with herself to object to a little coarse jesting at her expense.

"It's such a relief," she exclaimed. "You can't imagine. Now I'll be able to look after myself."

"And a couple of others," said Apollo.

Venus smiled at him coyly. "You fresh thing," she said.

Mr. Hawk examined the arms critically. He was scientifically interested.

"Excellent technique," he remarked at last. "Very well done indeed. A little out of proportion, but no one would notice that." Venus was gazing at him with glowing eyes.

"Want to see how they work?" she asked suddenly, and throwing her arms round his waist strained him to her. It was a hug that would have done credit to a bear in the pink of condition.

"Oof!" grunted Mr. Hawk. "They're a complete success. In fact, they work too well. Let me go while life remains."

"I guess I'll do," said Venus, releasing him.

"What?" asked Apollo.

"None of your business," said Venus. "Let's go out and meet a lot of men."

"I'd like to go out and meet a lot of fish," put in Neptune.

"And I suppose you'd like to go out and crack a couple of safes," Mr. Hawk said to Mercury. "I hope you'll remember to keep your hands in your own pockets, and if you must steal things, don't pick on me. You'll merely be fouling your own nest if you do."

"Oh, I wouldn't for the world think of doing a thing like that," replied Mercury with an embarrassed little laugh. "That would be going altogether too far."

"Suppose they get lost or separated?" Meg demanded suddenly. "They wouldn't know where to go or what to do with themselves. They'd get into all sorts of trouble."

"That's easily remedied," replied Mr. Hawk. "We'll tag the lot of them."

He telephoned to the porter for tags, and when they had been brought he wrote down the name and address of the hotel on eight of them. The gods and goddesses, rather than feeling humiliated by the tags, seemed to regard them in the light of decoration. They inspected them with childish pride and compared them to see who had the best.

As Mr. Hawk led them from the room he heard a

175

seething noise behind him. Turning, he was confronted by the snaky head of Medusa held carelessly under the left arm of the stalwart professional hero. Hawk turned the snakes to stone.

"Aw, what did you want to do that for?" complained Perseus. "They weren't bothering anybody."

CHAPTER XVI

Neptune Gets His Fish

THE OLYMPUS MOB WAS FOREGATHERED AT WHAT is perhaps one of the world's fishiest eating establishments. There might be places equally fishy, but certainly no place could get itself fishier. It far surpassed the sea god's fondest expectations, for more fishiness per square foot was crammed into the shabby, antiquated room than he ever believed possible outside of his spray-crested realm.

The room was not lacking in personality. It had an atmosphere entirely its own. In it were to be found some of the smartest and most desperate fish eaters in the city—fish eaters in on the know.

Whereas fish fanciers congregated at the Aquarium a few blocks south to gaze ineffectually at humiliatingly indifferent fish, the habitués of this river-front room—the real natural-born fish eaters of serious purpose and honest intent—came here with much heavier business in view. Their object was not merely frivolously to contemplate fish. Far from it. They came here to do something about fish, something positive and definite, something held clearly in mind. In short, to eat the things.

One cannot tell by observing a person looking at a fish whether that person is genuinely fond of fish or thoroughly detests them—loathes them, in fact. The fish watcher might be doing either one of two things—gloating over the incarceration of the fish, or deriving enjoyment from the contemplation of their stupid activities. No such doubt can exist when observing a person eating fish. One can tell at a glance whether that person is sincerely fond of fish or is merely tolerating the

176

fish until something less disagreeable turns up, such as tripe.

The true fish eater never hides his light beneath a bushel unless it happens to be a bushel of oysters or clams. Fish eaters are frank about it. And if not extremely careful they can develop into terrific bores.

The restaurant was redolent of fish. Outside, the streets were slippery with them—lined with fish markets. Pretty nearly every water-loving creature that ever swam, crawled, oozed, or drifted seemed to have settled in the neighborhood. In this district no fish need ever feel lonely. Few ever did, because most of them were quite dead.

The Hawk party was seated at a large round table. There was ample elbow room and a feeling of spaciousness. It was a table designed to hold a great many fish or one lightweight whale—as many as a party of ten could decently eat at one sitting. Perseus had placed his head beside his chair on the sawdust-sprinkled floor. He had done this because the negro waiter had refused to approach the table until the disconcerting object was out of sight. Mercury had laid aside his caduceus and Neptune had slipped his trident under the table. Diana had left her bow at home.

"To begin with," began Mr. Hawk, "does anyone here want fish?"

"The very word revolts me," Venus declared. "This is no place for the goddess of love. I belong in a night club."

"Ask the waiter to bring us a cup," said Hebe in a low voice, "and fill it from that flask you have on your hip. The gods are getting low."

Neptune was too bemused to answer his host's question. His eyes were fixed on an ice-filled tank on the top of which reposed in horrid state a number of ill-tempered-looking lobsters. Unable to bear the sight any longer, the great man left the table and laid violent hands on two of the ugliest, most anti-social-looking crustaceans Mr. Hawk remembered ever having seen. With this wickedly animated pair of pliers he returned to the table and prepared to do battle with them there and then in cold blood.

"Those damn things are worse than my snakes," Perseus complained. "Look at the faces on them."

"I can't bring myself to look at him," said Diana. "He's actually going to eat the things alive."

The negro waiter's eyes were doing something good in the line of popping.

"Gawd, brother," he muttered to an associate, "that pitchfork-toting party sure is one tough gentleman. See him snapping at them great big green rascals."

"Would you mind going away to some secluded corner and fighting out your battles alone?" Venus asked her uncle.

"Tooth against claw," observed Mercury. "I bet on the teeth."

"What's wrong with the lot of you?" demanded Neptune, sighting at the table between the jagged claw of one of his opponents. "I always tackle 'em this way."

A few of the more advanced fish eaters in the room were regarding the sea god with attentive admiration. They had never tried lobsters quite so fully alive themselves and were anxious to see just how one went about it. Although aware of the attention Neptune's impulsive action was attracting to the table Mr. Hawk retained his self-possession. He reached over and quietly but firmly removed one lobster from Neptune's grasp; then with his left hand he removed the other. The god was too astonished to protest effectively. The scientist nodded to the waiter.

"Take these things outside," he said, "and cook them."

Neptune gazed after the departing waiter in speechless indignation, then turned to Mr. Hawk.

"What did you want to do that for?" he demanded.

"Had I known previously," replied Mr. Hawk quietly, "that you wanted to fight lobsters I'd have made more suitable arrangements."

"But I always polish off a couple of live lobsters before I wire into the fish," the god protested.

"I was unfamiliar with your habits," the scientist explained with a faint smile. "However, I think you're going to enjoy these lobsters just as well. They're delicious when they're broiled."

178

"Are they?" Neptune exclaimed, his face brightening up. "I can hardly wait."

"You didn't," remarked Mr. Hawk briefly.

Hebe was cheerfully moving round the table with a cup full of cocktails. A rose-pink gown adorned her exquisitely feminine figure. A beatific smile wreathed her lips. She was happy. She was bearing a cup.

"Bear your cup to me, sweet wench," said Mr. Hawk. "My nerves need a little bolstering up. I wasn't counting on a lobster fight."

Hebe eagerly complied. "Go on," she urged prettily. "Get a little bit that way."

"How about yourself?" he asked.

"Someone has to bear the cup," she answered simply.

"You'd make an ideal wife," he observed as he swallowed a drink.

"I've never found it necessary to marry," she answered with a look too innocent to be true.

"It is rather an ostentatious gesture," agreed Mr. Hawk. "Never tried it myself."

"It all comes to the same thing," remarked Hebe, and moved gracefully away.

Across the table from him Mercury was showing Meg a new way to steal knives and forks.

"Of course," he explained, "these things are hardly worth the trouble, but you never can tell who's going to ask you to dinner. Just as well to keep your hand in."

"Oh, quite," replied Meg. "Is this yours?"

With a puzzled expression Mercury took the proffered wallet and examined it.

"Haven't had it long enough to get used to it," he explained with an embarrassed laugh. "Originally it wasn't mine, but I thought I'd just bring it along to see what was inside. How did you come by it?"

"In a like manner," she answered. "You see with you stealing is merely a diversion; with me it's been a means of existence."

"You must have made out well," Mercury remarked dryly.

Meg acknowledged the compliment with a slight bow.

"They're here! They're here!" cried Neptune as the waiter placed the lobsters before him. "Broiled, you say? Well, it doesn't matter. Dead or alive, they're the same to me."

The deep-sea god fell to with avidity, as did the others. Years of enforced fasting had put an edge on their appetites. Mr. Hawk, watching them, decided that one of the most likable features of the Olympians was that they put their whole hearts into whatever they chanced to be doing. Their enjoyment of life had the added zest of complete self-absorption which, paradoxically enough, is the same thing as self-forgetfulness. And taking everything into consideration, their table manners were not bad, with the possible exception of Neptune who insisted on casting his lobster shells to the floor with truly godlike indifference.

The only really unpleasant feature of the dinner occurred when Perseus reached down and placed the head of Medusa in the center of the table. Meg, who had been one of Hebe's best customers throughout the course of the repast, decided in her elevated condition that it would be an amusing thing to bring the whole head back to life. This she did, and it was bad enough, but matters became even worse when Perseus began feeding Medusa with bits of fish snatched from various plates. Mr. Hawk was so gripped by the weird spectacle that his own powers became for the moment atrophied.

Medusa fairly snapped at anything that came her way. She had to be fast about it, because the snakes had little ideas of their own. Many a choice morsel they snatched from the lips of the head they graced. Even the gods were a trifle upset by what they saw.

"Where does the damn stuff go to?" demanded Bacchus. "She hasn't any stomach."

"Hebe," said Medusa with her mouth full of fish, "what you got in your cup, dear?"

"This," replied Hebe emphatically, "is the one time I refuse to bear. Here."

She passed the cup to Perseus who in turn held it to Medusa's lips. She thirstily drained its contents, then blinked rapidly several times.

"Whee!" she cried suddenly in a hoarse voice,

180

causing the gods to start in their chairs. "That's the kind of stuff I like. You're a good sort, Perseus, even if we did disagree. You couldn't dig me up a body somewhere, could you?"

Mr. Hawk shuddered. Medusa's form of expression was a little too vivid for a man with an active imagination.

"Will somebody please tell me where she put that last drink?" Bacchus asked in a discouraged voice.

"Why don't you ask me, you tub?" snapped Medusa. "If you must know it went straight to my head. I don't need any stomach."

The burst of wild laughter that followed this grim sally horrified the entire room. In one corner the negro waiters were grouped in a dark mass.

"When Ah think that ma ten toes were within nibbling distance of that mouth it's pretty nigh mo' than Ah can bear," said the erstwhile attendant at Mr. Hawk's table. "Toes, toes, stop tremblin' in yo' boots. The lady like to got you."

Hunter Hawk took a swig from a second flask without waiting for a cup to be borne.

"Ah, there," said the head. "At it again, I see. How about a little drink for baby?"

"Let her have just one more," pleaded Perseus. "I'll look after her."

Without a word the scientist relinquished his flask to the god, who thrust it between Medusa's distended lips and tilted it at a generous angle. The owner of the restaurant took one good look at what was going on, then tightly closed his eyes.

"Does anyone want to buy this place?" he asked. "You can name your own price. When things like this begin to happen, it's time to quit. I know when the stuff's got me." He laughed a trifle hysterically. "Go on, everybody, have a good time. Have a fish on me," he shouted. "I've gone ga-ga." As he passed through the service door he was heard to remark to himself, "A disembodied, rum-drinking head, smartly trimmed with snakes." The poor man's voice rose to a yell. "Break out a couple of quarts, Steve, I want to get blind drunk."

181

"But I saw it, too," said the unseen person addressed.

"What!" screamed the owner. "Trying to humor me, are you?"

Further discourse was drowned by the sound of breaking plates.

"I can stand very little more of this," said Diana. "Won't you turn that head back to stone, Mr. Hawk?"

"If I had my old cunning," retorted Medusa, "I'd damn well turn you to stone."

"Don't turn her back to stone," put in Perseus. "Please don't, Mr. Hawk. She's having such a good time, she and her little snakes."

"Do you expect to go about town with a boisterously drunken snake-bearing head under your arm?" Mr. Hawk asked mildly.

"Certainly not," declared Apollo. "The damn thing gives me the creeps."

Medusa, indifferent to her fate, had begun to sing in a deep bass voice. This decided Mr. Hawk. He raised his right hand and returned the head to stone in the middle of its most ear-piercing effort. Meg immediately turned it back, and the interrupted voice continued to tell the world all about silver snakes among the gold.

"Hey, quit that," protested Medusa. "I don't know whether I'm coming or going. You're making me dizzy."

"You're going," replied Mr. Hawk, and once more returned the head to stone. "Lay off that head, Meg," he continued, "or I'll have to do the same thing to you."

Meg's brow darkened rebelliously, but she made no further attempt to interfere with the head. Mr. Hawk, observing her expression, suspected her of designs as black as the glances she cast him from time to time.

"Can you eat any more fish?" he asked Neptune.

"If I did," the god retorted, "you could play the scales on my back."

"The old boy's getting funny," observed Diana.

"Fish affect me that way," he replied. "You should eat more of them, my dear."

But Neptune received his biggest thrill when the party, well primed with food and drink, had shaken the sawdust of the restaurant from its feet and was walking cheerfully along the waterfront. Mr. Hawk was determined to leave no stone unturned to give the sea god his fill of fish. It was the scientist's private hope that Neptune would become so sick of fish that the mere sight of a tin of sardines would revolt him. He little suspected, did Hunter Hawk, the profound depths of the god's fondness for the dumb creatures of his realm.

As they passed by the fish markets, busy even at that hour of the night, the sight of so vast and so varied a quantity of fish, rather than exerting a soothing and reassuring influence on Neptune, seemed only to excite him, to arouse in him that latent spark of cupidity without which no person, whether god or mortal, can struggle along with any degree of enjoyment. The more fish Neptune looked upon, the more he wondered why these people should have so many fish while he himself could lay claim not even to a minnow. Surely no one had a better right. Was not he the great Neptune, the boss of all the damn fish that swam? This matter would have to be looked into, the situation rectified. Now, if he could only bring a fish home with him. That would be a start at least.

He stopped before a large box of fish and picked up one of the slippery objects. Now, it just so happened that the man who had things to do with that particular box of fish, whatever it is one does with a box of fish, was in an atrocious humor. Perhaps a fish had bitten him, or he was tired of looking at fish lookers, or fish had simply gotten on his nerves. Whatever the cause may have been, the fact remains that the man was in no mood to take any shilly-shallying from Neptune. He approached the god and addressed him with brutal directness.

"Put down that fish," said the man.

"Why should I put down this fish?" asked Neptune with deceptive mildness. "Is it your fish?"

"Don't ask foolish questions," replied the man. "Of course it's my fish. Put it down."

"Who gave you this fish?" asked Neptune. "Where did you get it?"

"Nobody gave me that fish," declared the man.

"No?" said Neptune, slightly elevating his eyebrows.

"Do you mean to say you didn't come by the fish honestly?"

"Say," retorted the man, "what are you trying to pull, anyway? I haven't time to stand talking to you all night long. Put that fish down."

"Are you busy?" inquired Neptune. "Busy about fish?"

"What's that to you?" snapped the other. "As it happens, I am busy. It's fish, fish, fish, morning, noon, and night."

"You're fortunate," observed the sea god. "I envy you your agreeable occupation."

"What are you trying to be, funny?" demanded the fish-weary individual. "Are you going to put that fish down?"

Mr. Hawk and his party had stopped at the street corner and were clustered there, looking back at the apparently harmlessly conversing god.

"Did it ever occur to you," Neptune asked of the man, "that I might grow tired of hearing you tell me to put this fish down?"

Here Neptune gently shook the fish under the man's affronted nose.

"And did it ever occur to you," sneered the man, "that I might grow tired of having to tell you to put that fish down?"

"Do you happen to know," demanded Neptune, drawing himself up to his full height, "that I am the god of all fish?"

"You're not the god of that fish," the man replied with absolute conviction.

This piece of defiance infuriated Neptune. "What!" he exclaimed, raising his voice slightly. "Not the god of this fish? Do you mean to stand there and tell me that?"

"That fish hasn't got any god," said the man.

Neptune examined the fish with renewed interest. "Do I understand you to say that this is a godless fish?"

"I don't know what you understand me to say," replied the man, "or what you don't understand me to say, but I wonder if you understand me when I tell you to put down that fish?"

"I understand you well enough," said Neptune, "but I'm not going to put down this fish. That's flat."

"What are you going to do with that fish?" asked the other, growing pale from exasperation.

Once more the god examined the fish as if seeing it for the first time.

"What am I going to do with this fish?" he repeated in a slightly puzzled voice. "Well, I don't know exactly what I'm going to do with this fish, but I do know one thing, and that is, I'm not going to put it down."

"Oh," said the man, "you're not going to put it down?"

"No," replied Neptune with great dignity. "I'm not going to put the fish down."

"Oh, for God's sake," exclaimed the other, casting all hope of patience to the wind, "you're not going to stand there all night long holding that damned fish, are you?"

"No," replied the sea god, "I'm certainly not going to do that."

"Then just what do you intend to do with that fish?" asked the man in one of those deadly calms that presages a complete abandonment of reason.

"I don't just know what my intentions are regarding this fish," declared Neptune with cocktail begotten ponderosity. "I don't care to hold the fish, neither do I feel at all inclined to put it down. Furthermore, I'm extremely tired of observing your silly face. If you want to know what I think of you and your fish—watch!"

With this Neptune threw the much-discussed fish into the astounded man's face. It was a telling shot, and it landed fairly. With the unpleasant sound of a solidified splash the fish impinged on the man's left cheek and a considerable portion of his nose.

There is something in being hit with a fish that arouses all that is worst in human nature. A pie or a brick may affect different persons in different ways, but with a fish it is always the same. There is only one result—homicidal rage on the part of the recipient of the fish. This invariably happens.

For a moment the man stood stunned; then quite automatically he dipped his hand into the box and hurled several fish into Neptune's face.

"Just what I wanted," cried the god with a nasty laugh. "I love fish."

"Oh, you do, do you?" panted the other, more from anger than from exertion. "Well, how about this one?"

He picked up a fish that barely missed being a whale and flung it with all his might at Neptune. The sea god dodged nimbly, and the fish took up its position in the gutter. As the man bent over to seize upon another fish, Neptune prodded him in an investigatory spirit in the part thus prominently exposed. It was not so much a painful act of retaliation as it was a degrading one. There was something about it that the man found intimately insulting. He snapped erect with another large fish in his hands and this time his aim was more accurate. The fish descended heavily on the sea god's head, and for a moment the Olympian was dazed. He staggered back, then relieved himself of a roar that meant nothing less than war to the death.

The gods and goddesses gathered at the corner observing that all was not well with their fish-inclined relation, and recognizing from eons past the nature of his bull-throated roar, legged it down the street without even pausing for the formality of a huddle. They were filled with fish and grog, which make a fighting combination. Mr. Hawk, despairing of peace, cast his lot with the gods and bounded down the pavement in the direction of this novel altercation.

Perseus, the professional hero, was the first to arrive at the scene of action. His movements were precise and definite. It was like a smooth first night after weeks of conscientious rehearsals. He picked up a barrel of fish and permitted the silvery shower to play over the head of his uncle's adversary. The man went down under a deluge of fish. From his clammy place of confinement his head emerged and began to make significant noises. He was earnestly summoning aid. And aid was not long in arriving.

It so seems that men who spend much of their time in the company of fish either dead or alive are strong, hostile, and active men. The group that joined battle with the Olympians were of this type, at any rate. They emerged from many doors, and Hunter Hawk, who

186

was ever interested in experimenting, wrapped a large eel round the leader's neck. So far eels had not entered into the battle, but from now on they played an important part.

Even a man most accustomed to fish does not like to have his neck adorned with an eel. Proceeding on the assumption that one cares for eels, it is only a person with a perverted taste who cares for them that way. This man did not care for them that way. He unwound the eel from his neck and, twirling it round his head with the dexterity but not the charm of Will Rogers, released it to its own devices. The eel sped over the immediate area of conflict, and as if spying Venus, who was pantingly bringing up the rear, sought seclusion down the bosom of her dress. It was then that this ravishing creature performed on the sidewalks of New York and in sight of the battling multitude what could only be classified as a lascivious dance. An eel on the exterior of one's stomach is even less agreeable than an eel twined round one's neck, and a lady finding herself in such a predicament may be forgiven for dancing almost any dance that pops into her head at the moment. So effective were Venus's convolutions that each faction paused in its effort to outfish the other until the eel had been dislodged from its intimate place of concealment.

Having successfully rid herself of her uninvited guest Venus turned her thoughts towards methods of reprisal. With a critical observation regarding the casual parentage of the eel slinger, she hurled herself into the forefront of the conflict and, disregarding the aid of fish, knocked the man flat with one Olympian blow. Couched on a layer of slippery fish the semiconscious individual made a surprisingly neat exit towards the gutter, where he remained. Undiscouraged by his enforced absence, the fight continued with, if anything, augmented abandon.

Megaera, with her usual resourcefulness, had endeavored to equalize the discrepancy in cubic stature by arming herself with a swordfish, with which she was doing painful execution. Mr. Hawk, clearing a fish from his eyes, caught a glimpse of her industriously

187

sawing away on the leg of a large party upon whose face Bacchus was comfortably seated while searching about for a certain kind of fish he had in mind. Hawk laughed madly and dispatched a flounder with scientific accuracy into the face of his nearest adversary. Apollo and Diana, from behind a barricade of barrels, were methodically emptying them of their salty contents by leveling an effective barrage upon the enemy. Perseus, having retrieved his head which momentarily he had laid aside, was holding single-handed three stout fish flingers at bay. Everyone seemed to be conscientiously doing his or her bit. They would have done even more had it not been for the intervention of the police. These civic joy killers arrived in a body of three. Mercury, from his point of vantage on the driver's seat of a cart, was the first to be aware of their arrival. Mistaking them for partisans, he discharged two handfuls of fish stingingly upon them. The officers of the law were both annoyed and disgusted. Somebody was going to pay for this indignity. A few revolver shots they might have overlooked, but fish, never. One of them sprang to the seat by Mercury and raised his night stick on high. Mr. Hawk broke through the seething crowd and turned the god to stone. The club descended with a loud report and snapped in two. The blank astonishment written on the officer's face repaid Mr. Hawk for many fast-traveling fish. Incredulously the policeman reached out a hand and felt Mercury's face. The hand was swiftly withdrawn.

"Be God," muttered its owner, "it's the first case on record of a fish-flinging stone."

For a moment he stood amid the din and confusion, completely submerged in his thoughts. Then with a sigh he decided to dismiss the incident entirely from his life and let one of his brother officers carry on where he had left off. However, he was too late. Mr. Hawk reversed the order of things. He petrified the policeman and released the messenger of the gods. Then, above the shouts and imprecations and the steady patter of fish, the scientist made his voice heard.

"Cease firing," he shouted, "and follow me. Don't lose your tags."

Picking Meg up bodily, he sprinted down the street and turned a corner. The Olympians streaked after him, and after them the policemen, frantically blowing their whistles. This would never do, Hawk decided. There was enough noise already, without the policemen adding to it. He jumped into a doorway, and as the officers rushed past at the heels of the gods he added two more impressive-looking statues to the police force of New York.

Into a cruising taxi he bundled as many gods and goddesses as he could find. He gave the driver the address and told him to drive like hell. He then hurried down the street in search of another taxi. Behind him the two petrified members of the city's finest looked as if they were playfully indulging in an adult game of Still Water, No More Moving. Later, when two members of the Flying Squad came across their statuesque colleagues, they did not have the temerity to report their find to Police Sergeant Burk, the officer in charge.

"It would sound too damned silly," said one of the discoverers, "to report to him that Officers Sullivan and O'Boyle had been found turned to stone."

"We wouldn't have a button left," agreed the other.

Police Sergeant Burk, however, had discovered strange things for himself. When he had demanded of the petrified figure on the driver's seat of the wagon just what was all the trouble about and received no answer he had climbed up beside the figure and examined it closely. It was an odd coincidence that Sergeant Burk, like his two subordinates, made no report of his discovery. He felt that it was one of those things that might lead to profitless discussion. Let others find out for themselves, was his not unwise decision. Thoughtfully he climbed down from the wagon and ordered the arrest of every living being in sight. After that he went home and got speedily into bed. The next day he put in an urgent request for a long vacation. What subsequently became of the three petrified officers was never officially recorded, although rumor has it that they were successfully used as shock absorbers on several important raids. Neither is it known whether they still received pay for their services or were ever carried to visit their respective families. Such purely irrelevant considerations are merely matters of conjecture.

In Mr. Hawk's arms Meg was singing "Rock-a-bye, baby, on the tree top," while above her the scientist's lean face peered into the darkness for a possible means of escape. Presently he spied a taxi, and toward this yellow hope he dashed, head on. It was not until he was seated with his burden in the cab that he noticed she was clinging to a swordfish.

"What do you want that thing for?" he demanded.

Meg looked at the fish in surprise. "I don't know," she said. "Didn't realize I had it. Let's bring it home to Neptune."

It was then that a harmless citizen was given something to talk about for many weeks by the sudden appearance at his feet of a swordfish which seemed to have descended from the sky.

"Is anyone in?" Mr. Hawk asked the operator of the private elevator.

"Yes, sir," replied the operator, then added after a moment's hesitation. "Ever so many."

The Olympians, virtually stripped to the skin of their fish-battered garments, had distributed themselves clubbily about the lounge and were thirstily watching Mr. Betts as he diligently mixed cocktails. Hebe was standing by with a trayful of cups.

Meg and Mr. Hawk were greeted enthusiastically upon their entrance. Inquiries were made regarding the probable whereabouts of Neptune, the missing cause of all the trouble. "Probably in jail," said Mr. Hawk wearily. "If so, Betts will have to bail him out."

"A well chosen word in connection with Neptune," observed Mercury whose mind was ever alert for trifles.

There was a hint of dawn in the sky when the sea god finally put in an appearance. He walked jauntily into the room with a huge fish over his shoulder impaled on the prongs of his trident.

"That elevator boy seems to be upset about something," he told Mr. Hawk.

"I can't imagine what," that gentleman replied.

With a dignified bow to the assembled company

Neptune hastened to the telephone and removed the receiver.

"Hello," he said, "I have a fish up here I want you to put on ice. It's an unusually large fish, and I want it served whole for breakfast. How big is it?" He paused and looked appraisingly at the fish, then turned back to the telephone. "Oh, I'd say about six feet six," he announced, not without a note of pride. "What's that? Too big, you say? Then I'll eat the damn thing in the bathtub."

He hung up the receiver with a snap and accepted a cocktail that Hebe bore him. Extending his cup courteously towards Mr. Hawk, the god of the sea addressed him.

"My regards, Mr. Hawk," he said. "This is a splendid town for fish."

"I'm glad you like it," said Mr. Hawk rather lamely.

Venus had to be forcibly restrained from attacking her uncle.

In such a strained situation Hebe the cup bearer and Betts the cup filler proved themselves invaluable in restoring congenial relations. By the time the members of the party sought their beds the hint of dawn in the sky had become an open avowal.

CHAPTER XVII

Meg, Mercury & Betts, Inc.

MR. HAWK WAS SITTING IN HIS BEDROOM, AND HE was a little bit drunk. It was five o'clock in the morning. He was still clad in evening clothes. A high silk hat, straight black stick, and a bottle of Scotch formed a swagger group on a near-by table.

Hawk was looking mildly at nothing. His eyes shifted to the bottle of Scotch and refused to budge therefrom. As if impelled by a desire to satisfy his eyes rather than his thirst he rose from his easy chair and arranged himself a drink. This accomplished he reseated himself, glass in one hand and cigarette in the other.

For the past half hour he had been vaguely troubled by the need of something, the exact nature of which he had not been able to discover. Only a few minutes ago he had succeeded in doing this. Hunter Hawk knew now that he needed a little more Blotto. He missed his dog. Also, he missed Daffy. Several times he had rung for Betts to tell him about his discovery, but either the bell or Betts was out of order. For once the old gentleman had failed to answer the summons. Neither was Meg anywhere to be found. She and Mercury had gotten separated from the party. Hawk was more nervous about this than he cared to admit. Not that he suspected the loyalty of either one of them. What he did suspect most definitely was their honesty. Now that Betts was among the missing, Mr. Hawk's suspicions became more firmly rooted.

"Meg, Mercury, and Betts," he said to himself with a hopeless shake of his head. "A bad lot. A very bad lot. They will come to no good end."

Such bleak reflections quite naturally led to another drink of Scotch. He enjoyed this. He enjoyed being alone. It was the first spell of solitude he had had in the last five days. Since the return of the gods life had whirled at hurricane velocity. There had been little time for reflection. The Olympians were all in bed now, if not asleep.

Mr. Hawk knew for a fact that with the exception of the first night not one of them had slept alone. How they managed to gather in transient guests was still a mystery to the scientist. He had grown quite accustomed to entertaining perfect strangers of both sexes at breakfast. The gods, in spite of the late hours they kept, were early risers and insisted that those who shared their beds should be early risers also. Breakfast over, past favors and friendships were callously forgotten and the guests summarily dismissed. Mr. Hawk ascribed this to a delicate disinclination on the part of the Olympians to be reminded of their delinquencies, whereas the truth of the matter was that they were very easily bored by mortals and were constantly seeking fresh fields to conquer. Venus, Diana, and Hebe, in the order named, had made a strong play for Mr. Hawk, Venus being the strongest, but he had successfully resisted their blandishments, more from a desire for peace than a love of purity. With Meg the gods showed a little more self-restraint. True enough, Apollo had made advances, but they had been tentative to the point of being perfunctory. Meg had found no difficulty in telling the so-called irresistible god to go to hell. Although he had not gone, he had desisted from further endeavors. They were now the best of friends. Although Meg greedily laid claim to virtually every known vice, she scornfully excluded cheating.

"Sex," she said, "according to our advanced thinkers, is the most important single factor in life. Having gotten this bearded profundity off their chests they sneak down a dark alley and proceed to test the truth of their theory with some other person's husband or wife. I believe in giving sex its due importance. If you can't get along with one man or one woman at a time, then hang out your shingle and make a business of it."

This sort of thing, of course, meant nothing to the gods. They listened to her with polite interest and said, "Quite right," soothingly, after which they went cheerfully about their own disreputable affairs just as if Meg's gratuitous moralizing had been an incentive to their misconduct.

Mr. Hawk had been good to the gods. He had stinted them in nothing. He had gone far out of his way to be decent and had done his utmost to satisfy their every whim and fancy. When Mercury had stepped on the dance floor of a night club and spilled out an assortment of knives, forks, and spoons to which he had taken a fancy, Mr. Hawk had not been stuffy about it. In fact, he had joined in the general laughter the incident had evoked, not heartily, to be sure, but he had done his best. When he had come upon Diana shooting arrows from her window into an office building across the street and causing consternation among the staff, he had made no outcry or hotheaded protest. He had helped her with the aid of innumerable pillows to rig up a dummy figure in the lounge, where he silently hoped she would shoot her damn head off. When Perseus, during the most exciting moment of a talkie, had leaped to the stage and attacked the screen, mistaking it for the villain, Mr. Hawk had allowed himself to be ejected with the rest of the cheering Olympians and later had done his best to explain to the overemotional god that the characters were not real and that even if they were they were only fooling. That time when Hebe, unable to restrain herself, had snatched a wine-filled goblet from the hand of an indignant cloak-and-suit buyer from St. Louis and then sweetly held it to the amazed man's thick lips the scientist had casually flung out the suggestion that hereafter she should limit her cup bearing to her own party. On the occasion when Venus had insisted on entering an impromptu beauty contest clad in little more than her garters it had been Hawk who had carried home the prize for her. Of all the Olympians, Bacchus and Neptune were the least bother. After his first fling with the fish Neptune had settled down to a comfortable humdrum existence. He loved to potter about, and after Mr. Hawk had bought him an attractively decorated miniature aquarium full of gold fish the sea god was as pleased as a pup with a greasy piece of rope. Nor did Mr. Hawk make any reference to the constantly diminishing supply of gold fish, although he was convinced that Neptune was cheating on him. He tactfully passed over the bearded god's little weakness and gave instructions to Betts to see that new gold fish should be acquired.

"A man as large as he is," said Mr. Betts tolerantly, "needs a little snack between meals."

"Snack," replied Mr. Hawk with a slight shiver of revulsion, "is the one word next to tasty I dislike most. Make a strong effort, Betts, to find less repellent substitutes."

As for Bacchus, that jocund god was hardly any trouble at all. He required only a sufficient abundance of wine, women, and song. These innocent pastimes he indulged in for nearly the twenty-four hours of the day.

"You're the most godless gods I could have possibly selected," Hawk told them on one occasion, "but I'm responsible for getting you here, and it's up to me to do the right thing by you. If you have any complaints or suggestions to make, don't hesitate to let me know."

The Olympians were loud in his praise.

"You're a good sort, Hunter," Venus had replied, "even if you did practically kick me out of your bed."

"Listen, my dear," Diana had put in, "if you held a

grudge against every man who had been forced to kick you out of his bed at one time or another, virtually every member of the male population of Italy and Greece would be in your bad graces."

"I'll have you to know I've been kicked out of very few beds, all things considered," had been the lovely goddess's hot retort.

"All things considered covers a multitude of kicks," Diana had shot back.

As usual Hebe had restored the quarreling goddesses to good humor with her inevitable cup.

Only one thing was making Mr. Hawk uneasy. He had noticed that of late his guests were not carrying their liquor well. The stuff seemed to be making inroads on their systems. They bickered more in the morning and were becoming more critical every day. Modern night life was evidently not agreeing with them. They were making a practice of getting themselves half lit before breakfast in order to be able to eat it. Sometimes Neptune would lie all morning completely submerged in a tub overflowing with water. In addition to its being rather a ghastly sight—particularly the floating beard—it was also terribly messy. It became even more so when the sea god insisted on taking his goldfish into the tub with him. As a result of this childish caprice Venus slipped on a straying gold fish and was inconsolable until almost every male member of the hotel staff with the possible exception of the manager had tenderly rubbed the injured spot. When, not satisfied with this, Neptune suggested that a couple of large live eels might add to the gayety of his morning tub, Mr. Hawk demanded bitterly if he would like to bathe in clam chowder or perhaps oyster stew. When Neptune told him that would be just great, the scientist turned on his heel and left the god bubbling merrily beneath the water.

As he sat there now in his luxurious armchair with the strains of a waltz from the last night club still knocking about his ears, Mr. Hawk decided that perhaps his Olympians needed a change and that he himself needed another drink. He would have liked to show them his place in the country had it not been for the threat of arrest hanging over his head.

195

He rose from his chair and mixed himself a stiff drink, but paused with the glass at his lips. A knock had sounded on the door. The next moment Betts had entered the room.

"There's a cow outside, sir," he announced with a slight show of embarrassment.

The scientist gave no indication of surprise other than to toss off his drink at a gulp.

"A cow," he repeated thoughtfully. "Do you know what it happens to want, Betts, or rather, what she wants?"

"I think she wants to come in, sir," the servant replied.

"Have we any spare rooms?" asked Mr. Hawk.

"Sometimes we have and sometimes we haven't," said Mr. Betts. "You know how things are, sir. Never can tell from one night to another. Some nights they bring home one. Some nights they bring home two."

"Exactly," commented Mr. Hawk dryly. "Well, don't keep the cow standing there in the hall. Bring her in here temporarily."

"Thank you, sir," said Betts.

"Don't thank me, Betts," replied Hawk. "Have you any personal interest in this cow?"

Betts hastily disclaimed having any interest in cows in general and in this cow in particular.

"You must admit," Mr. Hawk observed mildly, "that it is rather unusual to have a cow calling on one at this hour of the morning. Not that I find it so," he added, deliberately replenishing his glass. "I find nothing unusual any more. If a herd of bison should come stampeding across this floor I wouldn't turn a hair. If an ostrich should approach me right now and ask me if I could lend him a pocket in which to hide his head I wouldn't be able to dig up even so much as an attenuated exclamation point. But bring in this cow, Betts. I run on."

The servant retired, and the next moment a large, gentle-looking cow walked with stately self-possession into the room. Behind the cow came Meg and Mercury, pushing its rump diligently. Once in the room the animal looked back reprovingly, as if all this pushing were entirely uncalled for.

"Close the door behind you," said Mr. Hawk quietly. He returned to his chair, sat down with elaborate caution, and leveled his eyes on the cow. A look of mutual respect and understanding passed between them. At that moment a friendship was established. So far neither Meg nor Mercury had offered any explanation. They stood bunchily together looking about them uncomfortably. Mr. Betts stood a little apart steadily refusing to meet their eyes. They seemed to regard him as their leader and protector, and it was evident that Mr. Betts had no desire to be regarded in either capacity.

Mr. Hawk cleared his throat, and the three figures started visibly. He inspected them each in turn and decided that they, too, were not quite sober. He forgave this. He forgave everything.

"Did you just happen to run into this cow by chance in the hall?" he asked, fixing Meg and Mercury with a speculative eye, "or did you think that I wanted a cow—that I stood in need of a cow?"

He spoke slowly and reasonably, as if addressing small and not overintelligent children.

"We thought it would be nice," offered Meg after a hopeful look at Mr. Betts.

"Nice for whom?" continued Mr. Hawk in the same tone of pleasant inquiry. "For me or for the cow?"

"Sort of all around," said Mercury. "Nice all around."

"I see," went on Mr. Hawk. "Then, I take it, you did not meet this cow by accident?"

"Oh, quite by accident, sir," hastily interposed Mr. Betts. "I mean, sir, we didn't plan the cow."

"You couldn't plan a cow, Betts," Hawk told the old gentleman. "That requires a bull."

"Yes, sir. Certainly," agreed the servant. "That requires a bull."

"To say the least," put in Mercury, hoping to please Mr. Hawk.

"Not to say the least, Mercury," the scientist replied. "Just a bull, neither more nor less."

"And a cow, perhaps?" suggested Megaera.

"Oh, a cow by all means," replied Mr. Hawk. "That

197

goes without saying—but to return to this specific cow. How did you get her up here, may I ask?"

"We crammed her into the private elevator," said Mercury with almost brutal directness.

"It must have been pretty," observed Mr. Hawk. "And the elevator boy, did he offer no feeble objections?"

"That's a funny thing," said Mercury, grinning for the first time. "He didn't seem to have an objection left. Said he'd carried up so many strange things since we'd been here that one cow more or less made no difference to him. We gave him quite a lot of money."

"And where did you get the money?" Hawk demanded, then added quickly, "It doesn't matter. I don't care to know. Let us say you found it—as usual. An ill wind and all that sort of thing."

"It's a nice cow," Meg advanced timidly. She suspected her patron's calmness.

"An excellent cow," said Hunter Hawk, regarding the animal with frank admiration. "One of the best, no doubt, but hardly the cow for a bedroom, do you think?"

"The fact is," supplied Mr. Betts, "we didn't know exactly what to do with her after we'd got her here."

"So you thought you'd give her to me," said Mr. Hawk sweetly. "You probably decided there had been too few cows in my life. Got yourselves all worked up about it. But, tell me, how did you get the cow here and why did you get the cow here?"

"You see," replied Mercury with a winning burst of confidence, "we met her quite by chance wandering drearily about over by the river. She was lost—without a home, and of course, she couldn't sleep in the park."

"Of course," said the attentive scientist. "They don't like cows in our parks."

"New York," observed Betts in a sorrowing voice, "is a lonely place for a single cow."

"I should imagine it would be twice as lonely for a two-headed calf," Mr. Hawk commented. "Continue, please. We were up to the point where you had met this cow and received the impression that she was rather low in her mind. Then what happened?"

"Meg here said," Mercury resumed, "that you'd

198

never stand for seeing a cow wandering round the city without a place to lay her head and insisted on bringing her along with us."

"I wonder how she knew that?" mused Mr. Hawk. "She must be clairvoyant."

"Then I told her," continued Mercury, "that that wouldn't be at all a nice thing to do and that you wouldn't be expecting a cow. I pleaded with her, Mr. Hawk, but you know how she is. She just laughed rather derisively and said that if you didn't like it you could jolly well lump it. So that's——"

"Oh, what a liar you are!" exclaimed Meg. "I didn't say any such thing, did I, Betts?"

"I was holding the cow, Miss Meg," the old servant replied. "But it certainly doesn't sound like you."

"There, what did I tell you?" said Meg. "The man's a natural born liar and a congenital thief."

"And that's how it happened," finished off Mercury rather lamely.

"It seems to me, Mercury," Mr. Hawk remarked after a thoughtful silence, "that there's some truth in the old saying yet—'There's no honor among thieves.'"

Mercury smiled faintly. The truth of the matter was fairly obvious. Meg, Mercury, and Betts, the latter having accompanied the party to the night club so as to be on hand in case of emergency, had become bored with the forced gayety of the place and had withdrawn in search of fresh pockets to pick. The course of their wanderings had at last brought them to the west side of the city in the very heart of the cattle-car district. Here they succeeded in losing themselves quite thoroughly. Picking in this quarter of the city so far as pockets were concerned was not a flourishing business, so Mercury, who was leaning against a freight car when he came to this conclusion, decided to pick its lock. This he did with masterly skill and no little enjoyment. Sliding back the door the deft messenger of the gods thrust in a nimble arm.

"Oh, look what I got," he announced triumphantly. "I've found a cow."

"Seems to me you've found a great many cows," rejoined Megaera as a stampede of cattle came pouring down the broad runway which the ever efficient Betts had hooked over the steel ledge of the door.

"Almost too many cows," murmured the servant as he jumped back just in time to avoid the mass of released animals falling and staggering from the car.

In the story he told to Mr. Hawk the god had omitted to mention the fact that there were a number of homeless steers and cows that night wandering about New York. As a matter of fact, had the scientist been fully acquainted with the true facts of the situation, he would have congratulated the three thieves on the restraint they had exercised in bringing back only one cow.

The general confusion that followed the escape of the cattle served as a cloak for the further activities of the unholy three. They drove a well favored looking animal down a side street and in the darkness held a hurried consultation. In justice to the abductors of the cow it should be stated that Mr. Betts was carrying two large flasks of rye which were seldom if ever in his pockets for more than a moment at a time.

"This," said Meg, gazing with bright eyes upon the cow, "is the very biggest thing we've stolen yet."

"By far," agreed Betts in an awed voice, "and furthermore, Miss Meg, it lives, breathes, and moves."

"We just can't let her go," continued Meg pleadingly in the darkness. "We must bring her back with us."

"I have a rope," said Mercury. "I found it under here." He indicated the loading platform of a warehouse squatting swartly in the night.

It must also be said in justice to the three semi-sober conspirators that no cow was ever more willing to be abducted than was this one. The creature actually thrust her head through the noose that Mercury had cleverly contrived. How so gentle and home-loving a creature could have strayed into a car filled with reckless, devil-may-care steers remains one of the unsolved mysteries of cattle transportation. Perhaps some dim, maternal instinct had moved her to follow the destiny of some beast she mistook for her son, or rather, for one of her sons. However that may be, she seemed to realize now that she was in a decidedly unhealthy neighborhood for cows of any description. It was due to her strong desire to remove herself from this neighborhood that the team of Meg, Mercury, and Betts was able to return to comparative civilization. They followed the lead of the cow and triumphantly circulated the flask.

"It's a funny thing," Meg said in a subdued voice as they moved behind their leader down the dark, uneven street, "but a cow like this, a great, dumb, gentle cow, always makes me wish I had led a better life. I can't bear her eyes."

"I've led a fairly decent life," Mercury replied complacently. "Apart from a little plain and fancy stealing I have nothing to regret."

"Why, I've always considered you as the world's leading procurer," answered Meg. "Please don't disappoint me. Weren't you always arranging parties for the gods?"

"Only as a gifted amateur," responded the messenger of the gods. "Never professionally."

"But you would have made a good professionl, don't you think?" Meg asked hopefully, still clinging to her girlhood illusions.

"Oh, if you put it that way," replied Mercury modestly.

They crossed a wide, gloomily reaching avenue and continued on.

"I've never been able to sin very effectively or consistently," came the rather depressed voice of Mr. Betts. "A good bodyservant unconsciously absorbs the character of his master. Mr. Hawk has always been until recently an exceptionally clean-living man."

"Well, I like that!" exclaimed Meg. "Do you mean to imply I've soiled him?"

"I hope so, Miss Meg," answered Betts. "I hope you've blackened him. You see, I don't hold with overclean living. I think it sort of paralyzes one's moral sense. Morals should be kept in a state of constant circulation to be healthy. All progress is due to unmoral persons turning over new leaves."

"That observation is especially applicable to my time when people wore hardly anything else," put in Mercury. "Turning over new leaves in my day was of all sports the most popular."

Betts and Meg laughed politely at this little sally of the nimble-witted god.

"Sin," continued Betts, not to be deflected from his train of thoughts, "that is, so-called sin, is the working capital of religion—all religion. It would sound very presumptuous, wouldn't it, to assure some god every morning and night in your prayers that you were every bit as good as he was? No. The whole system works on sin, and I haven't done enough of it."

"Well, if stealing's a sin and it goes by size, you've made up for a lot of lost ground," Meg told the old man encouragingly.

"I certainly hope so, Miss Meg," he replied seriously. "I want it chalked up against me."

Thus philosophically conversing, the little party came to Broadway. There was not much traffic here at this hour, but there was too much for the cow. In the middle of the crossing she sat down behind a policeman and gave vent to a plaintive moo. Interested to see the automobile that carried such an unusual horn, the policeman turned round and found himself looking into two preternaturally large, humid eyes. He jumped back several feet and startled the cow nearly out of her wits.

"Sweet St. Patrick!" breathed the policeman. "What are you doing with that, lady?"

"That's a cow," Meg informed the officer.

"I know, I know," said the policeman impatiently.

"You didn't seem to when you first saw her," the girl replied accusingly.

"Well," admitted the officer, "I did get quite a start, but you've got to admit, lady, a cow is a queer thing to come staring you in the face at this time of the morning on Broadway."

"What is the most popular cow hour on Broadway?" Meg inquired.

"Any hour but this, lady," the officer replied wearily.

"Okay, officer," said Meg snappily; "then we'll come back some other time. Tweak her tail, Betts."

The cow responded to the tweaking, and before the policeman had the time to formulate any convincing objection the cow and its three escorts had crossed the wide thoroughfare and were heading towards Sixth

Avenue. At Fifth they were once more checked. Mercury had come to know well and hate heartily the uniform of the law. He decided to outface this one.

"Now, no questions, officer," he said in a voice of extreme annoyance. "We're very busy."

"I'm not going to ask any questions," replied the officer, looking the party over with an unfriendly eye. "I'm going to do things and issue orders. The first one is that you can't cross Fifth Avenue with that cow."

"Why not?" demanded Meg. "They let us cross every other avenue."

"Fifth Avenue's different," the officer replied boastfully. "Better."

"Oh, come now, officer," Meg continued sweetly. "If you'd say that about Park Avenue we might agree with you, but not Fifth. You know yourself that Fifth Avenue is nothing more than a vulgar commercial racket. It's just a great gully, officer, filled with envious and acquisitive humanity."

"Well, it ain't going to be filled with cows," replied the officer, "and that's flat."

"Just one cow, Mr. Policeman?" said Meg, her smile fairly dazzling the man. "Just one little girl cow who doesn't know her way about?"

The officer began to grin.

"You see," put in Betts respectfully, "my mistress just got this cow from the slaughter house."

"Snatched it from under the blade of the knife," added Meg.

"And it's going to be raffled off this evening at a charity bazaar," continued Betts. "A very fashionable function."

"So you see, officer," said Meg with sweet simplicity, "we have to get this cow across the Avenue. Both she and myself are losing our beauty sleep as it is."

"All right, lady," replied the officer. "Things can't be much worse than they are. Take your cow and raffle her off."

"Oh!" exclaimed Meg. "You startled me. I thought you were going to tell us to do something entirely different with our cow."

With a coy laugh she bade the puzzled policeman good-bye and the party continued on.

It was fortunate for the success of the expedition that the private entrance provided by the hotel for the exclusive use of Mr. Hawk and his guests was situated on an unfrequented, narrow side street and involved no traversings of halls or reception rooms. A small door gave directly to the elevator, and in the elevator dwelt a youth who apparently had no interests in life, not even in his elevator. When a full-grown cow was tightly wedged into it he looked away as if to rest his eyes. And when Meg, Mercury, and Betts filled in the chinks not taken up by cow he closed the cage doors and informed them dispassionately that in all likelihood the elevator would refuse to lift. It did not quite refuse, but its ascent was of a hesitating, uncertain nature.

"It will probably drop," said the boy as they passed the tenth floor.

"You waited for the right time to tell us," replied Meg. "This is just a nice height for a perfect open break."

At the fifteenth floor they pried the cow loose and Mercury gave the boy much stolen money for his silence.

"I never say anything, anyway," said the boy, "to anybody. A cow more or less makes no difference after all the queer things you people have brought up."

And this was how it came about that a cow was brought to call on Mr. Hawk between five and six in the morning.

"I'm very much obliged," he said at last, looking up from his thoughts, "for thinking of me in connection with this cow. Did you happen to find out her name?"

"No," replied Meg, "but I think she would like Dora."

"Very good," continued Hawk. "The cow's name is Dora. Pour some drinks, Betts, and tell me, Betts, do cows lie down?"

"Well, yes and no, sir," the old man answered.

"Not yes and no, Betts," the scientist objected. "It has to be either yes or no."

"I mean," said the servant, looking up from the glasses, "they don't rightly lie down like a dog. You can't just tell 'em to lie down and expect to be obeyed. It has to come to them, sort of."

204

"I have a dog," observed Hawk, "who has never lain down once when I've asked him to during the course of our long years of association. He doesn't seem able to get those two words through his brain."

"He's very much like a cow in that," commented Betts with a wise shake of his head.

"Perhaps he was already lying down when you first told him to lie down and he mistook it for get up," said Mercury. "I did that once to a dog and forever after I had to tell him to get up whenever I wanted him to lie down."

"I don't know," said Mr. Hawk. "Let's get back to this cow, Dora. She'll have to stay here until more suitable arrangements can be made for her. We'll keep this room locked to prevent the chambermaid from finding out."

"She has a key," said Mercury.

"Then we'll tell her to stay out," replied Mr. Hawk, "and later we'll padlock her in her own room. Do you think you could make her lie down now? We should all be getting some sleep. Not much, but some."

"Why don't you petrify her?" Meg suggested.

"A good idea," said the scientist, "but she's only just come. Doesn't seem very hospitable, and it might sour her milk."

"We can make her lie down," declared Mercury. "I'll take her back legs, and, Betts, you take her front, and, Meg, you and Mr. Hawk can push. She'll topple over very nicely."

"Sounds rather brutal," remarked Mr. Hawk, "but the damn fool should lie down. I suspect she's been traveling for several days and stands in need of a rest."

Dora, with a look of mild astonishment on her kindly face, allowed herself to be assaulted and toppled over. Once lying comfortably on her broad side she wondered why someone had not thought of it before. With a deep sigh, she fell asleep and dreamed fitfully of slums.

Half an hour later, after the consumption of several more than enough highballs, Meg and Mr. Hawk flung themselves down on their beds. Mercury and Mr. Betts were already slumbering peacefully, their heads cushioned on Dora's tan-and-white flank. It was a scene of

happy domesticity not usually to be found in a bedroom of a New York hotel.

Meg rolled out of her bed and, slipping off her excuse for a dress, curled up beside Mr. Hawk.

"I never could understand the reason for twin beds,"
she murmured.

"Suppose you had an enemy or a girl friend?" asked
Mr. Hawk, sleepily speculative.

"That," she replied, "would be a horse of another
color."

He dropped an arm across her and whispered,
"Sleep."

Betts and Dora contested bitterly for the audible
sleeping honors.

CHAPTER XVIII

A Demoralizing Tank Party

NEPTUNE HAD BEEN DRINKING HEAVILY ALL MORN-
ing and had eaten up all the goldfish. He was now
ranging through the rooms making himself a general
nuisance. Venus had caught him at a bottle of her most
dependable perfume. After she had driven him off with
the aid of a long nail file the thwarted god had sneaked
into Apollo's room and finished off that immaculate
Olympian's hair tonic.

"How do you expect your nieces and nephews to respect you," Mr. Hawk had asked him, "if you make a
practice of drinking up their toilet preparations?"

"I only wanted a little sip," Neptune had defended
himself, "but they had to get stuffy about it. And
besides, my nieces and nephews have no respect for
anyone. They're hard, Mr. Hawk. They're hard. Like
that," and Neptune extended a huge clenched fist.
"Like that, Mr. Hawk," he repeated.

"But why don't you stick to whisky?" asked Mr.
Hawk. "Isn't that strong enough?"

"It is, my dear sir. It is," the god assured him. "I am
very fond of whisky. I might say I love it. It was
merely a passing whim. The stuff smelled so damned
good. But to return to whisky. Where is some?"

Mr. Hawk provided him with a bottle, and Neptune

retired with it to his room where he could drink in peace and security.

"They get that way," Mr. Betts sympathetically observed, looking after the huge figure of the bearded god. "It's this stuff—the official poison of a free country. It's so bad that those who drink it begin to experiment after awhile, because they feel that nothing could be worse. These gods of yours are not used to the idea. They keep on hoping."

"It's worse for Neptune than for the rest of them," said the scientist. "He's more out of his element. A man who's been used to taking his morning dip in any one of the seven seas can hardly be expected to adapt himself overnight to a tub."

Betts nodded wisely and placed a cool shakerful of cocktails on the table beside his master. Mr. Hawk swallowed one of them and returned to his morning paper. He was interested to find out the latest news from the Metropolitan. At first the amazing disappearance of the statues had been withheld from the press, but after the museum had been inexplicably closed for several days the truth had leaked out and an official statement had been issued. Mr. Hawk had been relieved to find that his name was not mentioned in connection with the case. Apparently the guard who had visited him in the lower corridor and the man to whom the guard had shown Mr. Hawk's cards had decided that safety lay in silence. A world-wide search for the lost gods was already under way. Thousands and thousands of persons who previously had felt no qualms from their inability to tell one god from another were to-day discussing with intense interest the removal of the statues from one of the world's most scientifically protected treasure houses of art. Mr. Hawk had contributed this much to the advancement of learning, at any rate. He had furnished the world with a pretty problem.

He poured himself another drink, and after sitting quite motionless for a few moments decided he was feeling a little better. It had been a hard night and an irritating morning. Neptune was not the only god who was acting up. The whole disorderly lot of them had gotten out of the wrong side of the bed. Diana's transient guest had departed screaming down the hall with one of her arrows planted firmly between the tails of his hastily donned dress suit. Venus had loudly refused to take her shower unless Mr. Hawk turned it on for her. When finally he had consented to do so for the sake of peace and quiet, she had pulled him under the downpour and playfully mauled him about. In addition to this he had been unable to dislodge Mercury from the flank of the recumbent Dora, although Betts had responded at the first summons. It had been a morning of constant interruptions through which Meg, cuddled up like an abandoned doll, had slept quite undisturbed. Even Perseus, who usually was rather quiet and self-satisfied in the morning, had made himself particularly disagreeable because he had been unable to find any soap sufficiently gritty with which to wash Medusa's face.

Mr. Hawk looked enviously at the peacefully slumbering Meg and felt the need of privacy.

"I might as well be the purser on a ship full of lunatics," he mused. "Why do they have to drag me into all their arguments and expect me to humor their every damn whim? Olympus must have been a madhouse."

At this moment Dora decided to call it a sleep and managed to get herself to her hoofs by a series of heaves and jerks. Mercury remained behind her, sprawled on the floor. The cow greeted her host with a low moo. Mr. Hawk returned the greeting with a thoughtful gaze.

"Betts," he asked, "what do cows usually have for breakfast?"

"About ten square feet of meadow," Mr. Betts replied promptly.

Mr. Hawk considered this in silence. "That would be hard to arrange," he said at length. "Don't they ever vary their diet?"

"We might give her some Puffed Rice or Shredded Wheat, sir."

"A good idea, Betts. Telephone down for a dozen orders of each and take the tray from the waiter yourself outside. Don't let him come in."

While Mr. Betts was telephoning Hebe tripped rosily into the room. She gazed at the cow in delighted surprise.

"What a sweet cow!" she exclaimed. "Why, the poor thing needs to be milked. It's 'way past her time."

"Do you expect me to take up cow milking in my old age?" Mr. Hawk demanded. "And besides, she hasn't had her breakfast yet."

"Of course not, silly," laughed Hebe. "You're not expected to milk her. Cows are always milked before they've breakfasted."

This struck Mr. Hawk as being another example of man's inhumanity to beast.

"Damned if I'd go through such an ordeal on an empty stomach," he said.

"You'll never be called upon to do so," the cup-bearing goddess assured him, whereat Mr. Betts barked sharply into the mouth of the telephone.

"And if you'd like to know," continued Hebe, "cows like to be milked before breakfast."

"Did anyone ever hear a cow put herself on record to that effect?" asked Mr. Hawk. The cocktails were taking effect.

"No, but——" Hebe began.

"I knew it," Hawk interrupted. "You can't name one cow. It's all a piece of propaganda gotten up by farmers to excuse their unchivalrous conduct."

"Be that as it may," replied Hebe with a determined light in her young eyes. "I'm going to milk this cow right here and now. She needs it. May I use that large cup you didn't want me to bear?"

"Oh, certainly," replied Mr. Hawk with a broad grin. "I don't like milk anyway. The cow's name is Dora. I think you should know at least that much, if you are going to become so intimate with her."

Hebe became busy and efficient. In a short time the sound of milking could be heard. Dora still holds the unique distinction of being the only cow that was ever milked in a hotel bedroom. Whether the cow considers this an honor or a matter to be hushed up is not known.

In the midst of the milking Meg awoke and sat up in bed, her eyes gradually growing larger and rounder as the true importance of what she was witnessing dawned upon her.

"A person has to get used to some weird and incredible awakenings," she said, "to live at all comfortably with the gods. What's happened to Mercury? Did he die?"

"Not quite," came feebly from the floor. "If someone will provide me with a strong, chilled drink, I'll make a game attempt to lift my head off the spot where I was under the impression a cow by the name of Dora used to live."

The news of the milking of the cow spread rapidly through the apartment, and the Olympians, forgetting their various grievances and quarrels, dropped everything and hastened to the spot. They seemed to be the sort of people who hate to miss anything, even though they find no enjoyment in whatever it is.

The milking finished, Hebe generously passed the cup and was greatly disappointed to be met with polite but emphatic refusals from all present.

"Perhaps Dora might like some milk," suggested Mr. Hawk.

"Cows don't drink milk," was Hebe's scornful reply.

"This one might," said Megaera. "She seems to stand for anything."

"If a cow drank milk," the scientist advanced thoughtfully, "it would be something like discovering perpetual motion."

"But what earthly use would a cow be if she drank her own milk?" asked Bacchus.

"She could pose for the news reels," said Mr. Hawk, "or go into vaudeville, maybe."

"Not a constructive sort of a life for a cow," put in Mercury from the floor, reaching out a hand for the cocktail shaker.

"Better than reading want ads, isn't it?" snapped Neptune.

"I hate these nutty discussions," said Meg. "They never get you anywhere, and they always make me feel much worse than I really am. Don't let's go on with it. Send that shaker along, Mercury. I feel like one myself."

"I have a suggestion to offer," announced Mr. Hawk. "Surprised I never thought of it before. Why don't we all go swimming? This hotel sports a tremendous tank with Turkish baths and everything."

"Oh, let's," breathed Neptune, his eyes gleaming wildly above his flowing beard.

"I'm jolly good at floating," remarked Bacchus.

"Then fill up your flasks and come along," said Hunter Hawk. He rose from his chair, and picking Meg up in his arms, tossed her back on the bed. "Slip on a dress," he told her. "And pry yourself loose from that cocktail shaker. Betts is waiting to fill it."

At the entrance to the pool the Olympians good-naturedly accepting the conventional order of things, split up according to sexes and under the guidance of Meg and Mr. Hawk retired to the dressing rooms where they were provided with suits which also elicited a certain amount of subdued merriment. Previous to donning them, however, the attendants put them through their paces. Mr. Hawk was hurled to a table by a Swedish giant and his lean body subjected to the most brutal treatment. Nor was he alone in his suffering. All of the gods were receiving like punishment, beneath which their good-humor was gradually giving place to amazed indignation. In their untutored minds the impression grew that their assailants were grimly determined to do them in, and with equal grimness the gods were determined not to be done in. Strangely enough, it was Mr. Hawk, who should have known better, who first broke into rebellion. After repeatedly asking his furious Swede not to do a certain thing to him and receiving no satisfaction he petrified the man in his tracks and painfully rose from the table, leaving the Swede standing in a half-crouching position, his huge, torturing hands impotently pawing thin air. The scientist was just in time to witness Bacchus's quaint idea of retaliation. The fat god, red in the face and kneaded beyond further endurance, suddenly placed a foot in the earnest face of his attendant and pushed it with truly Olympian vigor. The man slid across the floor and landed with a thud against the tiled wall, many feet away.

"That," said Bacchus, rolling himself off the table, "will teach you how to handle a gentleman and a god. What a way to carry on!"

From the table on which Neptune was contorted came the sound of unpleasant squabbling.

"Keep your horrid talons out of my beard, I'm telling you," the sea god was saying.

"Then why don't you hold your beard up like I asked you?" demanded the man.

"I'd look pretty lying here, wouldn't I, holding it up in the air?" Neptune scathingly retorted. "I won't do it."

"Well, if you don't hold up that beard you can't blame me if I get my hands all tangled up in the damned thing," said the man, making a lunge at the prostrate god, who grunted beneath the impact.

"One moment, my good man," Neptune continued. "Be a little more careful how you address this beard. I feel like knocking your block off as it is."

"Try and do it," said the man.

Neptune did not try. He did it. The block was not exactly knocked off, but it and its owner found themselves crumpled up on the floor beside the body of their still dazed fellow countryman. The discovery of Mr. Hawk's petrified attendant was attracting increasing attention. The rubbers of the gods gave up their rubbing and hurried to inspect the solidified figure of the ex-mangler.

Taking advantage of the lull in the hostilities, Mr. Hawk led his gods into the steam room, which was immediately filled with their cries and imprecations.

"Who in Hades thought of this one?" demanded Apollo, springing up from a flesh-searing deck chair and regarding parts of his scorched self ruefully. "Plato himself would object to this."

"Will you kindly turn me to stone?" pleaded Bacchus, wallowing through the vapor towards the faintly amused Mr. Hawk.

Neptune, his beard glistening with moisture, was addressing himself to a perfect stranger who had apparently just awakened from a comfortable nap.

"My dear good sir," asked Neptune, "how the deuce can you lie there sleeping when people are dying all around you?"

"I don't understand," gasped the man.

"Neither do I," said Neptune, turning his back on the man.

Mr. Hawk could tell at a glance that the steam room

was not going to make a hit with the gods. Accordingly, he led them from the room and induced Bacchus to get himself under a stinging shower of ice-cold needles.

"More punishment!" screamed Bacchus. "Howling Cerberus, what a day!"

The Titanic laughter of the Olympians resounded in the room. Bacchus staggered from the shower and made for the dressing room. The gods were at his heels. They, too, had just remembered the flasks.

"This," said Bacchus, removing one of them from his lips, "seems to me to be about the only reasonable thing we've done since we were lured into this small but efficient hell. What happens next?"

"This way," replied Mr. Hawk. "Follow me."

"One moment," said Bacchus, holding out a restraining hand. "This way to what? We've just followed you through enough."

"The swimming pool," he was told.

They helped each other into their bathing suits, greatly deploring what to them was an exceedingly prudish precaution. Neptune seized his trident and followed Mr. Hawk from the room. They were joined in the pool by Meg and the goddesses, and experiences were excitedly exchanged. A group of swimmers stood listening close by and marveled at the innocence of the gods. It was a surprising thing to them how such a splendid-looking body of men and women could display such profound ignorance of Turkish bath technique.

"We locked all those female murderers in a room and had a swell time," giggled Venus. "Slipped down a lot of cocktails. I feel dizzy as anything."

Apparently so did everybody, including Mr. Hawk and Meg.

"Here I go on the crest of a wave!" cried Venus and flung herself with a splash upon the contented face of an elderly gentleman who immediately disappeared from sight. When at last he came up for air, his face did not look nearly so contented.

"Sorry I got my face in the way," he remarked bitterly. "Why don't you hold me under the next time? Make a thorough job of it."

"Why, you seductive old duck," smiled the goddess, "I do believe you bit me right there of all places."

The old gentleman paddled disgustedly away.

Diana, poised on a high springboard, dived gracefully into the tank. The other gods and goddesses unceremoniously followed her. Meg sought a shallow corner, where she did considerable splashing, to the annoyance of all in her vicinity. Mr. Hawk launched his lean frame into the pool and swam about with dignity and concentration. While thus engaged he received a violent slap in the face delivered by a lady who had suddenly and spasmodically leaped half out of water. When Mr. Hawk came up the lady was glaring balefully at him.

"Take that," she said, and down went Mr. Hawk again.

"Before I go down for the third and last time," said the scientist when he had once more reached the surface, "I would very much like to know for what reason I'm being drowned?"

"You know already," snapped the lady. "Keep your hands to yourself."

"What did he do?" asked an interested bystander.

"He gave me an awful pinch below the surface," the lady announced in a loud voice. "I don't know how I'll ever be able to explain the mark to my husband. Such a place to pinch."

Mr. Hawk felt like going down for the third time of his own free will, but he gamely trod water and faced the mysteriously assaulted woman.

"I don't know what place you are speaking about," he told her, "but I want to assure you it wasn't I who took the liberty of pinching it."

"Isn't he the roguish devil?" a feminine voice exclaimed.

"You did pinch it," retorted the woman.

"What?" shot back Mr. Hawk.

"You know what," she answered.

"My dear lady," Mr. Hawk said pleadingly, "I don't know what on earth you are talking about."

"I can make a pretty close guess," observed Venus, swimming up to the little group that had gathered round Mr. Hawk and the affronted woman.

At that moment she uttered another startled cry and made a frantic attempt to rise from the pool. She only half succeeded and fell back with a splash.

"I suppose I did that?" demanded Mr. Hawk. "I wasn't within three feet of you."

"He did it again!" gasped the woman.

"Not that gentleman," said another woman. "I was watching his hands all the time."

"Then there must be a gang of them," the twice pinched lady replied. "I felt it distinctly. One can hardly make a mistake about a thing like that."

"Hardly," smiled Venus sweetly in her most insinuating voice. "I should say not."

The goddess had scarcely finished speaking before she herself made an earnest effort to project her flexible form into the air.

"Well, whoever is doing all this pinching," she said, tenderly rubbing herself below the water line, "should certainly get his nails cut if he intends to keep it up."

"How do you know it's a man?" asked a voice from the crowd.

"There wouldn't be any fun in the thing if it wasn't," she replied innocently, and was surprised at the general merriment that followed her answer.

"Oh, look!" cried a young lady standing at the edge of the pool and pointing down into the water. "Look! Am I going crazy?"

Mr. Hawk looked down through the clear water and received a decided shock. Neptune, his beard floating wildly about him, was grinning up at them in malicious glee. He was seated comfortably on the floor of the tank and in his right hand he held, deftly poised, his three-pronged trident. As Mr. Hawk gazed the sea god made a feint in his direction, then opened his mouth and rocked himself from side to side. Evidently he was roaring with laughter and enjoying himself thoroughly.

"There, madam," said Mr. Hawk, "is the person you should have slapped and then publicly rebuked for pinching you in some rarely named part of your anatomy in which I am not at all interested, if the truth must be known."

The woman uttered a shriek and climbed out of the pool.

215

"But won't he drown?" someone called in an excited voice.

"I hope to God he does," said the woman. "The dirty dog."

An individual with a reasonable mind and a pair of knees that knocked as he ran appeared with the swimming instructor. This noble youth, realizing that something must be done in front of so many eyes, dived into the water and seized Neptune by the beard. For a moment the two seemed to be arguing, both gesticulating angrily, then the interview was terminated abruptly by the intervention of the trident in the pit of the instructor's stomach. He shot back to the surface and became busy about filling his lungs.

"He won't come up," he announced when this necessary precaution had been taken.

"That seems fairly obvious," said the dignified-looking gentleman, "but does he give any reason for his extraordinary conduct?"

"He tried to tell me something," the instructor replied, pulling himself out of the pool, "but I couldn't understand him. That must have made him furious, for he jabbed me with his pitchfork."

"But my dear fellow," the gentleman protested, "you can't expect us to enjoy our swim with the knowledge that a fellow creature is drowning before our very eyes. The poor chap's probably mad or something."

"He's mad all right," said the instructor, "but he doesn't seem to be in any danger of drowning. Look at him now."

Neptune, pleased by the presence of so many interested spectators, was doing his best to entertain them. His best consisted of sliding industriously down the steep floor of the pool, then stopping himself grotesquely with his feet at the end. It was an extremely childish performance for a bearded god to give, but Neptune was at that stage of inebriety at which everything seemed convulsing. Growing tired of sliding, Neptune played dead. It was a horrifyingly convincing demonstration. Gasps came from the audience. Several women were led screaming hysterically from the room. All they had seen was the whites of Neptune's eyes, his matted beard, and his lifelessly swaying limbs. The general effect was quite enough to unnerve the staunchest of souls. After this the sea god lay down on the floor of the tank and went to sleep, his massive head cushioned on his arms.

"The most amazing thing I've ever witnessed," remarked the dignified gentleman at last. "The man must be part fish. He couldn't drown if he wanted to, and I have no intention of letting him frighten me out of my swim any longer. One must look facts in the face."

With this he pointed his hands over his head, gave snappily at the knees three times, rose froglike into the air, and entered the water in the good old-fashioned way. Many of the spectators followed his example, if not his quaint style, and soon the tank had resumed its normal appearance.

Mr. Hawk looked up from his contemplation of the recumbent god just in time to see the lady who had so thoughtlessly assaulted him poised on the end of the springboard. It was an ideal set-up for his purpose. As she curved in the air from the board the scientist turned her to stone. In that position she struck the water a smashing blow and continued on to the bottom of the tank, where she remained without budging.

Screams and shouts once more attracted the swimming instructor, who, since the advent of Neptune, had been seriously considering throwing up his job. Realizing that he could not follow his natural inclination and let the woman drown in front of so many witnesses, he dived into the water and tried to move her. Looking up through the water at the blurred faces peering down at him, he shook his head in a gesture of discouragement. Then, as if seized by a new idea, he swam over to Neptune and once more tugged his beard. The god awoke with a furious churning of water and looked about him wildly. With bursting lungs the instructor pointed to the figure of the woman on the bottom of the tank. With a shrug of his shoulders the god removed his beard from the clutching hand and lay down beside the woman. The instructor popped to the surface with an expression of utter bewilderment on his strained face. For a few seconds he clung to the side of the tank gasping for breath. Then he pulled himself out and sat down heavily, his feet still dangling in the water. He

217

was through with that tank forever. He even doubted if he would ever swim again or have anything to do with water even to the extent of taking a bath.

"What are you going to do?" asked an indignant lady. "That woman's drowning."

"Search me, lady," said the instructor. "That's not a woman down there. She's a rock in female form. If anybody else wants to save her they're welcome to the job."

A number of men jumped into the pool, and Mr. Hawk petrified them for their pains. Down they went to the bottom of the pool in all sorts of odd positions. Soon the tank was filled with the petrified bodies of dozens of men and women. Neptune woke up and looked about him with a pleased expression on his face. Thrusting out his trident, he struck one of the bodies and was surprised to discover that the blow took no effect. He rose and jabbed viciously at several others, with the same result. Those watching from above were overcome with horror. Fainting and hysteria became the order of the day.

"Open all outlets," called the instructor to one of his assistants. "We'll have to drain the tank."

He rose wearily and sauntered away to supervise the execution of his order. As far as he was concerned everybody present could drown to their heart's content. He washed his hands of the whole business. It was a damn queer pool, and it was filled with damn queer people. Saving pieces of statuary was not in his contract, and no one was going to tell him anything different.

The manager and several members of his staff arrived on the scene of action just as Neptune's head and the business end of his trident emerged from the rapidly receding waters of the tank.

"My God! Who is that person?" asked the startled official. "Looks like old man Neptune himself."

"Don't know what his name is," replied the instructor, "but he's been making a public nuisance of himself on the bottom of that tank for the last hour or more without coming up once to breathe."

"Then the man must be drowned," said the manager decisively. "That's all there is to it."

"I'm afraid there's lots more than that," the instructor muttered.

"And who are all these other persons lying about down there in those ridiculous postures?" demanded the manager impatiently.

"I didn't ask them their names, sir," said the instructor, "but a short time ago they were all alive and kicking. Now they're just so many rocks."

"Then they're all dead, too," the manager snapped out. "This is really too bad. It would have to happen on a hot day just when we need the pool. Can't you hurry up with the bodies?"

"Can't even lift them," was the reply. "We'll have to use a derrick."

"Nonsense," replied the manager. "The excitement has affected your brain. I'll go down myself and investigate."

There was no foolishness about this manager. A dozen or so dead bodies in his tank meant little to him save trouble and unfavorable publicity. He was a man of action and quick decisions, the majority of which were bad. When the pool was empty he descended the ladder and seized the first body he saw. The body failed to budge. He then laid violent hands upon another with the same result. After he had wasted his energy on a third he stopped and looked up with a frown.

"Who's been chucking all these statues into the pool?" he demanded.

"They might be statues now," replied the instructor, "but they were living men and women half an hour ago. Ask anybody here."

"Impossible," said the manager. "Never heard such rubbish in all my life. These things were never living beings. They're just plain, everyday statues, and not very good ones at that. Some prize ass has been having a bit of a joke at your expense.

As if to refute the manager's words Mr. Hawk released the figures. They rose from the floor of the tank and angrily confronted the manager.

"We'd like to know the meaning of this," one of them demanded.

"Of what?" replied the manager, breaking out in an opulent sweat.

219

"We don't know," replied the other.

"Neither do I," said the manager. "Let's get out of here."

In the meantime Meg and Mr. Hawk had piloted their charges safely away from the observation of an altogether too inquisitive public. The company was now assembled in the lounging room of the luxurious suite. Hebe and Mr. Betts were busy at their appointed tasks. Everyone looked more refreshed and in better humor.

"When you're feeling low in your mind," Mr. Hawk observed, momentarily freeing himself from the strangle hold Meg had on his neck, "there's nothing like a good swim if you can only work up the energy."

"Well, you and Whiskers did your best to make a go of it," said Meg. "Both of you."

"Thanks," replied Neptune, "but if you don't mind I'd prefer not to be called Whiskers. Don't ask me why, for I haven't the vaguest idea. If you call me just plain beard it doesn't seem to matter. How did you like my dead man? Was it good or just so-so?"

"It was perfect," said Diana. "Too good to last."

"I'm not so bright," answered Neptune, "but even I can feel dimly that your last remark was not all milk and honey."

"Say beer and skittles," amended Bacchus. "It sounds better."

"When do we eat?" asked Perseus. "You gods keep the most irregular meal hours. Now, when I was in training for monster baiting——"

What Perseus did when he was in training was never learned, for at that moment Dora thrust her head through the door and mooed wistfully.

"Come in, Dora," said Mr. Hawk politely. "You make the party complete. Wonder if she wants a drink."

"Mr. Hawk," protested Mercury, "she's the only lady in the lot. Don't get her started."

"Well, I like that," drawled Venus. "How about our little Phoebus Apollo?"

"Come. Come," put in Mr. Hawk hastily. "Let's all have another little drink and think up something else to do."

220

"Glasses, Miss Hebe," called Betts cheerfully. "We've got a lot of customers."

With sweet, glowing eyes Hebe passed among the gods and deftly collected the empty glasses. The sound of tinkling ice made music for her feet.

CHAPTER XIX

The Gods Leave Town

"So THIS IS THE HOME OF OUR HOST," OBSERVED Bacchus, gazing placidly from the Emperor at the gracious lines of Hawk House. "We should do very nicely here. Did you say there was a cellar? A cellar with wine and things?"

"One of the most businesslike in many miles around," Hunter Hawk assured the god. "My father and his father before him drank on a generous scale, but fortunately for us their flesh failed before their thirst."

Mercury was taking the lie of the land with a practical and swift shifting eye.

"I notice," he said, "you have a high and comfortably protective wall on three sides of the place but none in front. Why is that?"

"Never got round to it," Hawk briefly replied. "Intended to some day, then forgot all about it."

"Walls not only protect but also conceal," the light-fingered god observed significantly.

Mr. Hawk grinned. "Had I known sooner that you Olympians were going to visit me I'd have had one thrown up if only for the sake of concealment."

Mercury hummed a thoughtful snatch of a song he had heard at some night club.

"The man across the way has a nice stone wall," he remarked. "The stones are well selected. You see," he added, "I know quite a lot about stone walls. I've climbed over so many of them."

Blotto, like a red mouth shot from hell, hurled himself into the car. So furious and inclusive were his emotional demonstrations that Mr. Hawk, for the sake of convenience, momentarily turned him to stone.

When the Olympians piled out of the automobile Al-

221

ice and Alfred Lambert, ably assisted by Junior, were entertaining some friends on the veranda. Alice had just been telling them that she had recently received a letter from her brother announcing his intentions of living in Japan. His unexpected arrival with a flock of boisterous men and women did not work in so well with her story. Her face grew set and determined. Something would have to be done to put an end to this. A certain detective by the name of Griggs was still interested in the movements of her brother. Perhaps a telephone call might——

Her thoughts were interrupted by the Olympians as they came charging noisily up the steps.

"Hello, all," said Venus including Mr. and Mrs. Blythe-Brown and Miss Amelia Blythe-Brown, age thirty-eight, in her genial greeting. "Not drinking, I notice. We'll have to remedy that. Hey, there, Mr. Hawk, how about some grog?"

"Betts is already mixing them," shouted Meg above the racket. "He went round the back way. Hebe went with him."

Alice Pollard Lambert, in spite of the healthy dread in which she stood of her brother, could not bring herself to receive his disorderly guests with any display of cordiality. Junior was openly snobbish, while his father, Alfred, stood by, speechlessly humiliated. The Blythe-Browns, of course, did not quite know what it was all about, but they were secretly delighted, for radically different reasons. Mr. Blythe-Brown hoped to get a drink. Mrs. Blythe-Brown to get a fresh scandal. Miss Amelia Blythe-Brown hoped—and how she hoped—to get an introduction to any one of the stalwart gods. Thirty-eight years is a long time for a girl to keep her patience. Amelia had recently decided after a private inventory of her rapidly fading allurements that her supply of patience was just about exhausted. She was out for business now, and she did not intend to be finicky any longer about partnership arrangements.

Strangely enough, Perseus took an immediate liking to Amelia. Perhaps something told him she was a woman in distress. He worked quickly and smoothly. After a brief conversation the two of them retired indoors. In the general confusion their absence was not noticed except by Mrs. Lambert and the eagle-eyed Mercury, who smiled cynically to himself.

"Keep your places," Mr. Hawk courteously begged his sister and her company. "I'm going to show my friends over the house a bit."

"How is dear Reverend Dr. Archer's case of squats getting on?" Meg asked sweetly from the doorway. Receiving no reply, she added a little less sweetly, "I hope it doesn't strike any members of his flock."

"We'll slide you out a bucket of cocktails," Venus called clubbily over Meg's shoulder. "Just keep your shirts on. Pip! Pip!"

Alice Lambert's face looked frozen. She was fairly snorting from injured dignity, but she was keeping a strong check on herself.

"What were you saying, dear?" she inquired, touching Mrs. Blythe-Brown's black satin dress with the tips of her carefully manicured nails. "Oh, you weren't saying anything. Then if you'll excuse me for just a moment I'll run in and telephone. Some man is so anxious to meet my brother. He would never think of doing it himself. Lost in his science."

At that moment her brother was lost in something a great deal more interesting than his science. His face was partially submerged in a glassful of cocktails, and the Olympians were cluttered round him. The kitchen presented a homelike scene. In one corner old man Lambert was seated in Mrs. Bett's own rocking chair. Near him stood the maid Stella, to whom he had been telling some particularly spicy stories gleaned from the unedifying recesses of his wicked old memory. Mrs. Betts was examining her husband with impersonal disgust. Daffy and Cyril Sparks, with Blotto dangling his tongue between them and trying to give the impression that he had arranged everything, were seated on the kitchen table. Grandpa Lambert was waving a half-empty glass in his clawlike hand.

"And since you went away," he was saying, "this has been the only comfortable place in the house to sit. Mrs. Betts has been very kind to Daffy and myself. That boy Sparks is always hanging about. I think he wants to marry her or something."

223

"Probably something," put in Venus, "if he's like the boys I used to know."

"You're wrong," declared Daffy. "I've already suggested something, but he insists on leaving me untaken-advantage-of."

"My poor dear child," said Venus sympathetically. "What a rotten shame. I'll have to have a talk with him."

"Don't let her," warned Diana. "He won't be the same man."

"Betts," said Mr. Hawk, "take a shaker full of cocktails to the veranda and see that Blythe-Brown party transfers its contents to his skin. He's a sadly overwifed man."

When Betts had departed on his delicate mission, the scientist led the Olympians to his partly demolished laboratory. Cyril Sparks took Bacchus and Neptune aside, while Mr. Hawk was explaining to the others scientific apparatus in which they displayed a polite but wavering interest. Cy took down several bottles and mixed a synthetic highball. Its effects on the two gods completely revolutionized their conception of drinking. After that powerful drink the fish and grape fanciers wandered round the room looking speculatively at the shelves filled with jars. They were thinking dangerously. If a mere mortal could mix such a drink as that what couldn't they accomplish if they set their minds on it? Stimulated as never before by the drink now leaping inside them, and fired with ambition for the drink yet to be created, these two ample gods discussed in undertones the possibilities of various jars containing liquids of unknown potency.

While Mr. Hawk was becoming more hopelessly tangled in the intricacies of the generator of the atomic ray, or whatever the remarkable gadget was called, Neptune and Bacchus sought a quiet corner of the laboratory and there prepared to mix themselves what they fondly hoped would prove to be the strongest drink ever sampled by man or god. Each selected a jar of liquid which for some reason appealed to them; then together they selected a third. Pouring the first two liquids into a large container they sniffed the results delicately.

"It's going to be good," murmured Bacchus.

"Shall we keep it to ourselves or whack it up?" asked Neptune.

"Pour in that other stuff, and we'll find out," replied Bacchus.

When this was done the sea god's question was immediately answered, immediately and unequivocally answered. The drink they had mixed so expectantly in the innocence of their godlike hearts turned out to be one that they could not keep to themselves. Whether they liked it or not, that drink was whacked up not only among those in the laboratory but also among persons some distance removed from the immediate neighborhood.

After picking themselves up from their overturned chairs on the veranda, the Lamberts and the Blythe-Browns, with the exception of Mr. Blythe-Brown, rush-rushed to the scene of the explosion. The exception remained behind comfortably seated in his chair. In one hand he held the cocktail shaker, in the other a large goblet. In his eyes was a gleam of deep satisfaction. Explosions were rare occurrences, but a shaker full of powerful cocktails was rarer still and should not be neglected.

Betts, closely pressed by the others, was the first to reach the smoke-filled laboratory. He was armed with a fire extinguisher which he began to play indiscriminately about the room.

"For God's sake," came the voice of his master. "Isn't it bad enough to be blown to hell and gone without having a heaping portion of chemicals squirted in one's eye?"

"Pardon me, sir," Mr. Betts replied, politely addressing the smoke in the direction whence the voice had sounded, "I suspect there's a bit of a fire about."

"I suspect so, too, Betts," Mr. Hawk answered gloomily. "I seem to have sat on much of it."

"But not all," came the voice of Meg. "Not all, my good man. My sitter is quite singed."

"Where are we?" demanded the voice of Neptune.

"I don't know and I don't care," was Mr. Hawk's heartfelt reply.

"If the lady who is sitting on my face would move

225

about three inches to the right," observed Mercury from the far end of the room, "I'd feel a little less destroyed."

"Sorry," said Diana calmly. "I thought it was a piece of glass."

"That was my teeth," said Mercury.

"Where's that head?" demanded Apollo out of the gloom.

"Whose?" asked Meg.

"Medusa's," the god replied. "Perseus asked me to hold it for him."

"Now, who the hell cares about that?" asked Mr. Hawk. "Where's my dog?"

"I have him," called Daffy. "Right in the pit of my stomach. He made a fair landing and has remained there ever since, together with the heel of a certain Mr. Sparks."

"Sorry, Daffy," was the conventional retort of Cyril. "It's twisted."

"What? My stomach?" exclaimed Daffy. "You would complain."

"No. My ankle," said Cy.

"Well, keep on twisting it off my stomach," replied the young lady. "That fair region has troubles enough of its own."

"Mr. Betts," asked a faint voice which sounded as if it belonged to a terribly enfeebled Bacchus, "would you mind squirting that stuff in another mouth for a few minutes? I can't swallow another drop right now."

"How's that?" inquired Mr. Betts.

"You're bathing my eyes now," said Bacchus.

"Any better?" asked Mr. Betts, changing the direction of the stream.

"Not so good!" shouted Neptune. "My left ear is sinking."

"Better take it away, Betts," advised Mr. Hawk. "Your efforts are not appreciated. Let the house burn a little, and do something about all this smoke."

In spite of this illogical suggestion the smoke eventually did drift unfragrantly through the shattered windows, leaving the Olympians disclosed in shreds. The Lamberts and Blythe-Browns gave off a series of shocked gasps when their eyes fell on the denuded gods. Megaera, looking at the smoke-blackened faces in which glittered large questioning eyes, began to laugh softly.

"Looks like a minstrel show," she said to Mr. Hawk. "The poor dears have never seen one."

"I see nothing to laugh at," declared Mrs. Lambert cuttingly.

"Neither do I, lady," agreed Bacchus, a fair portion of whom had been blown through the wall of the house and was now dangling over the lawn. "Life to me at present is a very earnest affair."

"Hunter," went on Alice Lambert, ignoring the fat god. "This really is too bad."

"It will be a damn sight worse," snapped Hunter, "if you don't pipe down."

And strange to say, as he finished speaking, the situation did get worse. That is to say, another complication was added to it. From the already weakened ceiling large slabs of plaster began to descend with increasing weight and rapidity upon the inquiringly upraised faces of the gods. Thrusting themselves weirdly through a white powdery cloud, the four legs on a bed hesitated modestly above them a moment, then continued to the floor of the laboratory with a crash. From one side of the bed Miss Amelia Blythe-Brown, clothed in little more than confusion, was bounced to the floor. From the other side Perseus rose and fell and then remained, thoughtfully clutching a pillow to him.

"What happened?" demanded Mrs. Blythe-Brown when she had recovered a little from the shocking revelation.

"Nothing," replied her daughter with a discouraged droop to her shoulders. "Absolutely nothing."

"Then how did you get into bed with that man?" the mother continued. "Surely not for nothing."

"I didn't say that," said the girl wearily. "You asked me what happened and I told you. Nothing happened. But," added the young lady, a reckless light in her eyes, "if it hadn't been for that explosion——"

Perseus made a frantic gesture intended as a plea for caution.

"This lady," he said hastily, "was blown into that

227

bed and I was blown after her. From the violence of the blow both of us lost much of our clothes, as apparently did everyone else."

"Very nice and neatly put," drawled Venus. "That explains everything."

"Why does he have all the breaks?" protested Bacchus. "He gets blown into bed with a woman while I get blown through a bed of stone."

"You were merely on the wrong end of that ill wind you've heard so much about," Mercury explained.

"I'm not quite satisfied about all this," Mrs. Blythe-Brown said in a puzzled voice.

"Neither am I," answered Amelia. "It seems as if fate were against me. If someone will toss me a sheet I'll withdraw and let you figure it out for yourself."

"There wasn't any hole in that ceiling when we came in," the mother of the girl mused aloud, lines of perplexity still wrinkling her face.

"You couldn't see the ceiling when she came in," retorted Mr. Hawk. "They were the very first to go up."

"Seems odd," continued the woman, "that the rest of you should have conveniently remained behind."

"Are you deliberately trying to make your daughter a loose woman?" demanded Meg.

"Certainly," replied Mrs. Blythe-Brown in a surprised voice. "Wouldn't you? She's thirty-eight as it is, and this is the nearest she's come to it yet. Never did have any get up and go. She's just like her father. I wish you'd postponed your explosion, Mr. Hawk, for at least fifteen minutes."

"My watch was fast," explained Mr. Hawk in a tone of apology.

"I'm afraid that doesn't help Amelia very much," replied the mother.

"Why, my dear Mrs. Blythe-Brown!" Mrs. Lambert exclaimed in a shocked voice. "Can I believe my ears?"

"Not if they're like your tongue," the lady replied. "Catch you waiting thirty-eight years. Why, you wouldn't wait thirty-eight minutes."

The Olympians to a god looked up at Mrs. Lambert with awakened interest not unmixed with approval.

"I'm sure I don't know what you mean," began Alice Lambert, but was interrupted by the rushing appearance of Stella.

"Mr. Blythe——"

"Mr. Blythe-Brown, Stella," Mrs. Lambert corrected.

"Well, whoever he is," continued the girl, "he's just knocked a man down on the veranda who says his name is Griggs. He's got an awful-looking badge on his vest, Mr. Hawk."

"My family seems to be going to hell," Mrs. Blythe-Brown remarked complacently.

"My brother's going to jail," announced Mrs. Lambert with equal complacency. "That man's a detective. He's been here several times."

"If I do," replied Mr. Hawk, "I'll turn you and your family, with the exception of Daffy and the old man, so solidly to stone you wouldn't even melt in hell."

Alice Lambert turned white.

"Stella," continued Mr. Hawk, "you go back and tell that guy to get up and that we'll deal with him in a minute." He paused and looked about the room. "There's a man out there who wants to lay violent hands on me," he went on. "He's a dumb, self-important detective, and he might have his gang with him. Will you gods stand by me?"

Loud cries from the gods and goddesses alike.

"Yank me out of this hole," shouted Bacchus. "I'll pound the beggar to pulp just as if he were so many grapes."

Bacchus, together with a circle of adhering bricks, was hauled into the room, and a motley crew of disheveled figures rushed from the laboratory to interview the already assaulted Griggs. Before the grim advance of the Olympians the detective stepped back a pace and dropped his hand to his pocket.

"I don't want any more trouble," he said warningly. "This drunkard has already knocked me down once."

"And he'll knock you down again," Mr. Blythe-Brown replied thickly from his chair. "Have a drink, somebody—I mean, everybody."

"What in hell do you want here?" demanded Mr. Hawk. "You'd better get out now, while you're well and healthy. We don't like you worth a damn."

"I'll go all right," replied Griggs, "but Mr. Hunter

Hawk goes with me. I've a warrant here for his arrest, and I'm going to serve it before I leave this house."

"Do you mean me?" asked Mr. Hawk, stepping towards the man.

"No, I don't mean you, and you know it," answered the detective. "Don't try to pull any of that stuff on me. You know who I mean just as well as I do."

"You're mad," said Mr. Hawk. "If you don't mean me, whom do you mean?"

Griggs laughed nastily and turned suddenly on the amazed Neptune.

"It's no use, Mr. Hawk," he said. "The game's up. You can't fool me. I know you were wearing a false beard."

Before the great sea god had a chance to know what was happening to him the detective reached up and gave a violent tug at his beard, several tufts of which came away in the dumbfounded man's hand. With a roar of rage and pain Neptune flung himself upon detective Griggs and whirled him about in the air; then, as if not knowing what else to do with him, he released his hold on the man and allowed his limp figure to loop through the air and land on the gravel path. Neptune in all likelihood would have let matters stand at that had it not been for the excessive merriment of the Olympians, not to mention the group of mortals, among whose loud laughter the whoops of the drunken Mr. Blythe-Brown led all the rest.

Seizing his long trident, the bearded god charged down the veranda steps. Griggs, observing the terrifying spectacle, bounded to his feet and sprinted down the drive, his flat feet spraying out gravel behind him in the face of the pursuing god.

Neptune had never boasted of his speed on land. Had this scene been enacted in the Atlantic or Mediterranean it would have perhaps had a more tragic and satisfactory ending. As it was, the detective gained the security of his waiting automobile and drove off at top speed amid the cheers of the delighted company assembled on the veranda.

"I'll be back," Griggs shouted at Neptune. "The boys will drag that funny-looking beard off your ugly face then."

The god, with a scream of baffled fury, hurled his trident at the moving car. The spare tire on the back popped, but the detective did not stop to find out what had happened.

Picking up his trident, the god returned to the house, tenderly stroking his beard and planning the death of Griggs and the various indignities he would practice on his remains. By the time he had reached the house he had become quite cheerful again.

The gods, though intellectually juvenile, had facile minds and were especially quick at picking up new methods of torture and mutilation in connection with their enemies. Formerly they had considered it no end amusing to change their victims into cows, dogs, snakes, Harpies, Gorgons, and such like, but of later years such relatively painless retaliations had begun to pall on them. No mortal had yet pulled Neptune's beard and gotten away with it. Neptune, one of the kindest-hearted gods that ever drew breath when not crossed, had thought up some pretty mean things to do to Mr. Griggs, if and when their paths ever crossed.

As he heaved himself up the steps he overheard Mr. Hawk saying to his grimy and tattered guests: "Take my word for it, he'll be back with his gang before morning."

"Damned if I would," said Mr. Blythe-Brown decidedly. "Not after such a reception as he got. What's this I hear about my daughter being blown into bed with a man? Where's this explosion anyway—it might do something about me? I'd stand for a lot of blowing if that half-clad lady over there would get in on the blow."

He waved the cocktail shaker at Venus, who dropped her eyes girlishly.

"Oh, Mr. Blythe-Brown," she gushed, "what things you say!"

"Put down that shaker, you decrepit old lush," came the calm voice of his remarkable wife. "It's empty."

"That can be rectified, my dear," he told her.

Betts removed the shaker from the waving hand and hurried into the house. Hebe hurried after him, gathering glasses on the way. Mrs. Betts had taken a fancy to the cup-bearing goddess. Stella was not so fond of her.

Hebe was usurping her place. Suspecting this reaction on the part of the maid, Hebe asked her to share in the bearing and immediately won her heart. She had already opened tentative negotiations with Mercury, who had always had a weakness for domestics, and now fair Stella wanted to perfect them.

At the moment Mercury was holding forth. "What we need," he said, addressing his remarks to the Olympians, "is a high stone wall. I know all about such matters, and if you'll all bear a hand we can throw one up in no time."

The deliberations following this proposal exhausted the contents of three shakers, after which the gods and goddesses alike hurried enthusiastically to the uncompleted section of the wall. Sand and cement were brought from the work sheds, and rocks were collected with feverish energy. The gods were good workers once their minds had been set on a task to accomplish. Mr. Betts, realizing the futility of mixing drinks in a shaker, began to use a bucket which Hebe carried along the line of activity whenever she saw an Olympian's ambition flagging through lack of fuel. Mr. Hawk regarded the whole affair as being quite in keeping with the unstable enterprise of the gods, but as it kept them happy and out of other and perhaps more disturbing pursuits, he gave them a free hand.

It was pleasant to sit on the veranda with Meg, Blotto, Daffy, and Cy Sparks and observe the labors of the Olympians. Not every man could boast of having a bunch of real authentic gods build a stone wall for him. True enough, Mr. Hawk never expected to see the wall finished, but the idea was refreshing. They seemed to be happy in their occupation, for the deep booming bass of Neptune harmonized agreeably with Apollo's ringing tenor as they sang some unintelligible song, probably dealing playfully with bloodshed, pillage, and rape, pastimes in which they were chiefly interested.

"They're a great crowd, your gods," remarked Cyril Sparks, rather wistfully. "Wish human beings could be more like that."

"Go ahead and invent a new economic system," said Mr. Hawk, "and you can have your wish. How can a man be happily irresponsible or develop the really charming possibilities of his character when the fear of losing his job through no fault of his own is constantly in the back of his mind? A man who gets up in the morning, washes his face, kisses his wife, and catches his train is not nearly so interesting as the man who gets up around noontime, mixes himself a cocktail, kisses someone else's wife, and misses his train. Yet under our present economic system the train misser loses out unless he is privately endowed or subsidized."

"Does a man necessarily have to kiss someone else's wife to be interesting?" asked Daffy, not without a thought to the future.

"By no means," replied Hunter Hawk. "I'm glad you checked me up on that. As a matter of fact, the man who kisses someone else's wife is hardly interesting at all, because he is usually following the line of the least resistance. A large quantity of married women are much easier to kiss than single ones. Although most women seem to make no objections to getting married, a whole lot of them hate to withdraw permanently from competition, and one of the most practical methods of getting the best of her unencumbered sisters is to offer a little more and to suggest a great deal more. That type of woman isn't interesting either, although she has her uses."

"Seems to me you're talking a hell of a lot," cut in Meg. "To what nurses' weekly do you subscribe? Don't think I've forgotten your conduct with that Brightly woman. You weren't following the line of least resistance then. Oh, no, dearie. You were following the line of no resistance, you big stiff."

"A mind so steeped in depravity as yours," replied the scientist, "can put but one interpretation on that unfortunate occurrence. You can neither understand nor appreciate a really pure-minded man, you common thief."

Meg grinned. "Listen, my good man," she said, "I'm probably almost everything, but I won't admit to being common about anything, and most emphatically not, when it comes to thieving. In that I know from experience that I'm a really exceptional woman."

"Are you proud of it?" asked Mr. Hawk.

"Naturally," answered Meg. "Can you pick a pocket as clean as I?"

"My ambitions have never led me in that direction, thank God!" said Mr. Hawk.

"And if they had," Meg retorted scornfully, "your victims would have souned like sleigh bells, your hand would have shaken so."

"Shall we take a walk to the village?" asked Mr. Hawk, dismissing Meg with a lordly gesture that was especially irritating to her. "I have a little business with my lawyer I'd like to put through before I make my last stand and leave the field to the train catchers and window watchers and mirth controllers, and all the rest of the filthy, criticizing, vice-coveting tribe that at present sets the standard of life."

Both Meg and Daffy looked up at the lengthy man, who had risen from his chair and was gazing unseeingly at a very busy and none too sober group of gods. In his words the girls had detected a note of bitterness. If such a thing were possible, Hunter Hawk was an idealist in loose living and straight thinking, and such a person is almost as difficult to bear as an idealist in anything else.

"Why don't you call them lousy and save yourself a lot of words?" asked Daffy.

"It's too fashionable," replied Hawk. "And I hate conformity. Before the word was taken up, so to speak, and made smart, I used to get a great deal of comfort out of it. Now the damn thing's been ruined for me, and I can't think up another."

"You have a terrible time of it, don't you?" asked Meg, sarcastically sympathetic.

"I do," said Hawk briefly.

"Well, if you ask me," she continued, "you're just a pair of stilts in human form."

"I don't ask you," Mr. Hawk snapped back. "Shake a leg there and let's get started. I can't leave those gods by themselves too long or they'll be swarming all over the countryside, leaving ruin in their wake."

At this moment Mercury was questioning Mr. Betts closely regarding the possible whereabouts of the owner of the wall across the road.

"His name is Mr. Shrewsberry," said Betts, "and

he's on the Continent, I think. The house has been closed all summer."

"It's a nice wall, Betts," remarked Mercury.

"Yes, sir. It's a nice wall. Certainly is."

"Do you see that sort of peculiar shaped, reddish rock in it, Betts?" continued the god, gently edging the old man across the road.

"My eyesight is not so good as it was," replied Betts. "You'd better point out to me with that sledge hammer, sir."

"I mean this rock, Betts," explained Mercury, bringing the great hammer against the side of the rock with a smashing blow. "Why, the damn thing's fallen inside!" exclaimed the god. "I'd better go over and get it."

Mercury showed his godlike prowess by the ease with which he scaled the wall. Presently he thrust his head through the opening he had made when pointing out the rock to Mr. Betts.

"Hand me the sledge, Betts," he said. "I can't climb back. It's harder that way. I'll have to tap a small hole in the wall to let myself through."

"That's the only thing left to do," agreed Betts. "Tap yourself a comfortable exit."

Within a few minutes a considerable pile of choice rocks had fallen at the waiting servant's feet. Through the place where these rocks had once been, Mercury emerged, carrying a rock in one hand and the sledge hammer in the other.

"Whew, Betts," he observed. "Thought I'd never get out. Why, what a lot of rocks! Where did they all come from?"

Mr. Betts shrugged his shoulders. "Must have been lying here, I suppose."

"How do you think the wall looks now?" asked the god.

"If anything, better," said Betts.

"I knew you'd say that," exclaimed Mercury. "Of course it does. That wall didn't need all those rocks, to begin with. The thing was just full of rocks, quite unnecessarily so."

"For a rock wall," agreed Betts.

"Yes," said Mercury. "I think you're right. Do you see this one?"

"Don't tell me," cried the old man. "I know just what you're going to say. I noticed the spot myself. It would fit perfectly there. Too bad to waste it and these other rocks too."

As a result of this hypocritical colloquy Mr. Shrewsberry's wall eventually was moved across the road and neatly rearranged on Mr. Hawk's property. Mercury's bright idea was enthusiastically taken up by the other gods and goddesses and put into execution. Soon they became so adept at wall moving that whole sections of the wall were transferred in a single operation.

"Don't know what use he has for a wall, anyway," panted Bacchus, "seeing that his house is all locked up and everything."

"You're right for once," agreed Apollo. "That wall of his was a lot of unnecessary ostentation."

"A vulgar pretense," grinned Neptune.

"Yes," remarked Diana, her hands resting lightly on her beautifully moulded hips. "Mr. Shrewsberry certainly has a lot to thank us for."

"He probably wouldn't," commented Venus, momentarily lifting her head from the bucket. "All men are ungrateful."

"What I'd like to know," asked Perseus, skillfully balancing a column of well cemented rocks, "are we wall movers or wall builders?"

"You would ask a question like that," observed Mercury. "But it does raise a nice point. To Mr. Hawk, our unexcelled host, we probably appear in the light of wall builders, whereas Mr. Shrewsberry might be inclined to call us wall movers or even wall snatchers. It all depends on from which side of the wall you consider the question."

It really doesn't matter what the gods decided they were. The important fact remains they had arranged a strong protective barrier for their host. If the latter part gave the impression of a wave done in stone or if they did omit the insignificant detail of providing some sort of a way to get in other than by scaling, these slight defects should be laid to the enthusiasm of Hebe and her bucket rather than to the craftsmanship of the stout-hearted Olympians.

On the way back from the village Mr. Hawk led his friends past the picturesque rectory of the Reverend Dr. Archer. The man himself was sitting on the veranda in some sort of a trick chair. He looked for all the world like a person nerving himself to jump down the steps in front of him to the path below.

"I can't stand that," remarked Mr. Hawk in a low voice, as he considered the man of God from the tail of his eye. "I'd be a nervous wreck if I had to live in the same house with him."

"Must have gotten used to it by this time," said Meg. "He's been squatting like that for many weeks now."

"After a life devoted to non-squatting could you get used to such a posture in a few weeks?" asked Mr. Hawk.

"It might be easier for me than it is for him," replied Meg thoughtfully. "You see——"

"We won't go into that," Mr. Hawk interrupted. "Let's call on the Reverend Archer."

They turned up the path and saluted the afflicted man.

"Pardon me for not rising," apologized the rector in his beautifully modulated voice, "but God in His wisdom has seen fit to visit me with this rather unprepossessing malady. I feel no pain, but the mental anguish is terrific."

"The seats of the mighty are sometimes hard," was Mr. Hawk's pious observation.

"That is especially true in this case," replied the Reverend Archer a little bitterly.

"I wonder what His idea was?" asked Meg innocently.

"My dear," returned the rector. "I have sat, or, rather, squatted here for many a long hour endeavoring to answer that question myself. I can only conclude that God has his lighter moments, for surely no deity in a serious mood could wish anything so utterly silly on a man. In spite of the humiliation through which I have passed, it has somehow brought God closer to me. He seems much more human now."

237

"That's all pure gain," Mr. Hawk assured him. "It will probably influence your sermons and your relations with the individual members of your congregation for the rest of your life."

"It has already begun to do so," said the Reverend Archer. "I see many things differently now. In many instances I have completely reversed my attitude. Previously I believed that the majority of the members of my congregation, which is, as you know, a fashionable one, did not need saving. Now I feel that they are not worth saving." The Reverend Archer consulted the faces of his visitors rather anxiously to ascertain the effect of his words. "I trust," he added, "my opinions do not shock you?"

"Not at all," replied Mr. Hawk. "I've always felt that way about it myself. But, my dear Dr. Archer, are you sure you won't backslide upon the restoration of your middle section to its former flexious condition?"

"Frankly, Mr. Hawk," replied the rector with a charming smile, "I shall carry on much as usual, but with certain mental reservations, if you get what I mean. My life here is fairly comfortable. I see no reason to change it. No good would be accomplished."

"And again," put in Daffy quite calmly, "after having been deprived of the advantages and slight compensations of a group of important functions one appreciates them more upon the resumption of their pleasurable activities."

For a brief moment the Reverend Archer looked startled, then once more he smiled even more charmingly.

"Admirably expressed, my dear young lady," he replied. "I feel somewhat that way about it myself. One should not, so to speak, look a gift horse in the teeth."

"That's right," put in Meg. "Don't pass up a thing."

"He's a good guy," muttered Cy Sparks, whose sympathies were easily aroused. "How about it, Mr. Hawk?"

"Right," replied the scientist. "I feel that I have accomplished some good in this world after all."

Slightly altering the position of his left hand, he directed the restorative ray against the mid-section of the Reverend Dr. Archer.

"Dr. Archer," he said, "I have reason to believe that if you rise now from that impossible-looking roost of yours you will find upon closer examination everything is as it should be."

The delight of the rector was a pleasure to witness. Abandoning for the moment all consideration for the respect due to his cloth, he executed several rather snappy dance steps, the knowledge of which he could not have come by honestly. After this surprising display of gratitude he took his guests into the house and treated them to a couple of stiff hookers of excellent cognac.

"You know," he announced, when they were leaving, "I think I'll run over to see dear Mrs. Brightly. She'll be so interested to learn that——"

"Your mid-section has been restored," cut in Daffy. "I'm sure it will be an occasion for mutual congratulations."

Once again it was the turn of the Reverend Archer to look startled; then his smile came to the rescue. "Prettily put, young lady," he said, "but slightly tinged with malice. By the way, does anyone know if Mr. Brightly is still absent from his home?"

"I know he is," replied Meg.

"Good," said Dr. Archer involuntarily. "I mean, I hope he is having a pleasant vacation."

So much for the mid-section of the Reverend Dr. Archer. The party strolled homeward feeling a little more cheerfully disposed toward life in general. It is always more pleasing to see a good man going wrong the right way than a bad man going right the wrong way.

Immediately upon his return Mr. Hawk was surrounded by a noisy group of gods and goddesses all talking at the same time and greatly exaggerating their individual contributions to the building of the wall.

When Mr. Hawk made a tour of inspection, the sight of the imposing barrier vaguely reminded him of something he had seen before. When occasionally he paused to examine a weather-seasoned bit of mortar, he noticed a decided tendency on the part of his escort to hurry him past that section of the wall. And when finally he climbed a ladder and looked over the wall, the Olympians made every effort to discourage him.

"It's just the same on the other side," Mercury suavely explained. "One rock is very much like another."

"So true is that," replied Mr. Hawk as he mounted the ladder being held by Perseus, "that it really doesn't matter where you pick up your rocks."

"Makes no difference at all," agreed Mercury, anxiously watching the expression on Mr. Hawk's face.

If the god had expected to see some sudden and alarming indication of the scientist's true feelings he was quite mistaken. Mr. Hawk merely glanced across the road, saw exactly what he had expected to see, then looked down into the innocently uptilted faces of the wall builders.

"There are a couple of good rocks over on Mr. Shrewsberry's property you might use if you happen to need them," he remarked casually. "Not many, but still you never can tell when a good rock will come in handy."

"But don't you think he would mind?" asked Mercury.

"No," replied Mr. Hawk with perfect gravity as he descended the ladder. "I don't think he would mind—now. You see, by the time he's gotten round to missing those few rocks, he'll have become so used to missing rocks—whole walls of rocks—that their absence wouldn't be noticed."

CHAPTER XX

Battle and Flight

SECTIONALLY FOLDED IN A DECK CHAIR, HAWK SAT that evening on the broad veranda of his old home. He was waiting. He was waiting most unpleasantly. He was waiting for the return of Griggs, an avenging Griggs reinforced this time with great quantities of highly explosive state troopers.

Of course, he could petrify the lot of them, but who wanted a small army of petrified policemen scattered about one's lawn in various bellicose attitudes?

Lumps of darkness surrounded Mr. Hawk as he sat there in brooding silence. These lumps bore names. The oldest and darkest lump was Grandpa Lambert. Then there were Daffy, Cyril Sparks, and Meg—an exceedingly small lump, Meg, quietly observant.

The excellent Betts, with the devoted assistance of Hebe, was engaged in transferring bottles from the cellar to the capacious body of the Emperor. The car had been parked in a back lane ready for instant action.

Diana was sitting on the veranda steps. As she whistled a song of the hunt she cleverly fashioned arrows with the aid of a bread knife. The gods were knocking about outside the great wall which had once been the rightful property of one Mr. Shrewsberry. The gods also had done some considerable transferring of bottles. But not to the Emperor. Not the gods. Within their huge bodies surged and seethed an amazing mixture of wines and spirits, for the gods were by nature indefatigable experimentalists. Their stomachs now represented so many chemical experiments, the vast cavern of Bacchus being perhaps the most interesting—a complete laboratory in itself.

Venus was attempting to carry on with the father of Amelia. That poor mortal was at present only fit for carrying.

Out of the darkness came the voice of Mr. Hawk.

"How's your old man?" he inquired of Meg.

"About the same as yours," she replied.

"No. I mean it."

"If you really want to know, it grieves me to state that the ancient sot was so busy counting the roll of bills you sent him that he didn't even have time to say good-bye to me when I left."

"Your parental thief is an excellent rogue. I like him."

"Yes. He steals and drinks, but still I am fond of him, myself," mused Meg.

"So do you, my speck, but still I am fond of you," replied Mr. Hawk.

"With me it's an art. With him it's a vice," said the girl.

"A distinction without a difference," observed Mr.

Hawk. "Did you tell him to consider my house his own?"

"He told me to tell you he always had."

"Then he won't feel out of place."

Once more silence settled down on the group. There was a feeling of tension in the air, a sort of anxious expectancy. Presently Hawk spoke again.

"I created an irrevocable trust to-day," he announced.

"Not in me," snapped Meg. "I wouldn't trust you out of my sight."

"And I don't trust you even when you're in my sight," replied Mr. Hawk, with dignity. "But that is neither here nor there. You fail to understand. I have disposed of my property. I am now a comparatively poor man, most of it goes to you, Daffy, and to Cy."

"Thank God," breathed Cy. "Now for the booze and bugs."

"Sweet boy," remarked Meg.

"How about me?" demanded the old man Lambert. "Am I to be left to the tender mercies of three who should be dead?"

"By no means," replied Mr. Hawk. "Daffy will care for you. She'll buy you a lovely pornographic library and read to you every night."

"Sounds good," admitted the old man.

"And Daffy," continued Mr. Hawk, "I'm afraid you'll just have to marry Cyril. Here it is the end of summer, and he hasn't ruined you yet. I doubt if he ever will, this side of wedlock."

"I'll wed the beast," Daffy agreed after a moment of thoughtful silence, "but I'll jolly well hold the key to the lock."

"What are you going to do?" asked Cy Sparks. "Die on us or something?"

"Something," said Mr. Hawk, sitting up suddenly and listening. "And all of us are going to do something else pretty soon. The time has arrived. Let us gird our well known loins for battle."

From the other side of the wall came the sound of much evil speaking—the voices of coarse men making no attempt to disguise their hostile feelings. The lumps on the veranda became animated with life. Diana, with

242

her bow and fresh supply of arrows, was already streaking across the lawn.

"I'd like to get in on this myself," grated old man Lambert, struggling to his feet.

Betts, flanked by Hebe and Venus, popped from the house and made after the flying goddess. From an upper bedroom window Perseus carelessly hurled himself and hit the ground running. Amelia's voice floated sweetly after him.

"Murder them all, my dear," was her Spartan injunction. "Then return to me."

"Shall we go?" Hunter Hawk asked in the most casual manner in the world. "Let's take a last crack at the forces of law and order. Events march to a grand and inglorious climax."

He rose, and followed by the others, hurried across the lawn in the direction of a burst of unpleasant words crackling in the air near the wall.

Thus opened the final stage of Mr. Hawk's classic contest with organized society—the Battle of the Stolen Wall, perhaps one of the most wonder-provoking conflicts of its kind ever to go officially unrecorded. Had Hunter Hawk been less of a philosopher, victory would have gone to his forces. There is no question of that. However, the man was what he was—an anti-social moral objector, and being such he was growing a little fed-up with many things. He had no intention of being further fed. It was not that he was too proud to fight. He was too bored or, perhaps, too detached.

At the start of this weird encounter most of the action was confined to the opposite side of the wall where, judging from the oaths and cries of anguish of the enemy, the gods fought fiercely and well. Presently, however, the scene of the conflict shifted. The gods, apparently growing weary of smiting the foe, began to cast them bodily over the top of the wall. Soon state troopers were raining down on the heads of Mr. Hawk and his small contingent like maledictions from on high.

"You damned fools," came the voice of Hawk, "you're chucking 'em in, and we want to keep 'em out."

"Our mistake," shouted Perseus, who had joined his

243

brother gods on the opposite side of the wall. "We'll be right over and chuck the beggars back."

"Gord," a voice complained in the darkness, "are we going to be pitched and tossed over this damn wall all night long?"

It seemed that they were.

Perseus, accompanied by the mighty Neptune, swarmed over the wall and laid violent hands on two of the prostrate figures.

"Hold on, Brother," one of them managed to get out. "This is the strangest way of fighting I ever saw. First you heave us in, then you heave us out. It might be a game to you, but it's a pain all over to us."

"All we want is Mr. Hawk," wheezed the other.

"Is that all?" grunted Perseus, feeling deftly in the darkness for the seat of the man's trousers. "Well, my man, you're going to get much more than you wanted. Over you go."

And over he went. Likewise the other.

It was a battle marked by many novel methods and hitherto untested forms of attack. Things were done that night that had never been done before.

Above the swish and thud of falling bodies sounded the deep voice of the sea god.

"Where's Griggs?" he shouted. "I want Griggs."

Hebe looked up from something she had been doing and peered mildly through the darkness.

"Does anybody want Griggs?" she inquired. "I think I have him, but he doesn't seem to go any more."

Neptune rushed to her side and found the dawn-bosomed bearer of the cup methodically churning Griggs in the back with the trident the great god had cast aside on his way over the wall.

"Is he any good?" asked Hebe. "When I first started doing this to him he sort of moved about, but now he doesn't do it hardly any."

"I'll make him move," gritted Neptune, seizing the trident from the accommodating goddess and plunging it deep into the most mountainous part of Griggs.

"There he goes!" exclaimed Hebe, highly pleased. "He's working beautifully now."

"But not enough," muttered Neptune. "No man can pluck at my beard with impunity."

While these two Olympians were carrying the battle into Griggs's quarter or quarters, Venus was doing a peculiar thing. Having found a man sitting up in a dazed condition, she had promptly thrust a bucket over his head and then proceeded to beat upon the side of the bucket with a large stick. It was like some new musical instrument. Every time the bucket resounded the man inside emitted a piercing scream. Venus seemed to derive no little enjoyment from this.

The tactics employed by Meg and Daffy, although totally different, were equally novel and effective. These two enterprising young ladies had seized upon an unfortunate trooper and were holding him well immersed in a trough of cement, discussing the while how long it would take for the stuff to solidify round him.

From the low limb of a tree Diana was sniping earnestly with her bow and arrows. So far she had succeeded in stinging Cyril Sparks as he was stooping over to ascertain if his victim still had breath in his body.

"That's not a nice thing to do," cried the youth, more outraged than injured.

"Pardon me," said Diana. "I was trying out my point of aim."

"Well, try it out on someone else's," retorted Cyril.

Naturally the state troopers were at a great disadvantage. Their plight was due not so much to their lack of courage as to their method of training. When they were studying how to state troop no one had told them how best to resist an infuriated bucket, or what would be the right thing to do when being flung into a trough of cement by two attractive young ladies. Such forms of attack were entirely new to them. Familiar as they were with clubs, machine guns, and revolvers, they were altogether puzzled by flying arrows and twisting tridents. All these things were not put down in the Troopers' Manual. How were they to know?

Old man Lambert's method of attack was of all the most difficult to anticipate. The devil himself would have been both shocked and surprised by it. Having observed a trooper descend heavily on the back of his neck and lie still, the dear old gentleman, in lieu of any other weapon, had fumbled out his fountain pen and

245

carefully seated himself beside the fallen enemy. Whenever the trooper attempted to open his eyes or mouth the venerable Lambert promptly shook red ink into the opening thus offered. Only a viciously senile mind could have conceived such a trick. Naturally the injured trooper was both enraged and amazed.

"Stop that!" he told the aged creature.

"No!" retorted the old man. "They gave me this thing for Christmas, knowing I never wrote. This is the first time I've had a chance to use it." He paused to try the point of the pen on the man's forehead, then continued, in a confidential tone, "Daffy wasn't in on it. She gave me a bottle of gin. A good girl, Daffy."

"I don't give a damn how good Daffy is," replied the man. "Stop doing things to my face."

This remark did not help matters any for the trooper. When they found him at last, he appeared to be the bloodiest of the lot.

Thrice had Mr. Hawk been brutally felled by the same man. The scientist was on the point of losing his patience. When he arose from the third felling he danced spryly away from his assailant, and at the same time vividly drew the man's attention to the evil nature of his parentage on both sides. Having thus successfully lured the indignant fellow to a soft spot in the wall, of which there were many, Mr. Hawk neatly sidestepped the next rage-blinded rush and permitted the man to pass partly through the wall. The part that passed through was immediately set upon by the gods without. The part that remained behind was roundly kicked by the avenging Hawk within.

"Who might this be?" asked Perseus, seizing the man's legs and inspecting all that could be seen. "Don't seem to recognize him."

"Do you usually recognize your friends that way?" asked Mr. Hawk mildly.

This question so upset the great hero that he pushed the man clean through the wall, where he was given an additional beating for having damaged the handiwork of the gods.

While this justly merited punishment was being administered, Mercury, always on the alert, glanced up in time to see a fresh contingent of motorcycle troopers speeding down the road.

"More law and order coming," he cried. "Much more."

"All right, boys," shouted Mr. Hawk. "Let's call it a day and make for the Emperor." Then he added as an afterthought, "It's full of wine."

Bacchus was painfully pushed through the wall by his loyal fellow gods.

"That makes two walls I've been through in one day," remarked the fat deity on all fours. "I fancy one can grow accustomed to this sort of thing."

He rose and wearily followed the line of the retreating Olympians across the lawn.

"It's now or never," thought Blotto to himself as with a tug of sheer desperation he secured what he had been after for some time. With this ragged prize held firmly in his mouth, the souvenir hunting dog raced after Bacchus. The trooper, relieved of the weight of Blotto, felt what little was left of his trousers and fervently thanked his patron saint the dog had gone no farther.

Into the Emperor piled the Olympians. From the front seat Meg, Betts, and Mr. Hawk watched and counted them. Blotto hurtled after his friends. Mr. Hawk petrified the dog, but was too late. Blotto, a thing of stone, rainbowed through the air and landed with a dull thud on the heaving paunch of Bacchus.

"Zeus Almighty," groaned that god. "Am I giving this party?"

Mr. Hawk thrust a long arm through the window and beckoned to Daffy.

"Come here," he said quietly.

Across the lawn the troopers were speeding. Some enthusiast was working a gun. There was the sound of many voices. Mr. Hawk took the girl's face between his thumb and fingers and shook it gently.

"You're a good kid," he said in a low voice. "Take care of our pet drunkard and the Bettses. Also my friend Turner. We've had grand times together. I would like to think you'll remember them at times."

Daffy's throat grew tight. Her heart was filled with little inarticulate cries. She wanted to say something.

247

"I—I——" she gasped.

"Aw, go on," said Hunter Hawk, and gave her face a gentle push. "So long, consumer of my alcohol. Good hunting."

The car dashed down the lane, and Daffy stood looking after it, her hands pressed to her cheeks where the touch of her uncle's fingers still lingered. Old man Lambert and Cyril Sparks stood looking after the car over her shoulder.

"There goes the damnedest uncle a girl ever had," said Daffy.

"And the most useless, black-hearted brother of a daughter-in-law an old man ever had," observed old man Lambert, who seemed not to care how involved he became.

Daffy turned on him with a smile. "You old devil. You terrible old man," she said. "If you don't keep a civil tongue in your head I won't buy you that lovely pornographic library."

"Let's catch a drink," muttered Cyril. "State troopers are literally stepping on my toes."

Daffy turned back once more to the lane. The tail light of the Emperor had vanished.

"He's gone now," she said. "Gone for good."

Together the three of them made their way to the house where for some time they listened to the complaints of various representatives of law and order. Later they sat quietly on the veranda and discussed the battle. Amelia joined them and asked timidly about Perseus.

"Don't bother us," Daffy told her. "Perseuses can be had for the picking."

This cheered the girl up considerably.

Meanwhile things were none too good with the Hawk outfit. Once he had been forced to stop the car until Perseus had found his head, which he insisted had been left behind out of sheer malice. He had previously packed the thing in the car in anticipation of the flight.

"I hope you know what I wish you would do with that head," Mr. Hawk bitterly observed as he jammed the car into action.

The retreat of the gods was punctuated by the popping of many corks. They were flying hither and yon,

248

and foam soaked into the upholstery. If earnest, the re-treat was none the less a merry one.

Three yellow eyes were tailing the car. Meg looked back apprehensively at them and cursed under her breath.

"Darling," she said to the man beside her, "there are always too many cops and gods knocking about. I need a little cherishing."

"You'll get it soon enough," was the scientist's grim reply. "A judge will cherish you."

"I'd prefer to have you undertake the job," said Meg. "Let's give up this mad life and go back to the grotto, or visit Niagara Falls, or learn how to play the zither. I'm too old for this sort of business and far too much of a lady."

"I can believe the first, but the second part offends my ears," said Hunter Hawk. "But I'm with you, Meg, only I'm far, far older. However, just look at those gods. Think how ancient they are, yet they're having the time of their lives."

"Just wait," was Meg's reply. "In a short time they'll be pleading for their pedestals."

"One thing I know," observed the scientist, watching the following eyes in his mirror. "There's little room in this world for me, and damned if I blame the world."

For several miles he concentrated her attention on the wheel and the road ahead. He was looking for some unexpected byway into which he could heave his car, but no such fortuitous avenue of escape offered it-self.

"Evidently this road never gave birth to any pups," he remarked at last. "It's just road all the way through. And the Emperor was never built to retreat. It is essen-tially an advancing car. There are sinister lights coming towards us and equally sinister lights in the rear. The next town has a large jail, and that jail draws closer with every mile. I do not like jails."

"Are we licked?"

"Let us say delayed. I have a plan. Father Neptune is going to play Hunter Hawk. He has already been mistaken for me to the everlasting sorrow of Griggs. It was a lucky day when I donned that false beard. In

249

their present condition our Olympians will be just as happy in jail as anywhere else."

"You're not going to leave them flat?" Meg's voice was reproachful.

"Only temporarily suspended." Hawk turned a little to Betts. "Snatch a couple of bottles from those milling hands back there and stand by to abandon ship."

He stopped the Emperor and turned to the gods.

"Listen," he said. "Pipe down, you gods and you goddesses. Venus, for the memory of your long lost maidenhood, please stop singing the Roman equivalent of Frankie and Johnnie. Perseus, please interrupt your maudlin sobbing for a moment. Thanks."

He paused to look back at the lights, striving to judge their distance and the speed of their approach. He would have to hurry. That was evident.

"In a little while I must leave you," he resumed.

Shouts of protest from the Olympians.

"Half a minute," pleaded Mr. Hawks. "Give me a chance. We won't be parted long. Neptune, I depend on you. You must play you're me, Hunter Hawk. I'll slip all my papers in your pocket. It's because of your beard. Mine was false and not nearly as splendid as yours, but yours looks too good to be true, at that. When we slip out, you take my place behind the wheel and just sit there doing absolutely nothing until they come to arrest you."

"Good Zeus!" exclaimed Neptune. "Are we all to be arrested?"

"Only for one night," explained Mr. Hawk soothingly. "To-morrow I'll get you off. It's an experience."

"Why don't you want to share it, then?" demanded Mercury, suspiciously.

"I don't need it."

"What makes you think we do?" asked Apollo. "We've had lots of experience already—centuries of it."

"Are jailers nice?" inquired Venus.

"Do they have cups in jail?" asked Hebe.

"Sure," Mr. Hawk assured her. "Cups and everything."

"Then I'll go," agreed Hebe.

"We're all with you," rumbled Bacchus. "You've been a father to us, so we'll be felons for you."

"Don't recognize me in court to-morrow," said Hawk as he handed Neptune a few of his personal papers, such as bills and dunning letters. "And remember—I'll see you through. Wait right here, and don't worry. The officers will take care of everything.

"You're painfully right they will," was Mercury's cynical observation, as Hawk, followed by Meg and Betts, slipped from the car and faded into the bushes.

The approaching lights swooped down on the Emperor and came to a halt. From behind the glare a number of officers with guns in their hands advanced on the Olympians. This time the law was taking no chances. The loud pop of a champagne bottle momentarily brought everything to a standstill, but the loud laughter of Bacchus reassured the enemy. The car was boarded and captured. Neptune, drunk as only a god can be, had no difficulty in playing Mr. Hawk. He actually thought he was Mr. Hawk.

From the security of the bushes the three watchers saw the car drive off down the road. Venus was still singing her wild pagan ballad. When the last light had vanished, the three of them sat down in a field and drank wine. Presently they rose and moved off carefully in the direction of the town. They were in quest of sleeping quarters.

In the town only a mile distant the police station gave the appearance of old home week. It was reeking with an assortment of sportive Olympians, one stone dog, and one stone head. The last two objects gave the captain behind the desk much to think about. He could not bear the head.

"A clean haul," he said, "but I wish to God you'd have left those two horrible things behind. This night's work will mean a boost all along the line."

The captain failed to state whether the boost would be up or down.

"That was a good idea of mine," said Mercury as he was being locked in his cell.

"Which, Son?" asked Bacchus.

"That idea about building a wall."

"Oh, that," said Bacchus thoughtfully as he felt his

251

steel-ribbed bunk. "That was a fine idea as ideas go. It was a funny idea. I enjoyed my trip through that wall."

In the bedroom of a near-by hotel Mr. Hawk suddenly clapped a hand to his forehead.

"What's wrong with you?" asked Meg, pausing with stocking in her hand.

"I forgot all about Blotto," said Hawk, "and the poor beast is petrified as stiff as a stone."

"That's the only way to be in jail," the young lady replied, and calmly continued making herself ready for bed.

CHAPTER XXI

The Gods on Trial

"BRING 'EM IN," COMMANDED EXAMINING MAGISTRATE Plenty. "All of 'em."

From a carefully selected seat in the courtroom Mr. Hawk, Meg, and Betts watched the Olympians, a fine, full-bodied, disorderly-looking lot, file into the room. The trio also noticed that Griggs, game but sadly crippled, was very much in evidence in this the hour of his triumph.

"Line 'em up," grunted Magistrate Plenty as he thumbed through a file of papers.

Before the seat of mortal justice the stalwart Olympians were lined. Hawk contemplated them all with a kindly eye, feeling somewhat the pride of a father in a nobly erring son.

"Your name?" snapped Plenty, pointing suddenly at the goddess of love.

"Venus," came the reply in a cooing voice, as the goddess smiled on the magistrate.

"Venus what?"

"De Milo," Venus startlingly answered.

"Hah!" almost gloated the magistrate. "That explains a lot. Foreign, eh? Italian. And yours?"

Plenty suddenly pointed to Bacchus.

"My name is Bacchus," said the god.

"Come, come, man! Your real name. This is neither the time nor place for levity."

"Bacchus has been my name for thousands and

thousands of years. Bacchus it is to-day," the wine god spoke with dignity.

Magistrate Plenty looked heavily at the stout fellow and pondered. He decided to bide his time. He passed more hopefully to the next offender.

"Your name?" he snapped.

"Mercury," said that god.

"See here. See here," cried the magistrate. "What are you all trying to do, hang yourselves or rattle me?" He pointed a trembling finger at the handsome god of music. "I suppose you'll be telling me you're Apollo next?"

"I am, sir," said Apollo simply. "I always have been and I always shall be, except on certain occasions of a nature well known even to yourself."

"Stop! Stop!" cried the magistrate. "Am I mad? Am I an ass? Am I clean gone?"

"Yes to all," smiled Apollo, who was at his best in public.

"Stop! Stop!" shrilled the magistrate. "Take 'em away. No, bring 'em back. What am I saying? Is this a court of law or a madhouse?"

As no one saw fit to enlighten the jaded magistrate he settled back in his chair and spent some time getting himself together. Finally he looked up and asked in almost a whisper, "Which one is Hawk?"

"There he stands, your honor," said Griggs, indicating Neptune.

"Why is he allowed to wear that loathsome looking false beard in court? This is no masquerade."

"He won't take it off."

"But he must take it off."

"We asked him to take it off."

"And he wouldn't take it off?"

"No, your honor," said Griggs indignantly. "He refused to take it off."

"Then," gritted the magistrate through his clenched teeth, half rising from his chair, "drag the thing off."

The scene that followed hardly befitted the dignity of the court. It goes without saying that Neptune defended his beard with all the spirit of a man who knows he is in the right. It further goes without saying that the court attendants under the eyes of the magistrate did their best to deprive Neptune of that which was rightfully his. The result was a decidedly awkward scuffle, during which Magistrate Plenty could be heard muttering from time to time:

"My God! to think of this. My God! Oh, that I must witness this!"

The decision must be called a draw. In fairness to all it should be called that. It is barely possible that if given enough time and opportunity the attendants might have succeeded in literally dragging off Neptune's beard, lock, stock, and barrel. It is also barely possible that Neptune might have killed them all and thus retained his beard. Magistrate Plenty could stand it no longer.

"Stop! Stop!" he shouted. "Come away from that beard."

"It won't come off," said one of the attendants, who had actually succeeded in laying hands on the beard. "I gave it a yank, a good one, and it wouldn't budge."

"Will you please shut up?" said the magistrate wearily. "If the beard won't come off, then I guess it won't come off. And that's all there is to it."

He sank deep down in the chair and brooded. Presently he raised his head and very calmly, very earnestly addressed Neptune.

"Mr. Hawk," he said, "let's forget the last few minutes. I think I know how you feel about it. But now I ask you as man to man and in all good faith, won't you please take off that beard? It does not become you."

Neptune by this time was so exasperated he was on the verge of tears. He in turn addressed the magistrate in a calm, earnest voice, almost as one trying to reason with a child or an inebriate.

"But I can't take off the beard," he said. "It's there. It's on me. I'll do anything else to please you—take off anything else—my coat or my trousers or my boots, but not my beard. That I can't take off."

"You can't take it off?" said the magistrate.

"No, sir. I can't take it off. Anything else, yes."

"Then," said the magistrate with a remarkable show of self-control, "let us say no more about the beard." Here his fine command of himself broke down. He rose from his chair and in a cold, white, passionate voice hurled at Neptune the last word, "Keep your damned beard!" he shouted, and collapsed in his chair. Only the top of his head could be seen above his desk.

"What the hell has he got against my beard?" Neptune whispered to Mercury.

"It's supposed to be false, you damn fool," the light-fingered god replied.

"Oh," said Neptune, and again, "oh. I see it all now. Well, it isn't a false beard. It's one of the realest beards alive."

"For the love of your brother Zeus," pleaded Mercury, "let us hear no more about that beard."

But more was heard about the beard, for unfortunately Neptune had a bright idea.

"Your honor," he called suddenly, "would you like to step down here yourself and handle this beard?"

"What!" the magistrate's head popped up as if blown from his body. "Me handle that beard? Oh—oh—oh—how revolting!"

For a moment the stricken man looked helplessly about the courtroom, then once more sank below the horizon of his desk top. No more was heard of the beard for the moment, but Magistrate Plenty steadfastly kept his eyes averted from Neptune's face. Whenever, as if fascinated, they strayed beardward, the gears of his brain seemed to begin to slip a little, his thoughts wavered, and his words dragged.

The examination that had opened so inauspiciously failed to improve with time. The magistrate hated everybody. Nothing seemed to go right for anyone concerned.

When Officer Kelly came to the witness chair another crisis was precipitated.

"I want to tell your honor about the conduct of these here prisoners," announced Officer Kelly.

For some reason Magistrate Plenty seemed to buck up a trifle at this suggestion. Perhaps he craved relief or was fond of bedtime stories.

"Tell us, Kelly," he said pleasantly.

"Well, your honor," began Kelly, "we had a terrible night of it."

"Too bad, too bad," murmured the magistrate.

255

"We did that," continued the encouraged Kelly. "This slick-looking party"—Kelly indicated Mercury—"kept unlocking all of his confederates' cells. Out they'd barge into the hall and go tramping about the place, laughing and scuffling like."

"Didn't they try to escape?" inquired the magistrate.

"No, your honor," replied Kelly. "They were thoroughly at home. Seemed to like it here."

"Good of them," beamed the magistrate, but the beam was laden with venom. "Go on, Kelly."

"Then they got the women over," said Kelly, "and had one high old time."

"Of course, it didn't occur to any of you to drive them back?" The magistrate's voice was soft and low. "Hated to spoil their fun, perhaps?"

"We did, your honor, repeatedly, but every time we did, out they'd bounce just as if they didn't know the meaning of a lock." Kelly paused for a moment to moisten his lips, then rushed right into trouble. "Then, your honor," he said, "they stole the stone dog."

The magistrate sat up. He was all attention.

"The stone dog, Kelly?" he said. "What stone dog? I have heard of no stone dog."

"Yes, your honor. There's a stone dog."

"What sort of a stone dog, Kelly?"

"Just an ordinary stone dog, your honor."

"There is no ordinary stone dog, Kelly. The very fact that the dog is of some stone makes it extraordinary, gives it a place of its own, makes it peculiar, unique, and arresting. But, tell me, Kelly. Is it a little stone dog or a medium-sized stone dog or, let us say, a huge stone dog?"

"Oh, no, sir," replied Kelly, somewhat confused. "It's a very lifelike stone dog, it is. Large and heavy."

The magistrate pondered a moment. This stone dog intrigued him. He had never seen a lifelike stone dog, a large and heavy one.

"Bring me this stone dog," he said at last.

It was unfortunate that the court attendant dispatched to fetch Blotto was nervously as well as physically fairly well wrecked. Merely to lift the stone dog was for him no small achievement. Nevertheless, he did lift the dog, and not only that, he carried the dog to the courtroom, but here his strength failed. The dog was about to slip from his numbed arms and would have crashed to the floor had not the quick wit of Hunter Hawk saved his old friend. As the magistrate was peering at the stone dog clutched in the arms of the failing court attendant, he was both startled and dismayed to see it wriggle impatiently and then bound to the floor.

"What!" ejaculated the good man starting from his chair and leaning far over his desk. "There's something funny about all this."

He removed his glasses and hastily rubbed them. The attendant took one look at Blotto; then, with a cry of sheer horror, fled from the room. Mr. Hawk swept the floor in Blotto's vicinity with the petrifying ray, thus turning the bottoms of the dog's feet to stone. For a short time the dog stood still, as if trying to get his bearings, then, spying his friends, the Olympians, set out to join them. It was a noisy progress. The placing of each paw occasioned a distinct little bang. The magistrate watched the dog with fascinated eyes. At last he turned to Officer Kelly.

"Kelly," he said, "that's the loudest-walking dog I ever heard. What's wrong with the beast? I thought you said that dog was made of stone. That's not a stone dog at all. That's a real dog with funny feet— very funny feet, if you'd ask me."

"It was a stone dog, your honor," declared Kelly. "All of the boys who saw it said it was a stone dog."

"Well, it isn't a stone dog now," said the magistrate. "It's some sort of tap-dancing dog. I really do believe that all this has slightly deranged my mind."

Blotto clattered across the floor and sat down by Neptune, leaned, in fact, a little against the sea god's leg.

"There are other things," offered Kelly timidly.

"Thank God for that," said the magistrate. "What sort of other things?"

"There's a head," gasped Kelly.

Once more the magistrate started.

"What sort of a head, man?" he gritted. "A calf's head, a horse's head, a fish's head—what sort of a head? Try to be specific."

"A human head," Kelly manged to get out.

"Your honor," broke in Perseus, unable to restrain himself, "it's my head."

A long, low, animal-like howl broke from the lips of his honor. He rested his forehead on the edge of his desk, and his hands fluttered helplessly above it.

"What is this?" he muttered. "Where am I? His head. His head. What does it all mean?"

"Your honor," came the voice of Hebe, "may we sit down somewhere? We're getting awfully tired."

"So am I," snapped the magistrate, looking dimly at the fair goddess. "Mortally tired. Yes, my child. Sit down. I'm going to charge you all with something in a few minutes. I don't know what, but now it looks like murder."

Suddenly he turned fiercely on Officer Kelly.

"Make yourself clear," he flung at the man.

"It's a stone head," said Kelly.

"I know. I know," replied the magistrate. "So was that dog. Is the head like that?"

"Oh, your honor," said Kelly, turning white. "I hope not. I do indeed. Not this head of all heads."

"Then bring it in, man, together with all of your other exhibits. Hurry."

Kelly brought Medusa and placed her on the magisterial desk. The honorable Plenty gave one look at the head, then twisted his own away, twisted it nearly off.

"O-o-o-o-o, what a head," he moaned. "I never saw a more unpleasant head. Thank God, it isn't alive."

Kelly then placed Mercury's caduceus on the other side of the desk and leaned Neptune's trident against it.

"That's all, your honor," he said.

"And quite enough, to be sure. You've done very well, Kelly! Too well, I might say. I'd like you all to know that this has been a terrible morning for me—a terrible trial. Come up here, Griggs. I want to ask you some questions."

Painfully but proudly Griggs mounted to the witness chair. It was plain to see he fully intended to do his worst for everybody but himself.

Magistrate Plenty looked long and with great distaste upon the red, raw face of Griggs.

"Griggs," he began heavily. "You got me into all

this, and I'm not grateful. I depend upon you to get me out and Mr. Hawk and his followers in. Now, listen to me and answer my questions."

"Yes, your honor," from Griggs.

"Yes what?" clipped Magistrate Plenty. "I have asked no question yet."

"I meant," said Griggs, "yes, I will."

"Yes, you will," repeated the magistrate. "Yes, you will what? Are you deliberately trying to puzzle me, madden me, infuriate me?"

"What I meant to say was, yes, I will get you out of it," stammered Griggs.

"Thanks," said the magistrate dangerously. "Answer this one. Does or did the prisoner Hawk wear a false beard?"

"Yes, your honor."

"Is that man there the Hawk in question?"

"He is, your honor."

"And is his beard false?"

"It is, your honor."

"If it is not false, Griggs, then it follows the prisoner is not Hawk. Am I right, Griggs?"

"You are, your honor."

"Did you ever tug at that beard, Griggs?"

"I did, your honor."

"And did it come off?"

"No, your honor."

"Would you like to take a tug at it now, Griggs?"

A deep growl from Neptune.

"No, your honor."

"How do you explain the fact that in spite of all our combined efforts we have been unable to dislodge that beard from the prisoner's chin?"

"I can't, your honor."

"Still you claim the prisoner to be one Hawk?"

"I do, your honor."

Magistrate Plenty scratched his head while Hunter Hawk played the petrifying ray across the lower part of Griggs, as that unfortunate individual sat perspiring in the chair. At last the magistrate spoke and said:

"I would like to help you, Griggs, but from all the evidence before us I am forced to conclude that the prisoner cannot be Hawk, and that, furthermore, you

259

have arrested the wrong man. You may step down, Griggs."

The stricken detective tried in vain to step down. He turned an ashen face to the magistrate.

"I can't step down," he got out.

"And why can't you step down, may I ask?"

"I don't know, your honor."

"You can't step down and yet can give no reason. That seems hardly reasonable, Griggs."

"Something has happened, your honor."

"What has happened, man? Tell us."

"I can't say what has happened, your honor."

"Do you mean you can't say or you won't say?"

"I'd like to say, your honor."

"Ah, you'd like to say but you won't say."

A long pause while Magistrate Plenty thought this out. Suddenly his face cleared, and he leaned far over towards the completely wilted Griggs.

"Do you want to whisper it, Griggs?"

The detective recoiled as if stung.

"Certainly not, your honor."

Control had long since flown from the courtroom. Tears were running down the faces of many present. The magistrate no longer seemed to care what happened. His one mad desire was to finish up this terrible business so that he could go home and drink himself into a state of completely forgetfulness. Looking about him for some source of inspiration his eyes encountered the baleful stare of Medusa. "Oh, God," he thought to himself. "Who would have thought up such a frightful face, such a completely devastating face? What demoniacal mind? I've been mad for at least two hours. Sanity will never return." With desperate self-control he faced Griggs and asked in a quiet, reasoned voice:

"Then do you want to speak right out here in court, Griggs, and tell us about it like a man?"

"I can't tell about it, your honor," Griggs was almost sobbing.

"Is it a secret, Griggs?"

"No secret, your honor."

"Griggs, you're being very stubborn about this matter. Something must be done. You can't expect to be allowed to occupy that chair forever, you know. Someone else might want to sit in it, Griggs. Won't you leave it quietly now instead of lumping selfishly in it as you are?"

"I can't, your honor."

"Then, Griggs," cried the magistrate in a voice that broke from sheer exasperation, "I'll have you dragged out of it. Understand me? Dragged out of that chair. Dragged bodily and brutally." He pounded on his desk with both clenched hands. "Drag him out, I say! Drag him out! Quick."

While Griggs was being removed from the chair Meg worked her magic on the head of Medusa and the serpent-twined caduceus. The hissing and crackling of the snake and the wild cries of Medusa caused the magistrate to turn from watching the dragging down of Griggs to see what was happening on his desk. He gave one swift, horror-stricken, incredulous look at the head; then his frenzied shriek rang through the courtroom. Still screaming like a soul in torment, he turned and on tottering legs disappeared through a door directly behind him. Nor was he alone in his flight. In a surprisingly short time the room was empty save for the Olympians, Mr. Hawk, Meg, and Betts.

Without undue haste they gathered up their possessions and departed. Betts led them to the Emperor. They entered the car in an orderly manner and drove off. That was all there was to it.

"Won't they follow us?" asked Hebe.

"No, dear child," said Hunter Hawk. "Settle back and think of cups. No one in that entire building could be induced to come within a mile of us."

"I say," said Meg, turning to Neptune, "you can take that beard off now. It doesn't become you."

The sea god's grin was expansive as he fondly stroked his beard.

CHAPTER XXII

The Last Sigh

HEBE WAS BEARING HER LAST CUP, AND THE Olympians, scattered round the lounge room of their suite in the hotel, were drinking their last drinks. The scene gave one the impression of a fancy-dress ball. All save Betts were in costume. Even Mr. Hawk, looking not unlike Abraham Lincoln gone Roman, was swathed in white drapery. To please the Olympians, and especially the lady Olympians, on this last evening he had allowed a little variety to be used in their costumes. The colors were riotous, but the costumes themselves were essentially the same—yards of material wound or draped according to the fancy of the individual wearer. Altogether the effect was picturesque.

Mercury was wearing his funny hat and Perseus had retrieved his heroic sword.

On the floor in their midst lay Dora, the stolen cow, who during their absence had been forced to remain in a state of acute petrifaction. She too was adorned gayly with ribbons which she failed utterly to appreciate.

The reason for the bizarre regalia of the outfit was that Mr. Hawk, for reasons of his own, wanted no marks of identification left behind when the Olympians returned to their pedestals, as they were just about to do. One by one they had rather sheepishly admitted that they were just a little tired. The world was too much with them, or after them. On all sides they either encountered trouble or created it. Then again, their stomachs were not what they had been. It was not Mr. Hawk's fault. No blame could be attached to him. He was not responsible for irresponsible persons who made ill advised laws.

"Volstead," said Bacchus, "must be a most remarkable fellow. I would have enjoyed a little chat with him in spite of the fact that we don't see eye to eye."

The discussion now centered round Dora. What disposition should be made of the cow?

"I say bring the old girl along and make her a gift to

the museum," suggested Mercury. "Petrify her along with the rest of us."

"You would say that, because you stole the cow," observed Bacchus.

"I found the cow," said Mercury. "Betts and Meg stole her. I merely came along."

"Then why not give her to Betts as a token of appreciation of his splendid mixing?" asked Neptune, idly dipping a hand in the goldfish tank.

Betts looked startled.

"Couldn't think of accepting her," he said hastily but modestly. "Mrs. Betts dislikes the idea of cows. Never got along well with them."

The heavy business of transporting the animal appalled the old man.

"Isn't there some society that does things about cows?" Meg inquired vaguely. "There seems to be a society for almost everything else either for or against."

"I don't think there's a Society for the Redemption of Lost Cows," volunteered Mr. Betts. "How about the Zoo?"

"Not a bad idea, that," said Mr. Hawk. "The Zoo might like to have a nice domestic cow just to make its collection complete. Tell you what we could do, though. We could write a letter to the Police Commissioner saying, 'If you will look in room 1537 you will find something to your interest.' We could sign it, 'A Well-Wisher.'"

In the end it was decided to do nothing at all about the cow, a decision that could have been predicted from the very outset of the discussion.

At the appointed hour the Olympians arose, drank a final toast and followed Mr. Hawk from the room. Hebe was bearing in triumph the cup she had originally wanted to bear. Mr. Hawk had not the heart to deprive her of this last pleasure.

"There's a cow knocking about my rooms," Mr. Hawk told the elevator boy, who did not seem greatly interested.

"Is that cow still there?" he asked carelessly.

"Of course it is," snapped Mr. Hawk. "What do you think we did with the animal, eat it raw?"

"I wondered what you were going to do with her in the first place," remarked the boy.

"Well, do something about it now," said Mr. Hawk.

"What, for instance?" asked the boy.

"Damned if I know," said Mr. Hawk as he stepped into the Emperor and drove off with Betts at the wheel.

It was late now, and no one witnessed the return of the gods to the Metropolitan. Mercury with his magic fingers had somehow managed the door. Before Hawk followed them in he pressed the restoring ring into the hand of the faithful Betts. Its usefulness was over. It could do no harm. The ray had nothing to operate on save the lower half of Griggs, a stone dog in the woods, a couple of policemen, a few waiters, and two fleeing figures by a woodland lake. Betts would never use it.

"Take care of things," Mr. Hawk told him as he squeezed the old man's arm. "That ring may serve to remind you of a few pleasant occasions."

Old Betts just looked at his master, then smiled.

"I may bring you back some day?" he said.

"By that time the ring will have lost its power," Mr. Hawk replied. "By the way, are you sure Miss Daffy picked up Blotto at the station?"

"Yes, sir," said Betts in a low voice. "I had her on the phone. She said, sir, to tell you—" the old man hesitated, then resumed—"I think the exact words were 'pip pip.'"

Hawk left the Emperor and crossed the short distance to the door. Inside the Olympians were waiting for him in the long corridor.

"I thought you were never coming," whispered Meg, looking like a small child in her white drapery.

Neptune was the first to mount to his stand. He settled himself properly and beamed down at Hawk.

"Thanks for the fish," he said.

"Good-bye, old friend," replied Mr. Hawk, shaking the sea god's hand. "You beard was a great help."

Meg did what was necessary, and the great god became even greater as he returned to his original state.

Thus passed the Olympians, one by one, mounting to their pedestals, to resume once more their rightful function of edifying and enlightening the general public. The world could stand for them in bronze or stone, but in the flesh it was an altogether different matter.

"We've had a nice clean time together," said Venus as she smilingly stepped up. "Oh, what about my arms?"

"Let the museum staff puzzle about them," replied Meg. "They're damn good arms, old girl, but they'll probably break 'em off."

Hebe returned, still clinging to her cup. It was this incongruous article that shocked and amazed the museum authorities, officials, and staff more than anything else connected with the whole strange affair.

"You can't say I didn't keep my head," grinned Perseus as he was about to go.

"You can keep right on keeping," said Mr. Hawk. "I'm sure Magistrate Plenty won't envy you."

"Well, my boy, I'm as near being a confirmed drunkard as I ever was in my life," observed Bacchus. "I don't know whether that's a compliment to your modern stuff or not. I think not."

"It's been nice to meet you both," murmured Diana. "I trust you will not judge me by the conduct of my sister. She really is a trollop. Thanks for a lovely time."

"If you meet a girl named Mabel," said Apollo, "just tell her not to worry. Not that she will. I wish to thank you, Mr. Hawk, for all of us, in case the others forgot."

"Good-bye, Mercury, old son," said Mr. Hawk when it came time for that smooth fellow to return. "You've been a great help and comfort. I hope you enjoyed your thieving."

"I did. I did," replied Mercury. "Meg's not so bad herself. Tell me, Mr. Hawk. Do you happen to remember in which hand I held this damn caduceus? I can't recall for the life of me. It really doesn't matter. The whole pose is ridiculous. Please hurry, or I'll fall on my nose."

"Well, thank God that's over," said Meg when the restoration of the Olympians had been completed. "Now we're alone at last."

She sank wearily to a bench beside the lean, white-draped scientist. In the vast hall the two figures looked like people from another age returned to claim their

265

own. Mr. Hawk looked thoughtfully round him at the dim, inanimate forms of the Olympians.

"Only a moment ago they were alive and active," he said in a low voice. "They were full of thoughts and ideas, of wants, likes, and dislikes. They could move and make themselves felt. Now—nothing. So much imperishable beauty."

"They played hard for a while and tired quickly," replied Meg, drawing closer to the man beside her. "Now they have gone back to rest. In a world that has forgotten how to play there was no room for the Olympians."

"Nor for us," said Mr. Hawk, taking the girl in his arms and slipping off her drapery as they sank to the cold stone floor.

And Meg took the man to her as a woman takes a man.

"Your lips on mine," she said. "Always."

As the current passed through the locked bodies a little sigh of ecstasy escaped the lips of Meg. The stone closed round them, shutting out the world. Nothing could get at them now. There was no time nor age. They had themselves forever, the man and the woman.

Yet through the deep silence of the vast hall something of them seemed to linger—Meg's last little sigh still floated like a mocking kiss on the cold cheek of convention.